The Hebrew Book of Revelation

"I Am the Aleph and the Tav"

English Translation

Miles R. Jones, Ph.D.

Preview Edition © Copyright 2024 Miles R. Jones
ISBN #   978-1-957488-09-7

"Yehovah gave the Word; Great was the company of those that published it!"
Psalm 68:11

Great Publishing Company
Benai Emunah Institute
Kerrville, Texas

Acknowledgements

Miles R. Jones, Chief Editor
Jonathan Felt, Associate Editor & Archivist
Pamela Lutzker, Associate Editor & Manager of Publications
Janice Baca, Senior Hebrew Editor
Patrick J. McGuire, Layout Design & Video Producer

—

MS Transcriptions: Caroline Shemesh, Deanna Amsler,
Stephanie Shiflet, Nigel Lloyd-Jones

—

MS Scholars and Committee Contributors for this Interlinear:
Alan Esselbach, aja-anon, Anna Knecht, Bryan Williams,
Caroline Shemesh, David Winer, Deanna Amsler, Diane
DeLeon, Janice Baca, Jennifer Webster, Jennifer Howell, John
Abel, Jonathan Felt, Jonathan Meyer, Kay Agnew, Kurt Sutton,
Kyle Gadd, Miles R. Jones, Naamah Hadi, Nick Strickland,
Matthew Chamberlain, Pam Lutzker, Rocky Webb, Sebastian
Rhinehart, Uwani Richardson

—

Other Active Contributors & Specialists world-wide as of
Aug 2023: Andreas Hurter (German), Anita Burke (h.t.),
Anita Jones (h.tr.), Anna Knecht (h.t.ldr), Arie Kralt (w.tr., MS
Research), Bel Guiste (h.t.), Bernardo Partida (Spanish), Bryan

REVELATIONS

Necrotic Apocalypse Book Six

D. PETRIE

MOUNTAINDALE
PRESS

ACKNOWLEDGMENTS

When I planned out this series, I always intended to end it with book six. Yet, when I got here, I wasn't quite ready to let these characters go. I wanted one more adventure together before bringing things to a close. There was still so much story to tell. So, I wrote an extra book. It's silly and weird, just like the rest, and I thank you all for coming along for the ride. This one is for you.

CHAPTER ONE

Being a kid sucks.

Hawk let that thought circle in his head as the red and blue flashing lights of a police car flickered in the night outside one of the many foster homes he'd lived in.

He was eight.

His toes were practically numb, wearing nothing on his feet but a pair of canvas sneakers. It had been one of those rare days in mid-December when it actually snowed in California. His winter jacket was fastened with the buttons misaligned so that an extra one hung at the bottom without a mate, while another flopped to the side of his collar. A social worker had put it on him in a rush, more concerned with the bruise on his face. They'd never asked him if it hurt. No, all they had done was write down the details. The size, location, and how it had happened. All the basics were noted so they could be added to his file. That way, whatever family he'd be sent to next would have an idea of his history.

The bruise looked bad but it wasn't a big deal. It hadn't even been caused on purpose. His foster father had started a fight with his foster mother. He'd been a thin guy with nerd glasses and a personality to match that had a job at the bank downtown. His foster mom had worked for a nursing home. She'd always worn long sleeves to hide the tattoos that covered her arms. They went all the way down to her wrists. In the few months that Hawk had lived with them, both of them had been pretty cool.

He never found out what the reason for the fight was.

It was one of those things that had already been brewing by the time he'd crossed paths with it. The reason didn't matter anyway. Every couple had problems. He had known that well enough.

The fight had started with a few mean comments from his foster father and escalated into shouting in under a minute. It was a common enough occurrence but it had never gotten violent, so Hawk had decided to slowly back out of the room as stealthily as possible to avoid the awkwardness of watching.

Unfortunately, he had just finished dinner and still needed to bring his plate to the sink. His foster father had gotten up at the same time, picking up a plastic bowl from the table that still had a few spaghetti noodles sticking to the side. Normally the guy would have placed it in the sink gently, but his head was running hot and he'd tossed it instead. The bowl hit the sink with a hollow clunk, bouncing around and splashing his foster mom with water from another dirty plate.

This did not help the situation.

She called him an asshole and he got in her face. Hawk hated it when people did that. It was like they were using the fact that they were taller to seem stronger. On reflex, his foster mom pushed the nerdy guy away. It hadn't been that hard. At least, not hard enough to be thought of as an attack. Just an attempt to take back a little space. Despite that, his foster father tripped backward, his elbow smashing into the side of Hawk's face while he was sneaking around the kitchen to get rid of his dish. The fight stopped immediately when they realized what had happened.

The rest of the argument could wait until later.

Whatever happened next didn't matter, because that was when a cop knocked on the door. A neighbor had called in the fight.

The rest of the story wrote itself.

That was how he ended up standing in the mid-December snow next to a suitcase holding everything he owned. Well, almost everything he'd owned. He hadn't known it at the time, but the stuffed bear that he'd been given by the state of California years before had never made it into his suitcase. It would be a day later before he realized it had been lost. By then, it was too late to go back. He was already be in a new home, with new foster parents.

Being a kid sucks.

The one good thing about living through the apocalypse was that growing up was the only option. The end of the world was no place for a child.

"Don't just sit there and mope. Come over here and breathe in this fresh air." Digby hung his head out of the window of the limousine.

"No thanks." Hawk remained where he was, slouching in one of the seats that lined the side of the vehicle with his arms folded.

"You realize that we have a horde of fifty zombies following us and the air smells like corpse, right?" Alex stared back over his shoulder through the open partition at the front of the car.

"Yeah, Dig. Plus there's probably more zombie assassins out there that you haven't brought under your Control yet. And they love to snipe at us from a distance." Parker eyed the necromancer from the passenger seat next to Alex. "So pull your head in here and close the window before you take a bone spike in the face."

Digby ducked back in to glower at her. "The last time I checked, you were no longer my keeper, Parker."

"That's true. But the last time I checked, you still had several war crimes to make up for. You know, like breaking my pinky finger. And let's not forget the murders." She turned forward again and slouched into her seat, putting her feet on the dash.

"Fine fine." Digby ducked down and practically threw himself into the seat opposite Hawk. "And in my defense, I was insane at the time. I can't be held accountable for my actions. For I am a new man now. Well, new zombie, at least." He turned his head to the back of the car. "Right, Becky?"

Hawk's adopted, vampire sister, lay across the rear seats on her back with a copy of Wired magazine, which had been published just before the end of the world, covering her face. A picture of Keanu Reeves was on the front. "Ask me again in…" She lifted the magazine off her face and looked out the window at the sun without sitting up. "Ask me in a half hour." She let her head flop back to the seat as if she couldn't be bothered to continue holding it up. Then she dropped the magazine back in place. "I'm not doing anything until the sun goes the hell away. I feel a little better inside the car, but that's still just a step above feeling like absolute garbage. And every time you open the window, I get a little worse. I swear, it's like you're letting in all the life essence out there. I don't even know why you brought me on a daylight mission."

"Excuse me for trying to get you out of your lair to get some fresh air." Digby pouted like a kid.

"Again, the corpse smell. The dead don't do much for air quality, so close the window," Alex commented.

Hawk laughed. "You're lucky we let you ride in here with us, Dig."

"I will have you know that I smell fine. I bathed just this morning and I haven't used my Body Craft or Necrotic Armor once today."

"You do have a smell, though." Becca peeked out from under her magazine. "If I had to describe it, I'd say it was dirt."

"Dirt? What have I done to you lately to merit such an attack?"

"It's not a bad smell." The vampire covered her face again, her voice sounding muffled from underneath the magazine. "It's just, I don't know, earthy."

"That doesn't make me feel better." Digby narrowed his eyes at the picture of Keanu Reeves extra hard, as if trying to make up for the fact that Becca couldn't see him.

"All I'm saying is that the air does smell fresher when no one is trying to kill you." The zombie held a hand out toward Hawk for some backup. "You all have to agree with me there."

He nodded.

It had been two weeks since Digby had led an armada of airships against Autem's imperial fleet and threatened them with a nuclear warhead. In the end, neither side could kill the other without destroying themselves in the process. The result was a fragile peace agreement.

"Can we really trust Autem to leave us alone?" Alex asked.

"It's been a couple of weeks." Parker pushed herself back up in her seat. "No one has come after us yet."

"Yes, I'd say that is a good sign that we are safe," Digby added.

"So why do we need the zombies?" Hawk tapped on the window where several of the dead walked outside as the limo hovered through the streets of Boston slow enough for the horde to keep up behind them. "If we don't have to worry about Autem coming after us, why are we gathering a horde?"

"That's the best part; we aren't." Digby held up a finger. "We're helping to remove a threat from the world. In time, people will come here in search of a place to live, and the less zombies there are lurking about, the easier that will be. This isn't about gathering a horde for war or even survival. This is about rebuilding. And that makes all the difference." A low cackle rolled through the necromancer. "The fact that these zombies can be added to our forces is just a bonus."

Hawk tried to imagine the world through the same hopeful outlook that Digby had gained over the last couple of weeks.

After his previous trip to Boston, when he had been temporarily stranded there with Alex, they had returned with the knowledge that the city had a larger zombie population than most. That was why it was the first place they had gone to gather more of the dead.

The job was easy. All they had to do was climb into a vehicle and drive around while Digby cast Control on any of the walking corpses that they passed. Then they just led them back to a mirror where they could transport them to Vegas.

Thanks to Alex, they could even do the job in style.

Before leaving Washington, D.C., where Autem's capital was located, they had made a point to take one of the presidential limousines from the White House. A few days later, Alex had applied everything he'd learned so far about runecraft to the car. The result was a flying, bulletproof, luxury vehicle with full altitude control.

It was better than the Camaro that had come before.

The only downside was that the heat and air conditioning didn't work. Alex was still figuring that part out. It would've been a problem if it had been a few months earlier and they had been in the middle of summer, but considering they were halfway through November, the temperature wasn't that big of a deal. Everyone just had to wear a winter coat.

Hawk had grabbed the first parka that fit him while Alex had looted a bomber jacket. Parker had been changing her coat at almost every store they passed, unable to decide which one she liked, and Becca just wore an oversized hoodie. Digby didn't need one, leaving him wearing the same clothes he always did, just a vest, pants, and a dress shirt with the sleeves rolled up.

Hawk let his hand rest on the handle of the pistol he wore at his hip, feeling comfortable with the weight of it. Everyone had been against him carrying it, but with everything he'd been through and the number of times he'd proven himself, they couldn't justify telling him no. Just like they couldn't say no when he had asked to go out with them on the mission.

Granted, he had been expecting to do more than just ride in the car while the rest of them chatted.

"Oh!" Parker suddenly slapped a hand to her window. "Stop the car."

"What is it?" Digby reached for his staff that was lying on the floor as Alex slowed the limo.

Parker popped her door open and jumped out before they had even come to a stop.

"What is that messenger doing? She's going to get herself grabbed by a zombie if she's not careful." Digby slid down the seats toward the door at the back of the vehicle and shoved it open.

Hawk followed, unfastening the snap that held his pistol in its holster as Parker weaved through a few of the zombies outside and shoved her way through the half-open door of a convenience store. By the time Hawk and Digby got out of the car, she was already exiting with an armload of boxes.

"What in the devil are you doing?" Digby tapped his staff on the ground while glowering in her direction.

Hawk kept his eyes on their surroundings.

Parker slowed to a stop, her mouth hanging open. "Oh, sorry. I just saw these in the window. They have several boxes in there."

Hawk looked down at what she carried. The words mini-pecan pie were written across the front beneath the logo for some snack cake company. It was the type of food that still had years before it would expire. Though, they probably tasted stale already.

Digby stomped toward her. "And just what is so important about," he looked down at the boxes before adding, "pie?"

"Because fall is almost over." She stared at him as if the reason should have been obvious.

"And?" Digbe made it clear that it was not.

"And you can't enjoy fall without pecan pie." She glanced to the side. "I suppose I'd rather it be pumpkin pie. But that isn't really an option right now."

Digby looked back to Hawk for answers, giving up on getting a clear explanation from her.

"There's, um, holidays in the fall. It's a lot of food and stuff." He couldn't help his tone from sounding sullen.

He'd always hated the fall. The only thing worse was winter. Everyone was always making a big deal about family gatherings. It was hard not to resent them as they ran around doing pointless things for the sake of tradition.

Parker caught the look in his eyes and lowered her head to the ground. "Sorry, I just always liked that stuff. You know, festive things. I thought maybe the people back in Vegas would like some pie to celebrate with. You know, after all they've lost."

Hawk nodded, trying not to resent her. He didn't know her that well, but it wasn't her fault for having a happy childhood.

"It's not just the holidays," Parker continued. "I used to go to the county fair every fall and try to steal a piece of pie from the baking competition. I got away with it most years, until that one time I ate too much and threw up on—" She winced and dropped the boxes before she could finish the sentence, raising a hand up to rub at her temples.

"You're still getting headaches?" Alex stood by the driver's side of the car, leaning on his open door.

Parker nodded. "I haven't been casting too many spells lately, so it hasn't been too bad. But the pain has been hitting harder whenever I think too much."

"Good thing you're adept at not thinking, innit?" Digby leaned on his staff and grinned at her.

Parker held up one of her pinky fingers and waggled it around as a reminder.

"I know, I know." Digby handed his staff to Hawk and went to help his ex-conscience with the load of pies she dropped without her needing to ask for a hand. The zombie had been like that for the last couple of weeks. Always quick to help Parker with anything she needed. He still complained constantly and said whatever sarcastic comment passed through his head with zero filter, but he never told her no. Hawk had even overheard him apologizing to her at one point when he hadn't known anyone was around.

Actually, he had overheard a lot of things since learning his Conceal spell.

The horde of zombies following the car let out a few random moans.

"We should get going." Alex patted his hand on the roof of the limo. "It will be getting dark soon."

"Thank god," Becca shouted from inside the car.

"Yeah, well, the vampire in the backseat may be looking forward to nightfall, but so are the revenants lurking in the surrounding buildings. So unless we want more to worry about than getting sniped by a zombie assassin, we really should be going. We gotta get the horde back to Vegas." Alex adjusted his eyepatch before dropping back into the driver's seat and closing the door.

Digby gestured for Hawk to pick up the rest of the boxes that Parker had been carrying while she rubbed her forehead. A minute later, they were loaded up with enough prepackaged pecan pies to feed half of Vegas. It wasn't enough for everyone, but there was plenty for every kid in Vegas to get one.

They got back to where they had arrived in the city earlier, a building called Faneuil Hall. The statue of Samuel Adams stood in the area outside. Hawk recognized the man's name from a book he'd been forced to read in school. Some shit about wanting to be a silversmith or something. He hadn't been paying a lot of attention.

Alex parked the vehicle off to the side as Parker opened a passage using a mirror that had been installed temporarily on the side of the building. It was big enough to get the limo through. Digby gave the order to send his zombies back to Vegas first.

Hawk shoved his hands into his pockets. The cold had begun to set in now that the sun was ducking behind the buildings.

That was when Becca decided to rise.

Hawk's vampire sister crawled out of the limo, yawning.

"You're all cutting things close. The revs will be out soon and I haven't killed a Guardian in weeks. I do not have the mana to fight anything right now." She shook her arms out, suddenly looking more alive than she had moments before.

"Yes, I know. You're likely to try to kill us if you use any magic." Digby continued waving more of his zombies into the mirror, barely looking in her direction. "You only remind us several times per hour."

"It's worth mentioning." Becca glared at him. "I am still the most dangerous threat in the area."

"I know you're a complete badass now. But even badass vampires can help carry these boxes." Alex smirked as he pulled a load of pecan pies from the back of the car only to drop two boxes when they fell off the top. "Aw, crap. Stupid brain cloud."

The artificer's agility was still impaired from the bullet to the brain he'd taken nearly a month ago. Ever since, Hawk had watched Alex trip over his own feet at least once every hour.

"I got it." Parker hopped out of the car and scooped up both boxes of pies from the ground. "We should probably stop dropping these; they're gonna be all crumbs by the time anyone eats them."

"They're probably crumbs already," Hawk added.

"I hope not." Parker held one of the boxes up to her ear and shook it.

That was when Becca straightened up and snapped her head to the side like a predator catching the sound of prey nearby. "Did you hear that?"

Everyone went quiet.

Parker lowered the box from her ear. "I don't hear any—"

Before she finished the sentence, Becca shouted, "Get down!" The vampire moved faster than any human could have, rushing toward Hawk.

For an instant, he thought she was going to attack. Then she plowed into him, throwing her body on top of him. The sound of something whistling through the air followed. Then a wet thunk. Hawk fell with Becca on top of him. The crack of bone hitting bulletproof glass came next. A jagged, white shape landed on the brick.

Hawk recognized it immediately.

It was a bone spike from a zombie assassin.

Boston was full of the things.

The monster revealed itself by lunging from a window three floors up, glass glittering through the air around it. The assassin landed on its weird hand-like feet near the statue of Sam Adams. Hawk scrambled to pull his hands from his pockets, regretting shoving them in there in the first place. With Becca's weight on top of him, he couldn't get to his gun.

"Get off of me!"

"Not a chance. Stay down," Becca said in a labored whisper.

Her breath huffed close to his ear, displacing his hair.

The zombie assassin let out a horrible roar as a glob of poison rose in its throat.

"No you don't!" Digby slammed the butt of his staff against the brick and threw his other hand out toward the creature.

The monster's roar stopped the instant he did. A water balloon-sized ball of poisonous, black goo popped out of its mouth with a fraction of the power it normally would have. It splattered on the ground a few feet away.

"That's better." Digby lowered his hand and gestured to the open Mirror Passage that led to Vegas. "Now go join the rest of the horde."

The zombie assassin turned and followed the rest of the dead as if nothing had happened. It vanished through the passage a moment later.

"Okay, now will you get off me?" Hawk pushed at Becca's shoulder to help roll her over.

She flopped onto the brick without resisting, landing on her side. The bottom dropped out of Hawk's stomach when he saw the blood on his hand. "Wait, Becca!"

Something white was sticking out of her back.

"Oh shit, someone help!" Hawk crawled toward his sister. She must have been hit by a bone spike when she dove into him. With her vampiric senses, she'd probably heard it coming a mile away. She'd just saved his life.

"I'm here, what do I do?" Alex stumbled toward them, landing on his knees behind her. For a moment, he reached for one of his flasks.

"Don't, healing magic will only hurt her," Parker shouted from where she stood near the Mirror Passage.

"Just pull it out." Digby rushed over, stopping to stand behind Hawk. "Her healing will do the rest."

"Wait, no." Becca shoved Alex to keep him away.

He fell back on his ass, crushing one of the fallen boxes of pies.

Hawk hesitated, waiting for one of the adults to do something. Then he realized he had to be the adult. Before he knew what he was doing, he reached out and wrapped his hand around the section of bone protruding from Becca's back. The thing was in there good. He didn't know that much about anatomy, but he was pretty sure it had gone straight through her heart. Becca reached for his hand, her body shaking with rapid shallow breaths. Her fingers fell just short of stopping him due to the awkward angle.

He yanked.

The spike held firm, stuck tight in the wound.

Becca let out a yelp.

He yanked again.

This time, the spike came loose with a sticky squelch and the nauseating sound of tearing meat. He tossed it to the side as soon as it was out, the piece of bone clattering across the bricks. Becca's breathing grew steadier almost immediately.

"You good?" Hawk leaned toward her.

She didn't even say a word before lunging at his throat. Shock crashed into him, unable to believe the level of aggression she threw in his direction. She had warned him. She had warned all of them. Still, he'd thought she had been exaggerating.

Her fingers swiped through empty air as he felt himself lift off the ground, Digby's hand tight around the back of his coat's collar. The zombie tore him from the brick with inhuman strength. The crack of a bone came from Digby's hand. He must've used his Limitless mutation. That was the only way he could have moved fast enough to beat Becca to him. The trade-off was that he had to go all out, literally throwing Hawk away from danger.

Digby let go of his coat, sending Hawk tumbling through the air. He slammed into the side of the limo and fell to the ground hard on his shoulder. Ignoring the pain, he got back up without hesitation.

"Becca, are you okay?" He stepped away, his back against the car.

His sister stood up with a wild hiss. Her shoulders were hunched like a tiger ready to pounce. Hawk flinched at the glowing embers drifting through her brown eyes. She stalked toward him, bearing her fangs.

Digby threw himself between them, dropping his staff and holding his arms out wide to block her path. Becca snapped her head to the side, in search of easier prey, finding Alex still sitting on the ground. He scrambled to the side and got to his feet. She lunged. The artificer stumbled and fell back to his knees. For once, his lack of agility had done him a favor as the vampire missed him by inches. Alex scurried toward the car after that.

"Get behind me." Digby shook a hand in his direction.

Becca skidded to a stop and spun, her eyes locked on Alex's back, her arms outstretched in his direction, her fingers curled like claws. A sudden burst of shadow exploded from her palm to send six or seven bats formed of pure darkness in his direction. The tiny shade formations pelted him in the rear.

He let out a random string of syllables, sounding like, "Whahaharl!"

Alex shoved himself up against Hawk's side a moment later in the safety provided by the zombie necromancer standing in front of them.

An annoyed hiss slithered from Becca's throat, only for her to turn back toward Parker who was still standing over by the open Mirror Passage.

"Go through the portal!" Digby swiped a hand through the air in her direction.

Hawk could practically see the gears turning in Parker's head. It was obvious she didn't want to abandon them, but they couldn't risk letting a rampaging vampire lose in Vegas on the other side of the passage. After a moment of hesitation, the pink-haired woman took a step backward to disappear through the rippling surface. The passage closed the moment she did.

A few zombies were left behind.

Becca hissed at the mirror before slowly turning back toward Hawk and Alex as they hid behind Digby.

"Now now, Becky." Digby's voice came out nervous as his attention darted around, clearly looking for a way to handle her. "I know how delicious these two humans look, but if I can resist these tempting morsels, then so can you."

"Don't call us delicious," Hawk groaned.

"Or tempting morsels," Alex added.

"This isn't time for complaints," Digby said through his teeth, tilting his head back toward them.

Becca stalked forward, her eyes flicking around as if judging the best angle to go at them.

"Now cut that out, Becky!" Digby tried to reprimand her into submission.

"I don't think that's working." Hawk struggled to keep Digby between them as she strafed to the side.

Alex did the same. "Can you use the zombies over there to grab her? Maybe pin her down or something."

"Good plan." Digby focused on his minions. "You heard him, capture this vampire. But don't hurt her!"

The zombies started moving, slowly, not having been enhanced physically yet. When the first one got close, Becca simply turned and ran her hand through its throat before ripping its head right off.

"Okay, that didn't work." Hawk's voice climbed with each word.

"Yes, but I don't want to do something that might kill her," Digby growled back.

Becca threw the severed zombie head she held in their direction. It bounced off the roof of the car.

"I think I'm more worried about her killing us." Alex flattened himself up against the limo.

"I don't see you coming up with any ideas," Digby snapped back at him.

"I just did. The zombie plan was mine."

"Yes, and that was a colossal failure."

"Will you two stop?" Hawk looked to the side for anything that might help, finding one of the doors near the front of the limo's passenger area ajar. It gave him an idea. "Never mind, I've got this."

Without another word, Hawk slipped out from behind Digby and rushed to the door. Pulling it open, he jumped inside. He glanced back at Becca as she locked her attention on him and broke into a sprint.

"Oh shit!" He threw himself through the car toward the back, nearly slipping on the magazine that lay on the floor.

The whole vehicle shook as Becca came after him through the door at the front. She slapped a hand down on one of the seats that lined the wall to stop herself. Her fingers dug into the leather so hard it tore.

Hawk popped the door at the rear of the car and shoved his shoulder into it. He rolled out onto the brick a second later and kicked it closed behind him. A ferocious snarl came from inside the limo as he stood up and threw his back against the vehicle to keep it closed.

"Lock it down!"

"On it." Alex dove into the open driver's side door and hit the button that secured the locks. Then he rolled out and slammed the door behind him before Becca could get at him through the open partition.

Hawk was pretty sure that even as a ravenous vampire, Becca still knew how to open door locks. Fortunately, the vehicle's security lockdown deactivated the buttons inside and out, so opening it required a physical key. Plus, the bulletproof glass was strong enough to keep her in.

Hawk stood next to the limo as it rocked back and forth in protest. Eventually, Becca settled down, pressing her face against the glass nearest him while biting at nothing.

"All right, I'd say that turned out as well as it could have." Digby clapped his hands as if they'd just finished a minor chore.

"Everyone okay?" Parker's face poked out through the surface of the mirror that had been mounted to the outside of Faneuil Hall. "No one got juiced, right?"

"Yeah, we're good." Alex sighed.

Hawk let himself fall back against the car, feeling the vibration of Becca pounding against the window. Hanging his head back, he stared up into the evening sky as a chill flowed through him.

A few tiny flakes of snow drifted down past the buildings.

He closed his eyes.

I hate this time of year.

CHAPTER TWO

"Here comes the helicopter." Parker held a pint bag of blood with a plastic tube sticking out in front of Becca's face.

She narrowed her eyes at her from the hospital bed she laid on. They'd gone straight to the emergency room the moment they returned to Vegas. Well, it wasn't exactly an emergency room. It had originally been a restaurant, but they'd converted it into a clinic over a week ago, complete with curtained-off beds and a waiting area. Most treatments didn't require more than a healing spell, but for Becca, healthcare was a little more complicated.

She leaned forward and took a sip of the blood that Parker offered. Then she adjusted her arms, trying to get comfortable with the handcuffs that secured both wrists to either side of the bed.

"Oi, you gotta put a little more in you." Harlow stood over her on the other side, looking strict. "You need a few more points of mana in that system of yours to make sure you don't get all murdery again."

"Are you sure that's enough?" Lana watched from the foot of the bed. "I don't actually know anything about a vampire's medical needs."

"I'll be fine." Becca sucked at the pint of blood that Parker was shoving in her face. It was nauseating yet wonderful at the same time. She didn't even know whose it was. Just that Lana had asked for volunteers after Digby and the others pushed the limo back through the passage to Vegas with her locked inside it. As far as how they got her out of the car, she had Harlow to thank for that.

The werewolf and last remaining member of the Fools had stayed in Vegas after arriving two weeks earlier. She mostly kept to herself, though she was always willing to help whenever she was asked.

According to Lana, Harlow had marched down to the parking garage the moment she heard Becca had lost control and declared that she'd wrangled a vampire before. She drew a pint of blood from Alex right then and there using nothing but a syringe from a first-aid kit and a Ziploc bag that had previously held a ham sandwich. Harlow ate the sandwich while they waited for the bag to fill.

After that, she'd opened the partition at the front of the limo just enough to toss it in.

A minute later, Becca regained control, though just barely. She needed around twenty-five mana points to keep from going on a bloodthirsty rampage. Anything less, and she would lose herself completely. Becca glanced to her HUD.

MP: 45/454

It wasn't a lot.

The moment blood left a human's body, the mana within it began to dissipate. Transferring blood from a human to her using a secondary container just wasn't efficient enough to give her much. Only biting was able to facilitate proper feeding, but there was no way to do that without spreading the curse or killing someone.

With just forty-five points of mana, it would only take one use of a high-cost spell to dip her below the threshold. It had taken two pints of donated blood to get her that high, too. Each one only gave her around twenty points. Unless someone wanted to open a personal blood bank just for her, she couldn't ignore the fact that she was in trouble.

Everything she'd been warned about was happening. She

couldn't keep her mana high enough without feeding. Even worse, the longer she went, the more points she lost from her maximum MP. It had been temporarily inflated past its maximum due to the swelling caused by killing a bunch of Guardians weeks ago. If she didn't find a way to maintain it, the added mana would dwindle back down to her original amount.

The more she thought about it, the less sense it made for her to take part in any kind of mission. It was just too dangerous for her to reasonably use her abilities. The only option was to try to live a normal life, never casting a spell or using any of her abilities. If she could do that, there was a chance that she could keep her mana high enough so that she could feel safe around people.

Who was she kidding?

A normal life?

That was impossible.

She was a vampire. The world she lived in would never allow for anything close to normal. Her only saving grace was that her abilities didn't work while she was in the vicinity of the sun goddess statue that kept some of the casino safe. The garage was out of range, but once she got inside, there was no chance of her losing control. Granted, that didn't mean she wasn't tempted by every human she passed.

Becca had hoped that reconnecting with the Heretic Seed would have solved some of the complications that had come with her new existence. Though, after regaining her connection to magic, little changed for the better. Her mana absorption rate was still terrible. Even worse, she was no longer an illusionist. Instead, the system had relabeled her as a nightmare.

The class couldn't have been more accurate.

STATUS
Name: Rebecca Alvarez
Race: Vampire
Heretic Class: Nightmare
Mana: 45/454
Mana Composition: Balanced (life essence incompatible)
Current Level: 33 (5,198 experience to next level)

ATTRIBUTES
Constitution: 51
Defense: 46
Strength: 45
Dexterity: 49
Agility: 46
Intelligence: 51
Perception: 77
Will: 47

AILMENTS
Life Mana Corruption

That last line was the kicker. Life corruption. Unlike Digby, whose body filtered out all types of essence except for death, her body let it all in. The caveat was that vampires couldn't process or use the life essence that came with it. Too much, and their entire manna system would become corrupted, essentially silencing her and taking away the supernatural abilities that came with her appetite for blood. During the daylight, it was impossible to keep the life essence in check. It just plowed into her system and made her feel awful.

Once the sun set, her body purged enough of the life essence from her system to regain its power. Her low absorption rate kept the rest in check until morning.

With the exception of a few, most of her previous spells had required an even mana balance to work, which included life essence. The result caused them all to fail when she tried to cast anything.

Lucky for her, she knew a zombie who had already gone through something similar. With a little encouragement, she had done some experimenting. According to Digby, if she kept trying, her spells would evolve.

And evolve they did.

Becca brought up a list of her new magic.

SPELLS

CONCEALING MIST
Description: Fill a space with an eerie mist. When entered, this mist will conceal your presence completely.
Rank: D
Cost: 50 MP
Range: 100 ft (radius around caster)

SHADE PROJECTION
Description: Project a shadow version of yourself visible to both enemies and allies. Shade projections may interact with their surroundings but will possess low strength values.
Rank: D
Cost: 25 MP
Range: Variable, dependent on the location of your target
Limitations: This spell can only be used with the intent to cause fear or psychological harm.

ABSORB
Description: Absorb the energy of an incoming attack. The absorbed energy may be stored and applied to a future spell to amplify its damage.
Rank: D
Cost: 30 MP
Range: 10 ft (radius around caster)

FICTION
Description: Increase the chance that your lies will be believed.
Rank: D
Cost: 30 MP
Range: Variable, dependent on how far your voice can reach.
Limitations: The likelihood that this spell will be successful or not will depend on how willing the target is to believe the lie. The effects of this spell may fade over time.

Becca sighed. She had regained a few of her spells as well. They were the ones that didn't require any life essence. Her primary offensive spell, Icicle, only needed fluid essence, and Cartography worked off soil and air.

The only spells that she had been unable to regain or evolve were her most important. Waking Dream, Ventriloquism, and Regeneration. Those had been replaced by her vampiric abilities. She willed the Seed to show her those as well now that they had official descriptions.

VAMPIRIC ABILITIES

SHADE CRAFT
Description: Form physical manifestations from the shadows around you, capable of damaging enemies.
Rank: D
Cost: Variable, dependent on the size of manifestations
Range: 50 ft (radius around caster)
Limitations: This ability can only be used with the intent to cause fear or psychological harm.

BANSHEE
Description: Allows the caster to project a voice or sound to another location.
Rank: D
Cost: 25 MP
Range: 100 ft (from caster or caster's projected shade)
Limitations: This ability can only be used with the intent to cause fear or psychological harm.

VAMPIRIC REGENERATION
Description: Automatically heal all damage upon receiving it.
Rank: D
Cost: Variable, dependent on the amount of damage
Range: Self only
Limitations: This ability cannot be canceled or delayed.

It was a lot to process. Even weirder was how her mind instinctively combined abilities to create the most dangerous and most horrifying results. It was like her instincts had shifted and terror came naturally to her.

The strange part was that she hadn't gained the blood sense ability that Digby had. She would have thought that would have been a given. Then again, being a vampire already gave her the ability to enhance all of her senses individually. Even her stats could be temporarily boosted. With all that power, blood sense wasn't really needed.

Her thoughts were interrupted by the sound of Parker mimicking the rotors of a helicopter as she poked her in the side of the face with the plastic tube that had been functioning as a blood straw.

"If you poke me one more time with that, I'm going to drink you." Becca gave her the harshest stare that she could.

Parker lowered the half-full bag of blood. "You know, it has been quite a while since I have gotten physical with anyone. And I'm gonna be honest here, biting is not a dealbreaker."

"That is," Lana paused, "more information than any of us needed."

"Well," Harlow patted the side of Becca's bed, "if you're in control enough to threaten people, then you're in control enough to not need me chaperoning you. So I'm going to go see about a spot of dinner." The short woman turned and headed toward the door of the clinic while Parker poked Becca with the plastic tube again. After another sharp look, the pink-haired soldier handed the half-full bag of blood to Lana and started for the door as well.

"On second thought, I haven't had dinner yet either."

As soon as she was gone, Lana pulled a key out of her pocket and slotted it into one of the handcuffs that secured Becca's wrists to the side of the bed. She hesitated before turning the key.

"You're sure you're in control, right?"

"Yes." Becca let out a long breath. "I just need to make sure I don't cast anything. And the sun goddess statue will prevent that as long as I'm in the casino."

"Alright." She turned the key.

Becca rubbed at her wrists, both glad to be free and afraid of what might happen. Still, she couldn't stay chained up forever. She gave Lana an appreciative nod and started for the door.

"Oh, don't forget this." Lana held out the half-full bag of blood. "You probably shouldn't waste it."

Becca took it, raising it like a glass of champagne and toasting sarcastically before continuing on her way. She hadn't actually been trying to be rude. She was just going through a lot.

Walking out onto the casino floor, she wandered through the rows of slot machines, sipping at her medicinal beverage and trying to pretend it was something else.

"I'm really going to need to find out whose blood this is."

She paused, not knowing what she was going to do if she found out. Should she thank them? Would that be appropriate? She shook her head and kept walking.

The activity on the casino floor had begun to die down for the night. It had already gotten dark back in Boston, but in Nevada, the sun was just setting. The strip outside was actually pretty safe. In the last two weeks, teams of artificers guarded by other Heretics had finished warding the entire place. After that, the rest of the casinos and resorts became usable again. No one had actually moved into them yet, since there was still plenty of room where they had started, but they were clear and safe. It all gave the city room to grow.

So far, they had assigned housing according to need, with the larger suites being given to families while individual rooms were assigned to people who wanted their own space. The fact that it was all free and safe kept anyone from complaining. Mostly they were just grateful. Eventually, the city might grow enough to a point where they started running out of room, but that was a long way off.

Walking towards the center of the casino, Becca stopped when she got to the statue of the sun goddess that had kept the revenants away. Technically, it wasn't even needed now that the strip had been fully warded. She grimaced, feeling her mana system twist itself in knots with the life energy present in the ambient essence around her. It was the result of the statue's mass enchantment. Having the sun goddess so close created the same conditions as natural daylight. Sure, it was great for the humans. Not so much for her. Walking around within its range wasn't so bad, but she got winded fast. Her only escape was to go outside or up to her room, which was high enough to be out of the statue's area of effect.

Becca did an about-face and headed back toward the casino's entrance.

Once outside, she kept walking all the way to the center of the strip where she plopped down on the curb to finish her drink. They hadn't lit up the entire area, but a lot of the lights had been turned on. People could get a lot done when they didn't have an empire trying to kill them. A part of her couldn't believe they had gotten so far. It almost seemed normal.

"Maybe there really is a chance I could live an ordinary life."

"Why would you do something so boring?" Digby's gravelly voice came from behind her, though she had heard his footsteps coming a mile away. The zombie wasn't exactly stealthy. More of a bull in a china shop type.

"It would be safer for everyone if I did." She answered without looking back at him. "That was how Leon got through part of the last century."

"I suppose I can understand that." He sat down beside her.

"You might be the only one."

The necromancer had gone completely off the rails in the week that he'd been walking around without a soul, but in the time since, after Becca had given him a part of hers, he had mellowed. He'd acted a little weird for the first couple of days, as if a little too much of her had become a part of him.

Fortunately, all that meant was that he refused to wear anything but pajamas on account of his pants becoming too uncomfortable and constricting. At one point, he seemed to be considering a switch to leggings, which probably would've made the goblin king proud.

After forty-eight hours or so, he began to even out. By the third day, he was back to being his normal, antagonistic self again. Though, he did retain her appreciation for music. She'd made a point to get him a phone and loaded it up with some of her favorite songs. He was quite partial to Bowie, which seemed appropriate somehow.

Music wasn't the only thing they had bonded over recently. The fact that Digby didn't sleep, combined with her aversion to the sun, meant that they had little choice in company. Oftentimes, they would cross paths like they were now and just hang out. She'd found out a lot about him in that time.

He had had a hard life and an even harder death. It almost didn't seem fair.

They still argued constantly, but she found herself blaming him less and less.

"We've come so far." Digby stared up at the lights. "It's almost hard to believe we were on the brink of annihilation up until recently."

Becca nodded silently.

"Glad to see you're getting used to your new place on the food chain." He gestured to the nearly empty bag of blood she was sipping on.

"Yeah, this is great," she said through a layer of sarcasm.

"Oh, stop sulking, Becky. You don't see me whining about my dietary restrictions."

"You don't try to rip the throats out of your friends and loved ones whenever your mana gets a little low." She chewed on the plastic tube that functioned as a straw.

"Yes yes, your existence is positively miserable. We all know." He reached a dead hand over and flicked her in the side of the head with a finger.

"What the hell?" She nearly spit blood in his face.

"Change is scary, Becky. I know it's easier to dwell on what you've lost. Believe me. I sure did." He gestured to the strip around them. "The world may have ended, but there are things to look forward to. If you spend all your time running from change, you'll never see any of it."

"You should get that written on a poster." Becca finished her drink. "I can put it up right next to that one of the cat in the tree saying, hang in there."

"I don't know what that means." He frowned.

"I'm going back inside." Becca stood up.

"Well, I never." Digby snapped. "Here I am, handing out the wisdom of my eight hundred years of existence, and all I get as thanks is sarcasm and snide remarks."

"Weren't you frozen for most of that time?"

"That is beside the point."

"Goodbye, Dig." She gave him a wave, which she knew would annoy him more than arguing back.

"Fine, I didn't want to sit around with you anyway." He stood up in a huff before shoving his hands in his pockets to retrieve a pair of earbuds that were paired with his phone. Then he stormed off.

Becca shook her head at the zombie and headed back toward the casino's entrance. He had been right about one thing, it was about time she stopped sulking. She crumpled the empty bag in her hands and shoved it in a trashcan on her way inside.

Putting up with the life essence flooding her system from the sun goddess's effects, Becca made a stop at the communal area at the heart of the building for a light dinner. She would have liked to have a larger meal, but being full of blood made the prospect less appetizing.

The space had been designed to look like the streets of Venice, complete with shops and restaurants. A fountain flowed at the center, surrounded by tables that had been set up for people to dine together, though many were used for playing board games as the evening set in. Most of the restaurants were closed since there wasn't a need for that many, but they had opened one as a buffet and another that sold simple meals that were already wrapped and ready to go, along with various snacks.

Thanks to some new developments in Hawaii, the restaurant now served a variety of fresh fruit. Mason had taken a team out to investigate some of the plantations on the island. To his surprise, there were already people there. The corporations that ran the farms had collapsed along with the rest of the world, but a group of ex-luau performers had taken over. The plantations were out in the middle of nowhere, so the revenants hadn't been that much trouble for them.

Due to the fact that the group was made up of descendants of the island's original inhabitants, it didn't seem right to try to claim any of the land. Hawaii had already been stolen once, so repeating history wasn't a good option.

Instead, Mason was able to negotiate an alliance. Vegas pulled out of the harbor and moved most of the warding there to the plantations to keep them safe. They were still allowed to return whenever they wanted, as long as it wasn't for any permanent occupation.

There was some discussion of offering magic to create a system of trade, but they had decided against it. Doing so would only create a power imbalance, since Vegas could take away access to the Heretic Seed just as easily as they gave it. It made more sense to produce warding materials to help the Hawaiians expand their territory to cover more of the island. In exchange, they supplied Sin City with produce, as well as some meat. Vegas hadn't run out of food yet, but they were still far from self-sufficient.

The alliance solved that problem.

Becca shoved her hand into her pocket and pulled out a few poker chips. The city's currency had already been adjusted several times, but for now, it seemed to be working for everyone. A base amount could be picked up once per week at the casino's front desk. It was enough to cover food and some basic items, with a little left over.

Beyond that, there was plenty of work to do to get more and the people were more than happy to do it. It didn't hurt that the work being done returned tangible results to the populace, giving them a strong sense of accomplishment. Even better, there was also a growing sense of community.

On her way in to look at the snacks, Becca passed a group of Heretics playing a card game after their shift and laughing. A few of them waved to her as she passed by. By now they had surely heard about her attempted rampage, yet they didn't bat an eye. She had Digby to thank for that.

After living in a community with a man-eating zombie that frequently reminded everyone that he was a man-eating zombie, vampires just weren't that extreme. Not to mention Union, Digby's animated skeleton, often interacted with the people. According to the infernal spirit, they were fostering a positive reputation with the rest of the working class. She had noticed an impact too. Union had picked up where Tavern had started, getting people used to living with the dead and the magic that had become a part of their lives.

Becca glanced back in the direction of the fountain near the entrance of the casino. It was where they had briefly stored a movie prop of the Holy Grail before it had been stolen by Bancroft before he disappeared. All they found in its place was the broken sword that Alex had used to cut her soul in two the week before. It had been lying on the edge of the fountain, along with a few drops of blood.

Bancroft must have used the artifact to break Digby's bond with Tavern. They had no idea what happened after that, just that they were both gone. She wasn't sure how she felt about it. The man that had arranged her murder had gotten away, free and clear.

Her feelings paled in comparison to how angry Digby had been that one of his minions had been stolen. The zombie had scoured the entire strip for three days in search of Tavern, but it was too late. Knowing Bancroft, she would never see him or the skeleton again. He'd probably snuck off to some airport or harbor, and gone to some safe house somewhere that he'd had waiting for decades.

Thinking about the man only annoyed her, so at a certain point, she decided she didn't care what happened to Bancroft. As long as he didn't come back, he wasn't her problem anymore. That was enough.

Becca stopped at a rack containing boxes of macadamia nut cookies that had been brought in from Hawaii. They were the specialty of a shop in Honolulu popular with tourists. So much so that a location had been opened at nearly every corner. She paid at the counter and left.

Nibbling on one of the cookies, Becca headed back out through the central area, passing a fountain. On her way, she couldn't help but notice Parker at one of the tables sitting with her head down.

Harlow sat across from her, working on a plate piled high with food from the buffet. It looked like Campbell had given her every-thing he could before closing up so that he wouldn't have to throw anything away. Harlow pushed a plate over to Parker, but the messenger barely looked at it.

The pink-haired soldier didn't look well.

It wasn't just the headaches, but her overall health had been declining as well. She was good at hiding the worst of it, like when a cat tried to keep an illness or injury secret. Thanks to the enhanced senses of a vampire, it was easy to see through her façade. Parker hadn't been eating much. Also, her movements were sluggish and unsteady. It was like her magic was draining the life from her.

They were going to need to find an alternative method of travel before they burnt Parker out completely.

They still had the cargo ship that they had used to transport Digby's horde during the battle with Autem. It was capable of flight, but just barely. Plus, if they were going to use an airship more regu-larly, they could do better than an empty cargo ship that smelled like corpses. That was why Jameson had taken two covens and a third of the city's artificers back to California to reclaim a new vessel. Alex had taken a few trips there as well in the last two weeks to help develop a better flight system now that they had more time to work the bugs out.

From the reports that Jameson had submitted, it sounded like the process was coming along well. Though, the information had seemed intentionally vague about what kind of ship they were working on. The last time she had asked Alex to clarify, he had winked and assured her it would be cool. She hadn't concerned herself with it any more than that. Whatever the ship was, it wouldn't be long before it flew over Vegas.

Becca shook her head at the thought, having trouble recon-ciling the fact that something so fantastical was now a part of everyday life.

Things had definitely gotten weirder.

Heading upstairs to her suite, she passed Hawk's new room. He had lived with her for a total of one night before she died. After she came back, it didn't seem safe anymore, so he moved a couple of rooms down the hall. She felt horrible leaving him on his own again, but there wasn't a better option.

Continuing on, she found Mason pacing the hallway. He was still wearing the hat that she'd given him before she'd died. She'd only seen him without it a handful of times since returning to Vegas. She wasn't complaining. Honestly, the rugged cowboy thing was working for her. She had a good mind to loot a duster from a store somewhere to complete the look.

The only thing that stopped her from pulling him into her room was the fear that she might bite him if she got too close.

"Oh, thank god." He rushed toward her the moment he saw her. "I heard about Boston. Is everything okay?"

She nodded, relaxing a little as he approached.

Mason had been her primary source of support over the last two weeks. There were obvious relationship challenges related to her new life as a monster that goes bump in the night, but Mason had been taking it well. He'd even been going above and beyond to accommodate her by adjusting his sleep schedule to match her nocturnal lifestyle.

He had also been patient with her about getting physical. They could still kiss, and there had been some cuddling here and there, but that had been it. It wasn't that she didn't want to do more, but she was still all too aware that he was food. It was an instinct that she just couldn't shake. She couldn't be sure that she wouldn't get carried away in the moment. Unlike Parker's little admission earlier, she was pretty sure Mason wasn't into biting.

"What happened?" He seemed to relax.

"One of those zombie assassins took a shot at Hawk and I had to jump in front of it. Healing the wound dropped me below my threshold and I ended up trying to kill everybody." She held the box of cookies out to Mason.

He took one. "No one got hurt, though."

"Just my pride." Becca sighed. "Fortunately, Digby had been there to get between us, and Hawk tricked me into trapping myself in the car. Apparently, I am not a genius when I'm hungry."

"Who is?" Mason laughed. "Glad Hawk is a smart kid. At least you know that he and the others can handle themselves when you get all…" He finished his comment by holding up both hands to mimic claws and hissing.

Becca glowered at him, annoyed that his impression was so accurate. "That doesn't make me feel better."

"It should." He lowered his hands. "You have been so worried about hurting everybody, but the first time things went wrong, you got locked in the car like a clown."

"Again, not making me feel better."

"My point is, you're not as dangerous as you think you are." He flicked the brim of his hat before snatching another cookie from the box in her hands.

"Oh really?"

"Really."

She lowered the box of cookies to her side. "Well, I'm glad that's what you got from my experience today. But what I got out of it was that it is way too easy for things to go wrong. Even now, I barely have enough mana to cast a spell without going on a rampage. Hell, if I cut myself on something, that might be enough to do it. And next time, things might not turn out as good."

"You're really going glass half-empty on this, aren't you?" He frowned.

"I'm being realistic." She put a hand on his arm. "But I am working on it. I just have to figure things out. I'll get there."

"I know you will." He leaned down to kiss her, sending her instincts into conflict.

A part of her wanted to push him away while the rest of her needed to pull him closer. Her mind settled on a compromise, leaving her standing awkwardly in place while dragging out the kiss. It ended when he pulled away.

"Hey, what happens if I scrape my tongue on your fangs?"

"Obviously, you would die instantly."

Mason laughed for a moment, letting it fade to an uncomfortable chuckle. "Wait, seriously?"

"No, not seriously. From what I was told, a bite has to be more significant to pass the curse." She smirked. "I have been waiting for that question, actually. It's one of those things that everybody feels the need to ask at least once. Well, that, and if it's safe to put anything else in my mouth." She rolled her eyes. "And I'll give you one guess who that question came from."

"Parker?"

"Parker." She nodded.

"That figures." Mason winced a second later. "But, is it safe though?"

Becca groaned. "I'm not into the rough stuff, so I think you'll be okay."

"Whew." He took off his hat and wiped his forehead with the back of his free hand in an exaggerated gesture. "Anyway, if you're feeling up to it, I stopped by the game library downstairs and borrowed a deck builder. Figured a board game was a good date activity with a low chance of getting bitten."

"Good call." Becca turned toward her room, stopping when she realized he had stepped in the direction of his door across the hall.

She froze. They had only been alone together in her room. She'd made sure of that. There was something about being within a space she controlled that made her feel more comfortable. Plus, she kept several bundles of warding rods in strategic locations so she could trap herself if the need ever arose.

He opened the door of his room and stepped inside without saying anything more. Becca debated on arguing but found the words missing. As scared as she was, she wanted to move forward. Too much of her life had been spent trapped in a room already.

Mason turned back to look at her with his hand on the doorknob.

Becca took a deep breath, then locked eyes with him. "Aren't you going to invite me in?"

"Very funny." He laughed and walked further into the room.

She frowned. "I… wasn't kidding. I need an invite."

His face fell. "Wait, really? That's a thing?"

"It is a thing."

"Wow, we are really in uncharted territory, aren't we?" He stood where he was for a moment before adding, "Oh, come on in."

Becca started to take a step forward but stopped when she glanced at her HUD. She still didn't have a lot of mana. If there was any kind of issue with his wording, the hearth ward active on his room could still be triggered. That would certainly wipe out the rest of her MP. The words, come on in, were clear enough, but they were far from a formal invitation. She couldn't take the chance that it was too vague. "Could you—"

He held up a hand before she could say more. "Sorry. You are hereby cordially invited into my room." He added a slight bow at the end, taking off his hat and placing it on his chest. He held the pose as he looked up at her. "Will that do?"

"That'll do." She stepped inside, relaxing when nothing happened.

Mason went about setting things on the table near the window as soon as she closed the door. "Do you want a beer or a soda? I should have some in the mini-fridge."

"No thanks, I'm full of blood." She dropped into a chair.

He froze. "Whose?"

Becca furrowed her brow. "I know one pint was Alex. I actually don't know where the rest came from."

"I'm just going to pretend I didn't hear any of that bit about the blood because I just kissed you and that feels a little weird."

Becca cringed, realizing she probably should've said something before she kissed him. "Sorry, I'll give you a heads-up next time."

"Yup, this is definitely uncharted territory." He continued setting things out on the table while making conversation.

That was when something caught her eye out the window on the horizon.

"What?" Mason asked, noticing that she was distracted.

Becca stood up, focusing on the night outside. It was normal to catch a revenant nightflyer flapping around out there, but this was something different. She stepped closer and pressed her hand against the glass. Without spending mana, she wasn't able to enhance her senses further.

"There's something out there."

Becca stared out at a white speck, waiting for it to get closer. The pints of blood in her stomach churned when she realized what it was.

An aircraft.

Autem was coming.

CHAPTER THREE

"I do not like this one bit." Digby stared up at the mana-fueled aircraft hovering over the strip.

After storming off from his conversation with Becca earlier, he'd been surprised when she'd come running back outside to find him. He'd been even more surprised when, instead of thanking him for his wisdom earlier, she just jabbed a finger at the sky and told him Autem was coming. He'd gotten on the radio immediately.

The entire city went into alert in under a minute.

The general populace had already moved to the casino's lower level where Parker was waiting to evacuate them to Hawaii if the need arose. As for their combat forces, they were armed and ready to go minutes later. They had made it out to the strip as one of the empire's mana-fueled aircraft approached. A force of over four hundred Heretics stood either behind Digby or were positioned in the surrounding buildings.

"What do you think they want?" Alex waited beside him, along with Mason and Becca.

"I don't rightly know." Digby kept his eyes locked on the owl as the aircraft began its descent toward the pavement. "Whatever it is, we are as ready as we are ever going to be."

The owl touched down, its rotating engines slowing to a stop. Digby narrowed his eyes. They couldn't have been there to attack. There was only one of them. If Autem wanted them dead, they would've sent the whole fleet. Then again, he didn't know what other weapons they had. Hell, there could be a nuke onboard.

No, Henwick would have to be insane to try that.

Digby still had a bomb of his own and he had made it crystal clear that if the empire made a move against Vegas, they would be sealing their own fate as well. Granted, the warhead that he had sitting in one of the vaults beneath the casino had been disarmed, and wasn't exactly in a state where it could be deployed quickly. Maybe Henwick had found that out somehow.

Perhaps they were no longer safe.

That was when the ramp on the owl popped open. He tensed as it lowered at an agonizingly slow pace.

"If things get bad, I only have about one spell before I lose control," Becca said. "After that, I need everyone to try real hard not to look appetizing. I'll try to take out a Guardian and get back up to full."

"It might not come to that," Mason said, his tone sounding hopeful.

"Just be ready for anything," Alex added.

Everyone collectively held their breath, staring at the open ramp. Digby worried that all the humans might just suffocate themselves if they didn't let it out soon. Then, a familiar figure dressed in white robes walked down the ramp.

He was old.

"Chancellor Serrano?" Digby watched as the elderly man strolled toward them before stopping about a dozen feet from the aircraft.

What the devil is he doing here?

Previously, he had only seen the empire's top government official through a Mirror Link spell when he'd negotiated the fragile peace that they had enjoyed the last two weeks. From what he could tell, Serrano was somewhat reasonable. Well, as reasonable as a person could be when also having had a hand in the destruction of the world.

Digby relaxed a little.

If Serrano was there, it was safe to say that whatever was happening wasn't an attack. He was just glad it wasn't Henwick that had shown up.

Everyone behind him let out the breath that they had been holding.

Then Henwick sauntered down the ramp.

A number of people behind Digby coughed out a gasp.

Six elite Guardians followed Autem's high priest out of the aircraft. Digby shouldn't have been surprised that he was there. After all, Henwick was the other half of the empire's governing body. He controlled the big stuff—like world domination—while Serrano handled the day-to-day and managed their citizens. The fact that they were both there raised the question, what could be so important to require an in-person visit from both of Autem's leaders?

They were taking a risk in coming there.

Digby had a small army at his back. In fact, it was possible that if he gave the order to attack now, they could kill them both and never need to worry about the empire again. The idea soured as soon as he'd had it. Even if they were able to kill them, the problem with attacking Henwick was that even if they won, they would suffer losses.

Digby glanced back at the men behind him. Could he really order an attack, knowing that many of them would die? It had been different when they had been fighting to defend themselves. He could accept the losses then. This was different. Ordering an attack would be the equivalent of throwing lives away.

"Hold your positions." Digby glanced to Becca. "No rampaging quite yet."

Serrano continued walking as soon as Henwick caught up to him. The pair continued toward them, the old man's robes fluttering in the breeze. Henwick was wearing an outfit similar to a modern suit, with a high collar. It looked like one of the uniforms he'd seen in the photos back on the naval base in Hawaii. The rest of the Guardians were dressed in full armor.

"Hello there," Serrano spoke first, gesturing to the army of Heretics standing behind Digby. "This is quite a greeting."

Henwick didn't say anything.

Digby eyed him before flicking his attention back to Serrano. "What is it that we can do for you, Chancellor?"

"Ah, yes." Serrano kept walking while Henwick and the rest of his men stopped. "With the way we left things the last time we spoke, I thought it best that we sit down and hammer out a more formal agreement. A treaty, if you will. If we are to enjoy a lasting peace between us, it's best to make things official."

"I was under the impression that not all of your side was on board with maintaining this agreement." Digby leaned to the right to look past the old man at Henwick.

"We have talked it through on our end," Henwick said from where he stood. "I may not like it, but I do have an empire to run. Sometimes the less palatable path is the only one that leads forward."

Digby chuckled on instinct. "That sounds an awful lot like admitting you were wrong."

"Now is not the time to gloat, Dig," Becca whispered from his side.

"Yes, well, obviously, we have had a lot to talk about." Serrano took charge of the conversation before it devolved into Digby and Henwick hurling insults at each other. "And I would like to think that we have a lot to talk about as well." He continued walking until he was standing just a few feet in front of Digby. "I must also admit, I have been looking forward to meeting you in person, Mr. Graves."

"Lord Graves," Digby corrected.

"Ah, very well." Serrano didn't bat an eye. "Lord Graves, then."

"I suppose it wouldn't hurt to have a conversation." Digby struggled to think of what to say next. The old man's polite demeanor had thrown him off balance. He wasn't used to being treated with respect. Insults, sure, he could do insults. But diplomacy? That was new.

He glanced back to the casino, realizing that they couldn't

negotiate something so important standing out there in the street. No, they needed to appear better prepared. Then again, he didn't want to allow Henwick or anyone else on Autem's side into any of the spaces that they regularly used. There was too much that they might see that could give them an advantage in a future altercation.

That was probably why they had come at such a late hour. To catch them unprepared and force them into letting them in to save face. That seemed like something Henwick would do.

Nice try. Digby cracked a grin.

If Henwick thought he could force his hand, he had another thing coming.

"I'm afraid you have caught us a bit unprepared. When we saw your craft, we were expecting a battle, not a polite conversation. If you could wait here for a few minutes while we prepare an appropriate venue." Digby nodded to himself as if congratulating his own ability not to put his foot in his mouth.

"Of course, say no more. That is to be expected." Serrano held up a hand.

"Good, good." Digby waited for a moment, hoping the old man would go back to wait in the aircraft he had arrived in. When Serrano didn't move, Digby cleared his throat and made a shoeing motion with his hand that he immediately regretted. Fortunately, Autem's Chancellor got the hint, turning back to the owl and gesturing for Henwick to follow.

The instant they disappeared inside the aircraft, Digby spun to Becca. "Holy hell, we need a place to take them."

"Ideally someplace that doesn't make it obvious how many people we have or that we are all living in one building," she added.

"I have a place." Alex stepped forward. "I've been doing some stuff in one of the buildings back that way. It's the one with the Statue of Liberty in front. I've been working on something in there, so I already cleaned up a little. As long as we take those guys in through a side entrance, it should look like we have ourselves put together as long as we finish tidying up."

"Perfect, good, that's why you're my apprentice." Digby turned to Mason. "Okay, you heard him, I want you to quietly assemble a team to get down there to start cleaning. Take Alex with you. Have everyone else disperse, and try not to make it obvious where they are going from here."

"Got it."

"And get Campbell to bring some food," Digby added.

"You want to offer Henwick food?" Becca eyed him sideways.

"Of course not, I hate the man. But if we offer them food, then it will look like the place is more operational than it is. Feeding Henwick is a small price to pay to maintain appearances."

"That actually makes sense." She nodded.

"Of course it does. Now let's go." Digby clapped his hands together and started casually walking away from the aircraft sitting in the street.

Becca followed while everyone else scattered.

Glancing back, he checked to make sure nobody was looking, Digby hastened his pace. At around a hundred feet he broke into a run.

"Come on, Becky, we have a lot of work to do."

CHAPTER FOUR

"Right this way." Digby stood as tall as possible as he led Serrano, Henwick, and their squad of Guardians through the side entrance of the casino that Alex had cleaned up.

"It is about time," Henwick commented in a voice loud enough to make sure everybody could hear. "You're lucky we didn't simply leave, Graves."

Digby ignored the comment, giving his primary enemy the silent treatment if only to annoy him. Instead, he responded to Serrano. "It would have been a shame to have turned back after coming all the way here."

The elderly man simply nodded as they stepped inside.

As it turned out, Alex's idea of clean left a lot to be desired. The main floor of the building still had a number of tables and chairs knocked over and other traces of the chaos that had passed through during the fall of the world. There was even a car parked in the middle of it that looked like it had been driven straight in through one of the rear entrances. Sure, the artificer had removed a few month-old corpses and tossed up some warding rods, but that was about it.

It took a crew of fifty to make the place presentable. The

process had stretched a few minutes into an hour faster than he realized. Hence Henwick's complaint.

Similar to the casino where everyone had been living up until now, the inside of this one had been done up to look like the streets of a city. Digby had been told that the real place existed somewhere in the northeast of the country.

The car that had been sitting in the middle of the space was still there. Digby would have liked to have removed it, but since it wouldn't start, there wasn't time to haul it away. To make the vehicle less conspicuous, Mason and a few other Heretics drove three more cars in through the doors where the first had crashed through. Parking them in a line next to the first gave the appearance that they were using the space as a garage where they could work on the vehicles.

After turning on the building's lights, and setting up one of the restaurants so that it looked like they had been using it, the staging had become somewhat convincing. Still, they took a path that kept most of the place hidden anyway.

An awkward silence followed the entire way up to the room that had been selected for the meeting. Digby didn't mind that part so much. He didn't want to talk to Henwick anyway.

Their destination was a smaller function hall, chosen because it was bracketed by a larger function hall on either side. This had been Mason's idea since he could fill both of the surrounding spaces with a hundred men each, all armed with swords, guns, and magic. Breaching charges had been placed along the walls that could be blown if something went wrong during negotiations, facilitating a surprise pincer attack.

Granted, when taking Henwick's level into consideration, his senses were bound to be strong enough to know how many men were surrounding them.

Digby watched as the man paused at the threshold of the negotiation hall. In the end, he didn't protest.

Inside, they had set up five comfortable chairs. Three on one side facing the doors, and two on the other. A space ten feet wide sat between them with a coffee table in the middle. A tray piled with some kind of food nugget sat on the table alongside a pitcher of water.

Digby walked in without hesitation to sit down in the middle of the three chairs that faced the doors. Alex sat down on his right while Becca settled in on his left. He gestured for Henwick and Serrano to take the remaining two across from him.

Their Guardians would have to stand.

Behind Digby, three covens of Heretics were already waiting, sitting at a few poker tables that lined the back of the room.

Serrano lowered himself into a chair.

Henwick dropped into the other, not waiting for the old man to get comfortable before speaking. "I'm going to put this—"

Digby interrupted him. "Can I offer anyone some refreshments?" He gestured to the tray on the table before looking to the back of the room where his covens sat. "What are they?"

One of the Heretics got up to check. "Um, those are dino nuggets."

"Yes, our finest dino nuggets." Digby nodded, not sure what that even meant.

"No, thank you." Serrano didn't look as impressed as Digby thought he should.

"Are you sure? We just had them made down in our kitchen."

"No one wants your blasted nuggets, Graves." Henwick slapped a hand on the arm of his chair. "This is serious." From there he launched straight into a list of demands. "You and your Heretics are not to show any aggression toward the Autem Empire. You are to stay out of our territory. You are not to interfere in our operations in any way shape or form. And you will allow a team of our specialists to examine the Heretic Seed. Only then will we agree to a permanent treaty."

Digby felt his mouth begin to fall open, but he stopped it a quarter-inch before it could qualify as hanging agape. His annoyance grew at not having been given any notice to prepare arguments of his own.

"Now you listen here." He prepared to unleash a string of insults, mostly to buy time to think, but Serrano held up a gentle hand before he could get rolling.

"First, I do want to say that you have impressed me, Lord Graves."

Again, Digby snapped his mouth shut to keep it from hanging open. "How's that now?"

"I was impressed with how you approached the situation two weeks ago." Serrano let his hand fall back to the armrest of his chair. "You could have killed me. You could have destroyed our entire capital. Yet, you didn't. You had a choice, and you chose peace. I realize the situation that you feel you've been put in, and the anger you must harbor, and you still chose a path of forgiveness."

"Bah." Digby scoffed. "Forgiveness has nothing to do with it. I chose not to kill the innocent people that your empire has gathered."

"Still, by offering us an open hand rather than a closed fist, it spoke to your character." He gave a kind smile. "I can't say I was too confident that peace could actually be reached between us until that point. In short, I believe that, despite our differences, you are someone that I can trust."

Digby eyed the man, searching for whatever trick he had up his sleeve. No one had ever spoken of his trustworthiness favorably before, it was hard to believe anyone would start now. Not to mention, this man was one of the empire's leaders. The same empire that hadn't batted an eye when wiping out billions to pave the way for their rise.

Becca spoke up before he had a chance to argue. "You can stop the good cop, bad cop act."

"Yes, I will admit that my ego may be easily stroked. But let me stop you right there." Digby leaned forward. "You talk as if the empire had nothing to do with the end of the world. As if we should just agree to your demands and become friends after every-thing your side has done."

Serrano let out a long sigh. "You are right, we have done things in the past that were regrettable."

"In the past?" Digby let out a mirthless laugh. "You destroyed the world little more than a month ago. I hardly think that's enough time to heal such a wound."

"I don't deny this." Serrano shook his head. "But I will say that not everyone within the empire desired such an outcome. Our goal has always been to protect mankind. And we will continue to do so."

When Becca scoffed this time, her reaction was followed by a brief hiss that Digby couldn't tell if was on purpose or not. "Protect? I've seen what you do to protect people. I saw what you did to the revenants. To the people who died to the curse that you modified and set loose. I saw the world that you are building."

"We are building a place where mankind will be safe to grow," Serrano defended.

"Only after you've erased everything that came before," Alex added half under his breath.

"What's done is done." Henwick stabbed a finger down into the armrest of his chair. "Arguing about it now will lead us nowhere. What matters is what happens next. And I think you would prefer an outcome that does not end with both of our cities being reduced to smoking craters."

Digby clenched his jaw, not liking the options before him. Henwick was right; destroying each other was obviously not a good option. Survival was what mattered.

No, it was more than that.

Everyone in Vegas was doing so well now that they weren't living in fear. He could tell just by looking at their faces. They had hope. He couldn't do anything to take that away. Yet, sitting in a room across from Henwick, being told that he just had to accept everything that the empire had done, left a bitter taste in his mouth. The idea that the empire could just get away with it all was unthinkable.

Unfortunately, they were not in any position to go about punishing them. A treaty was the only way to ensure Vegas's safety. At the very least, it would give them time to breathe.

"Fine." Digby rubbed the bridge of his nose. "The past, even the recent past, must stay behind us. But we can't possibly agree to all of your demands." He looked back and forth between Alex and Becca before adding, "And I think we probably have some demands of our own."

Serrano didn't seem surprised by this, his kind smile returning to his face. "That is what negotiations are for."

"And what are your demands?" Henwick asked in a tone that made it obvious that he was suppressing a laugh.

Digby narrowed his eyes at the man. "I will get to that if you could refrain from making your disdain for me quite so obvious. I say, you have pretty much made hating me your entire personality." He let a cackle roll through his throat. "Honestly, Henwick, you need to get yourself a hobby. I myself have found board games and music to be quite fulfilling."

"I don't need a hobby. I am eight hundred years old. I have had plenty of hobbies. Now what are your demands?" Henwick insisted.

The comment hit Digby with more impact than he'd expected, giving him a glimpse into the man's mind. Henwick had truly lived for centuries. For Digby, most of that time had passed in a flash. No wonder Henwick was the way he was. He'd already lived all that time. Enough time to do everything, see everything, and—most importantly—lose his connection to everything that mattered.

In short, he was bored.

The realization made so much sense, he couldn't believe he hadn't thought of it earlier. Hell, the only time he'd seen the man smile was during the battle two weeks ago. He was probably so desperate for something new that war was preferable.

At the same time, Digby found it all so unbelievable.

How could he be bored?

There was still much that Digby didn't know about the world, but what he did know was that it was amazing. Despite being technically immortal, it was hard to really think about it. So much had been created that he couldn't imagine getting sick of it. Though, he also knew how easy it was to get sucked into the minutia of everyday life. It was easy to forget about the wonders that the world had to offer. That was especially true for someone like Henwick, who had devoted his life to a set of ideals that forced his existence into a box formed of rules and guidelines.

He pushed the thought away, hoping that the same thing

would never happen to him if he was lucky enough to continue his existence that long.

Henwick was still looking at him expectantly.

"Yes, our demands." Digby went silent for a moment trying to think of what their most important concerns were while glancing to Becca for help.

"We can't let a team of yours anywhere near the Heretic Seed." The vampire stated the obvious.

Henwick started to speak up but Serrano beat him to it. "We understand your concern. However, as good as your intentions are, the Heretic Seed is a dangerous system, and we do need to make sure that its existence does not threaten the rest of the world."

The man may as well have erected a stone wall between them. They could never agree to let them anywhere near the Seed.

"It's that, or the smoking crater option," Henwick added as if sensing they were at an impasse.

Digby ground his molars together nearly hard enough to require repair. The man had backed them into a corner, using the threat of destruction to force them into agreeing to anything the empire wanted. It was the same tactic that Digby had used to stop the fighting. Having it used against him was infuriating.

Of course, he could simply say the same thing. The threat did go both ways, after all. His resolve wavered, remembering how much Vegas had gained in just two weeks of peace. The very idea of throwing its people back into the fight seemed cruel. That was where Henwick had an advantage. He didn't care if the empire's citizens were happy. They were just people that he'd gathered to fill his city and follow his rules. Hell, he lived on the moon, not among them. Serrano wasn't much better either. He may have been friendlier, but he had no problem sweeping away the atrocities that his side had committed.

Both of them wouldn't hesitate to bring suffering down on their own people.

Digby fought the urge to squirm in his chair. If he couldn't find some kind of leverage, he would end up giving Autem everything they wanted.

Then, he grinned.

Negotiations had never been his strong suit. No, he was more at home with scheming and trickery. There was plenty of room for that sort of thing in diplomacy, but not if he was trying to forge a lasting peace. Fortunately, he knew better than to try to do everything himself.

Digby clapped his hands together. "It seems we are at an impasse. Why don't we bring in a mediator?"

"A mediator?" Henwick folded his arms. "Who could you possibly have that could aid in this negotiation that is not already in this room?"

Digby gave a mental command to one of his minions without answering.

A moment later, the door opened. Both Henwick and Serrano turned around in their seats as a skeleton walked into the room with its skull held high.

"What is the meaning of this?" Henwick snapped his attention back to Digby.

"Allow me to introduce our mediator, Union." Digby gestured to the skeleton.

"I daresay I am confused as well." Serrano frowned.

Henwick let out a huff. "That is a minion, not a mediator."

"We are both." Union walked through the room and stopped in the middle, between their two sides.

"That's right, they are both." Digby set his hands down on the arms of his chair as if the matter was settled. "Now, if you could repeat your demands, my advisors and I will discuss the matter."

Henwick tapped his fingers on his chair, clearly getting impatient. Then he leaned forward and repeated their demands.

Union responded before he'd even finished. "Your terms are unacceptable."

Henwick ignored the skeleton. "Really, Graves, is this supposed to help the situation, or are you just trying to frustrate me?"

Digby chuckled. "Honestly both, but you are going to have to put up with it for now." He looked to Union. "What are your thoughts on how to move forward?"

His skeletal minion had spent the last two weeks trying to negotiate more favorable treatment for the horde, which didn't make a whole lot of sense considering they were dead. However, they had actually brought up a number of good points that applied to all of the city's residents, not just the reanimated ones. Digby had relayed many of the skeleton's arguments to Elenore. In turn, she implemented a number of new policies. Policies that had proved beneficial as their populace transitioned from survivors to citizens. The skeleton had a knack for negotiations. Digby was especially aware of that, considering he himself had made several concessions on how the horde was stored and how he called upon them for use.

Union tapped one bony finger against the side of their jawbone. "It is best to put all agreements into writing."

"That's actually a good point." Becca nodded.

With that, a desk and chair were brought into the room and placed off to the side where the skeleton had been standing. Union dropped into the chair without hesitation and Mason set a stack of loose paper down in front of them. They began writing immediately, only stopping briefly to look back at Mason when he leaned in to look over the skeleton's shoulder. A minute later, Union stood and handed the paper to Digby

He read over the suggestions that his minion had made, nodding along as he did. He folded the paper in half when he was finished and set it down on the side of his chair.

"Alright. First, we have the main sticking point, the Heretic Seed. At this time, we must remain firm in our insistence that none of Autem's people be allowed to access the obelisk."

Henwick let out a growl. "We are right back where we started."

Digby held up a hand. "I said we must remain firm at this time, but that does not mean there is no potential to revisit the issue in the future. If this truce holds and both of our sides are able to prove that we can coexist, then allowing your people access to the Seed is not out of the question. However, those people will be supervised and searched thoroughly prior."

"What difference does now versus later matter?" Henwick argued.

"No, that does sound reasonable," Serrano accepted. "Allowing time to foster trust is valid."

Union started writing on a new piece of paper, making note of the agreement.

"In addition," Digby continued, "if we are to allow you access to the Heretic Seed's obelisk, then you must also give us access to the Guardian Core."

Henwick gasped. "Absolutely not!"

Digby narrowed his eyes. "Why? Wouldn't that be fair?"

Serrano spoke up. "It would be, but as I understand it," he shifted his focus to Becca, "one of your people has already had access to the Guardian Core. Taking that into consideration, allowing us to inspect the Heretic Seed would be akin to paying a debt."

Becca sat forward. "That would be true if, when I was there, I had been allowed to inspect your system fully to gain a thorough understanding. But I was only able to secure a few brief minutes. If you want to count that as part of this agreement, then we would have to limit the amount of time that your people spend with the Seed as well. That would be fair."

Both Serrano and Henwick remained quiet for a long moment.

Then the elderly man spoke up. "Very well, you will be given access to the Guardian Core to inspect it at your leisure. Under supervision, of course."

"Of course." Union jotted down a few more lines onto the document in front of them.

Digby relaxed a little, glad that the worst of it had been avoided for now. "As per your request to stay out of your territory, we will agree, but with stipulations. First, your territory is not defined and there's nothing stopping you from staking claim wherever you wish. This makes it extremely likely that we will inadvertently break this agreement without knowing. Instead, we will agree to refrain from making any aggressive actions or attacks within your territory. And obviously, you would do the same."

Serrano nodded without putting up a fight, Henwick remaining silent as well.

Union added another line to the treaty.

"We will not interfere with your operations. Provided you inform us of such operations beforehand. Again, it would be very easy for us to disrupt something if we don't know what's happening."

"You expect us to pick up the phone and give you a call?" Henwick asked, his voice dripping with sarcasm.

"We would, if the phone still worked," Becca countered.

"I can set up a mirror that one of your people can touch before you leave. And we can give you one as well to take with you that our messenger has touched," Alex suggested. "That way we can communicate easily."

"That is… also reasonable." Serrano sighed, clearly hoping to have gotten away with more. "Now, that seems to be everything."

"Not quite." Digby gestured for everyone to remain seated. "We have one more demand of our own."

"And that is?" Henwick leaned to the side, resting his elbow on his chair as if bored.

Digby let his usual grin fade. "You will stop abducting children."

The room fell deadly silent until finally, Serrano spoke.

"But we aren't abducting children."

"The hell you aren't." Digby slapped a hand against his thigh.

"We are saving them." Serrano looked deeply hurt. "If it had not been for our efforts, hundreds of young lives would've been lost already."

"Yet you didn't rescue so many others. Others that were old enough to challenge your authority." Digby kept his eyes on the man.

"There wasn't time. Saving the children had to take priority. In time, we would have returned for others."

"Sure you would," Alex commented.

"I have seen the world that you are building." Becca dug her fingers into the cushions on the arms of her chair. "It is a world that erases everything that came before and replaces it with whatever version you believe the Nine wants. So don't pretend that you aren't taking children for a reason."

"That's right, you take the young and indoctrinate them into your beliefs while hiding from them anything that could make them question your authority." Digby remembered the teenager who had burned himself alive nearly a month ago rather than escape from Autem's clutches. It felt good to finally say something to the men that caused that death.

Serrano's face fell. "You're right. We do indoctrinate the young. And we do hide things that might hinder their faith in the Nine."

"Good, then you'll stop," Digby said with a sense of finality.

Serrano shook his head, adding a simple, "No."

"What do you mean, no?" Digby growled back.

"You have to understand, the Nine are real. They know what's best. We do these things because they are the right course of action to protect mankind's future."

"That is what you believe. But everyone deserves a choice." Becca stood up, the Guardians behind Serrano flinching at the sudden movement. She ignored them and continued. "By forcing your beliefs on others, you're taking away their free will."

"I see the Fools have gotten their hooks into you." Henwick eyed her.

"Well, maybe they have a point." A low growl rumbled through her.

Serrano stood up as well, stepping toward her. "Calm down, young miss. We may disagree, but no one is challenging your free will."

"But you would if I was still young enough not to have thoughts of my own." She eyed him, looking like she might lunge at his throat.

"Of course." He gave her a kind smile while admitting to it so easily. "I realize you want to paint the empire as evil, but we are not doing anything new. Everyone has free will, but that doesn't mean it's wrong to guide it. Everyone wants to have their beliefs and traditions preserved. Would you tell a Catholic that they can't raise their children in the church, or send them to a private school where they only interact with others born into the same beliefs? Would you stop the Christians from providing youth groups? Of course, you wouldn't. You wouldn't, because you respect their free will. All we are asking is that you respect ours, just as this treaty requires us to respect yours."

From the look on Becca's face, she wasn't finished. Yet she refrained from adding more and worsening the situation.

Digby let out a long sigh.

There wasn't much more they could argue about. Sure, he could insist that the empire give their citizens a choice in what to believe, but how would that work? If anyone within their capital denied the existence of the Nine and insisted on another path, Autem would just show them the door and send them out to die in the monster-infested world that they created. No one would give up the safety that they offered to retain their freedom.

"Fine." Digby approached the desk where Union was writing. "What we do with our respective populous will be left off of the current treaty. As for any new survivors that are found out there in the world, they must never be forced to go with your Guardians."

"We can agree to that." Serrano nodded. "Any survivors we find will be given the option to remain where they are or to join us in our capital."

Digby frowned at the willingness that the man accepted the demand. Of course, he did. All it meant was that they wouldn't outright kidnap anyone, but that didn't really mean much. No one was actually going to say no to them.

"The document is complete." Union handed Digby a piece of paper.

He took it and handed it to Serrano, feeling a little like he'd somehow sold out the rest of the world in exchange for Vegas's survival.

"I must say, you drive a hard bargain, Digby." The old man chuckled as if they suddenly became friends.

"That's Lord Graves," he grunted back, making it clear that they hadn't.

The sooner he was gone, the better.

CHAPTER FIVE

"Finally." Becca stood at the window as Henwick, Serrano, and their squad of Guardians walked back across the strip to where their aircraft waited.

"Agreed." Digby tapped his finger on the glass beside her. "The sooner they are gone, the better."

Becca shuddered, still bothered that they had even been there. After everything she'd seen, negotiating with anyone from Autem was like a poison pill. She stepped closer as the group outside traveled down the strip, growing smaller with each passing second.

Two of their men carried a mirror between them that Parker and Lana had touched to give them a means of communicating with the empire if need be.

"It all leaves a bitter taste in your mouth, doesn't it?" Digby grimaced.

Becca felt a hiss brewing in her throat but swallowed it back down. She had to stop letting her instincts get the better of her. No matter how much she wanted to resist the empire, the fact remained, she couldn't. Not without putting others at risk.

"Can a treaty really work?" Alex approached the window to join them.

The rest of the Heretics had already gone back downstairs to close up the building before turning in for the night. Now, it was just Digby, Alex, Mason, and herself. Union was there as well, but the skeleton hadn't moved an inch or spoke since the negotiations. No, they just sat at the desk with their fingers steepled.

"This feels wrong." Becca spoke her mind. "It's like we're letting them get away with everything."

"What choice do we have?" Mason dropped into one of the chairs that sat in the middle of the room and picked at the tray of cold dino nuggets that sat on the coffee table.

"And that is the crux of it, isn't it." Digby grimaced. "There is no choice."

"Are we really going to let them have access to the Heretics Seed?" Alex picked up the pitcher of water from beside the plate of nuggets and poured himself a glass.

"No." Becca sat down in a chair next to Mason. "And we have Union to thank for getting us out of that demand."

"You're welcome," the skeleton said without moving.

"Jesus!" Mason jumped. "I forgot Union was here." He gestured to Digby's bony minion. "Skeletons just blend in now whenever they're not moving. But how is Union's idea stopping Autem from examining the seed?"

"Simple. It's unlikely Henwick will ever allow us anywhere near the Guardian Core." Digby walked across the room to join them. "By making the same unreasonable demand as them, we created a deterrent that should prevent them ever requesting access."

"Henwick would never risk letting me near the Guardian Core again. Not when its caretaker is on our side," Becca added.

"What's on our side?" Parker wandered into the room to join the conversation.

"The Guardian Core's caretaker was created by the Fools. The empire stole it and used it to implement their magic system. Its capabilities are heavily restricted, but it will still do whatever it can to help us." Becca caught the pink-haired soldier up on the details.

"Well, that sounds like a horrible existence. Glad I'm not the Core's caretaker." Parker sat down and poked at one of the dino nuggets on the table without actually eating it.

"Was it just me, or did the list of demands that Henwick came in here with seem tailored to make sure we would break them by accident?" Mason leaned back in his chair. "It was all so vague."

"Indeed." Digby paced a few steps before turning back and going in the other direction. "I'm satisfied with the details that we were able to hammer out to avoid misunderstandings. However, it does seem that Henwick's demands held a secondary objective to spark a new conflict."

"But we still have the nuke." Alex joined Digby, pacing in the other direction. "Even if we broke the agreement, Autem can't do anything to us without risking nuclear retaliation. We should be safe. It's not like they can restart the war."

"I wouldn't be so sure. I'm sure Henwick is looking for a way around it as we speak." Becca considered the situation. "Plus, if we break the agreement, they could try other avenues to reprimand us. Small things that might chip away at our capabilities. We have to make sure not to let them get the upper hand. The nuke is a significant deterrent, but it would be best not to rely on it. It may not remain viable forever."

"Forever, no. Long enough, maybe." Union spoke up.

Digby turned abruptly to face his minion. "What the devil do you mean?"

"Empires are often mistaken." Union leaned forward on the desk, placing their hands down so that their bony fingers interlocked in front of them. "People will revolt."

"Like a rebellion from within Autem?" Alex set his glass of water down on the skeleton's desk.

"Control through force will not work long-term," Union added.

"That is a good point." Mason nodded. "Countless governments throughout history have tried to rule through rigid control systems. There will always be people who want the guidance of something like the Nine, but there will be others who will push back when it becomes too restrictive. That kind of situation doesn't tend to end well."

"People will organize." Union stated the outcome as if it was a fact. "A spark is all that is required."

"That's when they break out the Molotovs." Parker poured

herself some water from the pitcher, spilling a fair amount on the floor in the process.

"So if we sit back and wait, the empire might doom itself." Digby paced in the other direction. "If Autem's populace stirs up trouble for Henwick, we could always swoop in and lend them a hand. Might even come out of it looking good." The zombie stood tall, with one hand on the lapel of his vest like a leader standing for freedom and justice. Then he ruined it by saying, "That would really drive Henwick mad. It would be worth it for that alone."

"How noble." Becca placed a hand over her eyes as she shook her head. She dropped it back down a second later. "Wait, they still have magic."

"What's your point?" Digby dropped his hand from his lapel.

"The Guardian Core isn't like the Seed. They have it rigged to control who can and cannot use magic, or take it away from their own people if they need to. It can even alter the chemical balance in the brain. Hell, magic has completely replaced medical care at this point. If Autem can deny their undesirables basic medicine, the uneven power dynamic in play may not be something a rebellion can overcome."

"I'm afraid all this conjecture might be more than we can take on right now." Digby shoved his hands in his pockets. "Imagining the empire collapsing due to its own arrogance is a fun thought experiment, but we have a city of our own to worry about. And after these last two weeks of peace, it's clear that we have a duty to maintain this treaty for as long as possible. If that means abiding by this agreement, then that's all we can do. It's not like any of us wanted to fight a war, anyway. I would much rather never fight again."

"So you just want to wait and see?" Alex asked.

"As Mason said earlier, what else can we do?" Digby shrugged.

"It still feels wrong." Becca leaned forward to rest her chin in her hand. "I saw the city that they plan to build. They had a model of it there in the capital. I can't believe there's nothing that can be done to stop them from building it."

"I don't like it either, not one bit." Digby lowered his head. "But we have little room to challenge the status quo." He looked up a moment later. "At least, we can't right now. But that doesn't mean we can't explore other options. There is a lot of magic out there, and we have yet to discover much of it. There is sure to be something that can even the odds. And if Henwick begins to lose the support of his people, then we just need to beat him."

"Maybe," Alex said. "But where do we start?"

"I haven't the slightest idea." Digby shrugged. "That's why I want you all ready to gather more zombies first thing in the morning. We can discuss things while we are out." He turned toward the door. "So get some rest. I know you humans still require sleep."

Everyone got up and motioned to follow.

Everyone except Becca, who was not one of the humans in question.

"About tomorrow…" she trailed off.

"Yes?" Digby turned back to stare at her expectantly.

Becca swallowed before answering. "I'm not going tomorrow."

"Why? What could you possibly have to do?" Digby snapped back.

"No. I mean, I'm not going on any more missions." She struggled to look anyone in the eyes. "I've been thinking about my situation, and it just doesn't make sense to bring me with you. I'm a liability."

"What will you do then?" Digby threw a hand out. "Putter around the casino?"

"No." She balled her hands into fists. "I'll find something to do. I have other skills beyond ripping people's throats out, you know. I just want to try to live a normal life. And before you complain, I'll still be here to help in a non-combat capacity."

"And what does that mean?" Digby growled back.

She shrugged. "I don't know, I can give advice or something."

"Oh goody, words of wisdom. I'm sure that will mean a lot the next time we're surrounded by revenants." Digby frowned.

"Hear her out." Mason held out a hand to help.

"Yeah, don't be a dick, Dig," Parker added.

"Agreed." Becca folded her arms. "I have thought about this. And it's what's best for everyone."

Digby's frown grew more severe, looking like he might explode as silence fell over the room. Then, he just deflated. "Fine. Do what you want."

Becca raised an eyebrow. "Is that a, 'fine, do what you want,' meaning fine, do what you want? Or is it a, 'fine, do what you want,' and you'll be pissed for a week?"

"Honestly, a little of both." He shoved his hands in his pockets. "If I can't change your mind then there is no sense in trying. I don't like it, but I will accept it. Otherwise, I would be being..." He glanced to Parker before adding, "A dick."

"It's true." The pink-haired woman nodded.

"Indeed." Digby spun on his heel and continued walking only to stop when he reached the doorway. "A normal life, you say?"

"I'd like to give it a try." Becca took a step forward.

"Alright." Digby glanced back. "But when you get sick of it, we'll be waiting."

CHAPTER SIX

"This day just gets longer and longer." Digby stood at the fountain that had become the casino's town square.

He sighed. With Becca backing out of missions, he was running out of reliable allies. Things hadn't gone well the last time everything had been left up to him. A part of him wanted to march back to the vampire's room and try to convince her to change her mind. Though, that would probably have the opposite effect. He was finally starting to understand that pestering people only served to push them away.

It wasn't that he even disagreed with her.

Well, it was.

Yet it wasn't for the reason she seemed to think.

Sure, he didn't want to go on missions without her. Becca had become powerful enough to rival even him. It made no sense to leave her home. More importantly, it didn't feel right. A normal life? Bah. That was never going to work. It was like she was trying to deny what she had become with the hope that it would go away.

Becoming a monster was hard. He knew that well enough. He knew how easy it was to hide from the truth and pretend he was still human, or that he could become human again. In the end, he was only able to move forward when he'd accepted what he'd become.

He was pretty sure it was the same for Becca.

The only way forward was to embrace her new existence. At the very least, she would be happier. The bottom line was that she was his friend, and he wanted to help her. His mind circled around the issue, trying to come up with a way to explain that to her without sounding like he just wanted her help on missions.

Even worse, everyone else needed to rest for the night, leaving him to wander through the late hours alone. Sometimes he wished he could sleep like the humans that surrounded him.

A few patrols of Heretics were still out and about to keep the city safe, but Digby didn't want to disturb them just because he was a bit lonely. No wonder Henwick had ended up the way he was.

"If I'm not careful, I might become just as bored and isolated as him."

Then he shook his head.

"Bah, that will never happen. Not when there's a whole world of interesting things that I have not yet discovered. And I'm never alone. Not really. Not when I have a minion that would be happy to spend time with me."

Digby reached out to Asher across their bond, getting a cheerful flutter in return. The zombified raven cawed as she swooped in over rows of slot machines to join him moments later. She landed on his shoulder as soon as she reached him.

"There you are." He patted her side. "What do you say we go find ourselves something to do?"

Digby retrieved his phone from a pocket, along with the little white earpieces that were paired to it. Popping them in, he tapped play on the device's screen. Then he tapped it several more times when it failed to respond to his dead fingers. It was a common issue. Eventually, he gave up and retrieved a pen that had a pad on the end that connected to the screen better. The voice of David Bowie flowed into his ears, reminding him of the goblin king whose pauldron he sometimes wore. He'd listened to several artists, but Bowie was one that he kept returning to.

With that, he turned and headed off toward the function hall that they had converted into a library. It had been one of the first services that they had set up after putting down roots in the city. Survival was important, of course, but with so many people living there, they couldn't overlook entertainment. The library had filled the void to become one of the most important places in the casino.

There were many books but there was also much more. Shelves upon shelves, actually. They had been reclaimed from various shopping centers in the area. Occasionally, he would read to Asher in the late hours of the night. The raven always hung on his every word.

In truth, Digby didn't care much for reading.

The problem with being eight hundred years old was that there was so much he'd missed. He couldn't make it more than a page into a book without the mention of something that he lacked the context for. Without visuals to clue him in, frustration would always set in. That was why he stuck to movies. At least with video, he could see what was going on. If he didn't understand something, he could still work it out.

Asher seemed to enjoy movies as well, and was always happy to perch on the back of a sofa while he watched one.

The library was filled with row after row of shelves. They held everything from collections of ongoing episodes divided up into seasons, to full-length movies. As a backup, a small team had been put in charge of recordkeeping and preserving history. It was their job to copy everything in the room onto multiple computers, just in case something ever happened.

On the far end of the function hall was a section devoted to board games as well as some tables to play them. That had been the most popular area. Opposite that, there were a few shelves holding a different type of book. Digby didn't mind those since they had pictures filling the pages. Comics was what the sign affixed to the shelving called them.

Alex had recommended a few, but Digby had yet to check them out.

"Maybe I should give one of those a try tonight." He strolled down to the end of the room and reached out for the spine of a particularly colorful volume. Then he stopped and looked down at his hand. "Maybe I should wash first."

He wasn't quite sure when the last time he'd washed his hands had been. Surely it had been earlier that day, but he'd touched many things after that. Obviously, it didn't matter to him what he'd touched. He was dead. It wasn't like he could get sick. Yet, the library was a public resource, and anything that he handled was bound to be borrowed by someone else later.

He forgot all about the issue a moment later when his blood sense picked up something coming from the other side of the room.

It wasn't anything significant, just the sensation of someone moving mana through their body. At first, Digby didn't think anything of it. There were plenty of Heretics around, and it wouldn't be out of the ordinary for any of them to be casting a spell. Then he remembered that the room had been empty when he'd entered. With the majority of the settlement upstairs in bed, it was unlikely that somebody had come in behind him.

Digby pulled out one of his earpieces and listened. He didn't hear anything.

"That's odd."

With a thought, he told Asher to fly up and land on top of one of the shelves to get a look at the rest of the room. She sent a sudden feeling of concern across their bond as she did.

Alone, we are, she reported back through their link.

"We'll see about that." Digby turned around pulling his other earpiece out and pocketing them. "Who's there?"

Nobody answered.

The only one Digby could think of who might be sneaking around in the middle of the night would be Hawk. The young rogue was casting Conceal constantly, even when there was no need. It seemed like snooping was his favorite pastime. He'd already got the spell to rank B. Which was impressive, considering how little experience Hawk had with magic.

"Hawk? That you there?" Digby ambled to the side to look down one of the other aisles of shelves.

Again, there was no answer. Though, that wasn't enough to

rule things out. It wouldn't have been out of character for Hawk to remain silent. Especially if he was up to no good, which was also entirely possible.

Digby glanced to the information ring that floated at the edge of his vision, willing it to show him a log of Hawk's recent spell uses. He arched an eyebrow. The rogue hadn't cast anything for the last couple of hours. Next, he checked the Seed for all spell uses within the last five minutes. His HUD showed the results. There were only two, a Regeneration and a Mirror Link.

That's not good.

Neither of those spells would explain what he had sensed coming from the same room as him. The information brought up the obvious question; if he had noticed a spell being cast and it wasn't one of Las Vegas's Heretics, then who was it? The fact that Henwick had landed an aircraft on the strip not too long ago stuck out as entirely too suspicious. Autem's people may have left, but that didn't mean none of them had stayed behind.

The thought actually made Digby feel a little better. After meeting with his enemies and hammering out a peace treaty, he had been waiting for something more to come of the visit. Henwick had to have something else up his sleeves.

Digby checked his mana.

MP: 502/502

He checked his resources as well.

Sinew 55

Flesh 33

Bone 42

Viscera 74

Heart 43

Mind 57

Sparks 3

Digby willed his Body Craft mutation to shift both hands into claws. He wasn't about to let anyone get the drop on him. Then again, he wasn't about to lash out prematurely either. The last thing he wanted was a repeat of the murder he'd committed a few weeks back. He hadn't been careful then, and he'd regretted it ever since. Everyone might have written it off as something he'd done while his mind was impaired, but that death still weighed on his mind.

A small part of him wished he still had Sax as a minion. The elite zombie had been a powerful asset. Despite that, he'd released the soldier's corpse shortly after the battle two weeks ago, and laid him to rest. As strong as the minion was, it was clear that reanimating the body of a friend was not something that the rest of his allies would ever be comfortable with. Not to mention Sax had already fought long enough. The moment Digby regained a soul, he understood that the soldier deserved better.

Still, it would have been nice to have some more backup.

"If someone is there, speak now, or I can't be held responsible for what might happen."

Digby tapped a claw on one of the shelves as he slowly made his way toward the door that he had entered through earlier. It was propped open so that anyone could have followed him without making a sound. Reaching it, Digby flicked the little hinged stopper that kept the door from closing. The function hall had two more exits, but both were closed. If someone was hiding in there with him, they weren't getting out without him knowing. It was possible that he'd already scared them off by calling out earlier. If so, they would be long gone.

Then again, if they were there to harm him, they might be preparing to attack at any second.

"Who sent you?" He stalked back down one of the aisles of shelves, sweeping his gaze back and forth. All he had to do was doubt what his eyes showed him. That would be enough to unravel a Conceal spell.

That was when he sensed more mana flowing. He spun. This time, it had come from somewhere near the board game section of the library. Digby's mind raced to the possibilities of what the spell could have been. Whoever his opponent was, they were either an illusionist or a rogue.

"So you're a rogue, then?" A cackle rumbled from Digby's throat, his assumption based on the information that if the foe had been an illusionist, they probably would've cast multiple spells by now. A rogue, though, had fewer options. If he had to guess, the first spell he'd sensed had been to refresh their concealment. The second had been that agility enhancement one that he'd run into while he'd been trapped within the Seed. That jester he'd met had used it. At the time, he'd barely been able to fight against that spell. Though, he'd grown much stronger in the weeks since.

Digby prowled his way back to the board game section. The shelves of the area lined the room's walls to create a formation like the letter U. In the middle, three tables filled the space where people could play if they didn't feel like bringing the games some-place else. On one of the tables, a box lay open, the cover sitting by the side. The name Lords of Waterdeep was written across the front. Inside was a plastic organizer with several indented compart-ments, some filled with multicolored, wooden cubes while another held a deck of cards. Digby reached in and scooped up all the cubes before picking up the cards carefully with his claws.

Then he took a moment to consider where the invisible threat in the room might be. Would they be moving around? Or would they stay in one place? They could be directly behind him for all he knew. In the end, he had to take a risk.

"Last chance. I would prefer not to kill anyone tonight, but I suppose I can always interrogate your corpse." He gave a final warning, then he threw the deck of cards behind him.

A shower of paper flew into the space, fluttering through the air end over end, unimpeded by anything in their way. Digby didn't hesitate before spinning and launching the handful of wooden cubes in the opposite direction, opening his hands slowly so that the game pieces were released in an arc. The majority of the cubes continued on into the isles of shelves, but a dozen impacted with something in midair before trickling down to the floor.

"There you are!" Digby grinned as the air rippled and fell away to reveal a shocked man dressed in the armor of one of the empire's Guardians.

Now that he had confirmation, he flicked his eyes to the floor and opened his maw to send a spike of necrotic blood straight up at the man's crotch.

The rogue leaned backward, nearly throwing himself on the floor. His arms snapped out to catch himself using the shelving on either side. They creaked under the strain of his weight.

Digby's forged spike surged up from the floor, nearly skewering the foe's left thigh. He didn't let up, snapping his maw shut to sever the formation of black blood from its base. He caught it as it toppled over. Then, he opened his maw on the floor again, the rogue dangling from the shelves directly over it. Another Forge spell sent a new spike straight up toward the man's spine.

The rogue twisted his body to the side, letting go of the shelf to his right and pulling himself to the left with his other hand. The formation of blood skimmed his armor as it passed through the space where he'd been. An instant later, he kicked off in a seemingly impossible motion, aided by the enhanced agility of the spell that he had cast. His feet flew upward as he put his free hand down to the floor. For a brief moment, he balanced upside down on his fingertips, then he tucked his legs and kicked them back out. The momentum threw his body up into a flip with him landing back down in a squat like some sort of human frog.

Digby couldn't deny the rogue's movements were impressive, but it was going to take more than agility to keep the man alive. He closed his maw and caught the second spike that protruded from the shadowy opening as it snapped off. With blood formations in both hands, he spent the additional mana needed to reshape each into a stubby short sword.

Stalking forward, he glanced to the side at the shelves full of books and movies, hesitating. The rogue had him at a disadvantage. With all the power Digby had gained so far, there was a limit to what abilities he could use without damaging everything around him. Most of it could be replaced, but he was too aware of how important the library had become to the people of Vegas. Losing it would hurt. Even if it was just temporary.

I guess I'm going to have to do this the old-fashioned way. Digby raised one of his swords in front of him to strike while holding the other in a defensive position.

The rogue stood up and stepped back, eyes darting around as if looking for an escape route. A sword was locked into a magnetic sheath on the back of his armor, though he didn't reach for it. Instead, the man went for a pair of combat knives that were strapped to his thighs and raised them to match Digby. Then he spoke.

"We don't have to do this, Graves."

"I beg to differ." Digby lunged forward, taking a swipe with one of his blood swords.

The rogue blocked with a knife, chunks of blackish crimson chipping away from the edge of Digby's blade. The weapons were brittle from being re-forged, but they would last long enough for a few more strikes.

Digby pushed on his Limitless mutation to even the odds. He couldn't match his opponent's agility, but he could increase his own speed. Muscles tore and tendons strained as he thrust his other blade forward. He cast Necrotic Regeneration to repair the damage. The rogue dodged to the side, but Digby swiped with his other sword. Blades clashed in a blur, sending chips of hardened blood into the air. His weapons weren't going to last long.

Maybe I can use that to my advantage.

Digby jabbed one of his swords forward in a fast but weak strike, waiting for the rogue to deflect. The blade of his weapon snapped, leaving him holding the handle. He dropped it as he raised his other weapon high above his head and struck down with everything he had.

The rogue moved to block with the same supernatural ability.

Digby grinned as their weapons collided. The blade of his reforged sword snapped off, its edge continuing onward with the momentum of the strike. The tip hit the rogue in the forehead before slicing downward across his face in a diagonal line. A river of crimson flowed as the man cried out in panic.

"Wait, wait!"

Digby didn't wait. Instead, he snapped his free hand out to catch hold of the rogue's collar. His opponent may have had the agility of a much higher level, but it was useless if he couldn't break free.

Without a better option, the rogue plunged both of his knives into Digby, one into his abdomen and the other into the side of his rib cage. Digby felt the tip of the blade pierce his heart.

"Oh, I'm sorry. Was that supposed to hurt me?" He drew back his clawed hand, ready to strike.

"I said wait, this isn't what you think!" the rogue shouted, his voice climbing with each word.

"Really? Because it looks like Henwick sent you to spy on me."

The rogue squirmed against his grip. "That part is technically true."

"Good, so you admit it. That'll make this next part much easier." Digby motioned to drive his claws downward but stopped when the rogue spoke again.

"That's not the only reason I'm here!"

Digby hesitated. There was a time that he would have run the man through without a second thought, but after what had happened before, the rogue's words were enough to give him pause. The last thing he wanted was to commit another murder on impulse without all the facts.

"Alright, you have about one second to convince me not to kill you and add you to my horde."

The rogue responded with two words. "Analyze me."

Digby furrowed his brow, realizing that he hadn't already. Why would he have? He already knew what the man's class was. Beyond that, the fight had gotten started before he had time to think about anything else. Giving the rogue the benefit of the doubt, he focused on him.

He let go of the man's collar as soon as he did.

Guardian, Level 37 Rogue, Friendly

CHAPTER SEVEN

"Friendly?" Digby pulled his claws away from the rogue's throat.

"I can explain." The man gestured for him to move so he could get up, a river of blood still streaming from the cut on his face.

Digby hesitated, unsure what to believe. The man had admitted to being a spy for Henwick. Then again, the Heretic Seed didn't lie. If it had labeled a man as friendly, then he had to be an ally somehow. Digby pushed himself off the man and summoned one of his echoes. A glowing form resembling Henwick flickered into existence.

The rogue jumped in preparation for an attack only to relax when the figure raised a hand to heal the wound on his face. He rubbed at his forehead in disbelief a moment later. "That is freaky. That spell looks like Henwick."

"Indeed, I got it by eating his soul." Digby swirled one hand through the air as he glossed over the full explanation.

"You ate his soul?" The rogue stared up at him, looking concerned.

"It's sort of a long story." Digby nodded.

"I guess that explains why he wants you dead so bad." The

rogue stopped, his eyes glancing up to the side. "Or, I guess, he wants you more dead than you already are."

"Yes, he does seem to hate me quite a bit." Digby stated the fact as if it was something to be proud of. Then he flicked a claw in the direction of the rogue's feet and opened his maw. Casting Forge, he sent a tendril of blood weaving around the man's ankles to secure them together.

"Hey, wait." The rogue scooted backward on his rear, unable to separate his feet from each other.

"Don't worry, that won't hurt you." Digby crouched down to where the man lay on the floor. "The Heretic Seed might have labeled you as friendly, but I still need to take precautions. If you want to talk, then we can talk. I will decide what to do with you afterward."

The rogue sat for a second before nodding. "Fine, that's fair." He glanced back at the tables near the board game section of the library. "Could we sit down?"

Digby couldn't see a problem with that so he reached out to help the rogue up. From there, the man hopped back to one of the chairs and dropped into it. Sitting down opposite him, Digby leaned back.

"You… have a thing… you know, right there." The rogue pointed to the combat knife that was sticking out of the side of Digby's rib cage.

"Oh, yes." He pulled the blade out, as well as the second one that was still embedded in his abdomen. After dropping them both to the floor, he let his elbows rest on the arms of his chair and steepled his fingers. "Now, you are about to tell me why I shouldn't murder you. I suggest starting with your name."

"Will," he said without hesitation.

Digby arched an eyebrow at the quick response. He would've thought that someone in the rogue's position would be more hesitant. Unless Will wasn't his real name. He decided to wait and see what else to say.

"I'm what you would call a double agent. I was a member of Skyline before all this, and was recruited into Autem a couple of months before the world ended. I arrived tonight aboard the same aircraft as Henwick. My orders were to infiltrate this city and discover the location of both the Heretic Seed and the nuclear warhead that you used to threaten the capital."

"I had assumed that much." Digby dropped his hands to his lap. "None of that is going to convince me to keep you breathing."

"Yes." Will nodded. "But I'm telling you all this now so that you can move the Seed and the nuke. I have to protect my cover, so I will be telling Henwick where both of those things currently are."

"That is assuming that I will let you leave." Digby gave the rogue a predatory smile.

"You have to," Will said in a confident tone. "If you don't, then Henwick will know that I was killed and that might jeopardize the treaty that you have in place. Even if it is all fake to begin with."

"What's that now?" Digby leaned forward.

"It's all fake, the treaty, the negotiations, everything." Will held a hand out empty. "At least, for Henwick it is. Serrano is serious about keeping the peace. And as far as I can tell, the rest of the empire is happy to go along with it. However, Henwick has something up his sleeve. I don't know what it is, but he's only biding his time. So make no mistake. This war is not over, not by a long shot. Not if he has anything to say about it. It may not be soon, but he will find a reason to start up the fight again."

"I was afraid of that." Digby sat silently for a moment before letting himself sink into his seat. "But why are you telling me this?"

Will hesitated before answering, "Because I woke up."

"Woke up from what?"

The rogue leaned forward. "Do you know what it's like being a Guardian?"

"I assume you would have to have a sense of entitlement and willingness to grind the rest of the world beneath your boot," Digby said through a thick layer of sarcasm.

"You're not wrong." Will leaned back. "But you don't start that way. That's what the empire turns you into. Autem uses the connection with the Guardian Core to mess with your head. It alters the chemistry in the brain, but it's more than that. Being surrounded by their people, the way they talk, the way they think, the way they feel about anyone who isn't a part of the empire. It chips away at you little by little, stealing away the empathy you have for outsiders until you see the world as nothing but us versus them. It becomes normal. And they want this. They want you to feel that way. They train you to think this way, because it's the only way to make you willing to, as you said, grind the world beneath your boot."

"That does sound like Henwick's handiwork." Digby dragged a claw through the air between them. "And I take it that you have gone along with all of that up until now?"

A guilty expression fell across Will's face. "Unfortunately, I am not immune to that level of conditioning any more than anyone else. I joined Skyline as part of their youth program, like many of the other mercenaries I worked with. They got started young with me, and I did some... terrible things. This was before the apocalypse, mostly overseas operations. I was transferred to Autem to enter their Guardian program when the Core's connection to magic had become operational. I guess they saw potential in me, but that was when everything got worse. I was introduced to their belief in the Nine. I was always religious, so angels weren't that far-fetched, and it didn't seem that different from what I believed in before, so I let myself get sucked in. I started to grow numb as the atmosphere and attitudes of everyone around me gained influence. It all just felt right, so it wasn't long before killing off most of the population actually started to sound like a reasonable way to ensure a future where humanity could be protected and shaped by the Nine."

"But that changed?" Digby assumed.

"It's like I said, I woke up." Will gestured to the Guardian ring on his finger. "Or, more accurately, the Guardian Core's caretaker woke me up."

"Interesting." Digby tapped a claw on the table, realizing how powerful of an ally he might have within the core of the empire's magic system.

"I don't know when it happened, but at some point, my brain

chemistry returned to normal. I wasn't aware of what was happening, but I'd randomly break down, overwhelmed by my own emotions. The numbness that I had felt before was gone. After that, I started noticing differences in the Core's messages. It was subtle at first, just some changes in wording. It stopped reducing people to numbers. It started a conflict in my mind between the orders I was given and the people who found themselves in the way of those orders. I started having trouble with the us versus them mentality. And I started to question the empire and my place in it. I think the only reason I was able to break free of it all was because I hadn't been a member of their cult for that long."

"Better late than never." Digby chuckled mirthlessly. "Why didn't you flee or even defect to our side?"

"I could have. I even thought about it." He shook his head. "But by then I was too aware of what was happening and too complicit in it all. Running away wasn't going to fix what I'd done. So I decided to stay and do what I could from the inside. I figured every rebellion has to start somewhere."

Digby nodded along, remembering how Easton, Lana, and Campbell had come to the same conclusion when they had worked for Skyline. Perhaps Union was right. Maybe the empire's entire system was flawed. People would never truly be under their control. There would always be individuals like the Fools who would go against the grain.

"What kind of rebellion have you built so far?" Digby began to reach for the thread of hope that he and his Heretics were not alone.

Will yanked it away with a sigh. "Not much to speak of. Whatever exploit the Guardian Core's caretaker used to wake me up is closed now. I found a couple of others like me, but that's it, and we're scattered throughout the empire's forces. I'm the only one that has a position with any kind of access. Even that's limited. We were hoping to set up a system of hidden safehouses between the capital and Vegas to try to sneak people out of the refugee camps. That way, at least some of them would have a choice. Though, even with safehouses, the route would be dangerous. We're hoping to get some of the survivors we help to join us to help guide others."

"That's all well and good, but how does that help stop Henwick?"

"I wish there was more I could do. But there's too few of us to do anything on our own, and there's no way to organize something fast enough to have an impact right now." A somber look hung in his eyes. "That's why I'm telling you this. That's why I'm telling you that Henwick is still planning to destroy you. Because if I can't do anything from inside the empire, then you're the only hope we have at breaking their hold on the world. You have to keep fighting. Basically, I'm here to ask for help."

Digby scoffed. "I would love to, but what would you have me do about it? My side needs peace and I can't step out of line without jeopardizing the treaty. If you think I'm going to re-declare war, then you are sorely mistaken. I have gone to war already. Even with an army at my back, I wasn't able to defeat the empire. The best I could manage was this forced ceasefire."

"But you don't need to beat the empire." Will's tone grew hopeful. "You just need to beat Henwick. Without him, Serrano would be in full control and the empire would accept a lasting peace. More importantly, the people would have a chance at building a real resistance from within."

"Believe me, I would like nothing more than to assassinate Henwick." Digby chuckled. "But I don't have that kind of power. I can level up to close the gap between us. But if I am going to attack him, I need to be sure I can win. Because if I fail," Digby gestured to the city around him, "the people of Vegas will pay the price."

"But you have time." The rogue leaned forward, looking desperate. "Henwick may be planning to dissolve the treaty at the first chance he gets, but as long as you don't give him a justifiable reason to, the ceasefire will continue. You can use that time. You just have to find a way to fight him."

"Oh sure, let me just go get my secret weapon." Digby glowered at him.

"That's exactly what I expect you to do."

Confusion fell across Digby's face. "But I don't have a secret weapon. I believe I made that clear through my previous usage of sarcasm."

"You may not have one now, but there's more than one way to gain power. Take the time that you have now and put it to use. Find a way to kill him." Will stabbed a finger down onto the table. "You don't really have another option anyway."

"How helpful," Digby grumbled.

Will wasn't wrong. Digby had come to the same conclusion after the negotiations with Henwick. He might not have planned on striking first, but he had every intention of preparing for the inevitable.

"Alright, assuming that everything you've told me is true, I don't suppose you have an idea of where I can start looking?"

"Actually, I do." Will let a smug smile show for an instant.

"Why didn't you start with that?"

The rogue gestured to the formation of blood that was securing his feet together, looking a little nervous. "Because I thought I should save the most important information I had to bargain with. I will share it once you let me go."

"I think not." Digby folded his arms. "I will need to discuss this all with the rest of my people before letting you go anywhere."

"You can't keep me here. Not without jeopardizing the treaty." The rogue held firm.

"The hell I can't." Digby swiped his claws through the air. "All I have to do is have my vampire accomplice drain you to make it look like a revenant did it. Then I can cast talking corpse to find out what you know. Afterward, I'll just dump your body in the desert. Henwick might find it, but he'll never know I had anything to do with it."

The rogue started to sweat, then he shook his head. "You wouldn't do that to someone who is trying to help?"

Digby stared at him for a long moment before finally rolling his eyes. "Fine, no, I wouldn't. But I still need to discuss this with the rest of my advisors before deciding what to do with you."

Will's face grew even more concerned. "I only planned to leave you a note here. I never intended to show myself. I don't mean to question how you do things here. But professionalism is not exactly something you are known for, and I would prefer that as few people as possible find out about this conversation or be able to identify me. Plus, if I don't report soon, Henwick will know something's up."

Digby clenched his jaw. He didn't like the idea of letting the rogue walk away. Though, he did have a point. Professionalism was not their strong suit. Hell, he'd had to trap Becca in a car earlier to keep her from murdering the rest of his friends. Still, he couldn't just let the man go.

Will leaned forward to drop another tidbit into the situation, as if sensing that he might not get his way. "I understand why you would be reluctant to let me go. But I doubt I am the only spy that Henwick has keeping an eye on you, and I can't risk him finding out that we spoke."

"What do you mean you're not the only one?" Digby sat upright.

"I mean you have been taking in everyone that shows up at your doors." He glanced around. "I don't have any proof, but I wouldn't put it past Henwick to send a few loyalists in to keep an eye on you."

"I..." Digby trailed off.

The thought of spies infiltrating Vegas hadn't occurred to him before, but it was a very real possibility. Perhaps it was time to start making an effort to keep some things secret.

"Alright, you have a point there." Digby tried not to let on how worried he'd suddenly become. Then, he leaned back to where Asher had been perched on top of one of the shelves.

"What do you think?"

Asher responded with a caw and a gesture of her wings that resembled a shrug.

"Yes, I feel the same."

Despite that, he spent the extra mana to dissolve the formation of blood that he had wrapped around the rogue's ankles. In the end, the Seed didn't lie. If the rogue was really a friend, then he had to give him some element of trust. Besides, he hadn't said anything during their talk that Henwick didn't already know.

"Thank you." Will let out a breath, making it clear that he hadn't been confident that he would survive their conversation.

"Now, what is this lead of yours?" Digby stood up and leaned across the table to stare down at the man.

Will pushed himself out of his chair. "I got a message from the Guardian Core's caretaker when I was on my way here."

"And?" Digby swirled a claw through the air to urge him to hurry up.

Will answered him with another question. "Do you know anyone named Harlow?"

Digby froze. "I might."

Harlow, the last remaining Fool, had been down in the dining area the last he'd seen her.

"Good." Will nodded. "The caretaker's message said that she's your lead."

"That's it?"

"That's it."

"But I already asked her what she knew when she got here."

"Then there is something she didn't tell you."

"What reason would she have to lie?" Digby stared blankly at the wall behind him. "She wants Henwick dead as much as I."

"Well, the caretaker said to ask her about the truth. So I suggest you ask her again." Will started for the door.

"Or your caretaker is wrong," Digby called after him.

Will stopped and looked back. "The Core's caretaker is many things, but wrong is not one of them."

The rogue vanished into thin air as he continued walking again. A moment later, the door closest to him opened on its own and fell shut again to leave him and Asher alone.

Digby dropped back into his chair as soon as he was alone.

Asher flapped down to land on the table in front of him, clearly sensing his stress.

"I knew it was all too good to be true." He rested his forehead on the back of one hand while tapping the claws of the other on the table. The peace he'd found wasn't going to last. There was no way to know when, but something would go wrong, and when it did, he was going to have to be ready.

He stroked the top of her head for a few quiet moments.

"I suppose we should get to work."

Digby stood up from his chair.

"I have a werewolf to interrogate."

CHAPTER EIGHT

"Alright, if she tries to run, make sure to grab her." Digby stood in front of Harlow's hotel room door, ready to knock.

Asher nodded as she perched on his shoulder as if he'd been talking to her.

"I don't think that will be necessary." Becca stood behind him.

"But if the Guardian Core's caretaker says she knows something, then she must be hiding something," Alex added from beside her.

"Maybe it just slipped her mind." Parker leaned out from behind both of them.

"I doubt Harlow's mind is as slippery as yours." Digby glanced back at her, immediately doing a double take.

"What are you wearing, Parker?"

She looked down at the pink sweatshirt and matching fleece pants she was dressed in. "Pajamas?"

"You didn't think an interrogation merited getting dressed?" Digby glowered at her.

"What? You pulled me out of bed." She yawned. "What did you want me to wear?"

"For crying out loud." Digby rubbed at the bridge of his nose.

"Should I go back and change?"

"No, just try to act professional."

As soon as Autem's rogue left him fifteen minutes earlier, he'd rushed upstairs to get his inner circle. Alex had been awake still. As was Becca. Parker was the only one who had already gone to bed. Technically, he hadn't needed to wake her up, but after everything they'd been through, it felt wrong to leave her out of the decision-making.

The only one that wasn't present was Mason, who had fallen asleep. Digby opted to let him rest on account of the volume of his snoring. It was actually quite impressive. The entire floor had been vibrating. Besides, four should have been enough to interrogate one person, werewolf or not.

Digby raised his hand to knock.

"Wait, what if she's sleeping?" Parker asked.

"Then we wake her up." He brought his hand down only for the door to open before his knuckles could impact its surface.

Harlow stood in the entryway looking annoyed.

Digby let his mouth fall open.

Harlow stood silently for a moment, scanning each of her visitors one by one. Then she frowned and spoke through her teeth. "To what do I owe the pleasure."

Digby dropped his hand back to his side. "Ah yes, hello there. I was hoping you could help answer a question that has come up."

"I see, and at what point do you intend on grabbing me?" She eyed him.

"Uh, you heard that, did you?" Digby tried to act innocent.

"You weren't even whispering." She stared at him.

Her attention was soon pulled away by Parker as she waved awkwardly. "Hi again."

Harlow flicked her eyes down at the soldier's sleep attire. "Leave your room in a hurry, did you?"

She looked down at her outfit. "Sorry."

"Yes, Parker's clothing is an embarrassment." Digby shoved the distraction aside and got to the point. "May we come in?"

Harlow sighed and stepped back into the room. "Alright."

Digby couldn't help but notice that she held a knife behind her back when she turned around. The woman placed it on the table and sat down in a chair. She was dressed in a loose shirt and a pair of shorts, but her bed didn't look slept in. Digby glanced to the side at a number of maps scattered about the dresser. One of those tiny information storage devices that never seemed to be oriented the correct way sat on top. Obviously, the woman had been working on some plans of her own.

"Oi, I'm over here." Harlow snapped her fingers to draw his attention.

"Sorry to bother you so late." Becca sat down at the end of one of the beds. "But we just received a message from the Guardian Core's caretaker telling us that you had information that could help us."

Harlow furrowed her brow. "I suppose it's possible. I'm not sure what it could be, though. What is it you're looking for?"

"We need power," Digby answered matter-of-factly. "Enough to take down Henwick."

Asher cawed from her perch on his shoulder to back him up.

Harlow glared at the bird for a moment, looking uncomfortable. "Power? I thought your lot were working towards peace."

"That much is true. Though, it seems that Henwick won't allow for it to last. We need to be ready for whatever he has planned," he explained.

"I can't say that's surprising. The empire is too close to total domination to let this city exist outside of their control." She leaned back with a satisfied expression, as if confirming suspicions that she already had. "But I'm afraid the Fools have nothing to offer in the way of power. We were never ones to hoard strength."

"You must know something." Becca sat down on the foot of one of the room's beds.

Harlow remained quiet for a long moment, tapping one finger on the surface of the table in front of her. "Hmm."

"Was that a good hmm? Or a bad hmm?" Parker took a seat at the foot of the other bed.

"A bad hmm." Harlow leaned to one side to rest on her elbow. "I meant what I said. Nothing comes to mind."

"And would you tell us if something had?" Digby kept his eyes on her, watching for any sign that she was lying.

Harlow immediately slapped a hand on the table. "I have my secrets, sure. But none that would have an impact on you. And if I knew of a power that could rival Henwick, I would have fought him myself."

"Maybe it's something else." Alex stood to the side of the room. "Maybe it's not something that's obvious."

"Is there something that you might have overheard?" Becca leaned forward. "Something that the caretaker is also aware of."

Harlow leaned back to think. "What did this message say, exactly?"

"I was told to ask you for the truth?" Digby answered, having trouble making it sound less like an accusation that she hadn't been honest before. Then he stopped to think.

He'd never asked Will for the exact message, but was there something more?

Was there more to what the rogue had said?

Yes. His eyes widened. There was another word in there that he'd forgotten.

"Wait." Digby shook his head. "I wasn't told to ask you *for* the truth. I was supposed to ask you *about* the truth."

It was a subtle difference, but one that seemed to matter because Harlow's eyes grew wide as well. "That makes more sense."

"What does?" Digby asked.

"The Fools and Autem were not the only ones exploring magic throughout history. There was one other group that worked in pursuit of the truth of all things, magic included."

"Wait, are you going to tell us that there's another secret organization out there?" Alex stepped forward.

She chuckled and shook her head. "Not so much. And definitely not secret. You need to stop thinking too much and start looking at the obvious. Who do you think would have an interest in understanding magic?"

"The government?" Alex guessed.

Harlow shook her head again. "Nah, most governments are more interested in economics, business, and good old-fashioned war. All short-term stuff. Magic is a long game. If the governments of the world had invested in understanding the supernatural, they probably wouldn't have fallen so easily the first time a curse popped up. No, they never valued truth to begin with. So guess again. Who do you think of when you think of angels and Heretics?"

Digby felt a shiver run down his cold, dead spine, reminded of the fears that he'd had back when he'd first woken up. He'd been terrified that if someone found out that he had magic, he would be burned at the stake.

"The church."

"Of course." She nodded. "The Fools never really clashed with them. Nor did they ever work together. The church has always done its own thing, but there was one small sect that occasionally got involved. Mostly they acted as a silent observer to record what they called the truth. That was their whole deal. The last time the Fools crossed paths with them was decades ago. I don't think they're very active, but I know there's an archive in the Vatican. If there's information that can help you gain power, it might be there."

"The Vatican? What's that?" Digby looked back to Alex.

"It's the home base for the Catholic church. It's in Italy."

"Does that mean there might be people there with magic?" Digby asked in astonishment.

"I doubt it." Harlow gave a shrug. "The church was never on board with accepting or making use of the supernatural. None of them would have been willing to actually wield magic. No, they were pretty firm on that. But that doesn't mean they didn't research it."

"Maybe there are survivors there then," Parker offered, laying back on the foot of the bed that she sat on and yawning. "If they knew about it, they might have at least had some protection."

Harlow didn't look hopeful. "As far as I know, the Vatican fell along with the rest of the world. Though, that may work to your advantage. With no one there to guard the place, you should be able to walk right in, find the archive, and take what you need. Everything the church has researched about magic will be there. Mind you, I doubt you'll find anything that Autem doesn't already know, but you might find something that at least evens the playing field. It sounds like that's where you'll find a lead."

Digby considered the possibility. He'd never been religious. Hell, he'd always dismissed it all as a fairy tale. Stories that kings told to keep the peasants in line. Though, he couldn't deny that those stories still had an influence on the world. He'd noticed that much through the movies and other media that he consumed. The real question was how much of it was true and how much was just good storytelling.

Digby inclined his head to Harlow. "Thank you for the information." He turned toward the door. "I want everybody ready to leave first thing in the morning."

Parker let out a yawn. "Are we going where I think we are?"

"That's right, we're going to Europe."

He looked back to Harlow. "I don't suppose you would come with us?"

She shifted her gaze to the pile of maps and the data storage device on the dresser. "I'm afraid I have my own mission to worry about."

Digby frowned. "I don't suppose you will share the details."

She shook her head predictably. "It's a bit on the personal side of things. Besides, someone has to go out there and see if there's any more Fools still alive."

Digby debated on arguing but decided to let it go. The Fools really were allies and they had to take care of their own. With a little luck, Harlow would return with help.

"I hope you find them." He gave her a nod before turning to the door and beckoning to the rest of his coven. "Come now, we have an archive to search for tomorrow."

"I always wanted to go to Italy." Alex followed.

"Indeed." Digby looked back over his shoulder and raised a claw to his lips. "And tell no one."

CHAPTER NINE

"Okay, what else is there?" Becca closed the trunk of the presidential limo.

After leaving Harlow's room, she'd spent the rest of the night getting ready while the humans slept. She checked in on Mason at one point to wake him up so he could at least move from the sofa to the bed. She was pretty sure he wouldn't even remember the visit. Becca chuckled to herself. He was doing his best to switch to a nocturnal schedule but it didn't seem to be taking.

Hopefully, things would work out now that she was no longer heading out on missions.

Hence why she was packing the limo.

There was no telling what was waiting for them in the Vatican, and after the late night that everyone had, the others needed some rest. Hell, Parker hadn't even made it to her room. The pink-haired woman had fallen asleep before they'd even left Harlow's suite. Becca would have woken her up, but considering the toll that her magic had been taking on her, she'd left her there. Harlow didn't seem to care anyway. She was more concerned with preparing for whatever personal mission she was planning.

Becca tried not to think about that part. Harlow was the last remaining member of the Fools, and she'd done a lot to help her already. The idea that she would be gone soon left her feeling a little lost.

"That's probably how Digby feels about me staying home from missions." Becca sighed.

It couldn't be helped. A normal life was her only chance. She couldn't keep depending on blood donors to keep her in check.

"Where is Digby anyway?" Becca turned around.

She kept expecting the zombie to saunter into the parking garage any minute with a new argument to convince her to come along. The fact that he hadn't was starting to worry her. He was probably taking his time to come up with something that she couldn't say no to. She could see it now, the necromancer giving a five-point presentation with note cards and everything. There was sure to be plenty of guilt peppered in for good measure.

"Not looking forward to that." She pushed the worry out of her mind and went back to getting things ready.

By morning, she'd had the presidential limo all packed and ready to go. She'd also searched through the reference materials available in the library to find an image of a reflective surface in Italy. It was a polished bronze sculpture of a sphere within a sphere located in a courtyard at the Vatican Museum. Unless the area had suffered catastrophic damage, the giant metal object should still be there. With that, Parker would be able to open a passage straight to where they needed to go. Once they secured the area, they could transport a larger mirror to the other side to bring the limo through.

Usually, they had a support team to handle the installation of mirrors at their destination, but with the possibility of spies lurking in Vegas, they would have to do that themselves. From here on out, that was probably the new normal. If they were going to be researching ways to fight Henwick himself, they needed to keep their actions quiet. As far as anyone else was concerned, they were just heading out on another trip to gather zombies.

Becca checked the time on her phone.

It was already past eight in the morning. Digby had wanted to leave at dawn. If they didn't get going soon, they would have to postpone the mission until tomorrow. It was mid-afternoon in Italy, after all. If it got too close to nightfall, the Vatican would probably be swarming with revenants.

Becca stared at the doors that led into the casino. "Where are they?"

"Where are who?" A voice came from beside her as Hawk appeared out of thin air, releasing a Conceal spell.

Becca let out an instinctive hiss and jumped a foot in the air, not being used to having anyone sneak up on her. She may have had the enhanced senses of a vampire, but with the sun shining into the parking garage, her abilities and magic were useless.

Hawk smirked, clearly enjoying catching her off guard.

"Don't do that." She swatted at his arm weakly, lacking the strength that she was used to.

"Okay, sorry. And who are you waiting for?"

She swatted at him one more time before dropping her hands to her sides and growling. "I'm waiting for Digby and the others. They were supposed to have left already."

"Shit, I didn't know we had a mission this morning." Concern took over his face.

"Oh." She let her mouth hang open for a moment, unsure what to say.

No one had talked to him yet to tell him that he wasn't going. Hawk had proven himself a reliable part of the team, but a secret mission to the Vatican was still a little more dangerous than she was willing to send her kid brother on. Not only that, but they were on a need-to-know basis. She trusted Hawk, but she didn't want to tell anyone about where Digby and the others were going if they weren't already going with them.

"Actually, there's something else that I need you to do."

"You mean I'm not going out with you?" His tone immediately fell.

She shook her head. "No, and I'm not going either. But there's a more important job that you are perfect for."

"Okay, what's up?" He sounded a little more enthusiastic, though there was still a hint of skepticism in his voice.

"With all the new people that we've taken in, we suspect that at least a few might be working for Henwick as spies." Becca locked eyes with her brother. "We could be wrong and we don't want to cause a panic, so we're keeping the issue quiet. Only a handful of people know any of this. But what I need you to do is keep an eye on things. Just do what you always do, stay concealed and watch. Analyze people and make sure the Seed lists them as friendly. Report back anything suspicious."

Hawk went quiet for a moment before finally nodding. "Okay, will do. But if you need me for a mission, let me know."

"This is your mission now." Becky held his gaze. "And tell no one."

He nodded. "I won't."

The rogue vanished a moment later.

She was only able to enjoy a minute of silence before Digby burst through the casino's doors with Asher on his shoulder.

The raven cawed as he started shouting.

"There you are!"

Becca winced, expecting the argument that she had been imagining all night. To her surprise, there was none. Instead, he was too busy looking for Parker, who had been missing all morning.

"I've banged on her door. And checked with Harlow as well. She said she woke Parker up and kicked her out hours ago. So I have no idea where that messenger has gone." He continued to complain. "If we don't find her soon, we won't make it to the Vatican before dark."

"Shh." Becca cringed as he announced the destination of his secret mission, half expecting Hawk to reappear to ask questions. She had no idea if her brother was still in the garage or not. After a few seconds without Hawk's sudden appearance, she relaxed and returned her attention to the zombie in front of her. "We have no idea who might be listening, so maybe keep your voice down."

"Right right." He ducked his head. "But we really do need to find Parker."

Becca nodded. "Okay, I'll help look."

They parted ways a moment later as she entered the casino.

The muscles in her jaw tightened as she headed for the main floor. No matter how hard the messenger had been trying to hide things, her condition was getting worse. Hopefully, it hadn't taken a sudden turn. There was a second, worse, possibility. If that rogue Digby spoke to was right, and Henwick had planted spies into the city's populace, one of them could have made a move on Parker. It wasn't a secret that she was the source of their portal magic and that would place her at the top of the list of people to remove from the playing field.

Becca tried to deny the possibility. The idea that assassins and spies were walking amongst them was scary enough, but even worse, it was plausible. It was hard not to picture the messenger bleeding out in a hallway somewhere, still in her pink pajamas.

Becca parted ways with Digby to help him search.

It was a half hour later when Becca spotted something pink slumped over on the edge of the fountain in the casino's center. A trickle of crimson ran down the side of the tile.

"No!" Becca's heart jumped into her throat.

The messenger's hand dangled limp over the side.

Becca fought against the life essence flooding her mana system as she ran toward her. It was like running through waist-high water. Exhaustion hit her just as she dropped to her knees beside the fountain to grab hold of the messenger.

"Parker! Wake up!"

"Guh! What?" The woman jumped up in shock, immediately rolling off the edge of the fountain and into the water. She stood back up, her faded pink hair matted to her face and her soaked sweatshirt weighing her down almost enough to pull her back into the water. Confusion flooded her expression. "Where am...? Wait... Why are you...?" Eventually, she just trailed off before adding a single, "Shit."

Becca sat on the tile floor that surrounded the fountain, unsure what was even happening. Then she noticed something sitting in the space where Parker had been lying moments before. It was a crushed container of chicken tenders. It looked like a few had been nibbled at. Beside it sat a couple of open packets of barbecue sauce. The liquid from the container dripped down the side of the fountain.

Everything made sense after that. Parker had come down to the convenience store and bought one of the prepared meals they sold. After that, she'd sat down to eat it and then fell asleep on top of the container.

"What the hell, Parker? Were you sleeping here all night?"

The messenger glanced around as if trying to piece her night back together. "I think so."

"Are you feeling okay?" Becca stood back up.

Parker hesitated. She didn't look well. She was paler than normal and her eyes were a little sunken. From the looks of the package of food on the edge of the fountain, she had barely eaten anything.

"I'm fine." She sloshed her way through the water.

Of course, that was when Digby stumbled across the scene.

"What the devil are you doing in the fountain?" The zombie strode straight up to them.

"I fell." She gave a wet shrug.

"Of course you did." He stepped one foot onto the side and held a hand out toward her. "Come on then, let's get you out of there."

She grabbed hold of him and climbed out of the water. "Thanks."

"Now go upstairs and get ready to go." He checked his phone. "We only have a few hours left to get to you-know-where. I don't think we will have time to find what we need but we can at least secure our entry point."

"Okay, I'll be right back." Parker started to head for the stairs to the upper floors but Becca caught her shoulder.

"You're sure you're up for this?"

The messenger gave a smile and nodded, looking cheerful despite her skin's pallor. She was at least in a good mood.

"Okay." Becca let her go.

Digby blew out an exaggerated sigh as she walked away, which was strange considering he wasn't breathing to begin with.

Becca ignored him, assuming that the act had been performative.

Digby sighed again, this time, louder.

She ignored him again.

Finally, he gestured to Parker as the messenger dripped her way across the casino floor. "You see what I have to deal with."

Becca remained quiet, trying her best not to take the obvious bait that the zombie was laying out. One word from her and he was sure to break out the note cards and start his presentation on why she should be going with them.

"Welp, good luck with that." She turned and started walking before he had a chance to start up.

"Wait a second!" He threw out a hand to block her path, suddenly acting surprised, as if he'd just thought of something important.

Becca arched an eyebrow at his expression.

"I just realized something." Digby glanced in her direction for a second before looking away. "You used to be a drone operator."

"Yes." She frowned.

"Yes, well. It seems that if you are looking to live a normal life, then you could simply revert to your old job. That way you could still be involved without taking any risks." He nodded to himself at the end, as if finishing a statement that he'd rehearsed several times already.

Becca folded her arms. "That is true. But I wouldn't be able to send out a drone all the way to the Vatican. They only have a range of a few miles without internet access. But we can keep that in mind for a more local mission."

Digby's face fell in an overly practiced manner. "I suppose you're right. Maybe next time then."

Becca relaxed. "Sure, next time."

"Wait, is there a reason why you can't come with us and just stay in the car?" The corner of his mouth tugged upward for an instant. "It is armored, after all."

"You realize I know what you're doing, right?" She stared back at him.

"I have no idea what you mean."

"Don't play innocent. We both know you have been sitting around all night trying to think of a way to convince me to come with you."

The zombie placed a hand to his heart. "I am merely stating an option."

Becca flicked her eyes to the deceased raven on his shoulder. "How long did it take for him to come up with this idea, an hour?"

Asher hesitated for a moment, then she nodded.

"Traitor." Digby glowered at the bird before continuing. "Alright, I was hoping you would reconsider."

Becca opened her mouth to argue but he held up a hand.

"And before you say anything about me not respecting your wishes, let me say that my disagreement on this issue has nothing to do with what I want. No, it has to do with what is best for you. I understand how difficult a change like what you have been through can be, and I don't think hiding from it is going to make you feel any better in the end. Life may be different now, but it can still be good. You just have to allow what you think of as normal to change." He finished with a frustrated huff.

"Are you done?" Becca continued to stare at him.

"Yes."

"Good, because I haven't even slept yet so I can't possibly go on a mission now."

"You can nap in the car."

"I…" She struggled to think of another excuse.

Digby let a smug grin take over his face. "You see. There's no reason why you can't come along in a support capacity. Besides, this little excursion has to be kept secret. I can't take any of the other covens with us. Like it or not, you are one of the people I trust most. And that means I need you."

Becca closed her eyes and let out a frustrated growl. "I hate you."

"No, you don't."

"Alright, I don't, but I am annoyed."

"Does that mean you're coming?" He leaned closer, grinning.

Becky glanced at her HUD to check her mana.

MP: 175/454

She'd gained a little over a hundred points through the night. It was enough to keep her out of danger and she wouldn't need any of it if she stayed in the car.

"Fine. I'll go check a drone out of the supply."

"I'm glad you could see it my way." Digby spun on his heel and rushed off toward the parking garage. "Be ready to leave in ten minutes."

"Yeah, yeah." She waved over her shoulder as she made her way to the casino's weapon counter.

Ringing the bell, she waited for someone to come out of the back. Ever since Sax's passing, the area was manned by a guy named Bullock. He was a gruff gun enthusiast that seemed a little disappointed that people had begun to prefer magic over good, old-fashioned, American firepower. As such, he'd seemed to make it his mission to arm everyone that stopped by.

"Give me a drone," she said as soon as he emerged.

"Want a rifle with that drone?" he offered.

"No. I'll be staying in the car."

"You sure? You can never be too careful," he tried again.

Becca hesitated. He wasn't wrong. She probably should bring something. Especially considering she wouldn't be able to use any magic during the day. Not that she had much mana to do so with anyway.

"Okay, I'll take a bulletproof vest and a gun. One of the smaller ones, like an MP5 or something."

Bullock chuckled at the request. "You sure? I bet a lady like you can handle something bigger."

"Actually, no. I can't," she responded, annoyed at his response. "I am a vampire and I need a gun that I can handle during the day when I'm weaker."

He shrugged and walked into the storage area behind them. "Your funeral. I guess."

Becca hissed at his back as he left, already bothered by the way the day was going.

Then she leaned over the counter to add, "And grab me a sword too."

"Whatever," Bullock yelled from the back.

She didn't want to carry around something so heavy but she

could leave most of it in the car in case of an emergency.

Bollock returned with what she asked for. A drone, a submachine gun, chest armor, and a sword.

The armor was one of the black ones with a magnetic sheath on the back that had once belonged to Skyline. The sword, however, was a new creation of Sin City's own forge. The blade was heavy and unpolished, but bore a sharp, double edge. A long, leather-wrapped handle extended from the end, with a small cross-guard dividing the weapon. It was the kind of sword that could stand up to a lot of punishment. The balance wasn't great, but if she was to wield it at night when she had all the power of a blood-thirsty monster rushing through her, that wouldn't matter much.

Becca threw on the armor and snapped the blade into the sheath before tossing the strap of the MP5 over her shoulder. Finally, she grabbed the handle of the drone's carry case.

"Shouldn't you wear some real pants?" Bullock glanced at her legs.

She looked down at the leggings she was wearing, then rolled her eyes and walked away. He was probably right, but also, she didn't care. No one had forced her to wear pants since the world ended, and they were not about to start now.

Returning to the parking garage, Becca found Digby waiting with Alex, Parker, and Mason. Parker had finally changed out of her pajamas and into the Cloak of Steel that Becca had used back when she'd been human. The garment would protect whoever wore it with a near impenetrable barrier, so it made sense to give it to the messenger. Parker's safety was a priority, after all.

A small horde of twelve zombies stood by Digby. As soon as the necromancer saw her, he nodded in approval. In the same moment, Becca noticed her HUD update to show everyone's name along with hers. Digby's was on top to indicate him as the leader of their coven.

"I see you decided to come prepared for combat anyway." Asher cawed from his shoulder.

"Don't get excited." Becca gestured to the limo with her head. "I'm taking all this off and climbing in the car as soon as the destination is secure."

"Understandable." Digby picked up his staff from where it leaned against a wall and beckoned to his zombies. "And I've brought a little backup as well. If there is one thing I've learned, it's never travel without a horde." He turned to address the rest of the coven. "Now I assume everyone has kept their mouths shut about where we're going?"

"Yes, and I logged this mission with Elenore as just another zombie retrieval trip," Mason reported.

"Good, good." Digby flicked his eyes to Alex. "And you haven't said anything to that skull that you have been carrying everywhere, right?"

The artificer's eyes bulged as one drawn out syllable fell from his mouth. "Ahhhhhh."

Digby slapped a hand to his face. "Let me guess, it's in your bag."

"No." Alex hesitated before hooking his thumb back at the limo and adding, "She's in the car."

Becca looked in the direction he pointed in to see Kristen's skull on the vehicle's dash.

"But we can trust her." Alex held up a hand. "She's on our side now, and she's been extremely helpful in my exploration of magic. If it wasn't for her, the new airship that Jameson is working on wouldn't be ready for a test flight."

Digby eyed the artificer for an awkward moment before shaking his head. "Whatever. I suppose she can't tell anyone what we're doing if she's coming with us." When he was done interrogating everyone, he turned to the bay of mirrors that they had been using as a portal hub. "Parker, open a passage."

"Gotcha." The messenger pulled out the picture of the bronze sculpture that they were planning on using as an exit point and took a moment to study it before shoving it back into her pocket. "Hopefully this works. I've never opened a passage on something round before."

Becca approached the mirror in the center as it began to ripple. "I guess the shape isn't a problem."

Parker winced and rubbed at her head.

"You okay?" Alex asked.

"I'm fine." Parker gave him an unconvincing thumbs up.

"I'll take point." Mason stepped past Becca only to stop a second later and look to Digby. "Actually, you're coven leader. You call the shots."

"Oh, by all means." Digby waved him on. "You're welcome to go first. I shan't stop you."

Becca noticed Mason's shoulders relax. He was always more comfortable being in charge.

That was when Alex suddenly spit on the ground.

"Who cares who goes first? I'll do what I want."

Everyone turned to stare at him.

"Sorry." The artificer's tone grew sheepish. "That was for my eyepatch. I still have to rebel against authority every hour to keep my aim-bot active." He finished by giving both Digby and Mason the middle finger for good measure.

"Lovely." The zombie rolled his eyes and walked on toward the mirror.

Mason ignored the gesture and stepped through the portal. Digby followed with Asher perched on his shoulder. Alex went in after him, vanishing into the rippling surface. Becca glanced back at Parker.

"I'll be right behind you." She nodded.

The messenger waited to go last since the passage would close the moment she passed through it. Once the other side was secured, they could carry one of the larger mirrors through and find someplace to install it so that they could transport the limo.

Becca adjusted her grip on the submachine gun she carried, looking forward to abandoning it all in the limo. Hopefully things were quiet in the Vatican.

"Okay, let's get this over with." Becca stepped into the passage.

She sensed something was wrong the moment she exited on the other side of the world.

Both Mason and Alex were staring at the sky while Digby stood with one hand out as if feeling the air around him. Becca stopped dead in her tracks, raising her vision to a blanket of dark clouds that hung over the Vatican Museum's courtyard. The occasional flash of crimson lightning sparked within a layer of gloom to illuminate the buildings that surrounded them. That wasn't the strangest part either.

No, the strangest part was the mana.

Becca's strength began returning to her as her body purged the life essence that she'd absorbed back in Vegas. She dropped a hand into her pocket to grab her phone. Checking the time, she furrowed her brow. It should have been the middle of the afternoon, but somehow, her mana system was correcting itself as if the sun had already set.

"Is the sky supposed to look like that?" Parker asked as she stumbled out of the curved surface of the bronze sculpture they had exited. The passage closed the instant she did.

"No, I don't think the sky is supposed to look like that, Parker." Digby turned back to Becca. "Do you feel that?"

She nodded. "The mana balance is the same as it would be at night. I'm not weak here."

"Ah, guys?" Alex threw a finger out to the side.

Becca swept her eyes in the direction he pointed. A building loomed at the end of the courtyard, pillars lining its entrance like teeth in a skull. She noticed the figure standing at the center immediately. Squinting, she let a point of mana flow into her vision. The figure wore full tactical armor, including a police-issued helmet. Staring out from beneath was a pair of glowing eyes. A mouth full of jagged fangs and a bat-like snout made it clear what it was.

A revenant.

Then she noticed the rifle slung across its back.

"Since when do revs carry guns?" Alex dropped his hand to his side.

"Surely, it doesn't know how to use it," Digby added, his voice shaking.

Asher cawed from his shoulder as if to back him up.

The revenant proved them both wrong by reaching back to grab the weapon.

That was when Becca analyzed the figure.

Revenant, Uncommon, Thrall

CHAPTER TEN

"Thrall?" Digby stared out across the courtyard of the Vatican Museum at the lone figure standing between the pillars of a building at the far end. "What the devil is a revenant thrall?"

The creature answered the question by firing the rifle it carried in their direction.

"Holy hell! It's shooting at us!" Digby grabbed Asher off his shoulder and tucked her under his arm to protect her as bullets peppered the ground a few feet away.

"Get to cover!" Mason shouted as he ducked behind the bronze sphere that they had used as an exit for a Mirror Passage moments before.

"You don't have to tell me twice." Alex dove after him, landing in a roll as chips of stone sprayed into the air. The blue shimmer of a Barrier spell swept across his body as he came to a stop.

Ducking his head, Digby turned his back toward the gunfire to keep Asher safe and ran, carrying his staff loosely in his other hand. Bullets sparked across the side of the bronze sculpture as he rushed behind it. The instant he was safe, he leaned back out and tried to cast a spell back at the creature. He growled when nothing happened. "Blast! That damn thing's out of range for any of my magic."

"Somebody shoot it then." Parker sat on the ground with her hands on her head, taking rapid breaths as if she were struggling not to throw up. "But do it quietly, this is not helping my headache." Her Cloak of Steel fanned out around her. It would keep her safe, but she didn't look well.

"Returning fire." Mason stepped out from behind the sphere and dropped to one knee to steady his rifle before letting off a few shots. He ducked back behind the sculpture a second later. "I hit it, but it's armored."

"Who the hell equips a revenant with body armor?" Becca asked the obvious question.

"Probably the same person who gave it the gun," Digby stated the obvious answer.

"Fine, I'll deal with it." Alex stood up and pulled his pistol before stepping out from behind the sculpture. Bullets pinged off the ground around him, a few slamming into his Barrier with a burst of blue sparks. He braced against the impact and raised his gun in a single motion to fire one bullet.

The revenant at the end of the courtyard staggered back with a screech as the visor of its helmet shattered. A spurt of crimson poured from the opening to spatter the ground. The creature's cry echoed off the surrounding buildings and for a moment, it looked like the bullet had been enough to take it down. Then, the revenant reached out a hand to steady itself as the wound healed.

"At least we know the mana balance is the same for them," Becca noted the detail. "The clouds overhead must be canceling out the daylight."

Alex's hand flicked to the side, then he fired again. The bullet went straight through the same hole in the revenant's visor as the first. Blood poured from underneath its helmet as it toppled over. "That should do it."

An experience message ran across the bottom of Digby's HUD.

Revenant Thrall defeated. 640 experience awarded.

"What was that about?" He stomped out from behind the bronze sphere and started toward the body of the dead revenant.

"I don't know, but we need to rethink this." Becca followed after him. "Keeping this mission a secret is still a priority, but we need to bring a bigger team to secure the area. There's something more going on here."

"Indeed." Digby stopped when he reached the revenant.

It was dressed in full armor. Had it not been for the creature's screeching, he might have mistaken it for human. Around its waist, a belt of pouches carried additional ammunition. Someone had gone through a lot of trouble to outfit the foe and he was willing to bet there were more revenant thralls like it skulking about. "Alright, we must retreat for now. We'll return with a few covens and a horde of fifty."

Before he could say anything else, a screech echoed from someplace beyond the courtyard followed by another. A burst of gunfire erupted in the distance. He swept his gaze across the buildings around him to pinpoint where the noise was coming from. The fight a moment before must've alerted more thralls. They would be on top of them soon.

Digby stepped away from the corpse. "It's time to go. Parker, open a passage."

A sudden thud answered his request, like the sound of a body falling to the ground.

Digby snapped his attention back to the bronze sculpture at the center of the courtyard to find Parker lying on the stone. For an instant, he thought she'd been hit in the scuffle, but that was impossible. Not with the barrier provided by the cloak she wore. He glanced at his HUD to find her name listed amongst his covens. The word unconscious appeared after her mana value.

"What happened?" Digby rushed back to where the others stood.

"Shit, I think she passed out." Becca let go of her gun so it hung from a shoulder strap behind her and dropped down to one knee beside the messenger. She gasped when she placed a hand on her forehead. "She's burning up. Jesus, it's no wonder she slept by the fountain all night. She probably passed out there too."

"Why didn't she say she wasn't feeling well?" Digby hit the ground with the bottom of his staff in frustration, the gold-encased femur at the end clinking against the stone.

Asher peeked out from under his coat and cawed, sounding concerned.

"I don't know." Becca shook her head. "I could tell she was struggling, so I kept checking on her. But she just kept saying she was fine."

"Parker's always been like that. She doesn't like to be a burden." Mason dropped down beside her and threw a hand out toward Alex. "Give me a purified flask."

The artificer had one ready. Mason took it and tried to pour some of the healing water into her mouth. Most of it just ran back out. Digby couldn't be sure if she'd swallowed any. After that, Mason poured some on her forehead. The water plastered a faded, pink lock of hair to her skin.

Another screech echoed in the distance, followed by a burst of gunfire.

"What do we do?" Alex spun, searching for a threat. "We can't stay here."

"And we can't go back," Becca added.

"Then we run. We find somewhere to hide, ideally with a mirror, and we wait for Parker to wake up," Digby said just as another two revenants burst through the door of the building near where the first creature had fallen.

The pair howled at the sight of prey, each one raising a rifle. Their guns barked as bullets sprayed through the area. The creatures didn't have the aim of a trained soldier, but what they lacked in accuracy they made up for in quantity. Digby stepped in front of Becca. Bullets couldn't kill her, but there was always the chance that the damage they caused would take too much of her mana and send her into a bloodthirsty rampage.

"Get rid of them, Alex!" Digby ducked his head to keep his one vulnerability out of the line of fire and turned to keep Asher protected by his body.

"I'm on it." The artificer stepped carefully to the side to put himself between the threats and Mason who was trying to hoist

Parker off the ground. Just like before, Alex's hand snapped up to level his pistol at the threats. Then, he fired in a rapid staccato, his aim flicking back and forth between both targets. A final shot cracked into a stone pillar behind one of the revenants as his eye patch's Guiding Hand ability ceased to function once he no longer had a live foe to shoot at.

Digby's HUD lit up with another experience message.

Two Revenant Thralls defeated. 1,280 experience awarded.

"We've got to go. There's bound to be more of those things coming." Mason stood up with Parker in a princess carry, her head lolling to the side as one of her arms dangled.

"Give me your gun." Alex holstered his pistol and held a hand out to Mason, who couldn't do much while carrying the messenger. The soldier leaned to the side so Alex could pull the shoulder strap of his rifle up over his head.

Digby glanced at his mana.

MP: 502/502

It was plenty, but he didn't have a horde there to back him up. An image flashed through his head of his zombies standing uselessly back in the parking garage in Vegas next to the fully loaded vehicle that Becca had packed the night before. He cursed himself for not sending them through the passage before Parker.

"Go that way." Becca threw a hand out toward the opposite side of the courtyard from where the revenant had entered.

Digby picked up a flow of mana coursing through her body with his blood sense. She must've cast her Cartography spell. It was a heavy expenditure of her limited resources, but well worth it. He turned back to keep an eye on their rear as they moved, only to spin back around to the front when something screeched in their direction. Another revenant thrall had found them and was already raising a weapon. Fortunately, this one was in range of his magic.

"Keep running!" Digby raised his staff and summoned his wraith.

The rest of his coven rushed toward the creature even as it leveled a weapon in their direction. The flickering image of Jack the Ripper ran alongside them, a small blade gleaming as it darted past. The echo slashed upward into the side of the creature to throw it off balance. A burst of gunfire escaped its rifle, spraying bullets across the ground. The crimson echo winked out of existence for an instant before reappearing to bring a vertical strike down into the same place the creature had been hit before. Blood covered the stone at its feet, along with a coil of entrails that spilled from its abdomen.

Becca leapt over the revenant with the effortless grace of a vampire as Mason weaved around the fallen creature. The revenant reached out to grab its organs, shoving them back into the gaping hole in its side. Its wound sizzled and popped as it tried to heal.

Alex stumbled to a stop, nearly falling over a loop of intestine. Finding his balance again, he flicked the end of the rifle he carried into the revenant's face and fired. The creature went limp after that.

Revenant Thrall defeated. 640 experience awarded.

Digby blew past him, rushing into an archway that led to a door. Once inside, he skidded to a stop and released Asher from beneath his coat. The raven flapped up toward the ceiling as soon as she was free, drawing Digby's eyes upward.

"Good lord." His voice fell to a stunned whisper.

He had seen grand and spectacular buildings before, but this was on a whole new level. Nearly every surface was covered in some sort of relief or painting. Statues were positioned all along the walls, and a massive, vaulted ceiling hung overhead. The hours it must've taken to produce the art that covered the interior were unimaginable.

"There's more coming," Mason said, tearing his attention

away from their surroundings. The soldier stopped a second later to shift Parker's weight in his arms to keep from dropping her.

Digby snapped his attention to a group of seven or eight shadowy figures all carrying rifles and running toward them from the far end of the hall.

Becca threw herself against a wall, hiding behind a pillar as a torrent of uncontrolled gunfire poured in their direction. Alex's Barrier spell took a few hits as he ducked behind a pillar on the opposite side.

Three bullets slammed into the bone armor that covered Digby's chest. None of them penetrated, but one of the protective plates cracked. Not that he had any reason to worry about his chest. No, his only vulnerability was his head.

A squawk came from Asher as a sudden wave of fear flowed back to him across their bond. He found the raven a second later, hopping across the floor with a ruined wing. She'd caught a stray bullet. He used his Mend Undead mutation to fix her up, then ordered her to get behind a statue.

"We're pinned down!" Becca shouted.

"But we can't stay here," Mason added as he struggled to hide behind a statue while holding Parker's unconscious body. The messenger's legs still hung halfway in the open, the occasional bullet sparking off her cloak's protective shell.

"If everyone stays behind me, my Barrier can take a few hits while we run." Alex offered the only solution he could.

"Nonsense, you aren't nearly wide enough to supply adequate cover." Digby tried to hide behind a statue that was a few sizes too small for him.

"I suppose I have been getting a lot of exercise since the world ended," Alex responded with an awkward chuckle that was entirely inappropriate for the situation.

"That wasn't a compliment." Digby struggled to think of something as another bullet sparked off Parker's barrier.

That was when he got a brilliant idea.

Activating his Limitless mutation, he rushed across the hallway. With the increased strength, he grabbed hold of the front of Parker's cloak as well as the shirt beneath it. He closed his hand tight around the fabric and yanked the messenger out of Mason's arms. "Pardon me."

With that, he thrust Parker out like a shield.

Her cloak fanned out, its barrier shining as bullets slammed into her back, unable to harm her.

"Are you seriously going to use our most important magic user as a human shield?" Becca ducked as bits of plaster fell on her head from a priceless piece of art and history that had just shattered.

"Of course I am. Parker is the safest of us all right now. She won't even feel anything with this cloak on, and we can move while she gives us some extra cover." Digby thrust his staff forward past the messenger's dangling legs and summoned his wraith again. This time the crimson echo of Jack the Ripper rushed into the approaching crowd, slashing this way and that, only to vanish when the spell ran out of power.

"Damn, there's too many." Digby retreated. "I could use a little help."

Alex stepped beside him to help provide cover as everyone moved. Then he pulled his pistol and tossed Mason's rifle to him. The soldier pulled back a few more steps before leveling his gun at the enemy.

Becca raised her weapon as well.

All three of them fired at once, their bullets tearing through the oncoming group. Four experience messages flashed across Digby's vision by the time their guns clicked empty.

Becca let out a frustrated huff and raised a hand as three more revenants barreled toward them. The air grew cold as moisture flowed toward her to solidify into three spikes of ice. She let them fly as soon as they were fully formed. Two punched into the middle foe while the last sank into the throat of the creature on the right.

Digby peeked around his shield and flicked his staff toward the wall as the final revenant approached. Opening his maw, he launched a spike of blood from the side at an upward angle that punched through the last threat. It tore the creature off its feet like a ragdoll before slamming it into the opposite wall.

Lowering Parker's unconscious body so that her feet dragged

on the floor, Digby took a moment to find his bearings. "What the devil is happening here? Why on Earth is Europe overrun with thralls? And while we're at it, what the hell is a thrall?"

Asher stretched her newly mended wing, then flapped up to land on Digby's shoulder.

"I might have an idea about where these things came from." Becca stepped away from the wall. "I think there's another vampire here."

"What, really?" Alex reloaded and holstered his pistol.

"That's the only explanation I can think of. If a vampire were to bite a human without killing or turning them, I think a thrall is what you get. They can probably control them similar to how a necromancer controls zombies."

"That is downright unoriginal. Tell them to get their own abilities and stop stealing mine." Digby let out a huff.

"Do you want me to, maybe, take Parker back?" Mason motioned to pick up the messenger that was dangling from Digby's hand.

"Nonsense, I have her just fine." He raised her up and dropped her over his shoulder opposite Asher for easier carrying. It didn't hurt that her body served to protect his head. A screech echoed down the hall to remind him that they couldn't stand around and talk forever.

"Let's go. We still need to find someplace safe."

He took the lead from there, trying to move quietly to avoid any unwanted attention. Mason and Alex took a position behind him, with Becca bringing up the rear since her senses were sharp enough to catch anything that might try to sneak up on them.

Passing through another archway, they entered a gallery lined with art and statuary. Digby barely looked at his surroundings. The only thing on his mind was to find someplace where they could hide and deal with the unconscious messenger on his back. He skidded to a stop a second later when Becca let out a yelp.

"What is the matter?" He spun around.

The vampire stood on the other side of an archway that he had just passed through holding one hand like she had burnt it. A mix of shock and confusion hung on her face. "Shit, this room is warded."

"How could it be?" Mason stepped toward her. "Nothing else has been so far."

"I don't know, but I felt it the moment my hand went through." She let out a breath. "I was holding a rifle in front of me. Otherwise, I might've run straight through."

"Well, consider yourself invited inside," Digby barked and got moving again only to stop a second later.

She wasn't coming.

"An invite will only get me through a hearth ward. This could be something more. There is no way for me to pass a church ward, and considering where we are, it's entirely possible that's what we're dealing with."

Alex approached the archway and ran his hand along the side. "I don't see any engravings. So it's probably some kind of mass enchantment based on people's beliefs."

The sound of distant screeches echoed from somewhere behind them. They didn't have long to stand around.

"Is there a way to test if an invitation is enough?" Mason stepped into the archway as if standing in the space would somehow help Becca to pass through it.

"Yes, just dip a finger. That should clear things up." Digby adjusted Parker's body hanging from his shoulder as she began to fall off. Asher flapped her wings in protest, nearly sliding from the other side.

Becca nodded and raised her hand to extend a pinky. Then she yanked her hand back. "Shit. It's no good. Whatever this ward is, I can't pass."

"What do we do?" Mason placed his hand on her shoulder.

"You have to leave me." She looked back. "I'll run. I don't think the thralls are hostile to me if I'm alone."

"How do you know that?" Digby argued. "If there really is someone controlling those things, then you have no idea what kind of orders they've been given. So far, all they've done is shoot on sight."

"True, but I doubt that command would apply to other

vampires." Becca's tone wavered as if trying to convince herself as much as she was everyone else. "I mean, when they were shooting at us before, they were aiming more at the rest of you than they were at me."

Digby scoffed. "You don't sound very confident. And that proves nothing; those thralls are terrible shots. I think they only hit me by sheer luck and the volume of bullets."

Mason held onto her arm. "Digby's right. And I'm not losing you again. You weren't even supposed to come with us."

"I know. Unfortunately, someone just had to convince me to come."

"Oh, don't blame this on me," Digby started to argue. "I was trying to help."

"Now isn't the time for that." Mason put an end to the dispute.

"It's okay." Becca took his hand and squeezed it. "You won't. I'm not about to let myself get killed again. It wasn't fun the first time. You can trust me on that." She glanced back over her shoulder as the screeching of revenants grew louder. "I can do this. I'll figure something out." She slid Mason's hand from her shoulder.

His fingers held on for a second longer before letting go. "Okay." He reached into his pocket and pulled out a compact mirror. "Keep this on you. We'll have Parker contact you as soon as she wakes up. We'll find somewhere to meet up."

"I'll be waiting." She gave him a determined nod, then stepped away.

Mason stood watching as she turned and ran.

The vampire stopped to look back for a moment, then she vanished into the shadows.

"She'll be alright." Alex put a hand on Mason's shoulder. "I've seen what she can do with just a few dozen points of mana, and her MP is well over a hundred right now. She can survive anything."

"Indeed, and that's more than I can say for this one." Digby gestured to Parker dangling from his shoulder.

"I know." Mason adjusted his hat.

Digby turned as the soldier stepped away from the archway.

From there, they kept running until they came to another large room with four hallways extending from it. Like the rest, every inch was covered in art of some kind or another. It all must have been worth a fortune. Digby couldn't deny that there was still a little voice inside him telling him to hand Parker back to Mason so he could steal a painting. He shook off the thought. It wasn't like there was anyone left alive to buy anything.

Then again, everything within the museum would have value again eventually. Not necessarily monetarily, but it was valuable historically. Maybe taking something back with them would be a good idea, after all.

His attention was torn away by a lone revenant approaching from a side passage.

Unlike the others he'd seen, it wasn't armed. He swept his staff through the air, ready to cast an Emerald Flare at the creature, only to waiver. Not only was the art surrounding the revenant irre-placeable, but the building itself also held a historical significance. Casting his wraith would cause less damage. Then he got a better idea.

"What are you waiting for?" Alex started to pull his pistol.

"Let's wait for it to get closer." Digby watched the threat. "We don't know where the boundary of these wards lie. If it stops at the entrance to this room, that will tell us something. Not to mention I could use a new minion."

The revenant rushed toward them only to slow when it reached the archway.

"And there we are." Digby grinned.

With that, he marched toward the creature and shoved a hand through the threshold to plunge his claws into its chest to cast Fingers of Death. For a moment, the thrall seemed to be succumbing to the spell. Then it swiped a clawed hand in his direc-tion. Digby stepped back and held Parker out to block the attack.

"Why didn't it work?"

"Maybe you can't take a thrall as a minion, since someone has already claimed it." Alex shrugged.

Digby frowned. "Fine, then. If I can't have it, no one will."

He grabbed hold of the creature's hair and yanked it forward before it could put up a fight. The revenant spasmed the instant it passed through the archway, falling to the tile floor and screaming louder than anything he'd ever heard.

"Holy hell!" Digby stepped back as the creature flailed with such force it broke its own bones, its skin smoking and sizzling until a layer of blackened char began to spread across its body. After about fifteen seconds, it burst into flames. Digby stared down at the smoldering corpse. "Alright, I was not expecting that."

"Crap, is that what happens to Becca if she walks through a ward?" A horrified expression fell across Alex's face.

"It's like something out of a movie." Mason took a step back. "How can something like that happen just because enough people believe in it?"

"Mass enchantments are a powerful thing." Alex tapped on his eyepatch. "Trust me. A little bit of belief goes a long way."

"There's so much we still don't know about magic and how it interacts with the world." Digby tightened his grip on Parker's body. "We need to find this archive. If there's something in it that will grant us the power we need, then we must steal everything we can and get out of here."

That was when someone cleared their throat behind him.

Digby froze as an elderly voice spoke.

"I'm pretty sure there's something in the Ten Commandments against theft."

CHAPTER ELEVEN

"Please don't kill me, please don't kill me, please don't kill me."
Becca held her finger on the trigger of her rifle as she stood with
her back against a wall. She'd run outside after splitting up with
Mason and the others. As much as she would have rather stayed
inside, she couldn't take the risk of running into another ward that
she couldn't pass.

Once she was out of the building, it hadn't taken long to run
into another few thralls. None of them fired at her, but she'd kept
running regardless. She didn't want to fully test her theory of
whether or not they were hostile to her. Not yet, at least.

After a minute of running, she'd ducked around a corner to get
out of sight. The thralls continued on without noticing. She was
just glad that someone had blocked out the sun. Otherwise, she
wouldn't have been able to run for more than a few dozen feet
without getting winded.

She glanced at her HUD.

MP: 120/454

There wasn't much left after casting a couple of spells.
Certainly not enough to put up a fight.

"Stupid Digby. I can't believe I let him talk me into coming."

She felt bad for cursing the zombie immediately. He actually seemed to have been trying to help. Besides, he'd had no way to know that Parker was going to pass out at the worst possible time. If anything, Becca had only herself to blame. She'd noticed that the messenger's condition had been deteriorating and she'd trusted her when she said she was fine.

"Stupid me, I guess." She let the back of her head rest against the cool stone of the wall behind her. "Next time I am staying in the car no matter what."

The moment of peace was short-lived.

One of the thralls that had spotted her earlier rounded the corner on the far side of the building. It let out a screech the moment it saw her. A dozen more poured around the corner in seconds. Half of them raised rifles in her direction.

Becca flinched, ready to flick a few points of mana into her agility to get herself out of there. Then she stopped. They hadn't fired yet.

That was a good sign.

They were all dressed in the same tactical body armor as the others. She still had multiple magazines for the submachine gun she'd brought with her, but she'd never been a very good shot. It was unlikely she could cause enough damage with the weapon against armored targets. Revenants could heal most wounds anyway. Her only chance of winning would be to draw the heavy sword on her back, but that was out of the question. With the amount of mana it would take to wield, and the lack of humans to feed on, she would run out too fast.

"It is so much easier fighting humans. At least then I can bite them to refill my MP." She grimaced at her own words as soon as they came out of her mouth. "Is that really my first thought?"

Becca shook off her disgust and glanced to her right. The courtyard where she'd started stretched out before her. She could probably keep running. Looking back to the revenants, she realized that they were slowing in their approach.

"What would running gain?" she asked herself. "So I escape for another few minutes? What next?"

Becca shook her head. That wasn't going to solve anything. No, there were too many revenants and she had too little information. That last part needed to change.

"Okay, I surrender." She lowered her weapon and raised her hands.

It was the best option she could come up with. Thinking about the situation tactically, it was a good idea. If the thralls really were under the control of another vampire, there was a good chance they would bring her to them. That would let her gather intel. It could even help Digby and the others. Hell, the vampire in control of the thralls might even be willing to help them in the fight against Autem. Though, that was unlikely. Considering that the vampire in question had turned a ton of humans into thralls, she assumed they weren't concerned with saving the world.

The revenants stepped closer, entering melee range.

It was her last chance to draw her sword.

She resisted the temptation. "Take me to your leader."

That was when the thralls lowered their guns.

Becca arched an eyebrow. "So you have enough intelligence to understand me."

One of the thralls nodded while another snarled and raised a hand as if pointing in the direction they had come from. Half of the group began walking. The same revenant stabbed its finger at the air as if insisting that she obey as well.

"You want me to follow?" Becca eyed the creature.

Revenant Thrall, Uncommon, Neutral

Now that she was no longer traveling with humans, the Heretic Seed had updated the creature's relationship status. The knowledge scraped away the last of her apprehension.

"Okay, let's go." Becca lowered her hands and followed the first half of the group. As soon as she did, the rest filed in behind her as if escorting a prisoner. She just hoped whoever she was being brought to would be reasonable.

The thralls didn't take her far. Instead, they led her on a route that took her out and around some of the buildings of the Vatican before bringing her back toward St. Peter's Basilica. The domed roof of the enormous building nearly touched the canopy of dark clouds that blanketed the city. Its surface was illuminated only by the occasional flash of crimson lightning from within the hanging gloom. Becca followed her undead captors, expecting them to turn into one of the smaller buildings. She was taken aback when they continued on to the steps that led up to the basilica's entrance.

"Why would a vampire choose a giant church as a base?"

None of the revenants answered her. Instead, one of them approached to grab at her gun. She let the thrall snatch the weapon away without putting up a fight. It handed it to one of the other creatures that did not already have a rifle. It slung the gun over its shoulder, then came back to take the magazines that she had slotted into the elastic loops that were connected to her chest protector. Another of the thralls poked at the clasps that secured her armor while a third started to pull on the handle of her sword. That was where she drew the line.

"Hey! Cut it out." She shook them off, getting a screech in return. She hissed back, baring her fangs.

The thralls backed off as if she were speaking their language.

"That's better." She straightened her chest protector which had been tugged off-center.

Seemingly satisfied with only taking her gun, the revenants started up the stairs again. Becca followed, glad she had been able to keep her sword. She stopped when she reached the pillars in front of the entrance, a little concerned about what kind of warding the building might have. Then again, if a vampire was using it as their home, odds were it didn't count as a church anymore.

Becca waited for the first of the revenants to enter the doors just to make sure they didn't turn into a writhing mess on the floor. She'd stepped all the way through a ward by accident once before and it had not been fun. There was no way she was taking a chance now. When the thralls strolled through the threshold without issue, she started walking again.

Inside, the church was dark, save for the glow of candles.

A lot of candles.

They had been placed all over the floor in a seemingly random pattern, many burning down to nubs. She noticed a thrall placing and lighting new candles on top of the old, their wax dripping into multicolored pools that layered into mounds as they cooled. The entire floor was covered, turning it into a landscape of barren hills and craters. It gave her the impression that the building was rotting, like a scab forming over a festering wound.

There was something disturbing about being alone in such a large space. Sure, the thralls were there, but not really. The souls inside them were already gone. The thought struck her with a sudden, crushing loneliness that made her grateful for everyone back in Vegas. She hadn't thought of it before, but the absence of life around her weighed far more than she could've imagined. Silence raked its fingers across her mind as she stood in the dim light of the candles. After thirty seconds, she was practically begging for someone to speak.

Then someone did.

"Chi Sei?"

Becca nearly jumped ten feet in the air. The only reason she didn't was because she had enough control over her mana to keep from feeding it into her physical stats on instinct. She spun to find a figure of a man standing at the edge of the room, his voice echoing through the emptiness. It was gravelly yet sharp, like a knife being dragged against a stone to hone its edge. The candle-light couldn't reach him where he stood, leaving her to face his silhouette.

The man's posture was hard to read, with one shoulder hunched up, and the other hanging loose. It gave the impression that one arm was excessively long even though they both were the same size in reality.

Becca focused on the shadowy form, unable to get a good enough look for the Heretic Seed to analyze the man. Not that she needed it to. There was only one explanation for what he was.

A vampire.

"Chi Sei?" the figure repeated, remaining where he stood.

That was when she realized he was speaking Italian, a language that she did not. She knew a little Spanish from her parents but hadn't spoken it since joining Skyline as a teenager. Beyond English, she couldn't actually understand any other language.

"Sorry, I only speak English."

The figure immediately blew out a sigh. "Of course you do. And by the sound of your accent, you're American. The world ends and you still expect everyone to accommodate you, I see."

Becca frowned at the man's tone. It was clearly meant to be insulting. Granted, he wasn't wrong. She hadn't given any thought to the possibility that a language barrier would be a problem. She shook off her annoyance enough to pick up another detail. He had originally been speaking Italian, yet his English bore a French accent.

"You're a vampire, right? Like me?" She tried to build a connection.

The figure stood silently for a long moment before answering, "Yes."

"Oh good, I'm new here. And it's good to find allies." She tried not to leave any room for argument.

The figure argued anyway. "Allies? I'd say that's quite the leap."

"Ah, casual acquaintances, then?" she tried again.

"That depends on you and why you're here." His tone remained serious. "Someone has killed some of my thralls. And your arrival now is too much of a coincidence to be unrelated."

"Yes. That was my group," she answered without hesitation, adding, "However, it was your thralls that attacked first. All we did was defend ourselves."

"Your group? What sort of group?" The figure took a step closer, some of his details emerging from the darkness. She couldn't make out his face, but a wiry mess of blonde hair hung across one side.

"Yes, my group. We came to search for artifacts. The enchanted kind." It was a half-truth.

"And they abandoned you?" He took another step, the light revealing a three-piece suit that didn't seem to match the figure's posture.

"We had to split up. I couldn't pass through the wards."

"And they could? Meaning, they are human?" Excitement filled his voice as if she had just revealed something that she should have kept hidden.

She furrowed her brow. He had to know already that there were humans amongst her group. If they had all been vampires, then his thralls probably wouldn't have attacked. He was probably just trying to confirm his suspicions. Either way, he had no way to know she had a zombie on her side, and there was a good chance he didn't know any of them were Heretics. It didn't sound like he had been there to witness any of them use magic, and vampires didn't have a HUD to analyze anything with.

That was her advantage.

"Yes, they're human," Becca admitted what he already knew.

"You cooperate with them?" His tone grew suspicious.

Becca caught herself before answering. From what she knew of this vampire, he had turned a lot of humans into thralls. Not to mention she could smell blood in the room. It had been hard to pick out among the scent of candle wax, but now that she was getting used to it, the smell was hard to miss. None of the blood was fresh. It was more like a dried layer on a stained cloth. From that, she had to assume that humans did not have protected status in her host's eyes. The vampire before her probably viewed people as food.

That was when she asked herself, what would Digby do?

The answer to that was obvious.

He would lie.

"Cooperating is a strong term." Becca took a step toward him. "It's more like a convenient turn of events."

"Convenient in what way?" A conspiratorial hiss entered his voice.

"Well, it's relatively easy to get a few humans to trust you, especially if you save their lives every now and again. And they're not likely to suspect when one of them goes missing, especially when it's so easy to make it look like a revenant got them." Becca ended the lie with a predatory grin that showed her fangs. She cast her new Fiction spell to help sell the story, hoping the vampire didn't have a way to sense it.

"Well then." The vampire in the three-piece suit seemed to relax. "As long as you are willing to share, I'd say your assumption of you and I being allies would be accurate."

With that, he stepped forward into the candlelight. Becca tried not to react to his appearance. It wasn't horrific or anything disturbing. No, it just wasn't what she expected. From his voice, she'd thought he'd appear older. Instead, he looked to be around thirty. His suit, which had seemed fancy when he was standing in the dark, now looked disheveled and dirty. The fabric had been extravagant, with a shimmer of silver fibers woven into each piece of the outfit. Now, it was wrinkled and torn. There was even a bullet hole in the side. His tie was missing altogether, and a crimson stain covered the white shirt beneath his vest.

As he walked toward her, he straightened his shoulders to fix his posture. It didn't look natural, as if he was trying to force his body into a form that he considered normal. Suddenly, his reason for hiding in the dark for so long seemed different. Becca had assumed he had been lurking in the shadows to be intimidating, but now, she was starting to think that it might have been out of embarrassment.

"How does half of your group sound?" He held a hand out toward her. "Is that an amicable arrangement?"

"Half?" Becca stamped down her disgust and tried to play the role of an average murderous vampire. "Half seems a little steep, considering I've done all the work so far."

"I would agree if I had not set up such an inviting environment for our kind." He gestured upward. "Those clouds did not simply appear."

"How did they get there, actually?" Becca arched an eyebrow, hoping to glean a little more information from him.

"Oh, some artifact or another." He glossed over the topic. "But still, I'd say my efforts are worth an even split of the prey."

"You get one." She folded her arms. "But you can have the cute one with pink hair." Offering Parker seemed like the best strategy, since her cloak would protect her from most attacks. She would've offered Digby, but somehow she had the feeling that Parker would be more tempting to this particular vampire.

"That is an interesting offer. But I still have to insist on half." He grinned and stepped closer, leaning in as if trying to kiss her. Instead, he just bit the air near her throat. "Unless you want to just toss aside the prospect of being allies, then I can just bite you."

Becca resisted the urge to lean away. Not just because she found him repulsive as a person, but also because he smelled terrible. She had noticed the scent before, but thought it had been coming from the thralls in the room. Now that he was close, it was impossible not to notice. He smelled like he hadn't showered in weeks and his breath was terrible. It was like something had crawled down his throat and died before being reanimated and dying a second time.

"I don't think biting me would get you very far. A vampire can't feed on another vampire, after all." She forced herself to grin back.

He hesitated for a moment as if actually debating on biting her. Then he pulled away. "Of course not. Could you imagine? Vampires biting vampires."

She tried to laugh at the comment, but it only came out as an awkward chuckle. "So just one, then? You can take the pink-haired girl, and I get to leave with the rest of the humans to finish off when I choose to."

"Fine." He waved a hand through the air. "Provided you can find a way to get them out of those wards."

"I should be able to convince them to leave." She nodded. "And I'm Rebecca, by the way."

"Charmed." He stood a little taller, his shoulder popping as he forced his body to cooperate. "You may call me Lord Durand."

CHAPTER TWELVE

"Gah!" Digby spun to find an elderly man standing in the shadow of an archway behind him.

Asher let out a startled caw as Parker's unconscious body flopped to the side, nearly falling off his shoulder.

Both Alex and Mason froze where they were.

"I think this is what they call being caught red-handed," the stranger said.

Digby immediately regretted mentioning his intent to steal the Vatican's artifacts a moment before.

Granted, the man looked like he was in his eighties. If it wasn't for the heavy pistol that he'd casually leveled at Digby's head, he wouldn't have been concerned. It was one of those guns that could be loaded by sliding a magazine into the handle. It looked old and bore lines of engravings surrounded by filigree and other detailing. Even the wood panels that were bolted to the sides of the grip had decorative inlays of pewter peeking out from beneath the man's fingers.

Digby gulped audibly.

He had seen firearms like that before, back when he was trapped within the Heretic Seed, and knew enough to be wary of the engravings. There was no way to know what effect they had, but if they enhanced damage, a pistol like that could very well take his head off.

Digby tore his eyes off the gun and focused on the man holding it. Besides being old, he was dressed in a black button-down shirt with matching pants. An empty shoulder holster hung from one arm. The collar around his neck was odd, like that of the clergymen that Digby had seen in a few movies. The little white bit was missing.

"Now, now, there's no need to point guns at anyone." Digby glanced to the side at Mason and Alex to make sure their weapons were pointed at the floor.

"Stay where you are." The man's aim didn't waver. "I doubt this old Colt can put something like you down permanently, but it is certainly enough to ruin your day." Despite being in another country, the strange man's English was good.

"I assure you, I can explain." Digby made a point to keep his staff and claws low to remain non-threatening, not wanting to have his day ruined by a bullet.

"Good, you may start with your name." The elderly man remained calm, holding his gun steady as if he was used to the weapon's weight.

"My name is Digby." He decided to leave off the title of lord that he usually insisted on. "Beside me is my apprentice, Alex. And beside him is Mason. None of us are here to cause you any trouble."

"What brings you to the Vatican, Digby, Alex, and Mason?" The man flicked his eyes to each of them as he said their names.

"We need information," Alex spoke up.

"Indeed." Digby nodded. "We have people depending on us to protect them against a powerful enemy, and we were told there is an archive here where we might be able to find information on a way to gain an advantage."

"Is the young lady there on your shoulder injured?" The old man's tone softened as he shifted his gaze to Parker.

"Injured?" Digby shook his head, her body wiggling back and forth along with the action. "She just passed out. Bad timing, really."

"She has some sort of sickness that we don't understand," Alex added. "We didn't realize it was as bad as it is until now."

"We were looking for someplace safe where she could rest." Mason stepped forward.

The man stood for a long moment before lowering his gun. "Very well, follow me. But do not try anything sneaky."

"Of course, I would never." Digby glanced at the man's gun, debating whether or not he could get the weapon away from him before being shot.

Mason gave him a look that said, 'Don't.'

Alex gave him a look that said, 'Listen to Mason.'

"I am sure you wouldn't." The elderly man smirked as if knowing exactly what Digby had been thinking as well. Then he turned and started walking down the hallway. His pace was brisk, despite his age. "My name is Dominic. The sanctuary wards on this building will keep out most of the thralls for the moment."

"You know what these creatures are?" Digby asked, surprised that he had used the same word that the Heretic Seed had label the revenants with.

"I know plenty. One might say that it is my job to know such things." Dominic held his gun casually at his side as he walked.

"Do you know the location of the archive we're looking for?" Alex jogged a few steps to catch up.

"That might depend on what archive you are talking about. This is the Vatican, after all. We have many archives here. There is a lot to keep track of."

"Whichever archive has information about magic," Mason said while keeping an eye on the hall behind them.

Dominic let out an amused chuckle. "Oh, that archive."

"So you do know of it?" Digby tried to get more information from the man.

"Who do you think oversees it?" He stopped at a rather ordinary-looking doorway. "I dare say that is why I'm still alive now."

Digby stopped at the door, wanting to rush into the room. He stepped aside instead to let Alex take the lead since he had his hands full with Parker. His apprentice obliged without hesitation, yanking the door open. Digby followed him in only to stop just a few feet inside.

"What? This isn't an archive."

Surrounding him was nothing but a standard office space, the kind administrative staff would accomplish meaningless busywork in. A few desks filled the room as well as a meeting table. Unlike everything he'd seen so far, none of it was fancy. There wasn't even any art on the walls. It was all just... so mundane.

"Did you think I was going to lead you straight to one of the Vatican's most secret archives without asking a few questions first?" Dominic shook his head and pushed into the room. "Of course not. However, you may lay your friend down here on the table. There are some supplies here as well." He gestured to a corner where a plastic package of water bottles sat next to some basic food items.

Digby deflated, but couldn't fault the man for being cautious.

Walking across the room, he leaned his staff against the wall and set Parker down on the table. Alex removed his coat and balled it up to place it under her head. She didn't look well and her pulse was slow. Though, Digby wasn't one to judge since lacking a pulse was normal for him. Other than that, she seemed to be sleeping soundly. With a little rest, she might just wake up without a problem. There wasn't much else they could do but wait.

Asher hopped down to the table to perch on the back of one of the chairs to watch over her.

With their messenger sorted for the moment, Digby turned to Dominic. "Alright, if you need assurance before you take us to this archive, then ask whatever you need to."

"Not yet." He started back toward the door. "I am afraid that by coming here, you have compromised this place's safety. I must check the area and find an appropriate path for escape."

"But you said this building was warded." Alex looked up as he grabbed a water bottle from the package by the wall.

"It is." Dominic placed a hand on the door, letting his fingertip slide down its surface. "However, once Lord Durand learns that his thralls have chased someone into this place, he will take steps to negate the wards. He doesn't have an endless supply of minions or ordinance, yet a well-placed explosive will damage the wards as much as the structure they protect. Once he becomes aware that there is prey inside these walls, he will begin attacking."

"Lord Durand?" Digby stopped him before he could leave, trying to find out what was happening in the city.

Dominic scoffed at hearing the name repeated. "Yes. Can you believe it? He has declared himself Lord. Honestly, what sort of egomaniacal madman gives himself a title like that?"

"Ah, yes. A man of poor taste, it seems," Digby said, ignoring accusatory looks from Alex and Mason.

"Never underestimate a starving vampire's lack of sense," Dominic continued.

"Starving?" Alex twisted the cap off the water bottle in his hand and cast purify before pouring some on a cloth and placing it on Parker's forehead.

Dominic eyed the bottle as it glowed but said nothing about the spell. "Yes, Durand took control of the area as soon as the world fell. There were a lot of survivors around then, and I think he got a little carried away in building an army. He turned two of his victims into vampires and the rest into thralls. It seems he thought that the supply of humans would never run out, but, as you can see from the absence of clergy around us, we humans are not so limitless."

"He killed everyone?" Mason tensed, clearly worried about Becca who was still out there.

"Yes, the city fell to him almost immediately, as well as the other more common monsters. The result left him without anyone to feed on. Which is why he has been hunting me for weeks. Durand has been around for many decades, according to the records I have read. He was originally French nobility back when he was turned, the kind of man who never got his hands dirty. It's interesting how much things change when desperation sets in. It seems he has resorted to killing his newly created vampires after depleting the supply of humans to drink from."

"What?" Mason's voice climbed. "I didn't think vampires could feed on other vampires."

"It is not impossible for one of their kind to drink from

another, however, there are drawbacks. Killing their own can certainly replenish their power, however, it also poisons them. Feeding on the cursed impairs the mind and disturbs the body. The damage can be reversed by a more traditional feeding. That is why he has been desperate to get to me. As far as I can tell, I am the only person alive for miles. If he doesn't find prey soon, he will begin to lose control over his thralls."

"Shit." Mason gasped and looked toward the door as if about to rush out of there to find Becca.

Dominic's eyes followed him. "That is an awfully large amount of concern for someone who is currently safe within these walls. Would I be correct in assuming that there is another member of your group out there, one that was unable to pass through the wards?"

Digby tried to judge the man's expression. It was obvious that he already knew the answer. He must've overheard them talking about Becca while they stood over that burning revenant earlier. The man was surprisingly sly for someone his age.

"Yes." Mason lowered his head. "One of our friends was recently cursed. There has been a period of adjustment, obviously, but she has been doing well, all things considered. We were forced to split up earlier because of the wards. We thought she would be safe out there, since the revenants are not hostile to her when she is alone, but if this Durand guy is as bad as it sounds…" Mason trailed off. The concern on his face was obvious.

"I am so sorry." Dominic's tone grew sympathetic. "Being forced to separate aside, losing someone to a curse is never easy."

"She's not lost." The soldier shook his head adamantly. "She's just a vampire."

The old man's shoulders sank. "That is a heavier burden than you may realize. There are preventative measures that can be taken, but in the end, trying to live as one of the cursed without becoming a monster is a hard and lonely life."

"Is there a way to cure her?" Alex chimed in, sounding hopeful. "Something in the archives?"

"I am afraid the only true cure for a curse like that is death." His words carried an air of finality.

"Oh, boo-hoo." Digby rolled his eyes at the melodramatic statement. "Curses are no big thing. I'm living proof of that. Well, maybe not so much living, but still."

Dominic didn't look surprised. "I see. And you are, what? Some form of undead? I do not have much experience in that area, but I can tell when a corpse is walking around."

"Indeed, I'm a zombie." Digby puffed out his chest as he spoke. "It's a bit of a long story of how I got this way." He glossed over the rest.

"Well, that story will have to wait until I return." Dominic reached for the door handle. "You may stay here. This room should be safe until I return."

Digby looked to the others before snapping his attention back to the old man. There wasn't a chance in hell he was letting him out of his sight. Not when he knew the location of the archive they were after. "Wait, I shall accompany you."

"So will I," Mason volunteered.

"I…" Alex started to say before glancing back to Parker. "I should stay here to keep an eye on her."

"Very well." Dominic opened the door.

Digby grabbed his staff and followed him back out into the opulent hallway while Mason brought up the rear.

"This enemy of yours, the one that has forced you to travel here in search of an advantage, who might it be?" Dominic asked as he walked.

"Autem," Digby answered without elaborating. Odds were the man already knew of the empire.

His only response was a simple, "I see."

The conversation came to an abrupt pause when they heard a screech coming from a gallery off to the side. Dominic immediately pressed himself up against the wall and checked his weapon to see how many bullets were left. "The wards only cover part of this building. So the thralls still get in. They must be destroyed before they can return to Durand. Otherwise, he'll send them back with something that can damage the hallway's threshold."

"Save your bullets." Digby held his staff in front of the man to keep him from heading in first.

He didn't argue.

From what Digby could tell, it sounded like there were only two thralls. He stepped out into the gallery to confirm his assumption, finding a pair prowling around an archway on the other side. Digby raised his staff as soon as he saw them and summoned his wraith. The specter tore through the creatures in seconds, spraying an intricately carved wall in blood.

Digby frowned, still annoyed that he couldn't take them as minions.

"I assume you both are Heretics, then?" Dominic stepped into the gallery behind him along with Mason.

"Indeed." Digby turned to face him.

"Does that mean you are one of the Fools?" he asked.

"No." Digby held his staff vertically beside him, taking a statuesque pose. "We are on our own side."

Mason walked across the room to look down the next hall. "We were told about this archive you have by the last surviving Fool."

"Last?" Dominic chuckled. "No, their will is not so easy to break. There will be more Fools."

"It sounds like you think of them favorably." Digby tried to sort out whose side the man was on.

"I wouldn't go that far. But I think they have earned some respect." He nodded to himself.

"And Autem? Do they have your respect?" Mason asked.

Dominic frowned. "There were many here in the church that would have sided with the empire and its values, but I was not one of them."

"Is that why you seem willing to help us?" Mason asked.

Dominic shook his head. "I do not believe I have agreed to aid you as of yet." He gestured down the hall with his gun. "Even if I had, the archive you seek is not housed within this building. I am unsure if an old man such as myself would be able to reach it with the streets overrun with thralls."

"Then just tell us where it is." Digby took a quick step toward him. "We can make it there and we can probably pull the thralls away from you here."

"I wish that were possible." He sighed. "But the archive is

housed within a secure vault beneath the Vatican library. It requires a retinal scan of one of its keepers."

Digby arched an eyebrow for a second before tugging it back down.

Dominic caught the change in his expression. "Before you try to cut out my eye, you should know that the scan only works on a living retina."

"I would never." Digby held up both hands.

The man continued to stare at him.

Digby squirmed under his glare. "Alright, I would be lying if I hadn't thought of it. But that doesn't mean I would do it. I'm not a monster." He paused. "Well, you know what I mean."

"He's telling the truth." Mason backed him up. "Graves is definitely rough around the edges, but he's done more to save people than anyone I've ever met."

Dominic immediately held up a hand. "Hold on, your last name is Graves?"

Digby immediately sighed, knowing exactly where the conversation was heading. "Yes, I am a zombie, and my name is Digby Graves. The coincidence has been pointed out. It is... unfortunate."

"I should say so." Dominic chuckled as footsteps came from the hall where the thralls had been.

"Oh my, that is embarrassing," a new voice added.

Digby spun to find a man in a filthy suit standing just beyond the gallery's archway.

Behind him stood Becca, the Seed labeling them both as vampires. Dominic raised his gun without hesitation. That could only mean one thing.

Digby raised his staff toward the new arrival. "Hello, Durand. Nice of you to stop by."

CHAPTER THIRTEEN

"Everyone just put the weapons down." Becca stepped in front of Durand while Digby and some old priest stood ready to attack. She made sure to stop before she got close to the archway that separated the hall from the gallery beyond.

Crossing the threshold would probably kill her.

"Becca, you're okay?" Mason took a step forward, but stopped a second later when she shot him a serious look and flicked her eyes to the unstable vampire beside her. "I'm fine."

"We can see that." Digby lowered his staff. "Why don't you introduce us to your new friend?"

"This is Durand, and he's just here to—"

"Lord Durand," the vampire beside her corrected.

Becca rolled her eyes. "Yes, and we're just here to talk."

"Then speak." The old man beside Digby kept his gun aimed at Durand. He occasionally flicked his eyes to Becca as if debating whether or not to shoot them both.

"Very well. I wish to inform you that I have talked things over with Miss Alvarez here." Durand gestured to her. "And we have reached an agreement to allow you all to go free. I will call off my thralls and will not hinder you further."

"And what does your agreement entail?" the priest with the gun asked.

"Yes, Becky. I'd like to hear about this agreement as well." Digby walked toward her to stand on the other side of the archway. From the look on his face, he was considering throwing every spell he had at the vampire next to her and letting the chips fall where they may.

"The agreement isn't important, it's just a vampire thing. What is important is that everyone gets to live." She tried to convey the need for caution to Digby with her eyes the way she had with Mason. They had no way of knowing it, but Durand had around a hundred and fifty thralls waiting further down the hall, ready to pour in if anything happened.

Digby stood for a long moment, watching her. He would never suspect her of actually taking Durand's side, but she needed him to understand that there was something more going on. She needed him to stand back and follow her lead, and that was not always his first choice. Usually, he just did whatever he wanted.

"Fine." The necromancer stepped to the side to put himself between the old priest and Durand to ensure that no one would start shooting. He must have gotten her point.

"Good." She let out a breath before turning to Durand. "Now if you can make good on your half of things."

"Of course." He inclined his head. "I will recall all of my thralls for the next twenty-four hours, during which time your group will be allowed to leave unimpeded, and you may take the old man with you." He didn't wait for anyone else to speak before turning on one heel and sauntering back down the hallway. "I suggest you gather your things and get moving."

"We will." Becca waited to say anything else, feeding a few points of mana into her hearing to make sure that Durand had actually left and taken his thralls with him.

"Just what is going on?" Digby stepped forward through the archway to stand in front of her now that she was alone.

"It's just what it looks like. We're good to go," she lied.

Judging from the sound of Durand and his thralls, he was still in earshot. Though, he was moving away at least. It wasn't easy, but she could tell his heartbeat apart from the revenants that followed him. Becca dropped the act as soon as she was sure he was far enough away. "Okay, that was all a lie."

"What do you mean that was a lie?" Digby snapped back.

"I mean that I told Durand that I would convince you all that it was safe, and that I would lead you out of the building tomorrow morning into an ambush. I was going to let him have one of you in exchange for letting me go with the rest of you," she admitted. "He thinks I've been pretending to work with you all because I'm planning on killing you one by one."

"What?" Mason looked confused.

"Yes." Digby frowned. "That all sounds relatively counterproductive."

"I know that." She groaned back. "And that's why we're going to leave out the back door while he is waiting for us in the front. We can take the night to rest and prepare, then we'll leave just before dawn."

"I see, so it's a con then." Digby grinned. "I knew you had something up your sleeve."

"I'm just glad you're okay." Mason rushed forward and threw his arms around her. He squeezed her tight for a long moment before letting go.

"I am sorry, I do not understand." The old priest continued to point his gun in her general direction, though his aim did falter.

"You heard her, Dominic." Digby glanced back at him, letting out a chuckle. "We have a plan of escape. If Parker doesn't wake up in time, we'll make for the archives in the morning. If this vampire thinks he knows where we will be, then we just have to not be there."

The priest, apparently named Dominic, lowered his gun. "We will never make it. And I certainly wouldn't trust Durand to follow through with his word."

"He will. Sort of." Becca shifted her weight awkwardly, fighting the instinct to walk through the archway to join the rest of her group. "To be honest, I think he does intend to double-cross me. My guess is he'll kill everyone at the ambush, including me, but I think he bought my story. He seems like the type of person that backstabbing comes to naturally, so the idea that I would be planning on killing all of you fits with his worldview." She paced a few steps to keep herself busy. "That being said, he's definitely going to have a few groups of thralls watching the other directions as well."

"What is the point of this subterfuge, then?" Dominic's tone grew frustrated.

Becca stopped pacing. "Because it's the best I could do. This Durand guy is not all there. I'm lucky he didn't kill me already. At least this way, I was able to buy us some time and breathing room. He pulled his thralls back for now, so we can roam the building freely and get ready to make a break for it in the morning."

"How can we possibly make it?" Frustration filled Dominic's voice.

"He has a point. We can try to find a car, but a lot of the thralls are armed. They'll just unload at us on sight and we can't risk Dominic getting hit. We need his biometrics to open the vault where the archive is," Mason explained. "If we had an armored car like the presidential limo that we've been using, then we might stand a chance. But it's still back in Vegas."

"None of that will matter if our messenger wakes up." Digby leaned on his staff.

"Messenger?" the old priest asked.

"Yes, our unconscious ally is capable of opening passages between mirrors. If she wakes, then we can simply travel back home for reinforcements. This Durand person won't stand a chance against an entire horde of the dead."

"Passages? Good Lord." Dominic placed his free hand to his forehead to help process the information. "I knew such things were possible, but not that they could be wielded by the average human."

"Indeed, Parker seems to be somewhat special in that regard." Digby sounded a little like he was bragging on her behalf.

Becca ignored him. "We should be ready for a worst-case scenario anyway. If there's one thing I know, it's that things rarely go the way we would like them to. Besides, I have an idea."

"Yes?" Digby arched an eyebrow at her.

Becca willed the Seed to show her the map that she'd made of the area earlier. The Vatican cityscape filled the floor around her in response. She took a moment to orient herself. "Alright, there's a parking lot nearby that we need to get to. We'll have to split up because of the wards, but I can meet you there."

"No, I'll go with you." Mason didn't budge from her side. "I almost lost you twice now, I'm not sending you back out there alone again."

"I know." Becca's chest grew tight. "But I'm safe out there, you're not."

Mason stared back at her. She could practically see the gears turning in his head trying to come up with a valid argument. In the end, he just let out a frustrated sigh and turned away. "Fine, but I'm going on record that I'm not happy about it."

"I know." She gave him a sympathetic smile, appreciating the fact that he was always able to keep a cool head. Few men could put aside their emotions long enough to see the situation for what it was. That was one of the reasons she loved him. "It will be fine. I'll meet you in fifteen minutes."

"Wait." Dominic let out a sigh and holstered his pistol. "You can come with us."

"No, I can't. I've tested the wards already, I can't enter." Becca pointed to the archway standing between them.

"That is a sanctuary ward. Anyone may pass through if they ask for protection."

"Oh." Becca hesitated before adding, "Can I claim sanctuary?"

"Do you intend to harm anyone inside?" Dominic's tone grew serious.

"No," Becca responded matter-of-factly.

"Then you may pass." The old priest watched her intently as if expecting something to happen if she stepped forward.

Becca cautiously held out a finger, feeling nothing. Then she stepped through.

Dominic let out a relieved breath when nothing happened.

"I assume that was a test?" Becca narrowed her eyes at him.

"You assume correctly." He gave her a smile. "Words are binding. If you had been lying, the ward would not have allowed you in."

"I suppose I can't fault you for being careful." She shrugged.

"Thank you for understanding." He inclined his head. "You may be a monster, but your character seems to defy your nature."

"Thanks. I think." Becca frowned.

"Yes, we all feel very safe now." Digby put an end to the issue. "Now, what's this about reaching a parking lot?"

Becca started walking. "It's this way. There's a car there that we can use to escape."

"A car? But we need something tougher than that." Mason fell in beside her.

"Indeed, we can't have Dominic here getting filled full of bullets on the way there."

"I would like to avoid that as well," the old priest added, following Digby reluctantly.

"I think I have a solution for that problem." Becca flicked a few points of mana into her senses to scout the area up ahead as she walked. "If I'm right, the vehicle waiting for us should do the job." She picked up her pace.

"Pardon me, but I have not ventured outside in weeks. What kind of vehicle could possibly protect us against an army of thralls with automatic weapons?" Dominic asked, only to have the question answered when she stopped at a door and pushed it open. His face fell as soon as he saw what was outside. All he said after that was a quiet, "Oh."

The area was populated by a scattering of cars and surrounded on all sides by more of the museum's ornate buildings. At the center, a fountain stood, half-full of water. Beside that was the vehicle Becca sought.

It was a modified Mercedes.

The vehicle was laid on its side, as if its driver had taken a turn too sharp and lost control. Other than that and a few scrapes to the paint, it was in good condition. As far as how it got there, she had no idea. All she cared about was that the oversized windows were still intact.

They were.

Of course they were, they were bulletproof.

Becca stopped and turned with one hand held out toward it with a smile, one fang poking out the corner of her mouth. "Will this do?"

Mason let out a low whistle and took off his hat out of respect. "Well, damn. That's the Pope-mobile."

"The what?" Digby turned to him with a confused expression.

"It's the car that they use when they take the head of the church out into crowds. I've seen the specs. It's bulletproof and can withstand small explosives." Becca walked toward the vehicle. "All we have to do is get it right side up and get it open. We can drive it all the way to the archive. I assume there are wards there to keep us safe."

Dominic nodded. "The vault itself will keep anything out as well. If your messenger doesn't wake up tonight. We can wait there for help, provided you have a way to call for reinforcements."

"I'll start checking some of the other cars in the lot for tools. Pope-mobile or not, it's not good for a car to sit on its side. It's going to take some work to get it running reliably," Mason commented.

"That's a good point. Hopefully we can..." Becca trailed off and held up a hand, noticing the sound of something chittering coming from inside the vehicle as she approached. She slowed, just in case it was a threat. It sounded like someone had been trapped inside before becoming a revenant. The image of one of the creatures dressed in white robes and a big hat flashed through her head as she walked around to the front. She blew out a sigh of relief, finding nothing but a random man in a suit.

"He must've gotten bitten and trapped in there," Mason assumed, standing next to her.

"Thank God." Relief swept over the face of the old priest as soon as he saw who was inside. He whispered a quiet prayer a moment later.

Analyzing the revenant told Becca that the creature was not a thrall.

"Finally." Digby rushed over to press himself against the bullet-proof glass. "One of those things that has not yet been claimed. I will have a minion, after all." He stepped away a moment later. "Now, how do we get this thing upright?"

Becca stared at the heavy car, doing the math in her head. Dominic was a little old to help with the task and Parker was unconscious. That just left her, Digby, Alex, and Mason. Even with their enhanced strength, most of the work would have to be done by the nonhuman members of their coven. She glanced at her mana.

MP: 95/454

It wasn't much, but it might just be enough.

She turned back to Digby. "Come on, I'm going to need some undead help with this."

CHAPTER FOURTEEN

"Do you think she'll wake up?" Alex stood next to Digby back in the office where Parker lay on the table.

"There is no way to be sure. We don't even know what's wrong with her." Digby leaned forward, hanging over her. She still looked unwell, with beads of sweat on her brow. It had been a few hours since she'd passed out. Alex had kept watch over her while everyone else tried to get the vehicle that Becca had found upright. So far, they'd been unsuccessful since the vampire was trying to conserve what little mana she had. On top of that, the plan to make a run for the archive was reckless and desperate.

Though, if Parker didn't wake up soon, they wouldn't have a choice but to try it.

Digby reached down and picked up one of her hands, lifting it off the table and shaking it around. "Hello, Parker? Could I trouble you to wake up and pull your own weight?"

There was no response whatsoever. She didn't even stir.

"Is that helping?" Alex stared at him.

"Not so much." Digby dropped her hand back to the table

"It was the same back when she was trapped in the Seed with you. Nothing we did would wake her up." Alex placed another damp cloth on her forehead. "You don't think her mind is some-place else, do you?"

Digby shook his head. "This is something different. I can feel it with my blood sense. She's in there, alright."

Alex placed both hands on the table, sinking a little lower. "Magic has done so much good. It healed Jameson's heart condition, and we've used it to reattach limbs, but I guess that comes with complications of its own. We've traded one set of ailments for another."

"It's not that surprising. Magic interacts in so many strange and unpredictable ways. We can't expect them all to be beneficial." Digby checked his phone for the time. Doing the math in his head on what he understood about time zones, he figured that night had set in. Not that anyone could tell with the clouds blocking out the sky. Hopefully, someone back in Vegas would realize they hadn't come back yet. Maybe they would be able to send a few covens their way. Granted, Jameson had just scrapped the cargo ship for parts and was just entering the testing phase with their new airship. Digby was sure his team of artificers were working as fast as they could, but unless they'd made a lot of progress in the last day, it was unlikely that help could arrive in time.

It was starting to look like they were on their own.

Well, maybe not completely.

Digby clapped his hands together and stepped away from the table. "Alright, Parker may not be waking up anytime soon, but that doesn't mean she can't help."

Raising one hand over her body, he closed his eyes and reached into his pocket for the large diamond ring that contained his infernal spirit. Union was sure to be disgruntled after being left in storage for longer than they had agreed upon, but they were sure to understand once they became aware of the situation.

Digby cast Animate Skeleton.

With that, Parker's body sat up in a strange unnatural motion, her head and arms dangling.

"What did you do?" Alex jumped back from the table.

"I animated her skeleton," Digby explained as if it was simply the most efficient course of action under the circumstances, which it was.

Parker's head straightened itself while Union used her skull to look around the room. Her eyes remained closed the entire time, the infernal spirit inside her lacking the connections needed to control her muscles. One of her hands raised up to flex each finger in front of her face.

"We are alone." A dark voice came from her mouth.

"Indeed." Digby gestured from her head to her feet. "Parker is not currently available. We are in a bit of a dangerous situation, so I'm going to need you to operate her body and keep her safe until she wakes up."

"We agree. She will need assistance." Union nodded, using her head.

"She is going to be so pissed when she wakes up." A look of horror fell across Alex's face.

"I can't very well carry her around like before, can I? If we're going to escape this place, all of us will need to be on our feet. Plus, the spell gives Union the same physical attributes as whoever the skeleton they inhabit belongs to. That means she will be able to help lift that vehicle with the rest of us and spare Becca from using too much mana. You can judge me if you want, but this is merely the best option among worse choices."

"No, you're right." Alex didn't argue, though he didn't look comfortable with the situation either.

"Good, that's settled." Digby snatched his staff up from where it leaned against one wall and headed out into the hallway outside the office. "Now, come along. We have work to do."

Alex walked toward the door, keeping his eye on Parker as he moved. The messenger's body slid her legs off the side of the table to place her feet on the floor. Union pushed off and took a few wobbly steps before acclimating to their new form. Parker showed no sign of waking from the sudden movement. Her face remained blank and expressionless with her eyes closed. If Digby didn't know better, he would have thought her a corpse.

Alex shuddered.

"Oh, don't be so squeamish," he groaned before heading off down the hallway.

It wasn't long before he exited the building into the parking area outside. The sky somehow looked even darker than before, flashes of crimson lightning flickering across the buildings. Mason stood with a flashlight by the fountain at the center of the space. Becca and Dominic sat on the edge of it. The old priest and vampire seemed to be getting along fine. It had been touch and go for the first hour, but after that, whatever differences they had were tossed aside in favor of teamwork and having a common enemy.

"I've brought help," Digby announced as he approached. He was sure that Becca had heard him coming before he'd even exited the building, but sneaking up on Dominic in the dark was not a good way to make friends, and they weren't getting into the archives without his help.

"Oh, thank god." Mason rushed toward Parker as her body stepped outside. "You're awake. We can go—" He skidded to a stop when the beam of his flashlight met her face.

"'Fraid not." Digby gestured to the messenger. "I've just employed Union's services as a puppeteer."

"She is going to be pissed." Becca walked toward them.

"Yes, we have covered that." Digby waved his hand around in the air at nothing in particular. "This is the best way to keep her alive. I know I have a bit of a spotty history with the spell, but I assure you my intentions are just in this instance."

"We will keep her safe." Union backed him up, speaking through Parker's emotionless face.

"Incredible." Dominic approached, seemingly unfazed. "It is horrible. The very idea of magic being capable of such things. But to use an ability like this to protect an ally that is unable to protect themselves is an interesting turn of events."

"You seem to be taking all of this really well." Alex stepped toward the old priest.

"No offense, but the church hasn't been known for being very accepting of things," Becca chimed in.

"Indeed," Digby added, remembering the church full of

people in California who had turned his group away the moment they realized there was a zombie among them. Had they not, he might have been there to protect them. Instead, they all perished in the night. "I wasn't expecting a member of the church to be so cooperative with Heretics. Some would rather risk death than have anything to do with us."

"I cannot deny that." Dominic raised his head to the clouds above. "Fear is a powerful thing, and through it, faith can very often become a barrier to understanding as much as it can be a strength to aid growth. Hence why magic was never accepted by the church. There were too many conflicts and too many inconvenient questions. It is easier to deny and default to tradition. I, and many who served in my position before me, have tended to be more open-minded than what the church has a reputation for. I would say we have served God in our own way."

"And how do you serve God?" Digby stepped toward him.

Dominic lowered his gaze from the heavens, back down to Earth. "By seeking truth."

"Truth?" Digby furrowed his brow, remembering what Harlow had said about the purpose of the archive. Then he shook his head. "What the devil is that supposed to mean?"

The old man turned slowly, gesturing to the world around them. "God didn't give all this to us so that we could ignore it. We are supposed to learn. The truth is what He wants us to know. That is how I believe I can best serve, by understanding the gifts that we have been given."

"And what happens when that truth is not what you wanted it to be?" Digby asked.

"A valid question. Truth is scary and sometimes it is hard to face, but that is why we have faith. To carry us through." The old man walked slowly back toward the wall of the magnificent building that surrounded them and placed his hand against the stone. "There's so much history here. Yet, it is all recorded by mankind. And mankind is flawed. It is naïve to think that we have gotten every detail correct for thousands of years. There are mistranslations, irrelevant traditions, and assumptions that many base their entire existence on. And worse, there are those who knowingly twist God's words for their own gain or convenience. Many will tell of the importance of blind faith, but that defeats the purpose of faith itself. One cannot claim that their faith is strong if one turns away from truth whenever it is tested." He chuckled. "I have traveled the world in my lifetime. It was my job to investigate situations that were suspected to have ties to the supernatural. Some even turned out to be real. And a few," he gestured to the gun tucked into his shoulder holster, "required intervention."

"You mean like, exorcisms and stuff?" Alex perked up.

"Yes, and stuff." Dominic gave him a smile before sweeping a hand through the air to gesture at all of them. "I hardly think a zombie and a few Heretics will be what shakes my belief. If anything, this is an opportunity for learning. I might be old, but it is still never too late to grow."

"Too bad none of Autem's people feel that way." Becca folded her arms. "I've seen what they plan for their empire, and truth is not exactly a priority. It's more about rewriting history and erasing anything that conflicts with their version of it."

"That is regrettable." Dominic deflated. "The Nine certainly have done much to tighten their grip on the minds of their followers."

"Indeed they have." Digby nodded along, before doing a double take. "Wait, you know about the Nine?"

The last person that he'd spoken to who knew anything about Autem's angels had been the Heretic Seed's original caretaker. And she had been dead for thousands of years. He'd thought the truth had been lost. The only thing the caretaker had said back then was that the Nine were not a myth, or at least, not completely.

"A complicated question." Dominic rubbed at his chin. "One that depends on which of two theories is most likely."

"Spit it out then." Digby hit the butt of his staff on the pavement, getting impatient. "Are the Nine real?"

The old man held out a hand. "They are. That much I am sure of."

"Wait, you're saying that angels are real?" Alex hopped up to sit on the hood of a car.

"I believe God is real, or, as Autem calls Him, the One. It is not so hard to believe in angels once that much is accepted." Dominic stared at him for a moment before adding, "And seeing that God has been described as jealous, it could be possible that the Lord's angels have spoken to Autem's leaders and tasked them to guide mankind in rebuilding this world in their image. If that were true, then everyone who stands against them would be wrong. Including me, if I were to help you." He gave a slight shrug. "But that's just one theory."

"And what of your second theory?" Digby leaned on his staff.

"That is where it gets complicated." Dominic rubbed at his eyes. "According to the information stored in the archives that you seek, the Nine are, for all intents and purposes, angels. However, the important question is whether or not they started out as such?"

"You think they were people?" Becca followed along.

He nodded. "I will preface this by saying, I am not the first to value truth. As I said, others before me have investigated this as well and much information has been gathered. What I am about to tell you is just a theory. However, my own experiences suggest that it is the most likely possibility." He paused to let that sink in before continuing. "The Nine were a group of ten people."

"I think your math might be a bit faulty, there," Digby commented, his mind getting stuck on a detail.

Dominic shot him an annoyed look. "I realize the name is misleading, but I suggest that you allow me the opportunity to clarify before asking such minor questions." He didn't give Digby a chance to interrupt a second time. "Magic, as you know, is every-where. It surrounds us completely as a part of the natural world. What stops an average person like myself from wielding that power is that there is not enough compatible energy within me. Yet, that may not have always been the case. It's likely that, long ago, everyone possessed a larger quantity within them."

"Are you saying that everyone had mana similar to a Heretic?" Mason asked.

"Yes, but that doesn't mean that everyone could use it. Evidence suggests that magic was unfocused and disorganized. At least, it was before the Nine discovered what it could do."

"You mean the Ten," Digby corrected, still wondering about the discrepancy.

"Fine, the Ten." Dominic let out an annoyed huff. "They found a way to unlock this power. To control the mana, as you call it. In the archives, this method of control is referenced as the Word of God. It was something like a language that could organize and enhance the potential effects of magic."

"A language?" Alex arched an eyebrow. "You mean like runes?"

"Possibly."

Becca's ears pricked up. "I always thought the runes were a programming language for magic."

"Something like that," Dominic agreed.

"So the Nine were ancient coders," Alex assumed. "They found a process similar to the engraving spell that I have and learned from there."

"The Ten," Digby corrected.

"I am getting to that part," Dominic snapped back at him. "And I'm starting to see why you make enemies so easily, Mr. Graves."

"My apologies." Digby waved him on. "Please continue."

"The problem with power is that it corrupts. We all know that. And the Nine—or Ten, in this case—were no different. Not only that, but by abusing magic, it became too obvious to them how others might do the same. Or how they might be challenged for control of it. That birthed a fear of allowing anyone else the same access. So they began experimenting with ways to lock magic away from the rest of the world. That became the primary objective, for all of them, except one."

"The tenth." Digby nodded, finally getting an answer to the detail in question.

"Yes, the tenth member of their group disagreed. The rest, which became known as the Nine, cast them out and continued their work. Eventually, a spell was designed that could root itself into the soul and spread from one person to another. It could even be passed down from parent to child. It altered the amount of the world's essence that a person could take in and hold, making it impossible for anyone to ever wield magic without having that lock removed first. They cast this spell, without anyone realizing what they had lost. The only ones immune were themselves. After that, they hid the Word of God away, destroying all records of the language so that only those who remembered it could use it."

"That's why regular people don't have as much mana as we do. The Heretic Seed must have a way to remove the effects of that spell. It just resets us back to the way humans used to be." Alex's eyes widened for a moment, then he shook his head. "But then, who created the Heretic Seed?"

Dominic glanced to Digby. "That is where the tenth member, who was cast out, comes back into the story. They didn't agree that magic should be locked away from the rest of the world. I don't know if they tried to stand against the Nine, or if the Nine just hunted them down as a loose end. Either way, in a last act of rebellion before capture, the tenth member created a way to free mankind from the limits that the Nine had shackled it with."

"The Seed." Digby staggered, realizing how important the obelisk really was.

"Yes. There isn't much about this Seed in the archives, but I think it's safe to say that you know more about it than I do at this point."

"And what happened to this tenth member?" Digby shook off his shock. "If the Nine were real, then is it possible that the tenth is still out there. Maybe—"

Dominic held up his hand to stop him. "That is the last that the tenth member was ever mentioned in the archives. But needless to say, it did not end well for them. After all, it is not hard to find reference to a fallen one when angels are concerned."

"Oh shit! The Heretic's Seed was made by the devil," Alex blurted out.

Dominic chuckled. "I'm afraid the truth is a little less interesting. A lot of what we think of as the modern devil is really the result of text being translated multiple times and not having an exact word in each language. The character gained a life of its own after that."

"Good. You had me a little worried there." Digby chuckled

awkwardly at the thought that he was somehow an unwitting pawn of Satan.

"Then again, what people believe also plays a factor. That's why truth is so important," Dominic added. "You may still serve the devil by accusation alone."

"What the hell...? I mean, what the devil?" Digby shook his head. "I mean, what is that supposed to mean?"

"I did say that the Nine were angels. And if that's true, then the one you serve is..." He trailed off to let Digby fill in the blank.

He stomped across the parking lot. "Now, you wait just one second, you just said that the concept of the devil is a mistranslation."

Dominic chuckled. "I did, but I did say that the Nine were angels, and the same thing that gives them that status could technically work against you as well."

"How could someone become an angel if angels, no offense, may not even exist?" Becca asked.

"No offense taken. Everyone is free to believe or not believe what they wish. My faith will remain regardless." He gave her a nod in understanding. "Belief is, in many ways, self-fulfilling." He gestured to the clouds in the sky. "After all, the beliefs of people thousands of years ago were able to give an artifact the power to blot out the sun. It works the same."

"You're talking about mass enchantments." Digby followed along.

"Yes, I believe they were called that a few times within the archives."

"How could a mass enchantment make someone into an angel?" Alex leaned to one side. "I've seen plenty of powerful artifacts, but no enchanted people. I don't even know how that would work."

"It is simpler than one might think. All that is required is for an individual to perform the role that they desire in a believable way. In the case of the Nine, their chosen role was the Lord's angels. As you can imagine, by using magic, it was not hard to gather followers and convince them of their authenticity. And thus, the

Nine ascended from their human existence to the divine, and Autem was born."

"That's it?" Digby nearly dropped his staff in disbelief. "Do you mean to tell me that the Nine are merely con artists?"

"According to this particular theory, that is the gist of it. Manifesting a mass enchantment upon a person is not difficult for an individual who already has power, especially when the people they are trying to convince do not." Dominic turned and walked over to Becca. "For example, if a vampire desired to enter any home they wished without an invitation, they could do so by assuming the identity of an entity that is considered to have an open invitation."

"Wait, are you saying I could change the effects of my curse?" Becca reached her hand out toward him but stopped before making contact. "Is there a way to cancel it out completely?"

He shook his head. "I am sorry, but there is no way to truly change a curse. But it is possible to orchestrate a mass enchantment to gain new abilities and gain more specialized rules that apply only to you."

"Okay, so how do I do that?" Becca spoke quickly, as if suddenly in a rush. "I don't want the ability to cross a hearth ward but say I did. What would I have to do?"

Dominic went silent for a moment as if thinking. Then he chuckled. "How do you feel about teeth?"

Becca screwed up her eyes. "What does that mean? Teeth? I don't know. Why would that matter?"

The old man grinned. "If you were to find a way to locate every tooth lost by a child and claim them, then you would be no different than the fairy that parents tell their children of. In doing so, you would gain an open invitation to enter any dwelling, maybe even the ability to fly as well. Obviously, you would need to leave some sort of payment behind in exchange for the teeth."

"Obviously." Alex laughed.

"Seriously?" Becca stared at the old man, her face completely blank. "That's how it works? I just become the tooth fairy by convincing everyone that I am."

"What is the tooth fairy?" Digby looked back and forth between them.

"It's something parents tell their kids," Mason explained. "When children lose their baby teeth, they put the tooth under their pillow and their mom or dad sneak into the room at night to take it. They leave a dollar or something in its place and tell them that a fairy did it."

"A fairy that buys teeth?" Digby stared at the soldier. "That's horrifying. What the devil is wrong with you all? Teeth? What would a fairy even want with teeth?"

"You're getting a little off-topic, Dig." Becca blew out a sigh. "I am not becoming the tooth fairy."

"Obviously," Alex added again.

"The logistics of collecting teeth alone would be insane." The vampire groaned.

"But not impossible," Dominic commented.

"Yeah, well, that's probably not going to happen." She glowered at him.

"I don't know. You'd probably like the outfit." Mason laughed. "You'd get to wear leggings all the time."

"You are not helping."

"Yes, none of you are helping." Digby flailed his free hand at the group. "Now get back to the Nine."

"Apologies." Dominic chuckled, clearly enjoying the derailment. "It isn't surprising that the Autem Empire, or at least its leaders, chose to destroy the world to remake it in their image. There is power within the beliefs that mankind has harbored throughout history, but there's nothing stronger than the thoughts and feelings of those currently living. Especially if those beliefs are shared by a large percentage of the existing population. In the example of the tooth fairy, you might only require the faith of children to manifest an enchantment. However, in the case of the Lord's angels, Autem would need much more."

"Are you suggesting that Autem killed billions to make the ratio of those who believed in the Nine more manageable?" Digby knew the answer before he'd even finished the question. Of course they had.

"It seems it is far easier to remove the majority of nonbelievers from the equation than to force them to believe." Dominic held his hand up before letting it drop to his side. "If we accept the theory that the Nine were originally mortal, then several other details begin to line up. The power of the Nine most likely faded as the world's population grew along with other competing beliefs. It's possible that they may no longer exist as they once did. Some may have found a way to thrive impersonating other minor deities, while others may have been diminished into nothing but folklore. Thus, the end of the world and the rise of the Autem Empire may very well be an attempt at a ritual of resurrection."

Digby's blood ran cold. "Holy hell! Henwick is trying to bring back the Nine."

"What would that even mean for the world?" Alex's tone grew exasperated.

"More importantly, how close is he to succeeding?" Becca wrapped her arms around herself as if trying to chase away a chill.

"I'm afraid I am only operating on speculation and cannot predict what the Nine's return might mean for this world." Dominic closed his eyes for a moment. "But Autem would need to convert over a fourth of the world's total population into true believers to succeed. It would have been an impossible task in the world that existed before. Yet, by removing so many people from the equation, they have created an environment where doing so is now within reach."

Becca let herself fall backward to lean against an abandoned car. "That's it then. That's why the treaty doesn't stand a chance of lasting. Henwick will continue to gather citizens for his empire and indoctrinate them to follow the Nine. But if he can't get enough to reach the threshold, he'll need to remove those who don't fall in line, starting with everyone in Las Vegas. Hell, he'll probably eliminate the non-believers just to make sure."

"The war will continue no matter what we do." A grave expression spread across Mason's face.

"This changes nothing." Digby raised his staff and dropped it to the pavement with a decisive clang to snap his coven out of the sudden gloom that had settled in over them. "All this does is confirm what we already knew. More importantly, it gives us a timetable."

"How so?" Alex leaned to one side.

"The empire has taken in a lot of people and many of them are far from true believers in the Nine." Digby swept a claw through the air. "It will take time to win that many over. There will be those that go along with it, sure, but many will be doing so simply for protection from the dangers out there in the world. It could take years to convert everyone."

"I wouldn't be so optimistic." Becca shook her head. "You're forgetting, I was a part of Skyline. I saw how easy it was for people to drink the Kool-Aid. Skyline wasn't a religious organization, but it definitely had its own culture. It starts slow, but the more someone is surrounded by others who believe the same thing, the easier it is to become a part of it. Hell, the only thing that made me question my place there was when I found out they planned to leave me back in Seattle to die. I think the more people they get on their side, the more they will surround and influence the people on the fence. The Nine's true believers will grow faster as it becomes less and less acceptable to be an outsider."

"Alright, maybe not years, then." Digby frowned.

"I would say at least a few months, depending on how many people the Empire is willing to dispose of in order to increase their total percentage." Dominic spoke with a sense of finality.

Digby swayed from side to side, unsure if he should be crushed by the weight of the looming deadline or relieved to know for sure that they still had a few months left. Then he cracked his neck and relaxed his shoulders. They still had a chance. Henwick could be stopped. They just had to make full use of the time they had left.

With that, he started walking toward the vehicle laying on its side. If they were going to do anything about the Nine, then they first had to survive the night.

"That's enough talking. We can't allow some random vampire like this Lord Durand fellow to get in our way. We have an empire to fight. A few revenant thralls with machine guns are not going to stop us."

A moment went by when nobody moved. Then, one by one, his coven followed.

Digby set down his staff and crouched down to find a grip on the roof of the strange windowed vehicle. The revenant trapped inside scratched at the glass. Union, wearing Parker's body, joined him at his right. Becca took his left. Alex and Mason crouched down beside them. Last, Dominic pushed his elderly frame against the vehicle.

Then, they all lifted together.

CHAPTER FIFTEEN

"What do you mean you can't?" Digby growled at a tiny mirror in his hand as he stood in the parking lot of the Vatican Museum.

The exasperated face of Lana stared back at him.

It had taken most of the night before anyone back in Vegas realized that Digby and his coven had never returned. Kristen's skull had been screaming from inside the presidential limo for hours to no avail. As much as he wanted to be angry about the situation, keeping the mission a secret had been his idea. Most of his coven was carrying a mirror compact for communication, but with Parker unconscious, they were useless to contact home. Not that they could do anything from halfway around the world, anyway.

Digby had hoped that Jameson would have had the new airship in the sky by now. Then maybe they could load it up with Heretics and send it his way. Unfortunately, Lana had offered nothing but bad news. Jameson's team had been busy and hadn't given a progress report that day. She had been trying to get in touch with him but when she activated a link to the mirror in the workshop he'd been using in California, all she got was an empty room. It made sense. Jameson and his team must have turned in for the night hours ago.

There was no help coming.

Digby snapped his compact shut and turned to Parker who was standing beside him, still unconscious. Asher sat on her shoulder, occasionally cawing in her ear to try to wake her up.

They weren't going to be opening a passage home any time soon.

He checked the clock on his phone. There was an hour left before the time that Becca had set up with Durand to ambush them. With that in mind, they planned to head out early in the opposite direction in the hope of avoiding the bulk of the insane vampire's thralls. It would still be a fight, but they could make it to the archives. Once there, they could use the wards to keep Durand out. They would still be trapped, but the vault was more secure. They could hole up there for at least a few days. By then either Parker would be awake, or they could get help from their people back in Vegas.

"Come, it's time." Digby beckoned to Union as he walked toward the bulletproof vehicle that Becca had located.

Parker's unconscious body followed.

The car, the one that Mason had called the Pope-mobile, was their only saving grace. After seeing the icon embedded in the front grill, Alex started calling the vehicle a Mercedes. Digby had floated the suggestion of using the artificer's knowledge of runecraft to get the car in the air. Unfortunately, they didn't have the tools and materials needed to do the job. It had been hard enough just to get the thing upright and running. Becca had even been forced to spend a bit of her mana in the process.

Digby glanced at her name displayed on his HUD and the information beside it.

Rebecca MP: 71/454

She didn't have much left after using some mana to make sure neither Durand or his thralls decided to try to spy on them while they worked. He just hoped she could avoid using the rest. If there was one thing he knew, being locked in a bulletproof vehicle with a ravenous vampire would not be fun. At least, not for the humans that were coming with them.

On the upside, unlocking the car's doors had been easy thanks to the common revenant that had been trapped inside. All Digby had needed to do was access the vehicle's ventilation system and poke a finger in. From there, he had been able to use his Body Craft mutation to form dozens of new joints along with links of bone to extend the digit. His elongated finger snaked its way through the vents and into the cabin of the vehicle where the end split to create a hand with five clawed fingers.

It wasn't an attractive display, but it worked.

Once he had a hand inside, his Fingers of Death spell converted the revenant trapped within into a new minion. After that, all he had to do was command the newborn zombie to unlock the door.

Digby severed the finger snake from his hand and yanked it from the vents, then he turned to address his coven. "Everyone make sure you have everything we need. We shan't be coming back here."

"I'll drive." Mason pulled the driver-side door open.

"No, I will." Becca shooed him away before turning to Digby. "And you're riding shotgun."

He glanced back in confusion. "But I don't use firearms."

"It's an expression." She groaned. "It means you're sitting in the passenger's seat."

"I have to disagree with that." Mason folded his arms. "The windows in the back can be rolled down, but they're huge, and if we opened them to shoot out, that would defeat the purpose of them being bulletproof. Graves should ride in the rear since the windows won't stop him from casting spells. We should put someone with a gun in front where the windows are smaller. We can open and close them faster without leaving us as exposed."

"Oh, I suppose that's why they call it shotgun." Digby nodded, proud of himself for putting it together.

Becca ignored him, her attention still focused on Mason. "Yes, but I would rather keep the humans in the back where they are protected by bulletproof glass. That leaves me driving. And I hate to sound like a broken record, but if something happens, I don't want any tempting blood bags sitting next to me."

"By that logic, wouldn't we want somebody else driving?" Alex waved a finger between Becca and Mason. "You know, because if something does happen, having an out-of-control vampire at the wheel wouldn't be great either."

Becca's mouth fell open for a second. "I'll have Digby with me. He could take over."

"I don't know how to drive." Digby stared back at her as if her argument was the dumbest that he'd ever heard.

She just let out a frustrated growl.

The conversation was interrupted by Dominic, who took charge. "I fear it is unwise to operate off hypotheticals. It makes more sense to proceed as efficiently as possible."

"See." Mason held his hand out toward the old man. "We should listen to our elders. I'm driving, Alex has shotgun. All vampires, zombies, priests, and unconscious people with animated skeletons get to ride in the back."

"Fine." Becca groaned as she dragged her feet around the rear of the vehicle and pulled open the door. "It's going to be tight in there, though." She jabbed a finger at Digby's staff. "You're probably going to have to put that in your void."

"Nonsense, I'm sure there will be plenty of room."

"I do not think there will be," Dominic said as he leaned his head into the windowed compartment. Pulling his head back out, he turned to Alex and removed his gun and shoulder holster before offering it to him. "I would like to entrust this to you. I will be unable to make use of it from the back and I am told that you have the best accuracy of your group."

"I, ah…" Alex trailed off as he stared down at the old but well-cared-for gun. "Thanks, I'll get it back to you as soon as we get to the archives."

"Yes, take care of it until then." The old man pulled off his holster and handed it over. "And there are two full magazines in the pouch on the other side."

Alex slipped the holster on and adjusted the straps.

With that, they piled into the vehicle.

The rear compartment had been home to an ornate chair. Once they had ripped that out, Digby found the back surprisingly spacious. Although, Becca had been right about his staff. It wasn't that it didn't fit, but that he couldn't maneuver it about inside without hitting everybody at least a dozen times every ten seconds. He was eventually forced to store the weapon in his void after several complaints. There was standing room only, but handles had been built into the ceiling, giving something to hold onto.

"Everyone good back there?" Mason looked over his shoulder through the little window in the rear of the driver's compartment that connected it to the back.

"We will survive." Digby turned away from him and tapped on one of the large windows to get the attention of the revenant that he had converted into a zombie. "Hey you, get on the roof and hang on."

His minion obeyed, awkwardly hoisting itself up onto the hood of the vehicle and climbing onto the roof. He wasn't sure what a single zombie could do against however many thralls Durand had, but he wasn't about to leave the monster behind. He had already enhanced the zombie a bit to return its physical attributes back to what it had possessed in life, but he wasn't sure if he should push the monster further. He checked his void resources.

Sinew 55

Flesh 33

Bone 42

Viscera 74

Heart 43

Mind 57

Sparks 3

It wasn't enough to form his minion into anything huge like a zombie destroyer, but he could manage a brute or a bloodstalker. That would certainly get them out of a pinch. Though, he would have to rely on his magic for the most part. If his mana ran low, he would have to Leach more from his minion or Parker. The messenger might not have been able to cast any spells without being conscious, but she was still useful as a well of power that he could draw from if need be.

According to Becca, Durand's ambush point was half a mile away. From what she could tell from her enhanced senses, the mad vampire had made good on his promise to pull his thralls back. Kneeling, Becca gave Mason directions through the window that connected the front and rear sections of the Mercedes. Then, he started the vehicle and headed for the parking lot's exit. He kept the headlights off to avoid being noticed.

From there, they turned left to head in the opposite direction of the ambush.

Digby squinted into the night as the vehicle rolled on, looking for any sign of movement. Instead, all he saw was large buildings covered in decorative stonework. The streets were mostly empty, with few obstacles blocking their way. It was almost as if Durand had made a point to have his thralls clear some of the abandoned cars. Granted, that would require the creatures to know how to drive. Digby wasn't sure if that was possible. His zombies could, provided he used his Control spell on them to enhance their intelligence. There was a chance that the process of creating a thrall would allow the same. The more he thought about it, the more likely it was. They could fire guns, after all, so why not drive cars?

Mason kept the armored Mercedes going at a slow and steady pace until he came to a street with several trucks parked across it. It was nearly impossible to see in the dark. If they hadn't been so careful, they might have plowed right into it.

"I do not like the look of that." Dominic leaned against the front of the glass compartment.

"Neither do I," Becca agreed. "That wasn't there when I cast my Cartography spell. Durand must have blocked it since then."

Outside, it was dead silent.

Digby pressed himself against the glass, looking for movement. "If this road was intentionally blocked, then it's likely Durand left a few of his thralls to keep an eye on things as well."

"There!" Becca jabbed her finger into the window.

Digby flicked his eyes in the direction she pointed, finding a pair of figures moving in the dark behind the row of trucks. He raised a hand but hesitated to cast a spell, afraid of the possibility that they were just random people in the wrong place at the wrong time.

"What are you waiting for?" Becca snapped her attention back to him.

Digby winced and summoned his wraith, unable to wait until he could see the targets clearly. The darkened streets lit up with the crimson flash as the murderous specter streaked toward the figures. A wave of relief swept over him as the spell's light showed pale faces and jagged teeth. The Heretic Seed confirmed the targets the instant he got a better look at them.

Revenant Thrall, Uncommon, Hostile

The first of the creatures fell, its head nearly severed by his wraith's blade. The flesh of its throat began to knit itself back together before slowing to a stop, unable to repair such catastrophic damage. The second thrall started to run as the crimson specter darted toward it. Its blade sliced around one side before circling back, blood spraying through the air in an arc. The revenant spun as it fell, but not before letting out a tortured howl.

Everyone in the vehicle froze as the dying creature's cry faded into silence. Digby didn't dare move a muscle, the dead stillness outside returning for a moment. Then, another revenant screeched from someplace nearby, maybe one street over. Then another further away. A chorus of howling cries joined in, all sounding further and further from their location as if the entire city was screaming.

"Shit!" Becca slapped her hand against the glass. "They know we're here."

"We are boned," Alex said from the front seat as he pulled Dominic's gun from its holster.

"That's it, we go loud." Mason flicked the vehicle's headlights on and threw it in reverse.

Tires squealed as the car lurched backward. Parker's unconscious body fell against Digby's side as her animated skeleton stumbled. Asher cawed and flapped her wings, still perched on the pink-haired woman's shoulder. Parker's breathing was still shallow and unsteady. Digby did his best to help Union get a hold of one of the handles attached to the ceiling as the vehicle leaned to one side.

Mason reversed the car in an arc and put it back into drive. Then he stepped on the gas.

Digby slid one foot back to keep his balance as the vehicle lurched forward. Durand wasn't taking any chances. He must've blocked the roads just in case Becca decided to double-cross him. It was likely that more barricades had been set up during the night.

"Do you have enough mana to cast another Cartography spell?" Digby turned to Becca.

"I do, but it will put me dangerously close to the ravenous threshold. Plus, I would have to open a window to access the outside. Otherwise, the spell will only map the interior of the car."

"Do it. We need to know what roads are blocked."

The vampire turned to the window and slid the top half down. Digby grabbed the back of her armor as she hung half her body out. Of course, that was when the flash of muzzle fire lit up one of the side streets as they passed. He yanked back on her to pull her in, bullets peppering the street. Most missed, but a couple pinged off the vehicle's hood while another made it in through the open window. It cracked into the wall behind Digby's head, passing so close that it displaced his hair.

Union moved quickly, using Parker's body to close the window as soon as Becca was back inside to avoid any more close calls.

The vampire dropped back into the compartment, leaning against Digby's legs. She was unharmed.

"Did you get the spell off?" He stared down at her.

"Yeah." Her face went blank for a moment as if staring at a map that no one else could see. "Shit, he blocked all the roads. There's no way out."

"Yes, there is." Digby pressed his hand against the front of the compartment. "There's no need to be quiet anymore. The next barricade we run straight through. I will blast it to bits with a flare. We will be home free after that."

"How many times do we have to tell you to stop being so optimistic? It almost always invites disaster." Becca got back to her feet.

"I know I know. But no one was hurt just now, so I'm hoping luck remains on our side."

That was when Dominic fell back against the compartment window with a pained grunt. From there he slipped down to the floor, leaving a smear of crimson on the glass. "It seems that luck was never with us to begin with."

Digby flicked his eyes around the cramped space, unsure of what happened. The bullet that had hit the wall behind him must have ricocheted. He dropped down beside the old man and helped Becca turn him over onto his side. As soon as they did, she jerked her hands away and shoved herself to the other end of the compartment. She slapped one hand against a window, her fingers tense as if clawing at the glass. Her other hand was held a few inches from her face dripping with blood.

For an instant, she looked like she might lick her palm clean. Then, she lowered her hand and shoved it under her legs as if trying to hide it. "Sorry, I just got a little confused there." She shook her head, then returned her attention to the situation. "He's been hit in the back. I don't think I can help. I need to stay away."

"Well, we can't lose him. We'll never get into the archives without him." Digby looked down at the old man's face. "You hear me, you're not dying here."

"I do not think that is up to you," Dominic said with a pained chuckle.

"We'll see about that." Digby banged his fist against the divider that separated the front seat from the rear. "Alex, I need a flask of purified water, we have a man down."

"Way ahead of you." The artificer passed a container to him. "You need to get the bullet out first. Otherwise, the wound will just heal with it still inside and that could be worse."

"Yeah, I've been there," Mason added.

"Me too." Alex tapped a finger to his head.

Digby looked down at the man as the vehicle drove past a group of Durand's thralls. Another spray of bullets hit the car. One slammed into the window by Digby's face, creating a three-inch circle of discolored glass filled with tiny cracks. From the looks of it, the word bulletproof was not exactly right. It was more like bullet-resistant. There was a limit to how much the windows could take. He pushed the thought out of his mind as the vehicle swayed, and dropped his attention back down to the old man on the floor.

Placing his hand on the man's side, he tried to sense where the bullet was by focusing on the flow of blood. It was no good. He could get a vague idea of where it was, but he already knew that much simply by looking at the wound. Despite that, there wasn't time to wait. He waved a hand over the floor and cast Forge. Some of the blood that had begun to pool beside Dominic shifted and flowed up toward his fingers to form a narrow rod, the size of a pencil. If he could slide it into the wound enough to find the bullets, he could re-forge the object to grab hold of it and pull it out.

It wasn't the most sanitary of situations, but he was pretty sure Alex's purified water would take care of any infection that might set in. Digby tensed as he carefully examined the hole for the best angle to work from and moved the makeshift tool toward the opening. Almost as soon as he did, the vehicle swerved to one side. A thud came from the front, like the sound of metal hitting something soft. A revenant screeched a second later as the left wheels of the car went over a bump.

A kill notification passed across his vision, followed by a level up.

"Hold it steady!" Digby growled at the tiny window that led to the driver's seat.

"Sorry, but some of them are unavoidable," Mason said without looking back.

Digby let out a frustrated huff and dropped his extra attribute point from his level up into intelligence as he went back to work. Then he stopped. "Wait a second, what am I doing?"

He flicked his vision to the information ring that hung at the corner of his vision and willed the seed to show him Parker's attributes. He ignored all but one, her dexterity. The messenger had been dumping all of her extra points into it from the start, giving her the steady hands of a surgeon. Granted, she only ever used it to throw knives, but that didn't mean she couldn't help now.

It didn't matter that she was unconscious. Union would have

the same physical attributes as the body they inhabited, meaning they were much more suited to the task. Not only that, but the skeleton didn't need their eyes to see. Hopefully, that meant they could find the bullet through other means.

Digby handed the tiny rod of hardened blood to his minion. "Get to work. And be quick about it."

"We are not trained in medical procedures." Parker's mouth moved unnaturally upon her emotionless face.

"Neither am I. And that makes you this man's best hope." He looked down at Dominic's wound. "All you have to do is get that rod to touch the bullet, I'll do the rest."

"We will do our best."

"I assume it would be unreasonable to ask for a licensed medical professional." Dominic let out a chuckle followed by a wheeze. He was far tougher than he looked.

"Now isn't the time for humor, old man." Digby placed both hands on the man's side to hold him steady. "This is not going to be fun."

A few more bullets slammed into the rear of the compartment, covering the window in more circles of discolored glass. Digby struggled to ignore it, keeping his focus on his patient. Union readjusted the position of Parker's body to straddle the man's legs. Then, they slipped the rod of blood into the wound.

Dominic let out a pained grunt and sucked air in through his teeth.

The vehicle swerved to avoid a group of thralls blocking the road. One of the creatures slammed into the side of the car, cracking his head against the glass.

"Sorry," Mason shouted back.

"Just keep it straight," Digby responded without looking at him. Instead, he kept his attention on Union, giving his minion a nod to tell them to continue.

Parker's hands moved with the same dexterity that she used to handle her daggers. The infernal spirit shifted the rod around, pushing it deeper. Dominic kept his eyes closed tight, and his teeth bared. Digby wished he'd given the man something to bite down on. A second later, Parker's body froze.

"We have found it."

Digby didn't hesitate. He willed the rod of blood to change shape to coil around the bullet inside the man. "Now! Pull it out."

Union moved Parker's hands carefully, wiggling the projectile clear of the tissue inside. Then they popped it out through the wound.

Digby shoved the flask Alex had handed him into the old man's mouth. "Drink. All of it." Some of the water trickled down the side of the container to Digby's hand. His fingers sizzled on contact and pain shot up his arm. He ignored it and flicked his eyes up to the window that led to the front seat. "I'm going to need another flask."

Alex already had one ready, passing it through to Union.

"Poor that on the wound," Digby ordered before glancing to Becca who was still huddled in the corner of the compartment. "Be careful not to get any of the runoff on you."

She nodded and pushed herself up off the floor to stand.

Dominic opened his eyes. He didn't look well, but he was certainly better than before. There wasn't time to worry about him any more than that.

"Dig, we're going to need your attention on the road," Alex shouted back, his voice climbing with each word.

Digby saw the reason why as soon as he stood up.

Lights shined through the street from over two dozen vehicles, all blocking the road. They were parked at least four deep. It was the ambush. They must've circled around and driven straight into it.

Mason started to brake but Digby slapped a hand against the window. "Don't slow down!"

"But we'll plow right into them. This car is tough, but it's not that tough."

He was right. If they had run into one of the lighter barricades blocking the roads, they could blast their way through easily. Trying to plow through four rows of cars would be insanity. Glancing back through the rear window, the flash of muzzle fire lit up the street. Thralls were rushing into the road behind them.

Only about a third of their bullets hit the vehicle, but they would get through the glass eventually.

There was no choice. They had to push forward or surrender. It wasn't hard to decide which was a better option.

"Keep going!"

Digby looked down at Dominic, who was still sitting on the floor with his back against one of the walls, breathing heavily.

"If your faith is still strong, old man, I suggest you start praying."

CHAPTER SIXTEEN

"Everyone hang onto something!" Digby grabbed hold of one of the handles that were attached to the ceiling of the vehicle's bullet-proof compartment.

The blockade ahead rushed toward them.

Digby slapped a hand to the front window and focused on the first row of cars that blocked the road. Headlights shone in his eyes, a row of suns blazing in the dark. Another line of lights slipped through the gaps between the vehicles from a row of cars parked behind them. A third line of headlights marked another layer to the barricade, followed by a fourth.

Digby prepared to cast Emerald Flare, doing the math in his head with only seconds before impact. The spell required time to gather its power. He had to account for that. As soon as the bullet-proof Mercedes that he rode in moved within range of the barricade, he cast the spell three times focusing on the same point between two of the cars at the center of the obstacle. Hopefully, multiple explosions happening in unison would be enough to blast the road clear.

There wasn't time to come up with anything better.

He cast another three Emerald Flairs at the next row of cars only a second later. Tendrils of sickly green light were already slithering through the air toward the epicenter of the first wave. He didn't stop there, casting another round of flares as soon as he was in range of the third row of cars.

"This is going to suck." Alex put his foot on the dash as if bracing for impact.

The engine roared, Mason pushing the pedal to the floor.

Then, the first wave of spells detonated.

A blast of radioactive power lit up the street, its emerald light shining like a miniature sun as the two cars on either side of the epicenter flew into the air. They spiraled through the night to the left and right just as Mason forced the bulletproof vehicle through the gap that had been created. Kill notifications lit up Digby's HUD. Another explosion of power went off directly in front of them, launching cars out of their way. A third detonation followed, cleaving through the barricade to allow passage like Moses parting the sea.

The final wave of Emerald Flares threw a Jeep over twenty feet to the right, where it landed on top of a building. A cargo van that had been parked to the side was tossed only eight feet. It came down as the Mercedes pushed through the gap. The van crunched into their side for an instant, nearly tipping the bulletproof car over. Mason swerved to compensate, slipping out from under the van just before the weight became too much.

Another few lines of kill notifications streaked across Digby's vision. Unfortunately, none of them mentioned Durand.

A moment of silence passed.

Digby snapped his head from side to side to take stock of the situation. All of the windows were intact. The vehicle was still running. Everyone was alive. He glanced down at Dominic to double-check that last one.

The old man gave him a weak wave.

"I'd say that went pretty well." Digby raised his head to stand a little taller.

Then took a look at his HUD.

MP: 73/513

He cringed, realizing how much mana he'd spent.

"No matter." He immediately cast Leach on Parker to fill himself back up. She may have been unconscious and animated by an infernal spirit, but she was still a decent source of mana. He nodded along at his MP value as it ticked up to full, then gasped a second later when he noticed the word hanging beside every member of his coven's name except for his.

Poisoned

"Holy hell!" Digby dropped down to look through the window that led to the front of the car. "Alex, we're going to need purified water. I think casting twelve Emerald Flares in close proximity has poisoned you all."

The artificer was currently rolling down the window with a panicked expression on his face. As soon as he got it halfway open, he shoved his head out and threw up.

"Gah!" Digby recoiled.

At the same time, the vehicle slowed as Mason started to turn green. "Why did you have to hurl right next to me?"

He looked like he might throw up at any second. Before he had a chance to reach for the button, Alex shoved a flask in his direction, waving it around as it glowed.

The soldier snatched it with one hand and downed a mouthful.

Digby glanced at his HUD as the poisoned status vanished. He was just glad the ailment they had been inflicted with hadn't stopped Alex from casting his purification spell.

Mason handed the flask back through the window to Parker's outstretched hand. The messenger, herself, didn't seem bothered by the poisoned status, but she wasn't technically conscious either, so she probably wouldn't notice. Union tipped the flask back to give her a sip regardless. They immediately let out a croak of pain and began to shake.

"We burn." The shaking stopped a second later. "Yet, we survive."

"Good, now hand that to Dominic." Digby jabbed a finger at the elderly man at his feet. "We need him alive."

Then he realized something else.

Becca.

Flicking his eyes to her, he found the vampire clinging to the handle on the ceiling with her eyes closed tight, as if struggling not to be sick. If Alex's flask had caused Union pain, there was no telling what it would do to her. Hell, it would probably cause enough damage to send her off on a rampage. He checked her mana, finding it ticking down already. The poisoned status still showed next to her name. Her body must have been trying to cure it on its own. He hoped it could do so before she dropped below the threshold where she would lose control.

"You're going to have to restrain me." She glanced up at her hands. "Use Blood Forge. Bind my hands and my feet. Secure me to the wall or something."

Before he could do as she asked, a light shined into the rear window. The entire vehicle lurched forward a moment later, the crunch of metal coming from behind.

"Did something ram us?" Digby turned to find the headlights of a Jeep shining in his face. A second one followed behind that, along with what looked like a pair of motorcycles. "Well, I suppose that answers the question of whether or not thralls can drive."

The Jeep rammed them again, causing him to forget all about Becca's predicament. A burst of gunfire erupted as well, slamming into the glass behind him. The sound reminded him of a snowball hitting a wall. Digby threw a hand out and summoned his wraith directly into the driver's seat of the Jeep behind them. The crimson specter flickered into existence, already stabbing the thrall at the wheel. The Jeep swerved to the side before flipping into the air. It came crashing down behind them. Another three kill notifications flashed across Digby's vision.

Durand's thralls didn't give them a moment's peace. Another car was already surging forward to ram them. At the same time, two motorcycles pulled up along either side of their vehicle. Each raised a firearm and opened fire directly into the windows. Bullets punched into the glass one after another. The creatures' aim was terrible, but they were already so close they couldn't miss. Discolored circles of whitish gray filled the windows, making it hard to see out.

"Back off!" He swept his hand around him, casting Decay at the tires of the motorcycles.

They both collapsed forward to throw their rider off. One revenant smashed into the back of the Mercedes, leaving a bloody smear of gray matter and bits of skull down the rear window. The other thrall hit the pavement next to them. Both died on impact.

The Heretic Seed tracked each kill.

Again, the car giving chase slammed into them. Digby fell against the cloudy glass barrier behind him as a torrent of gunfire poured from a pair of thralls that hung from the windows. Each bullet punched into the reinforced glass hard enough to make Digby's teeth rattle. He pushed away from the window, feeling it bend and flex against his weight. It wasn't going to last much longer.

Glancing to his HUD, Digby checked to see if his minion clinging to the roof of the Mercedes was still with them. By some miracle, it was. He banged his fist against the ceiling.

"Time for you to get moving."

He didn't have a lot of resources to spare, but his void held enough to manage a bloodstalker. He willed his Body Craft mutation into action, sending the material needed for the transformation into his minion. The ceiling above began to indent as the weight increased. A zombified hand slapped against the side window, growing into a massive, clawed fist.

"We're slowing down!" Mason shouted from the driver's seat. "Get your pet off of us!"

"You heard him!" Digby pounded against the ceiling.

His half-formed minion lunged from the roof, one arm three times the size of the other. Its head was still too small for its body, making it look ridiculous. Despite that, it landed square on the hood of the car behind them and smashed its big hand through the windshield to wrap its fingers around the face of the thrall at the wheel.

"Yes, that's it! Rend!" Digby cackled as his minion attempted to rip the creature from its seat.

Surprisingly, the thrall was wearing a seatbelt, resulting in only the top half of the revenant being torn from the harness. The creature screeched and screamed as his minion yanked it free, ribbons of entrails dangling from its torso. Digby's bloodstalker simply shoved the unfortunate thrall into its mouth. Its jaws grew to fit the body just in time to bite down. Without a driver, the car slowed as the rest of his minion grew to full size.

Mason floored it, leaving the monster behind to slow the vehicles in pursuit.

Digby took the moment of peace to check on the rest of the passengers. He'd never had a chance to restrain Becca, and in the chaos of the chase, he'd forgotten about the predicament she was in. Looking down, he found her licking blood off the floor.

Dominic sat beside her, gently patting one hand on her back.

Digby checked her mana. She didn't have much left, but it had stopped ticking down. Her poisoned status was gone as well. Her body must've had just enough mana to handle it, but not before forcing her to fill back up on whatever she could get.

The vampire looked back up at him. "Don't judge me."

"I would never." Digby gave her a sympathetic smile. "I'm sure I've done worse."

"You poor thing." Dominic reached into a pocket and retrieved a handkerchief, offering it to her to wipe her face.

"Don't you pity me either." Becca shot him a look that said, 'Put the hanky away.'

"It is not pity." He placed the cloth in her hand regardless, clasping hers in his own. "I am sorry, but I have not heard of one of your kind capable of such control. Perhaps I was wrong when I said there was no hope for the cursed."

"I hope so." Becca repositioned herself to lean against one of the walls opposite the old man.

"Did we escape?" Digby leaned to the side to peer through one of the spaces in the rear window that hadn't been damaged.

"I don't know, but Durand doesn't seem like the type to give up." Becca shrugged.

"I'm heading for the Vatican library now, but we're not out of the woods. They'll catch up eventually," Mason added.

"My minion should be able to buy us a bit of breathing room, at least. Hopefully we will be within the archives walls before anyone finds us again." Digby nodded to himself before glancing to Parker. "It would certainly be nice if our messenger would decide to wake up, right about now."

"She cannot," Union said from within her.

"What you mean she can't?" Digby eyed his minion.

"We feel it." The infernal spirit answered. "There is an interference."

"Interference?" Digby arched an eyebrow, unsure what that meant.

"We do not know why." Parker's body shrugged. "Her body rejects her power. She will grow worse."

"That isn't good." Digby frowned. "If her condition grows worse, the only thing we can do is cut her connection with the Heretic Seed and remove her magic altogether."

It was an extreme solution to the problem, but the only one he could think of. He didn't want to lose access to her passages. Yet, if her power was killing her, removing it would be unavoidable.

His attention was torn away from the question and back to the road when Alex shouted. "Crap! Everybody grab on to something."

Digby barely had time to see what the obstacle was. The road was clear. It was only when he noticed the artificer pointing up that he realized the threat was coming from above. He flicked his vision to the top of the buildings, finding a lone thrall standing on a rooftop holding some kind of staff. The creature raised its weapon to its shoulder, pointing one bulbous end at their vehicle.

Then, there was a puff of smoke and a burst of flame.

The end of the staff shot off, propelled by some form of rocket.

"Incoming RPG!" Mason swerved just as the projectile streaked past the Mercedes to hit the street. It detonated in a burst of fire and force.

Their armored vehicle lurched to the right, tipping over. Digby flew across the compartment and into the opposite window as the entire car flipped onto its side. The bulletproof glass beneath him flexed and warped like a heavy fabric, barely holding itself together. Sparks flew from the metal frame as they slid another twenty feet before coming to a stop.

A moment of vertigo passed as Digby reoriented himself to a crouch. The window above hung halfway from its frame. He dropped his vision down to find Dominic. The old man was alright. Union had thrown Parker's body and her nearly invulnerable cloak between the man and one of the walls to keep them from smashing into it. Becca wasn't harmed either. Somehow, she had righted herself mid-crash and landed on her feet in a crouch.

Digby checked the front. "Is everyone alright up there?"

"Yeah." Alex held up a hand with one thumb raised so it was visible through the opening in the divider.

"I'm alive." Mason dangled from the vehicle's seat belt, still in the driver's seat. He fell directly on the artificer below him as soon as he unbuckled the harness.

"I take that back, I am badly hurt now," Alex croaked out from beneath the soldier.

"Quiet, you'll be fine." Digby ignored him, shifting his focus to the vehicle. "Can we get right side up again?"

"The engine's had it." Mason pulled himself off of Alex. "This is as far as the Pope-mobile goes."

"Damn." Digby stood up and activated his Limitless mutation to kick his way through the severely damaged window at the back of the car. It folded in on itself with a few good hits. He shoved his way out into the street as soon as the opening was clear. "Everyone out, we have to run."

"We still have half a mile to go." Mason climbed up to the driver-side door and popped it open.

"We can make it if we stay quiet and out of sight." Becca followed him out into the street.

Union helped Dominic through the broken window as Alex crawled out behind Mason.

Digby held his hand out as his maw opened on the pavement below it. Calling his staff forth, the weapon rose from the shadowy opening. He cast Blood Forge as soon as it was out, causing the necrotic blood that covered the shaft to flow upward to form a spearhead at the top.

"Time to go."

That was when a screech came from above.

Digby winced at the sound, realizing that the thrall that had shot at them from the rooftops was still there. Just like before, another cry answered back coming from a street away, then another and another. The whole city began screaming soon after.

"So much for doing this quietly." Mason pulled his rifle from the ruined vehicle.

"Here, take this." Alex offered Dominic his pistol back.

He shook his head. "I think I should leave the fighting to those more capable."

"Give me your other pistol." Becca held her hand out to Alex. "I don't have enough mana to use magic."

The artificer passed her the gun he'd been using the day before.

Digby turned to Parker. "Union, stick close to Dominic. That body you're in might be unconscious, but its barrier can still take a beating. Keep him safe."

The infernal spirit nodded and stepped to the old man's side.

With that, they were off and running.

Digby darted down a narrow street that led between two beautifully adorned stone buildings, hoping to stay out of sight. He skidded to a stop when he found three thralls blocking their path.

Union followed his orders, lunging in front of Dominic as each of the creatures raised a rifle. Becca ducked behind Parker as well. Mason took cover behind Alex as a Barrier spell swept over the artificer's body. Digby simply shielded his head with the blade of his spear. Bullets peppered the entire area, most missing them entirely while some sparked off Barriers or thumped into Digby's chest. He ignored them and raised his staff. Opening his maw, he sent a spike of blood up through the thrall in the center.

Becca crouched and fired a few shots from behind the cover provided by Parker's body. Mason did the same from behind Alex to finish them off.

Digby started running again just as another two thralls rushed in behind them. He spun as they raised their weapons. "I have this."

"Too slow." Alex was already raising Dominic's gun with one hand while pointing a middle finger in Digby's direction with the other. The weapon barked once with a burst of muzzle fire larger than any normal pistol. A white-hot streak shot out, so bright that it left an afterimage on Digby's vision. Both revenants' heads exploded at once, their bodies crumpling to the pavement.

Digby blinked, still seeing the path of the bullet that had been temporarily burned into his retinas. Instead of aiming at either of the creatures, Alex's Guiding Hand ability had aimed at a wall beside them to cause a ricochet that hit both targets.

"What did I just do?" Alex stood staring at the pistol in his hand. "It's like my eyepatch synced up with the gun's enchantments."

Dominic simply gave him a nod. "I think that old Colt has found a new partner."

"That's all very impressive, but more are coming and that weapon only holds so many bullets." Digby spun on his heel and continued running.

The rest of the group followed with Alex hanging back to cover their escape. He fired a few more times, the muzzle flash of the old pistol lighting up the narrow alleyway that ran between the buildings. Digby ignored it.

There wasn't time to look back.

They still had plenty of ground to cover and they were already close to being overrun.

Digby picked up his pace. Ahead, an alleyway bisected the narrow street they were on. If he could make it there, then they might just be able to find someplace to hide.

He crashed into a thrall the moment he turned the corner.

Digby cast Decay on instinct, shoving his hand in the creature's face. It recoiled in pain as its eyes began to rot. He followed the spell with a swift sweep of his staff. The blade of black blood at the end sliced straight through the revenant's decaying skull like a soft bit of fruit. Shoving the dying creature aside, he continued forward. Then he stopped. More thralls began to flood into the narrow street to block their path.

"Blast!" Digby turned to look down the alleyway to his side.

Inhuman silhouettes moved toward them. The thralls had stopped shooting, probably because they had been surrounded. No sense in risking the lives of their prey. Durand still intended on feeding, and that meant he needed the humans alive.

Another dozen revenants rushed into the street behind them. Alex held his ground at the back, firing occasionally to keep the creatures at bay. For every one he killed, it seemed two more took their place. There was nowhere to go but up.

Then, Digby snapped his head to the sky.

"That's it." He leapt toward the nearest wall and opened his maw.

He didn't have much in the way of resources, but he still had plenty of blood. Raising his claws toward the sky, he cast forge to send a river of inky black fluid flowing up the stone wall like a waterfall in reverse. The rungs of the ladder emerged from the blood positioned at every foot.

"Hurry, we might still have a chance on the rooftops!" He stepped away from his newly forged escape route to make room for the others.

Dominic approached the ladder and began trying to guide Parker's unconscious body toward it.

"No, you go first." Digby insisted. "We will protect your escape. This will all be for nothing if you fall now."

The old man hesitated for a moment. Then he nodded. "Very well."

Digby spun back to the thralls that were approaching from their front. He reached down and grabbed the half-decayed head of a revenant that he had killed a moment before. With a yank, it came loose from the rest of the corpse. It had been a while since he'd used his Cremation spell, but it was about time it made a comeback. The head ignited in emerald flames as he launched it at the oncoming swarm. It howled as the pressure of the molten gray matter inside built up, then exploded in midair to shower a handful of thralls in fire.

"That'll make you think twice about trying to corner a desperate zombie."

Glancing back, Alex still had their rear covered.

"I'm on my last magazine." The artificer was making every bullet count, but the moment he ran out, it would be over.

"I'm running low too." Mason fired into the alleyway to the side.

Digby glanced up at Dominic. The old man was halfway up the building. "Everyone get climbing! I will go last."

That seemed to be the only reasonable option since he was the only one other than Becca who wasn't in danger of being cursed. Mason gestured for her to go first, but a stern look from the vampire made it clear that wasn't going to happen. He didn't argue. Instead, he handed Becca his rifle and one spare magazine. He jumped up the first few rungs of the ladder after that. Union joined him, piloting Parker's skeleton.

"You too!" Digby summoned his wraith, casting the spell several times to guard Alex as he fell back. "I'll be right behind you."

"I know you will." The artificer made for the ladder, stumbling on the first few rungs.

"Don't try to stop me from heroically sacrificing myself or anything," Digby grumbled sarcastically as everyone left him behind without an argument. Then he summoned his crone to slow the oncoming swarm.

The echo's spectral hands reached out from the pavement to snag a half-dozen of the thralls coming from the front. Digby ignored them, sending his wraith into the alleyway. The flickering killer streaked into the narrow space, cutting through foe after foe. Digby turned and cast Decay to his rear to hold another dozen revenants at bay.

Despite his efforts, a pair of thralls managed to slip past him. They made straight for the ladder, lunging up the rungs after Alex. The artificer was only halfway up the building, moving slower than the elderly man who had gone before. Digby spent the extra mana to reforge the bottom section of the ladder into a dozen jagged spikes. The two revenants screeched as the spell turned them into pincushions.

With his escape route cut off, he spun in a circle, casting Decay in all directions to buy a few seconds. He followed the spell with an Emerald Flare focused directly on where he was standing. Then he opened his maw beneath his foot and forged a post of blood to launch him upward. He kicked off, using his Limitless mutation to throw himself higher as rivers of sickly energy flowed toward the place where he'd been. The thralls below converged just as it detonated.

Digby shot straight up, kill notifications flooding his HUD.

"Aw, come on, not more radiation," Alex complained as he flew past him. The artificer clung to the ladder as the street below exploded. "I don't have any more flasks to purify if I get poisoned again."

"Then climb faster." Digby slowed to a stop in midair a dozen feet above him.

He reached out and caught one of the ladder's rungs before falling back down. From there, he climbed the rest of the way up. Climbing over the side of the building, he tumbled onto the roof to find Becca running a thrall through with the heavy blade she'd been carrying. It fell back as she pinned it down.

"What the devil is going on up here?" Digby stood up.

"There was one of them up waiting for us on the roof." Mason stepped on one of the revenant's flailing arms to help hold it in place. "It was chasing Dominic when I got up here. It nearly got him."

"I think it's the rev that fired the RPG at us earlier. It must've been following us across the rooftops." Becca twisted the sword before flicking her attention to Dominic. "It didn't bite you?"

"I will be alright."

That was when Alex appeared at the edge of the building. He glanced back down as he climbed up over the edge. "We're good for the moment, but those things are starting to scale the walls in some places."

Digby ran to the edge and looked down. He was right. The thralls were more athletic than a normal human, and they were using every bit of strength they had to claw their way up. He cursed the building's architect for designing it with so many decorative elements to grab onto.

"Think, Digby, think." He struggled to get his thoughts moving.

Climbing to the roof had bought them a few minutes, but they were still no closer to the archives. Nor did they have any means to escape. He could always grow himself a pair of wings and fly away, but that would do nothing for the rest of his coven. If worse came to worst, he could probably pick up one of them, but which one?

He shook his head.

That wasn't even a question he could think about.

He tore himself away from the edge of the building and paced across the roof.

"Alright, I need ideas. Nothing is too stupid."

CHAPTER SEVENTEEN

Becca pulled her sword free from the corpse of the revenant at her feet. The thing had nearly gotten Dominic a moment before. She'd almost been too late. Not that it mattered in the long run. They were still surrounded. Digby had bought a few minutes by getting them to the rooftop of a building, but the thralls were starting to climb. They needed a way out.

Becca glanced at her HUD.

MP: 43/498

It wasn't enough to use any of her abilities.

"Alright, I need ideas. Nothing is too stupid." Digby spun away from the edge of the building and marched to the center of the group.

Both Alex and Mason started talking at once. Neither of them had a complete thought. They seemed to be throwing out anything they could think of to avoid doing nothing.

That was when the crackle of a radio came from Mason's waist. With all the commotion, no one else seemed to hear it but her. Her mind crashed to a halt. The radio shouldn't have worked at all. The other half was in the limo all the way back in Vegas.

"Everyone, shush." Becca snatched the handset from Mason's belt as a familiar voice came from the speaker.

"Is anyone there?"

It was Hawk.

Unsure if she should be relieved or horrified, Becca thumbed the button. "We're here."

"Where are you?" Hawk responded, the sound of wind in the background made it hard to hear him.

"We're trapped on a rooftop surrounded by revenants," Digby shouted over her shoulder.

"More importantly, how are you in radio range?" Becca asked.

"Never mind that." Hawk glossed over the question as if answering it might get him in trouble. "I need you to send up a signal so we can find you. Something that can be seen from the air."

Becca decided not to call him out on it. She could get mad at him later. "Okay, we need a signal."

Mason was already waving a flashlight in the air.

"I see you. Just hang on." Hawk went quiet after that.

A moment later, a shape appeared in the sky illuminated from above by the crimson lightning. Without being able to enhance her sight, Becca struggled to make out what it was. Then it got closer.

"The hell?" She stared up at the last thing she expected.

A lifeboat.

The tiny vessel floated through the air. It was only a dozen feet long with a white hull. She could just make out Hawk standing at the bow. As far as how it was flying, she had no idea. It was too small to have made it all the way there. Then she noticed a cable connected to the front. Checking the rear, she found another attached to the back. She followed the cables up until they both vanished into the clouds.

Becca stared into the sky, realizing that there must have been a larger vessel flying high above the gloom. So many questions ran through her head. She shoved them all aside. There wasn't time to worry about the how. All that mattered was that help was here. She glanced back to the side of the roof. The revenants would reach them soon, and judging from the speed that the lifeboat was travel-ing, it wasn't going to make it in time.

"We need to meet him halfway." Becca thrust her finger out toward the roof of the building next to theirs. There was only a narrow alley between them.

"Indeed, everyone start jumping." Digby waved Alex and Mason on before checking back on Dominic. "I'll stay to help the old man."

Mason hesitated.

"Go! Alex might need help." Becca urged him on while staying back with Digby to make sure Dominic made it.

Mason didn't argue. Instead, he went first, leaping over the alleyway to land on the rooftop on the other side. He immediately turned back and held out a hand to the artificer.

Alex made the leap as well, with Parker's unconscious body close behind.

"Alright." Digby threw a hand out to Dominic. "I can carry you if need be."

That was when the old priest let out a labored grunt.

"I don't think that will be necessary." He raised his head with an apologetic look.

Becca knew what he meant by the comment the moment she saw his eyes. She would have recognized the orange flecks of color in his irises anywhere. They were the same ones that drifted through hers when she used her more monstrous abilities.

"No." Her knees nearly gave way as despair threatened to crush her. "He's been bitten."

"I apologize." The old priest gestured to the revenant that she had killed with the sword moments before. "It seems that one got a bite in." He reached into the collar of his shirt to close his hand around a gold cross that hung from his neck. "I had hoped my faith would protect my soul a little longer. But it seems a few minutes is the best it can do."

Digby immediately shouted to Alex who was already running across the rooftop of the next building. "We need a flask, Dominic's been cursed."

"Ah…" He slid to a stop. "I don't have any left. But I can use any liquid." The artificer glanced around frantically, finding nothing. His face brightened a second later as if a brilliant idea had just occurred to him. Then he cupped his hands in front of himself and started spitting into them.

"What are you doing?" Mason turned around to stare at him.

"I need liquid to purify. So start spitting."

An instant passed when it looked like Mason was struggling to process the request. Then he just shook his head and started spitting into Alex's waiting hands as well.

"You too, Union." The artificer shot Parker's unconscious body an urgent look.

"We do not have control over those functions," the infernal spirit answered back, unable to move the internal tissues needed to help.

"Fine." Alex returned his attention to Mason. "Spit faster."

"I'm spitting as much as I can. I don't have much saliva. My mouth is all dry from running."

"I'm not sure this is going to work." A panicked expression took over Alex's face.

Dominic let out a gasp as his skin grew pale. He was holding off the change longer than most, but it was clear he couldn't resist anymore.

"No, no, no, no." Digby rushed over to him, grabbing hold of the man's shoulders. "You are not dying here, you hear me? I did not come all this way just to lose now."

"I'm afraid I am out of time. Though, I wish you luck in your efforts." Dominic held out a hand as if offering it to shake. "I am glad to have met you, Mr. Graves. It has been educational."

Digby took his hand. "Don't talk like that. You need to hang on."

The screech of a thrall came from the edge of the building.

The lifeboat hanging from the sky approached a few rooftops over from where Becca stood. Hawk shouted directions into a radio from the front, a safety harness securing him to one of the cables. The boat slid up against one of the buildings to drag itself forward. From the looks of it, stopping wasn't possible.

"Hurry up!" Hawk leaned over the side. "This thing can't circle around for another pass."

Mason and Alex both looked back.

"Go!" Becca waved them on. "Dig and I can fly."

Her statement was technically true. The zombie could grow wings and she could use her Shadecraft to get in the air. She left out the fact that she didn't have the mana to actually do it. Hopefully, Digby could carry her.

Mason nodded and leapt across to the next building as the boat slid past. Alex and Parker followed, all three of them tumbling into the tiny vessel just as it pulled up.

Becca let out a relieved breath as the humans got to safety. Well, all except one.

Digby let out a loud growl in frustration.

There was nothing they could do for Dominic.

The old priest suddenly lunged forward to grab hold of Digby's coat. Becca raised her sword, afraid he'd turned and was already on the attack. Dominic pulled the zombie close as if to tear out his throat.

"Wait!" Digby threw up a hand before Becca could bring her blade down.

The old man whispered something to the zombie.

Becca didn't dare enhance her hearing to find out what it was. Not when she had so little mana.

When he was finished, Dominic simply let go.

"You must leave." He reached for the crucifix around his neck, his ears stretching into wicked points.

"Alright." Digby turned away from the old priest. The bones in his back cracked and popped as a pair of leathery wings ripped through the back of his coat. "Come, Becky, we've done all we can here."

The hand of a thrall reached up over the side of the roof not far away.

"One more thing." Dominic groaned. "I request that you prevent me from becoming one of Durand's thralls." He shifted his gaze to lock eyes with Becca. "I think… that is a need that you are uniquely equipped to fill."

She knew what he meant without needing an explanation. Hell, it had already occurred to her that if he was already doomed, then there was no sense in letting the mana inside him go to waste. Now, he was offering it willingly. The idea of feeding both sickened and enticed her.

"Go," she said, only looking at Digby for a second. "I'll catch up."

The zombie remained where he was. "You cannot help what you are, and you do not need to hide it."

She groaned in frustration, not having time to argue. Then she flicked her eyes back to Dominic. His teeth were already beginning to shift into a row of uneven fangs. It was now or never.

"Don't you dare!" a familiar gravelly voice shouted as the twisted figure of Durand leapt up over the side of the roof to land on its edge. His thralls crawled onto the roof around him. A broadsword was sheathed at his waist. The vampire thrust a finger out toward Dominic. "That is my prey."

The old priest didn't even look at him. Instead, he kept his eyes locked with Becca's. He gave her a smile and a nod. "Perhaps a normal life may be impossible. But that does not mean that you cannot live despite your curse."

With that, she tossed her sword to Digby and lunged.

The necromancer caught the weapon and darted toward Durand to block his path. The insane vampire drew his sword and brought it down. Digby crossed the edge of his staff's spear with Becca's blade to catch Durand's in the center.

Becca took the moment for what it was and sank her teeth into Dominic's throat. He let out a gurgling croak and wrapped his arms around her. One hand patted her gently on the back as her jaws crushed his windpipe. Becca swallowed, taking everything he had. Her mana system reached out to connect with his and she caught hold of his spark as soon as she felt it. Then she yanked it away from the growing curse within him. His soul came loose in a flood of power that surged across the link between them. Her mana filled back up to full in an instant, swelling to increase her maximum value by five points. The excess of the man's soul burst into the air around her before dissipating into nothing.

Whatever existence came after death, he was already on his way.

Becca dropped the old man's body to the rooftop and wiped the blood from her face with a sleeve.

Digby stumbled backward, the head of his spear cracking under the force of Durand's strength. As soon as he saw that she was finished, he leapt back and tossed her sword to her. Becca caught it, flicking a few points of mana into her strength to bring the weapon in front of her.

Durand's blade tore through the air, crashing into hers with a burst of sparks. Saliva flew from the insane vampire's mouth as he shouted, "How dare you!"

"Will you just shut up?" Becca deflected his attack to the side and hopped back.

"I will not let you leave this city!" The twisted vampire held a hand out to his side as several thralls rushed past him to swipe at her face. "I don't care what it does to me, I will drain you dry."

"You have to catch me first." Becca simply jumped backward and snapped her sword into its magnetic sheath. Once she'd gained some distance, she raised a hand toward him and willed her Shadecraft into action. She cast Icicle at the same time to send a torrent of bats swirling around a core of frozen spikes in his direction.

Durand moved with inhuman speed deflecting the jagged formations of ice, but not before she had time to call to her shadows once again. Darkness swirled around her, lifting her up. She let it embrace her as tension grew, tendrils of gloom forming to launch her like a stone from a slingshot. She soared over fifty feet into the air before gravity began to claim her again.

"I've got you." Digby flapped up to grab hold of the back of her armor, his wings carrying them higher.

She watched the rooftop below as it fell away from her. Durand stood at its center, his thralls swarming around him; none of them were able to fly. He didn't shout or curse her. No, all he did was raise his sword to point it in her direction as if marking a target.

Something told her he wasn't going to forget about her.

He grew smaller as Digby carried them into the sky. The

vampire below vanished as they pierced the canopy of clouds above. Gray and crimson surrounded them. It seemed unending. Then, they burst through the top.

Becca gasped as soon as the sky was clear, staring out at the airship that had facilitated their rescue. Alex had said Jameson was working on something special, but she'd had no idea what to expect.

The ship was old, but more importantly, it was massive.

"What the...?" Digby nearly dropped her as he stared at the vessel.

It looked as though the Titanic had risen from the depths to claim the skies. A name was written across the hull. The Queen Mary. It sounded familiar, though Becca couldn't place it.

The lifeboat carrying the others was being reeled up to the deck by a set of heavy-duty winches.

"That is some ship." Digby adjusted his grip on the back of her armor.

"It's something, alright." Becca dangled below him, the taste of blood still lingering on her tongue. "At least we get to go home in style."

CHAPTER EIGHTEEN

"Welcome to the Queen Mary." Jameson, the old army vet turned airship captain, stood on the deck behind Hawk.

Digby still couldn't believe what he was looking at.

Becca and the rest of his coven stood beside him, equally dumbstruck.

The vessel was huge. Far larger than the ships that they had used in the battle two weeks before. The side of the deck was lined with dozens of lifeboats like the one that Hawk had been riding in. Though, only his had been outfitted with the heavy-duty winches that had been used to lower it up and down. The rest dangled more precariously over the edge; one was missing altogether with several more hanging by one side from damaged pulley systems.

"Please excuse the state of things. This ship is capable of traveling at extreme speeds, but it's sure as hell not made for it. We lost a few lifeboats trying to get to you in time. The wind speeds get a little ridiculous."

"That is understandable." Digby barely acknowledged the explanation, still astonished by his surroundings.

Three massive smoke stacks rose from the ship at an angle, spaced in even intervals. Digby swayed, letting himself get accustomed to the motion of the deck as the vessel turned to head back across the ocean from where it had come. The clouds that had plunged Vatican City into permanent darkness swirled beneath them. Crimson lightning flashed from within as the sun began to rise on the horizon to fill the sky with brilliant orange.

The view was impressive, but somehow the man standing before him was more so.

It had been two weeks since he'd last seen Jameson. The retired soldier had looked quite healthy for a man of his age with a heart condition. Now, he seemed like a different person altogether. A glance to his HUD told him that Jameson had reached level twenty-eight. Along with it, he'd practically doubled in size. The wool coat he wore looked like it could barely contain his biceps and the gold buttons that held it closed were at their limit. Even the white hat he wore looked a little small on his head.

Digby had heard of a similar phenomenon happening back in Vegas with some of the older Heretics. One effect of the Seed's power was that it returned people to whatever shape they had been in during their prime. Apparently, Jameson had been a mountain of a man back in his younger days. Digby certainly wouldn't have wanted to run into him on the battlefield, that was for sure.

He pulled his attention away from the old soldier and lowered his gaze to Hawk with a sudden frown.

Hawk held up a hand before he could say anything. "Okay, I get that you're mad, but I saved your asses. And really, you wouldn't have gotten in so much trouble if you hadn't kicked me off the mission and lied about it."

The young rogue wasn't wrong.

Digby sighed. Apparently, Hawk had been concealed in the parking garage back in Las Vegas before they left. After Becca had told him to keep an eye on things for her, he'd decided to eavesdrop a little on their conversation.

He'd heard everything about the mission.

After they'd failed to return for the limo and the rest of their gear, Hawk had gotten worried. After an hour of waiting, he was already working to mount a rescue operation. Unfortunately, because Digby had been so clear about keeping everything secret, the young rogue didn't know who to trust to go to for help. He'd thought about telling Lana, but decided against it on account of her past working for Skyline. He was pretty sure she was on the up and up but wasn't willing to take the chance with something so important. From there, he only told the people that he needed to organize a rescue mission.

The first thing he did was contact Jameson. The old soldier was the only one in a position to get him halfway around the world and he'd had no connections to Autem or Skyline. His experience in the military had given him an understanding of covert operations and rescues, so he'd taken over the rescue mission from there.

As for the Queen Mary, the ship had been used to transport people back and forth across the ocean for years before aircraft became popular. After that, it became a hotel and museum. Jameson had just gotten the vessel ready to fly when Hawk contacted him. The way he'd figured it, the airship needed a test flight anyway, so why not take it to Italy?

Jameson had taken a small team of artificers to crew the ship and launched. Sure, he'd planned on securing the rest of the lifeboats, but the mission took priority. He'd swung by Vegas to pick up Hawk on the way.

As much as Digby wanted to be mad about Hawk's eavesdropping, he couldn't find fault with it. He certainly wished the rogue had at least contacted him to tell him that a rescue ship was coming, but he only had himself to blame after taking the secrecy of the mission so seriously. Even if he had informed them of the situation, it wouldn't have changed much. The time constraints still would have forced them to make a run for it when they had, and Dominic's fate would have ended the same way.

After all was said and done, the rescue had been mostly successful and only a handful of people had become aware of their mission. It was safe to say that if Autem did have any spies in Vegas, then they were still in the dark.

Hawk had done well.

"So why the Queen Mary?" Becca asked as Jameson turned to lead them to the bridge.

"I figured that this was supposed to be a post-war vessel, so we should get something that provides a little comfort." He slapped a hand against the wall as he approached a doorway. "This here beauty has three hundred and some odd guest rooms. Not the tiny ones either, the first-class kind. There's also a dining room, multiple ballrooms, a fitness center, a full promenade level with shopping spaces, and pretty much everything else you could ask for. It's basically a flying city." He turned to Hawk. "Why don't you take Parker to one of the guest suites so she can lie down? I can't imagine having Union running around in her body while she's unconscious is helping the situation."

"Yes, we are overdue for a break." The infernal spirit inside the woman nodded before following the rogue in the other direction.

"How do you get a ship this big in the air?" Alex hung his head over the side, probably looking for engravings.

"The magic bits are all internal." Jameson stepped inside. "After you helped us understand the runes more, we spent weeks welding enchanted panels into the lower decks. Other than the altitude control system that we gutted from the cargo ship, it's all new runecraft. Plus, it's all self-sustaining so there's no need for our Heretics to feed their mana into its propulsion systems. It all pulls the ambient essence in from the sky around us and puts it to use."

"That's impressive. I could never figure that part out." Alex sulked a little.

"You did plenty. My team never would have gotten this far without the groundwork that you started us with." Jameson laughed. "This thing isn't perfect yet, anyway. It's fast and reliable, but its maneuverability is terrible. That's why we couldn't try for a second pass down there. We'd never get turned around in time. But I figure that's not so bad, since combat wasn't a part of the plan for this ship." He slowed and looked back. "It's not part of the plan, right?"

"We hope to avoid that, yes." Digby followed the enormous man into a room filled with brass fixtures and mechanisms.

"Captain on the bridge," a familiar Heretic called as soon as Jameson entered.

Digby recognized the man as Kim, one of the artificers that he'd helped gain a few levels a couple of weeks ago. He was dressed in a similar wool coat with gold buttons as Jameson, like it was a uniform.

Sweeping his vision around the room, Digby found the front lined with windows while wood paneling covered every other surface. A series of tubes capped with some kind of funnel hung from the ceiling, as if part of an internal communication system.

Another Heretic stood at a large steering wheel. Digby recognized her as well. She was another one of the artificers that he'd helped level weeks before. If he remembered correctly, her name was Thelma. She wore her coat unbuttoned and gave him a respectful nod before returning her gaze to the horizon outside the window.

Jameson had chosen their best engineers to make up his team.

"How many crew members do you have running this ship?" Digby turned back to the vessel's captain.

"Right now, it's just a skeleton crew." He pointed to Thelma and Kim then hooked a thumb back over his shoulder. "Mike is in the engine room handling things down there." He chuckled. "He's been insisting the ship is haunted."

Digby arched an eyebrow. "Is it?"

"Who knows?" Jameson laughed.

"That's where I've heard the ship's name before." Becca slapped a hand on her thigh. "I watched a documentary about the most haunted places in the world. The Queen Mary was on it. Along with Lizzie Borden's house, and an insane asylum."

"Should we be concerned about that?" Alex looked to Digby as the resident expert on the dead.

"Probably not." He hesitated. "I think."

"I'm more concerned with keeping this ship running. I would have brought more crew, but we were trying to keep this mission secret. As far as anyone else knows, this is just a test flight."

"Well, I appreciate your commitment to secrecy." Digby gave him a nod. "There's no telling how many spies Autem has sent our way. I fear that this sort of mission situation may become more prevalent in the future, provided we can improve our communication."

"And how did the mission go?" Jameson sat down in a chair

close to the back wall that looked about two sizes too small for him. "Or should I not ask, considering the circumstances?"

"It was a bust." Becca rubbed flakes of dried blood from her neck using her sleeve. "We were close, but we lost the one person who could've helped us get the information we needed."

She proceeded to give the ship's captain a brief explanation of what had happened back in the Vatican. Kim, the artificer standing by the door, got her a bottle of water from a cabinet to help her clean up. She seemed to relax after that. It wasn't just that she'd removed the evidence of what she had done, but she was obviously more comfortable now that her mana was full.

As she spoke, Digby dropped into a chair that was mounted to the floor to think.

"There might still be a chance." Alex stepped forward. "I know keeping things a secret might get difficult, but if we come back here with a large force of Heretics, we should be able to handle Durand and his thralls. Afterward, we can try to find a way to break into the archive down there." The artificer shrugged. "I mean, how hard can it be to break into a vault if we bring the right equipment? I know desecrating the Vatican library might not be a good look for us." Alex lowered his head and adjusted the old pistol that now hung beneath his arm from its shoulder holster. "But I have to believe that completing this mission would be what Dominic would have wanted."

"Yes, but you said it yourself, it will be impossible to keep an operation like that secret. Autem will find out what we're doing," Mason added. "Not to mention, I don't think we could go head-to-head with Durand's thralls without losing a fair amount of our people. That's not something to take lightly."

That was when Digby stood up again. "Indeed. But I don't think we will have to go to such lengths."

"Why not? Don't we still need to reach the archives?" Alex went to the cabinet to the side and got a bottle of water as well, using it to refill his empty flasks.

"No. Reaching the archives may no longer be necessary." Digby tapped a claw on the top of one of the brass levers that filled the bridge.

"Dominic said something to you, didn't he?" Becca dried her chin after scrubbing it clean. "I heard him whisper something to you down there but I couldn't make out what it was."

"Simple." Digby grinned. "All he said was that he'd already told us everything we needed to know."

Everyone in the room stared at him expectantly.

"I wasn't sure what he meant by it at first, but now that I've had a few moments to think, he may have been right."

"Sure, he told us about the history of the Nine." Alex shifted his weight to one side. "But how does any of that help us?"

"Dominic didn't just tell us about the history of the Nine." Digby turned to look out the windows that lined the front of the bridge, staring out at the rising sun. "He also told us how they gained their power."

"Wait." Becca took a few steps toward him, shielding her eyes from the light. "You mean how they became angels?"

"You're talking about mass enchantments." Alex leaned against a wall next to her.

Digby turned around slowly, holding both hands out to his sides as the sun flooded into the windows behind him to send his shadow stretching into the room. "That's exactly what I'm talking about."

Alex scoffed. "I'll be the first to admit mass enchantments are cool, but we've tried searching for artifacts. The results so far," he tapped on his eyepatch, "can vary. We can keep scouring the world for more and hope that we find something powerful enough to give us an edge, but most of it is a shot in the dark. And it's pretty safe to say that Henwick had already beaten us to the really good stuff."

"Yes, we've already discussed that option." Digby closed his hands and lowered them to his sides. "Which is why I'm not talking about artifacts. Nor am I referring to any mass enchantments that currently exist."

"Holy shit." Becca sucked in a breath, clearly following his line of thought.

Alex's eyes widened in recognition a second later. "You want to create a new one."

Digby let a crooked smile stretch across his face as he pointed to him with one claw extended. "Now you're on to something."

"I'm sorry, but what is this all about?" Jameson shifted his position in his chair, having trouble fitting his large frame into it.

"A mass enchantment is created when enough people believe in something," Alex explained. "The belief that they share is able to manifest an effect."

"That's what creates the wards that keep me from entering a person's house," Becca added. "Enough people throughout history have believed that vampires can't enter a home uninvited, so we can't."

"Which means, we just have to come up with a new enchantment that can tip the odds in our favor. Something that will grant me the power to take down Henwick." Digby let a cackle roll through his chest. "Then we just have to make people believe it."

"Are you insane?" Becca blew out an exasperated huff. "How could we possibly do that?"

"Dominic already told us." Digby waved a claw through the air. "Henwick has already done half the work for us. By decreasing the number of people in the world, he's brought something that would normally be impossible into our reach. We don't have to convince millions, or even everyone still living out there. Just the thousands that remain between the populations of Vegas and the empire's capital. We don't even need all of them to believe. Only enough to manifest an enchantment."

"And I'll ask again, are you insane?" Becca stared at him, her face blank. "Whether it's millions of people are thousands, what you're proposing is a—"

"A con." Digby finished her sentence for her, standing a little taller in the process. "Think about it, Becky. We have been wrong this whole time in assuming that the only way to fight is to build an army and go to war. We are not generals. All generals do is put their own people in harm's way."

"Amen to that." Jameson backed him up. "War just brings out the worst in humanity and leaves everybody worse off. Take it from someone who's been there."

"Yes. More importantly, we have been trying to be something

that we are not." Digby placed a hand to his chest. "We have been trying to fight a war, but we are not cut out for it. Not really."

"You're not wrong about that either." Mason flicked the brim of his hat. "Parker and I may have been in the military, but we were only privates. And I would hardly say that military strategy is the strength of anyone in this room."

"That's right. We are all just surviving. We do the best we can with what we have, and I think it's time that we all accept what we are." Digby swept his eyes through the bridge, making eye contact with everyone one at a time. "So I ask you all, what are we?"

A roomful of vacant expressions stared back at him.

Digby rolled his eyes. "To what do we owe every victory we've had so far?"

Another moment of silence passed before anyone spoke up.

"Theft." Alex shrugged.

"Right!" Digby pointed a claw in his direction again. "We pulled off the greatest heist in the history of the world when we stole the Heretic Seed's fragments from Autem." He flicked his attention to Becca. "And how did you get information from the Guardian Core's caretaker?"

The vampire gave him a puzzled expression before answering, "I don't know, breaking and entering?"

"Exactly!" Digby laughed. "And how did we escape from Bancroft when he had us cornered weeks ago in California?"

"We tricked him." Becca started nodding along.

"That's right." Digby clapped his hands together. "So I ask you again, if we are not generals, then what are we?"

"We're criminals," Alex said with a somewhat blank expression.

"Indeed." Digby puffed out his chest.

"You do realize that being a criminal is not exactly something you should be proud of, right, Graves?" Jameson eyed him.

Digby deflated. "Well, it's not like it really matters. There is no king to tell us what to do and there are no laws except the ones we make ourselves, but you get my point." He held out both hands. "All I'm saying is that we are not suited for war, so why would we ever think fighting head-on would be the answer? We need to stick to our strengths."

Becca continued to stare at him. "So what do you propose? That we con the world instead?"

"No." Digby closed his hands one finger at a time before spinning to stare out at the sun on the horizon.

"I propose that we pull off the greatest con the world has ever known."

CHAPTER NINETEEN

"Where am I?" Parker winced as light poured in through a nearby window.

Her head was still throbbing, but not as bad as before.

Sitting up, she found herself in a full-fledged hospital room surrounded by a variety of medical equipment. None of it was familiar. A little monitoring device was clipped to one finger, and she had an IV line running from a bag of clear fluid that hung near the top of the bed. Several carts sat next to her bed with more equipment and medical supplies.

Glancing around, she struggled to find a detail that would explain where she was. She'd been in Italy a moment before, so she could be anywhere now. If she'd been brought back to Vegas, she would have expected to be in the infirmary. The fact that she wasn't worried her.

"Maybe I'm still in Europe somewhere?" She rubbed her face with the hand that did not have tubes running from it. She had no idea where she was or how much time had passed. "What happened?"

The last thing she remembered was being under fire in the Vatican. She had been feeling worse and worse, but she had been trying her best not to slow everybody down.

"I guess I messed that up."

She must have been knocked out or passed out. Either way, she couldn't have opened a passage for anyone. Digby and the others must have escaped whatever was happening in Italy without her help. They must have carried her to safety after that. At least, she hoped she'd been carried. There was technically a way she could have walked there on her own.

"Union? Are you here?"

A sudden feeling of nausea coiled through her stomach as her mouth opened on its own to answer.

"We are."

She blew out a sigh. "I suppose I shouldn't be surprised about that."

"We apologize for the intrusion."

Parker choked down her annoyance. As uncomfortable as it was to have her skeleton animated in principle, it was probably the best way to keep her safe if she had been unconscious in a dangerous situation. Unlike the last time Digby had cast the spell on her, this time, he had probably saved her life.

That was when her arm started moving on its own.

"Hey! What are you doing?" She reached out to stop her hand with the other, accidentally pulling out the IV line in the process. "Oh crap." She froze in panic, unsure which problem to deal with first.

Union ignored her struggle and continued reaching for a box hanging from the side of the bed to press a button on it. Parker relaxed, realizing it was just an alert to get the attention of whoever was taking care of her. The sound of the door's electric lock announced the arrival of her doctor, or at least, the closest thing she had to one.

"Good, you're awake." Lana stepped into the room.

She was dressed in standard hospital scrubs and a white coat, looking like a real medical professional. The sight of her set Parker at ease. If Lana was there, then that meant she was back in Vegas. She furrowed her brow a second later. If she was home, why hadn't they brought her to her room or the infirmary? And where did they find a hospital?

"How long was I out? And where are we?"

Lana gave her a sympathetic expression. "It's been three days. You passed out shortly after you left for the last mission. And we're at an urgent care facility in Vegas that is better equipped than the infirmary in the casino. The building is outside the secured area on the strip, but it's warded and there's two covens downstairs to keep watch."

"That sounds like a lot of effort to go through for one person." Parker wrinkled her nose at the idea of everyone going out of their way for her.

"Not really." Not if there was a spy in the city. "Without your magic, we would have no way to deploy that nuke that Dig has. So we wouldn't be able to retaliate if attacked. If Henwick was to find out that you were out of commission, there would be nothing stopping him from voiding the treaty and coming after us. That's why we're keeping you in a secure location and controlling who knows what's going on with you. Everything is really hush-hush right now. Especially where you're concerned. Can't have assassins coming after you, right?"

Parker frowned, not appreciating that her life was the only thing standing between Vegas and certain destruction.

From there, the nineteen-year-old disguised as a doctor continued to recount everything that had happened while she'd been unconscious. Digby had brought her into his inner circle as soon as they returned. According to her, Parker had missed a fight with a vampire, an epic car chase through Italy, and some badass priest with a gun.

The priest didn't make it in the end.

Her eyes welled up as the priest's face flashed through her mind. She wasn't sure how she had been able to remember him if she'd been unconscious the whole time, but he'd somehow taken root in her mind. The throbbing in her head swelled, telling her not to think too hard about it. Parker let herself sink into the pillow as she pushed the memory aside and buried it along with so many others that hurt to think about.

She'd screwed up.

If it hadn't been for her, that priest would still be alive. "So everything went wrong after I passed out?"

Lana shook her head. "I don't know what the plan is from here on, but Digby seems to think they got what they needed from Italy. He, Alex, and Becca have been holed up in one of the casino's suites since they got back, bringing in cartloads of research materials. Judging from the amount of cackling coming from the room, whatever scheme he has cooking is something big. Actually, you woke up just in time. The three of them have called a meeting to present what they've got in mind later today. I'm sure they'll want you there as well. I'm pretty sure the only reason I was brought in on all this is because you're important and they need me to make sure you're okay."

"Yeah, I'm sure my magic is going to play a part in whatever he has planned." Parker stared up at the ceiling.

"You're probably right, but I think he's also worried about you." She glanced back to the door. "Digby has been checking on you at least every couple of hours. And he's been keeping Union with you so you wouldn't be left defenseless if anything happens."

"Cool," she said as sarcastically as she could. "I assume that means he knows I'm awake, doesn't it? You know, because of the bond that you share."

"He has been informed of your awakening," Union answered from inside her. "He is on his way now."

Parker shook her head. "Tell him to worry about what he is doing. I don't want to slow things down any more than I have."

"I would prefer that he stays out of here as well." Lana stared down at her as if looking through her face at the skeleton beneath. "I gathered every medical expert we have in Vegas and we are going to figure out what's wrong with you. I doubt having a zombie hanging over us and asking a million questions is going to speed that process up."

Parker's head nodded on its own. "We will inform him."

"While you're at it, can you ask him to recall you from my skeleton? It's not that I don't appreciate the company, but, you know, get out." Parker hooked a thumb toward the door.

"Yes, it is about time we took a break," her skeleton answered.

She laughed. "I'm surprised you've been with me this long. You're way past quitting time."

"When one falls, it is the support of others that gets them back on their feet," Union added. "We are only strong when we are together."

A moment later, she felt a strange sense of emptiness, like something inside her had vanished.

"Union?" Parker waited a second, then shrugged when the infernal spirit didn't respond. "I guess I'm alone again." She turned to Lana. "Okay, what do we have planned here?"

"Well, Digby said that Union sensed some kind of blockage in you. Now that could be anything, but we should rule out as much as we can." The cleric walked around the bed and picked up a clipboard from one of the carts in the room. "We've checked your vitals already and they are mostly normal. But it seems like headaches are pretty big symptoms, so we're going to start there and see if there's anything wrong with your noggin."

"Noggin?"

"I don't know why I said that. I'm nervous."

"You've checked me out before." Parker looked up at her. "Why be nervous now?"

"I know, but this all feels more formal. Everything I've done up until now was mostly simple first-aid or healing by magic." She gestured to the hallway outside with her head. "I have a couple of med techs out there ready to fire up an MRI machine, and a pair of actual doctors that know a lot more than I do. The only reason I'm the one in here with you now is because we have a rapport. They felt that would help you stay calm."

"Calm? Oh crap, should I not be calm?" Parker pushed herself up on her elbows. "Am I dying?"

"No!" Lana dropped her clipboard, flinching as it clattered to the floor. "I mean, we don't know what's wrong with you, so I can't say anything for sure."

"But you're gonna take a look at my noggin?"

"You're not going to let me forget I said that, are you?" Lana picked up her clipboard.

"Probably not." Parker slid her legs out of the bed and pulled the monitoring device off her finger. "Let's get this over with then. If I have magic cancer, I should probably find out about it."

From there, Lana let her out into the hall where she met her medical team. As the cleric had mentioned, there were two med techs and two doctors. One of them was an oncologist who had mostly treated pediatric cancer before the world ended, and the other was a plastic surgeon. Neither could be considered specialists in whatever was wrong with Parker's magic, but it was the best they could do with what they had.

They each took turns poking at her and drawing several vials of blood.

"How did you get this scar?" The plastic surgeon ran a latex-glove-covered finger along her jaw.

"Car accident. When I was a kid." She winced as he pressed a little harder; her headache swelled to join the party. She pulled away, uncomfortable with the surgeon's sudden interest.

When the pair of doctors were satisfied that they had prodded at her enough, and thoroughly annoyed her, Lana led her down the hall to the stairs. A pair of Heretics joined them as guards to keep the medical team safe, on account of the hospital being outside the strip's perimeter. It was unlikely that there were any revenants still lurking around, and most wouldn't be a threat during the day regardless, but it was better to be safe than sorry.

Parker followed Lana into a room with an MRI machine. It looked like a big, white doughnut. Lana waited for her to lie down before leaving the room. After that, her voice came from a speaker. She tried to keep Parker talking as the table she lay on slid into the claustrophobic machine.

"Make sure to hold still."

"Are these things all magnetic and stuff?" Parker tried to distract herself as the machine started to make noise.

"Yeah, I think so."

"I read a thing once about a guy who went in one of these things with a buttplug in. I guess the core of the thing was metal and he didn't know. So it went all crazy and nearly killed him."

A long pause came from the speaker before Lana said anything.

"Probably don't wear a buttplug, then."

Parker chuckled. "Yeah, probably a bad idea."

"Please hold still," one of the techs said.

"I know. I'm not moving." Parker kept quiet after that. Eventually, she started to get used to the noise of the machine and closed her eyes. She opened them again when the tech told her not to fall asleep. Instead, she sat there wondering how much all of the medical tests would have cost back before the world ended. She'd had enough problems getting healthcare when she was younger. It was weird to think that it was better in the apocalypse.

The ache in her head put a stop to that line of thought soon after.

After being allowed out of the machine and led back to her room, she was left alone to contemplate her mortality. It was possible that whatever was wrong with her could be fixed easily. Then again, the headaches were getting worse and she was passing out for days at a time. There was a chance that her time was limited. She frowned. Not just because she was scared, but because she didn't seem as worried or scared as she thought she should have been. Even if she was running out of time, it was more time than the rest of the world had been given. The fact that she was still alive at all was surprising.

In the end, there was no way to know how much time she had left. She decided to pretend that everything would be okay until she knew otherwise. Denial really was the easiest way.

Lana came back in after a couple of hours, holding her clipboard close to her chest.

"Well?" Parker braced for the worst.

The cleric answered her with a shrug. "Nothing showed up."

"What do you mean nothing?" Parker cocked her head to the side.

"We have run every test we can think of, and there is nothing physically wrong with you." She looked down at the clipboard for a moment before looking back up. "Whatever this is, it's purely related to the magic side of things."

"Great." Parker dropped back into her pillow. "At least I can still pretend nothing's wrong."

"Have you tried touching the Seed again?" Lana sat down at the foot of the bed. "That's where this all started, so maybe coming into contact with it again would help."

"Sure, why not?" Parker started to get up. "I'll stop by the obelisk on my way to this meeting that Dig has planned. Where is that by the way?"

"He said the parking garage."

"And where is the Seed now?"

"I think it was moved down to the casino's vaults." Lana got up from the foot of the bed and headed to the door. "With all the worry about spies, it probably wasn't a good idea to leave it sitting in the open. If you want to get dressed, I'll tell the guards that you're ready to head back to the strip."

Parker nodded and threw the covers off her legs. The Cloak of Steel that she'd been wearing was draped over the back of a chair in the corner, and a change of clothes sat on the seat. Someone must have gone into her room back in the casino and got them. She found her daggers beneath the cloak, still in their sheaths.

By the time she was finished getting dressed, a pair of Heretics was already waiting outside her room to escort her back to the warded section of the city. She felt strange having guards. It was like she was some kind of royalty.

Following them down to the lobby, they led her out the front doors to where an ambulance waited. Parker crawled into the back while the two Heretics climbed into the front. They dropped her off at the entrance of the casino.

Alone again, she headed inside and down to the lower level. Lana must have called ahead, because Alex was already waiting for her in front of the vault. The skull of Kristin, the deceased seer, was tucked under one arm.

"Hey." Parker waved.

"How are you feeling?" The artificer walked halfway down the hall to meet her.

"Like crap." Parker glanced down at the skull under his arm. "I see you brought a friend."

"Yes, and it is about time someone took me out." The skull let out a ghostly huff. "Do you have any idea how long I was locked in that limousine? I thought I would go mad with boredom."

"I said I was sorry," Alex groaned back, making it clear that it was not the first time he'd apologized that day. "Anyway, I brought Kristin since she knows a lot about magic."

"Yes, it seems my expertise has been requested. Lucky you," the skull added.

"So does that mean I don't have to worry about you sabotaging us?" Parker eyed her.

A moment of silence went by before the skull responded. "I have accepted that I am not the person that Graves murdered. I have become something else, and as such, I have no responsibility or loyalty to my previous incarnation."

Parker bent down to look into the hollows of the skull's eyes. "So you decided you like us, then?"

The skull clicked her nonexistent tongue. "I never said that." Another pause went by. "However, being around some of you does alleviate the boredom."

"That's good enough for me." Parker stood back up and held out her hand to shake. When it became obvious that the skull was not going to magically grow one of its own, she just poked one finger into an eye socket and wiggled it up and down. "Welcome aboard."

"Would you not do that?"

"Sorry." Parker turned away from the skull and headed into the vault where the Heretic Seed's obelisk waited. She stopped as soon as she saw it. The obelisk was no longer standing upright. Instead, it was lying on its side on a cart. It was wrapped in a moving blanket, the kind meant to protect furniture. There was something obscene about the lack of ceremony that left her staring at the Seed longer than she meant to.

Eventually, she took a step toward it. "So what do I do?"

Alex set Kristin's skull down on a block of shrink-wrapped dollar bills that sat on a nearby table. "I guess, just touch it."

"That is the only option," the deceased seer agreed.

"Okay then." Parker shrugged and crouched down before reaching her hand out.

She felt the pressure immediately.

The instant her skin touched the glossy black surface of the obelisk, the pain in her head exploded. It was like her brain had suddenly grown to ten times its normal size, threatening to spray out of her ears, mouth, and eyes. Instead, she felt something surge downward to spread out through her body like a shockwave that echoed back from her limbs to converge on her heart. She gasped and yanked her hand away so hard she fell over. Rolling onto her back, she clutched her chest to keep any of her organs from escaping.

Alex dropped to his knees beside her. "Are you okay?"

Parker took several deep breaths. The sensation began to fade, settling back down to the dull throb that had tormented her for weeks. "That sucked."

"That wasn't a reaction I was expecting," Kristin said from her place atop a block of cash.

"It felt like my body and my magic were trying to fight each other." Parker scooted away from the Heretic Seed's obelisk to make sure she didn't accidentally touch it again.

"Take it easy." Alex passed her a flask of water before looking back at Kristin's skull.

"I think this is going to require some research," the seer said.

"Sure, take your time," Parker commented with a heavy dose of sarcasm as she grabbed hold of a nearby table and hoisted herself off the floor.

Her legs wobbled like Jell-O.

Alex helped her over to a pile of cash to sit down. She remained there for around ten minutes while he and Kristin discussed a long list of possibilities for what might be wrong with her. Eventually, she began to feel a little more stable and pushed herself up.

"I'll leave you to think about this. I'm going to head to the parking garage and see what Dig's plan is."

Alex went silent as soon as she mentioned the zombie's mysterious strategy meeting.

"What?" She narrowed her eyes at him. "What do you know?"

He glanced around the room before responding. "Honestly, I think it's better if you let Digby explain it."

Parker wrinkled her nose. "It's that bad, huh?"

"Not bad." Alex held up his hand in defense before adding, "It's just... weird."

"Of course it is." She turned slowly, grinding her teeth as she did. The tension in her jaw only made her head hurt more. "I guess I'll see you there then."

Parker left Alex and Kristin behind and made her way to the parking garage. Well, she didn't go straight there. First, she stopped by the central area of the casino and popped into one of the shops to buy a tuna salad sandwich and a can of orange soda. Then, she headed to the parking garage.

Becca was already there sitting on the cement floor, leaning against one of the support pillars while looking through a binder of magazine articles and advertisements. Stopping to stand beside her, Parker unwrapped her sandwich and leaned over to see what the vampire was so interested in. The only detail she was able to see before Becca closed the binder was that the advertisements inside were all for various zoos. She decided not to ask questions. It was sure to have something to do with Digby's plan and it was sure to be so crazy that speculation was impossible.

Glancing around, Parker couldn't help but notice there was no one else there. She checked her watch. There were still fifteen minutes before the time that the zombie had set to meet, but it was weird for no one else to be there yet. Before she was able to ask where everyone was, the presidential limousine that they had been using hovered its way down the ramp from one of the upper levels. The vehicle stopped directly in front of them.

"That's our ride." Becca stood up and started for the back door of the car.

"Oh, the meeting is someplace else?" Parker hesitated.

"We figured if we are trying to keep things secret it would be best to keep all discussion contained at a more secure location." The vampire popped open the door and glanced back expectantly.

"This is getting weirder by the second." Parker followed and climbed into the limo.

Becca dropped into the seat beside her and closed the door. "You probably want to buckle up then, because it's only going to get weirder."

CHAPTER TWENTY

"Ah, here they come now." Digby stood on the deck of the Queen Mary as the presidential limousine rose up above the side of the ship and drifted toward him.

Asher perched on the railing nearby, cawing and flapping her wings to help welcome their guests. She flew up to his shoulder as the car landed on an open part of the deck. The vehicle had been traveling back and forth between the city of Las Vegas and the enormous cruise ship that floated a thousand feet above it.

"Holy fucking shit!" Parker burst out of the back of the limousine, practically spinning to take in the sights that the Queen Mary had to offer. "How is this even a thing?"

Digby relaxed a little as the messenger ran back and forth across the deck. She still didn't look great, but seeing her running around set him at ease. After she had been unconscious for three days, he had been beginning to fear the worst.

"Calm down. You have been aboard this ship before, Parker." He held up a hand to quell her excitement.

"Really?"

"How do you think we got you back to Vegas?" Becca asked as she exited the limo behind her and closed the door.

The vehicle floated away from the deck and dropped down

below the side of the ship to get the other members of the team that Digby had requested to join him. While he waited for the car to return, he gave Parker a brief tour of the ship. There wasn't time to show her everything, so he just brought her by the bridge before leading her to the ballroom where he planned to explain everything.

He still had trouble believing that he was on a boat. The ballroom was enormous, with a ceiling three times the height of a normal room. Nearly every surface was covered in polished wood paneling, save for the floor, which was mostly carpet except for a dance floor. He stopped at the center, surrounded by pillars on all sides, a pair of doors decorated with intricate filigree standing behind him. Above that, a mural of peacocks filled the wall from the top of the doorframe to the ceiling.

Digby turned to face the room. He'd set up three tables in the shape of a half circle facing the dance floor. Chairs had been placed along the opposite sides so that everyone he'd brought aboard could face the center. Currently, the only ones that had arrived already were Parker and Becca.

The ship's crew had also been invited. They arrived not long after, led by Jameson. The old yet burly captain had added six more members to the ship's staff to alleviate the stress of running the vessel on a skeleton crew. Digby had worked with him to make sure each new member was vetted properly.

Secrecy was still important, but he didn't want a repeat of what happened in Italy. Not to mention he was going to need a lot more help if he was going to pull off the con that he had planned. That was why he'd expanded the team. Each member had been hand-picked by him. Most had been with him since the early weeks of the apocalypse, and had proven their loyalty time and time again. The rest had been investigated thoroughly.

"So what's all this about?" Parker took a seat at one of the tables off to the side.

"All in good time." Digby gave her a self-satisfied grin.

His smile faded a second later when he felt the sensation of someone moving mana through their blood to cast a spell. He wasn't a hundred percent sure where it had come from, but it was definitely inside the room. It hadn't been cast by anyone sitting at the tables in front of him, which meant that the only explanation was that they had another rogue sneaking around.

Digby glanced to his HUD and willed the Seed to show him the log of every spell cast in the last minute, as well as which Heretic had cast it. There were twelve entries listed but only one was of consequence. He cleared his throat before calling out the name of the culprit.

"Hawk, you can come out now."

The air rippled just beyond the dance floor on the carpeted section of the room as the young rogue appeared. "Oh, come on. I was using Sneak on top of Conceal. There's no way anyone heard me. I even fooled Becca."

The vampire scoffed. "That's not hard to do during the day. You should try it again at night."

"Well, it seems you still can't hide from me all the time." Digby chuckled to himself. A part of him appreciated Hawk's dedication to sneakiness, but there had also been a reason that he hadn't requested the rogue's presence. Sure, he trusted him, but if he was going to con the world into manifesting a mass enchantment, he had to fool as many people as possible. In this case, that included Hawk.

Digby gestured to the door. "I hope you enjoyed your stay aboard the Queen Mary, but I think it's time to head home. The limo will take you back down to the strip."

"That's bullshit and you know it." Hawk held his ground but remained calm. "I know what you're doing is supposed to be secret, but I think I proved that I can keep things quiet. Plus, I can help. Becca can't Conceal herself anymore now that she's Dracula, and you might need someone who can."

"Can you not call me Dracula?" The vampire glowered at her brother.

"Sorry, Vlad." He gave her a sarcastic grin before returning his attention to Digby. "You know I'm right."

Digby hesitated, unsure how to respond. He had a point. Having a rogue on his team might be helpful. Not only that, but much of the preparation for his plan would not be dangerous.

Though, none of that negated the fact that Hawk was a valid target of the con. Allowing him to help would certainly stop the child from believing the con in the end.

"I'm afraid my decision not to include you has nothing to do with trust." Digby took a few steps toward him. "It's just that this mission does have a bit of an age requirement."

"Seriously? That's it? You know I'm not a kid anymore." Hawk let out a long sigh before saying the last thing Digby expected. "Fine. I'm not gonna argue about it. And I don't want to complicate whatever plan you're cooking. I'll see you when you're done here."

Digby's mouth fell open as Hawk turned toward the door.

It had been an argument that he'd had with the rogue numerous times. Yet, this time, he'd accepted it so easily. No, it wasn't just that Hawk had accepted it. He was actually acting like an adult. There was no tantrum or complaint. Just a strange air of maturity, as if Hawk really had put his childhood behind him.

Digby considered how that development would impact the plan. He might have been too hasty in marking Hawk as a target.

"Wait." Digby held a hand up.

"Yeah?" Hawk turned halfway to look back over his shoulder.

"You really believe that you've grown up?"

Hawk held both hands out to his sides. "It's the apocalypse, growing up is kind of the only option."

"I wouldn't say that." Becca stood up from her seat at the table. "The city below us is thriving. It won't be long before we have schools open and you can make friends your own age. It's not too late for you to be a kid."

Hawk lowered his eyes to the floor. "I know, but right now, I'd rather help. I want to go forward, not back."

Silence fell across the room until Digby finally broke it.

"Take a seat, then." He gestured to one of the tables to the side. "I suppose this plan will still work if there's one stray teenager in the mix."

Hawk nodded, looking a little more mature than he had in the weeks before.

After that, the other members of Digby's crew filtered in through the doors at the end of the room.

Mason took a seat next to Becca. Combat wasn't going to be important, but having the soldier with them was still a good idea. Not to mention they were going to need a lot of support in other areas.

Alex entered next, setting Kristin's skull on the table in front of him as he sat down. Digby had been unsure about the seer, but it wasn't like she could run off to tell anyone anything. As long as Alex didn't take her off the ship, there wasn't much to be concerned about. In addition, the knowledge of enchantments and magic she possessed was invaluable.

Lana poked her head in the door after that and rushed in to find an empty seat. With Parker's magic being as unreliable as it was, it was a good idea to have a second Heretic with the Mirror Link spell. Plus, it couldn't hurt to have a cleric aboard the ship to heal if the need arose. Of course, she was under strict orders not to tell her brother anything. Alvin's loyalties had shifted back to their side, but he still didn't want to take any chances.

After Lana, Easton entered the ballroom. Sadly, his connection to the world's magic had been severed during the week he'd been held captive in Autem's capital. Those bastards had tattooed runes all over his chest that prevented the Heretic Seed from finding him. Even after being rescued by Becca, they were unable to find a way to fix the problem without removing the man's skin. Nevertheless, he was trustworthy and a good communications officer. That would come in handy during the final execution of the plan.

Finally, Elenore completed the team. He was going to need someone to handle things down in Vegas when the time came, and there was no better choice than her. Not to mention, her organizational skills would go a long way in figuring out the logistics of what was to come.

Digby allowed everyone to settle in and get all their questions about the miraculous flying cruise ship out of their system. Jameson was happy to answer everything. It was going to be a long meeting, so Digby had made a point to have a tray of baked goods and drinks brought up from the city below. Once everyone had something to eat and the chatter had died down, he took the floor.

Asher flapped down from his shoulder to land on the table near Alex, where she pecked at the shiny forehead of Kristen's skull.

"Begone, you feathered menace." The deceased seer did not appreciate the attention.

Asher responded by cawing in her face.

Digby ignored them and opened his mouth to speak. He closed it again when Parker raised her hand.

"What?" He frowned.

"Is this everyone?"

"Yes." He opened his mouth to say something else, but her hand was in the air again. "What?"

"Shouldn't we get Harlow up here? She seemed pretty knowledgeable, and she has experience with covert missions."

Digby frowned. If he was honest, he would have liked to include Harlow for the same reasons Parker had mentioned. Unfortunately, the woman had vanished while they were in Italy. After the way she had been talking about having her own mission, he wasn't surprised. In the end, all he could do was hope she would return when she was ready.

Parker dropped back into her seat, looking sullen when he told her. "And here I thought we were hitting it off."

"Yes, well, too bad." Digby rubbed his hand on his forehead. He had a whole speech planned but the messenger had just thrown everything off. "Anyways, I've asked you all here to help con the world into giving us the power we need to defeat Henwick when the time comes."

Elenore raised her hand now that Parker had set a precedent. "And just how do we do that?"

"Mostly through lies and deceit." Digby went on to explain how the Nine used a mass enchantment to ascend from their human existence and how Henwick intended to return them to their full power. "With your help, I intend to do the same."

Lana threw a hand up. "You want to become an angel, like the Nine?"

"What? No." Digby growled back. "That would be ridiculous. But there are other legends, myths, and demigods that I could impersonate. All I have to do is fulfill their role as publicly as possible so that people begin to believe I am real."

Elenore briefly waved a hand through the air as a formality before asking another question. "Assuming we can actually do that, which is a big assumption, will that give you a mass enchantment powerful enough to kill Henwick?"

"Indeed. As long as we can do so in a convincing enough manner. Provided we pick a demigod that has a job easy enough for me to complete." He gestured to her. "With everyone's help, of course."

"That's the stupidest thing I have ever heard," Kristin said without raising a hand on account of the fact that she was a skull and did not have any.

"I agree." Elenore slouched back in her chair. "There is no way to convince the world that you are a demigod. It is insanity."

"Not quite." Alex stood up and joined Digby on the floor. "One thing to remember is that we have plenty of time to prepare before Henwick is ready to resurrect the Nine."

"And how much time will that take?" Hawk leaned forward with his elbows on the table.

"A few months, we think," Alex answered. "There's no way to be sure, so we're trying to be conservative with our estimates."

"Oh good, a few months. That's plenty of time to create a demigod from nothing." Elenore folded her arms.

"See, I knew you'd come around." Digby smiled at her.

"I was being sarcastic."

"Oh." Digby's face fell.

"The sarcasm is warranted," Kristen added. "A mass enchantment is exactly what it sounds like, with emphasis on the mass. I doubt you would have to travel to every settlement around the world, but at the very least, you would have to convince everyone here in Vegas and the thousands of people over in the empire's capital that you are whichever demigod you claim you are. That would take months or years, and Henwick would be sure to kill us all before we finished."

Digby scoffed. "That's why we're going to pull off this con in one night."

Several gasps echoed through the cavernous room.

"One night?" Jameson leaned to the side, his chair creaking under the weight of the old man's oversized body.

"For the plan to work, we have no choice but to do it in one night," Digby added.

"Yes, we went over our options and most demigods and other mythological figures require acts that are beyond our capability. For example, Zeus would be a possibility since calling lighting down from the sky is possible with magic. But at the same time, the fact that people know about magic now makes it hard to convince them of something like that."

"Plus, Dig can't go around impregnating people." Parker chuckled for a second before stopping. "Wait, can you? I don't know."

"Never mind what I can and can't do." Digby stomped his foot at the idiocy of the question.

"Yes, let's maybe move on." Alex tried his best to push past the thought. "We went over other options. Some are just impossible, and others are unlikely to manifest abilities that could stand against Henwick. For example, Dig could try to impersonate Cupid, but there's not much of a power increase there."

Mason let out a sudden laugh. "How would Graves do that? By playing matchmaker?"

"Yes, we crossed that one off the list for a variety of reasons," Becca added from her seat beside him.

"We crossed off a lot of things." Alex held up a finger. "But then we started to think about entities that might have a lower burden of proof."

"What kind of demigod has a low burden of proof?" Easton asked.

"It means that we don't need to make everyone believe. Just the ones that matter." Digby paused to let that sink in.

Parker threw her hand up again. "I'm not following any of this."

"What he means is that some legends, by their nature, require a much smaller portion of the population to believe in them." Alex held out a hand. "For example, an angel generally considers itself part of a religion, and religion doesn't jive well with conflicting beliefs or nonbelievers. Because of that, the burden of proof is high. For Henwick to resurrect the Nine, he needs to convince at least a quarter of the world's total population. That's why he's so quick to kill off anyone that he can't get on board." He lowered his hand and held up his other one. "But some myths are not aimed at the entire population. When this was explained to us back at the Vatican, the example that was given was the tooth fairy, which is only believed in by children."

"So you want to become the tooth fairy?" Hawk asked.

"Not this again." Digby groaned. "I don't even know why you all invented this insane tooth collector, but I don't think it would give me the advantage over Henwick that I need. No, I need something more powerful."

That was when Elenore slapped a hand on the table. "The boogieman."

"Yes." Alex held out both hands. "If there is one thing that falls in our wheelhouse, it's terrifying children. Between Digby's Body Craft and Becca's shadows, we could strike fear into the hearts of every kid in the world. Not to mention the powers of such a monster would offer a wide array of viable combat capabilities."

"You'd need my passages to get into people's houses though," Parker assumed.

"Unfortunately, there's no way around that." Digby pointed a finger at the messenger. "That is why your only job throughout the preparation process will be to rest. I don't want you casting anything or lifting a finger."

"I can do that," she chirped with a happy nod.

"So that's it? You are just going to scare kids?" Elenore folded her arms. "Is that really the right thing to do? After everything that the world's children have been through, this idea seems a little cruel?"

"We thought of that too," Alex added. "Although the bigger obstacle is that impersonating the boogieman might be too risky when we get to Autem's capital. The treaty specifically states that we can't do anything hostile within their territory. So, this must be a completely non-violent operation. With that in mind, we were forced to cross the boogieman off the list."

"Could we just ignore Autem's territory?" Hawk asked. "You said you don't need to scare all the kids, so couldn't we just find whatever groups are still out there on their own?"

"We don't have the resources to reach any survivor groups beyond this continent." Kristen answered the question. "The empire estimates fewer than one hundred thousand humans are alive out there scattered across the globe. Among that, the survival rate of children is low. And that's according to the data I saw before I was killed weeks ago. That number will have dropped significantly since then. Plus, the empire has been active in gathering the young that remain. There's still plenty out there, but a large percentage has already been relocated to their capital. Any way you do the math, we would be unable to ignore the empire's population."

"Alright, but what other entity could Graves possibly pull off?" Easton glanced between him and Alex.

"What we need is a demigod. Or something close to it." Alex continued, "One with powers and unpredictability that could actually help in a fight against Henwick."

"Oh my god!" A ghostly gasp came from Kristin's skull, making it clear that she'd just figured out the plan. "You're insane if you think you can convince anyone you are who I think you intend on impersonating."

Digby's grin grew wider.

Alex shrugged. "There is only one entity within our reach with a viable power level that won't be considered hostile under the treaty."

"What?" Parker looked back and forth. "What myth are you planning to invoke?"

"Think about it. We have to do this in one night, and Graves only has to convince children he's real." Kristen sounded horrified.

"That's right." Digby let a cackle roll through his chest as one by one the faces around the room grew wide-eyed in recognition. "We're going to save Christmas."

He folded his arms, expecting a moment of quiet awe at his declaration. Instead, the entire room fell into chaos. Kristen immediately started lecturing Alex and Becca. Hawk and Parker burst out laughing. Mason, Easton, and Elenore all asked questions at once. Then, for good measure, Jameson's coven of artificers all began pointing out the plan's flaws. It was possibly the worst reception that any of his ideas had received.

Deflating, Digby shoved his hands into his pockets as the opposition continued. He had spent the night before sitting in Parker's hospital room watching a collection of movies that Alex had gathered for him. Each featured a certain jolly legend. From that, he got an idea of what his plan required.

None of the traditions in the videos had been familiar to him.

Not only were the holidays different back in his time, but he'd never had anyone to spend them with. His mother had died in childbirth, and his father had hated him for it. There wasn't much cause for celebration throughout his youth. After he'd left home, he'd only become more alone.

Still, the plan was simple.

All they had to do was deliver gifts and look the part. As long as they kept all preparations aboard the Queen Mary and controlled access to the ship, they could ensure that no one beyond the crew would find out what they were doing. Compared to everything they had done in the past, this would be easy.

Then again, if he couldn't get his own people to believe he could pull it off, what chance did he have?

From the sound of continued arguing, it didn't look good.

"Alright! Everyone calm down and let me explain." Digby held up both hands to quell the chaos.

There was a brief moment of silence where the entire room looked in his direction. Then, they all just started talking over each other again, leaving him and Alex on the defense in the middle of it all. The only one who wasn't adding to the chaos was Becca.

That was when the lights in the room began to flicker, the shadows growing into a sudden swell of darkness that blocked out the light. It was just a few seconds, but when the gloom retreated to normal, Becca was gone from her chair. The room quieted down immediately.

"That's better." Digby dropped his hands to his sides just as he noticed the vampire that was now standing next to him opposite Alex. "Gah! Holy hell!" He jumped at least three feet, nearly knocking over the artificer beside him. Somehow, she'd moved without him noticing. He'd sensed her mana flowing, but that was it.

"Sorry, force of habit," Becca apologized without looking in his direction.

Digby glanced at his HUD; she'd only spent twelve mana which she could regain in a night. It was a small price to pay to get the room's attention. He frowned a second later, realizing that everyone had grown so accustomed to zombies that he didn't rate as high as a vampire on a scale of which was scarier.

Becca didn't give the room a chance to start up again. "I realize that this is easily the weirdest proposal we have come to any of you with, but the fact is, the math checks out. There are enough targets here on this continent, and we can realistically reach them." She glanced at Digby and Alex before looking back out into the room. "We have discussed everything at length and now we need your support."

For a moment, it seemed like everyone was willing to accept the proposal now that the vampire had appealed to their sense of reason and quelled some of their skepticism.

Then, of course, Parker decided to add something to the conversation. "You're Santa's elf."

"What?" Digby narrowed his eyes at her.

The messenger stood up and pointed at the vampire. "Becca is your elf."

The vampire tried to argue. "I don't think—"

"No, it fits." Parker stood up and walked around the table. "If we're going to do a Christmas episode, Santa, or in this case, Digby, has to have someone that he relies on. And that's Becca, his elf. She has pointy ears and everything."

The vampire took a step backward, suddenly looking

concerned as Parker's eyes began to sparkle. "Why are you looking at me like that?"

The messenger closed the gap between them. "You're gonna need a costume."

"Yes, yes. I'm sure we'll need several disguises." Digby tried to ignore her excitement. "We shall need many things." He turned to Alex, who walked over to one of the pillars to retrieve an easel that he'd left there the night before and dragged it to the center of the room.

Once it was set up, he placed a large pad of paper on it and flipped the cover page over to reveal a list of several items. Alex had compiled it over the last couple of days after watching every holiday-themed movie they could. The list contained every objective that they had to complete before executing the plan.

1. Disguises
2. A flying sleigh
3. Gifts
4. Magic reindeer
5. A bag of holding
6. A means of locating children

Most items on the list were mundane, except for the last two. Number five was easy. The bag of holding was just a sack capable of storing infinite presents. As Digby understood it, it was similar to the void inside him that held his resources. It wouldn't be hard to find a way to make that work for their purposes.

The sixth item, however, was a different story. If the plan was going to have a chance, then they needed a way to locate recipients for them to give presents to. Any way he looked at it, the only thing that could do that would have to be an artifact.

"Do you have a marker?" Parker leaned to Alex.

"Sure." He pulled one from a pocket and handed it to her.

The messenger proceeded to add a seventh item to the list, an elf. She checked it off as soon as she wrote it, giving Becca a thumbs up.

The vampire rolled her eyes.

"Well then." Digby clapped his hands together. "Now that

everyone has been brought into the loop, I suggest we start planning. Obviously, the hardest item on our list to find is the locator."

"Actually, that might not be so difficult," the ghostly voice of Kristen's skull commented. "I know of an artifact that is not currently in Henwick's possession that is capable of doing what you need."

"Is that right?" Digby arched an eyebrow. "What's the catch?"

The skull hesitated. "The location is… complicated."

Digby nodded, shocked at how unsurprised he was.

"Of course it is."

CHAPTER TWENTY-ONE

Digby leaned against the armrest of his seat in the back of the presidential limo as it lifted off the deck of the Queen Mary. It had been two days since the meeting in the airship's ballroom. There were still some lingering doubts about the plan, but everyone had finally committed to getting it done. Aside from Elenore and Lana who had family in Vegas to take care of, the rest of the team had relocated to the rooms aboard the ship.

He frowned as he stared out the window. It had taken a full day to travel across the country to the location of the artifact that Kristen had told him about. As comfortable as the flying cruise ship was, it wasn't fast.

He had Captain Jameson's overbearing sense of caution to thank for that.

At top speed, the ship could travel as fast as most modern aircraft. After pushing it well past its limits on the way to the Vatican, its elderly captain had been insisting on keeping the vessel's speed at a reasonable pace. This left them traveling about as fast as they would have if they'd been riding on the ship back during its time at sea.

It was agonizingly slow.

After an hour of nagging Jameson, he finally agreed to push

the ship up to half speed. Everything had worked out well, but Digby ran into a bit of trouble when he got lost in the middle of the night and accidentally exited the interior of the ship through a poorly labeled hatch. He hadn't even been able to set foot on the deck before the wind blew him straight off the ship. His only saving grace was the fact that he could grow himself a pair of wings. Well, that and the fact that zombies didn't get tired.

At half speed, the Queen Mary had left him behind rather quickly and it was at least an hour before anybody noticed he was gone. It then took another fifteen minutes to slow the ship enough to turn around and pick him up. After that, Digby stopped complaining about how fast they were going.

"You're sure what we need is down there?" He folded his arms and stared at Kristen's skull, peeking out of the open flap of Alex's satchel.

"Of course, I'm sure," she responded curtly, the sun reflecting off the gold that coated her forehead. "You should be more concerned about remaining inside moving vehicles."

"Oh, please, it happened one time."

"The artifact will be there." Alex ignored their argument, sitting at the back of the limo. "I have a good feeling about this place."

"Me too. My parents brought me here when I was a kid." Mason looked back through the open partition that separated the driver's seat from the rest of the vehicle.

The soldier had volunteered to drive, though Digby was pretty sure he just wanted to stay close to Becca.

"Well, you'll have to wait until I scout the area before reliving your childhood." Becca sat on the floor of the passenger compartment, connecting a surveillance drone to a laptop. "I don't want to repeat what happened in the Vatican. I want a full understanding of the situation before any of you set foot out of this car. No more walking in blind."

The only member of Digby's primary coven that was absent was Parker, who was still under strict orders to do nothing. She wasn't complaining, of course. Instead, she'd taken over one of the first-class suites and dragged Hawk along with her to explore the ship.

Digby leaned to one side, placing his chin in the palm of one hand as he stared out the window at the sundrenched land below. Then he looked back to Kristin's skull. "How do you know that the artifact we need is down there? And, for that matter, what is it?"

"It's a scrying mirror that allows you to view any person you wish. It's a fairly common enchantment. The same power can sometimes manifest in a variety of things, even on bodies of water. Though, there is usually an activation phrase associated with whatever legend manifested the enchantment. Which is why ordinary people don't find such things easily. The empire already has many scrying mirrors in its possession. And the reason I know about the specific artifact that we seek is because the empire knows about it as well."

"What?" Digby slapped a hand down on the seat cushion beside him. "If Autem already has several scrying mirrors of their own, then that would mean they could have been spying on us this entire time. Why didn't they use one to find us when we were in hiding?"

The skull let out a ghostly sigh, sounding bored. "Mostly because you were lucky. For the first two weeks that you were on the loose, Henwick believed you had perished in Seattle, so he wasn't looking. By the time he became aware that you had not, you had already reached a location capable of blocking a scrying mirror's ability."

"Wait, what?" Alex did a double-take. "How did we do that?"

"Scrying mirrors are not as reliable as one might assume." The skull clicked her nonexistent tongue. "There are numerous ways to ward against them, and countless locations that naturally block their scrying ability due to a common belief in confidentiality. Such as church confessionals, most law offices, various government buildings, and doctors' offices. Some mental health professionals exist within their own naturally occurring bubble that applies to any room they are in. Oh, also, the entire city of Las Vegas."

"Seriously?" Becca eyed the skull.

"Seriously."

"What happens in Vegas, stays in Vegas," Alex commented in a hushed tone.

The skull scoffed. "Yes, that slogan has certainly caused Henwick quite the headache. When he attempted to scry your location before and found the ability blocked, he assumed the Heretic Seed had a way of interrupting it. He never suspected it was just coincidental luck on your part."

"Holy hell!" Digby tightened his grip on the seat cushion beside him, realizing how close he had come to being found. "Wait, does that mean he can see us right now?"

"Right now?" The skull paused. "No, this vehicle, having once belonged to a top government official, also holds the ability to block a scrying mirror."

"What about the ship up there?" Alex jabbed a finger into the ceiling. "Henwick could see anything we do aboard?"

"Technically, yes, now that you have left Las Vegas's airspace. However, as I mentioned, Henwick has assumed that the Heretic Seed is preventing you from being spied on. So it is unlikely that he has tried again."

Alex's eyes widened. "We're going to have to get some sort of ward up just in case. At this point, he knows we were hiding in Vegas so he might have already realized his assumption was wrong."

"True, but I doubt it." An annoyed tone entered Kristen's voice. "Henwick can be a frustrating man. He does not doubt himself easily. This allows him an impressive level of confidence, but also makes it difficult for him to think of any possibility that involves him being wrong. But yes, it would be wise to ward the Queen Mary when we return."

"That is an understatement." Digby groaned. "It would have been nice if you had mentioned any of that before now."

"I..." Kristin trailed off for a moment. "I am still getting used to the idea that I am no longer the person I once was. I sometimes struggle to sever the old loyalties that linger. Also, I did not think of it until now."

"That's unhelpful." Digby narrowed his eyes at the skull.

"Neither was the fact that we had to stop the ship and turn

around last night because a certain zombie fell overboard," the skull spit back.

Digby just shrugged. "Indeed, that was unhelpful."

Mason slowed the limousine's descent as the buildings below grew. Digby arched an eyebrow at the strange cityscape. It was oddly reminiscent of the strip back in Vegas. They touched down on a wide area of red brick that looked out across a lagoon. He popped his door open as soon as the car came to a stop.

"Wait." Becca stopped him before he had time to put his foot out. "Let me do my thing."

The vampire activated the surveillance unit that sat on the floor and thumbed the sticks on the controller. The drone floated up to hover in the center of the limo's passenger compartment. Then it swooped forward toward Digby before turning to the side and slipping out his open door. From there, it flew up to take in their surroundings.

Becca kept her eyes on the laptop screen in front of her. "I'll give you the okay to move once I've had a look around."

Digby frowned. The area looked empty, and he didn't see the harm in just stepping outside. Then he thought of something else. "If Las Vegas has the ability to block scrying mirrors, do other locations have other powers that we haven't encountered yet?"

"Yes. Territory-based enchantments are quite common. Though, some can be more impactful than others." Kristin's skull answered in a tone that made it clear there was more that she wanted to say. "If you will remember when I first told you about this artifact, I also said that its location was complicated."

"Yes, that statement was uncomfortably vague." Digby eyed her. "And how would I be able to find out what enchantments this land might contain?"

"Simple. All you have to do is touch the soil beneath your feet."

That explained why Digby had never become aware of the enchantments that had been bestowed upon the city of Vegas. The area had been so heavily developed that it was rare to see exposed soil. Sure, there were a few areas of grass back on the strip, but he had never had the urge to bend down and touch it.

"Hmm." Digby leaned out through the open door beside him in search of open soil.

There was a landscaped section of small plants surrounding a sign reading Transportation and Ticket Center. He leaned back in the car and turned to Becca.

"I assume it is safe for me to take a stroll over to those trees."

She gave him a nod. "I've swept the immediate area."

"Good, good." He grabbed his staff off the floor and hopped out of the car without hesitation.

The sun beat down on him the instant he was in the open. Even this late in the year, the temperature was warm. Holding out a hand, he could feel the weight of the life essence in the ambient mana. It was even higher than the balance back in the desert. Fortunately, he could also feel a fair amount of death essence in the mix as well to balance it out.

Digby leaned back to look into the car. "What do they call this land again?"

"Florida," Becca answered without looking away from her laptop.

"Ah, yes, Florida." Digby pushed the door shut before turning toward the patch of grass not far away.

The golden femur at the end of his staff clanked against the bricks as he moved. Digby was just glad that this Florida place was far enough south to be out of Autem's general area. If he was honest, it was still closer than he wanted to get. He stopped walking when he reached the landscaped plants.

"Alright, time to see what that skull thinks is so complicated about this land."

Digby slid his fingers down his staff as he knelt to place his clawed hand in the dirt. Text immediately flooded his vision. His mouth slowly fell open as he started reading.

MASS ENCHANTMENT
Due to widely known beliefs or reputation, this land has gained a power of its own.

SUNSHINE STATE

During daylight, the ambient mana present throughout this land may contain a higher amount of life essence.
Bad place for a creature of the night.

FLORIDA MAN
During a state of heightened stress, all persons born within this land will have a .00001% chance of becoming a representative of Florida. This may result in a permanent increase in one or more attributes. The number of additional attribute points will be distributed amongst all existing representatives from this land's common pool.

TERRITORIAL ENCHANTMENT
Due to a widely known belief or reputation, this territory has gained a power of its own.

HAPPIEST PLACE ON EARTH
This enchantment will occasionally distract this territory's visitors from their problems and worries.

Oh good, you do have a lot of problems and worries.

"Territorial enchantment, indeed." The information faded away from his vision as he lifted his hand from the grass. Digby turned as the quiet buzz of a drone's propellers drifted into the space behind him.

"What did you find?" Becca's voice came from the speaker on the front.

"You're going to want to stay in the car. It seems the sunlight is more potent here."

"Shit, I could feel that something was off the moment you opened the door of the car." A sigh came from the drone's speaker. "It got a little better once you closed it again. The limo's bulletproofing and overall durability must be providing some insulation against the outside mana balance."

"Let's hope it lasts." Digby turned toward the entrance of the area where Kristin's skull said they could find a scrying mirror. "What did you find in there?"

The drone remained quiet for a moment before speaking. "It's odd. The place is empty. Almost too empty. I saw a few bodies from above, but that was it. There's very little evidence of revenants. Considering how many people visit this place, there should have been more damage."

Digby leveled his eyes at the entrance. "Perhaps something has scared them away."

"Maybe. But it also could be a good thing. You can just walk right in and get the mirror."

"Alright then." Digby glanced back at the limo as Mason and Alex got out. He could hear Becca yelling at the artificer over the distance as well as through the speaker of the drone.

"Close the door!"

"Sorry." Alex did so before jogging to meet Digby.

He'd left his coat in the car since the weather was warmer this far south. Instead, he wore one of those ugly floral shirts that he had been wearing weeks before. The pistol that Dominic had given him hung from a shoulder holster underneath. Mason followed behind, tugging down the brim of his hat to keep the sun out of his eyes. He carried his usual rifle and wore one of Autem's swords on his back.

Digby had opted to keep his coat on since the pauldron attached to its shoulder granted him an extra fifty points of mana. The unseasonably warm weather didn't bother him anyway. As long as he wasn't on fire, the heat didn't have an impact on him.

Walking through an area of turnstiles and ticket booths, Digby stopped to look up at the entrance before him. A wide area of well-manicured flowers lay before him in a raised bed of soil surrounded by a half wall. It had begun to grow a little wild after not being cared for since the world ended, but it was clear that the design was meant to be some kind of face. Beyond that, a train rested on a set of tracks that passed over the entrance, leaving two tunnels for people to walk through. A sign with gold lettering named the place.

"What exactly is this kingdom, and why is it magic?" Digby leaned on his staff and stared up at the sign.

"It's a theme park." Mason stood beside him.

"What the devil is a theme park?" Digby furrowed his brow.

"It's a place for entertainment, kind of like Vegas." Alex held a hand out at about waist height. "Except this place is more for kids."

"Tell that to the millions of obsessed adults that used to come here every year." Mason kept walking.

"I'm going to scout ahead and check out some of the buildings. There's got to be a rev or zombie walking around somewhere." The drone flew forward zipping up and over the train that was parked above the entrance.

With that, Digby pushed on, walking through the tunnel on the right. Posters lined the walls inside, each depicting a different attraction for visitors to play on. A part of him wished he could have come before the world ended, just to see what it was all about. The idea that families would bring their children to such a place seemed unreal. His father certainly never would have brought him anywhere.

I wonder if Hawk would have liked a place like this. Digby shook his head. *I suppose not.* The young rogue didn't seem interested in things meant for kids anymore. It was hard not to feel a little sad. Digby still remembered Hawk back when they'd met. The child had been interested in magic tricks and such. The world had really changed him since then.

Exiting the entrance tunnel, Digby found himself in a large area surrounded by buildings. Each one was painstakingly built with complex detailing. Yet, there was something off about the structures. It took him a moment to figure out what it was. They were fake, or at least, the upper floors were. The bottom of each building held a shop, but the rest seemed to be only there for decoration. It reminded him of the façades inside the casinos back in Vegas.

As he walked further toward the main throughway, another structure came into view to stop him in his tracks.

"That's a castle!" He threw a finger out in the direction of one of the most fantastical buildings he'd ever seen.

"Hence why they call this place a kingdom." Mason gestured to the street around them.

Before Digby was able to ask any more questions, Becca's drone flew out of one of the buildings through an open door.

"I've found bodies."

"What kind?" Digby turned to the hovering machine. "Human, revenant, zombie?"

Knowing what the remains belonged to would tell a lot about what potential dangers might lurk in the area.

"I'm not sure." The drone turned its camera back and forth as if shaking its head. "They're sort of half-eaten."

"Ah, good. Sounds like team zombie has come out on top in this territory." Digby marched forward toward the building the drone had exited, smirking at its camera as he passed by. "Sorry, Becky, but looks like your team has found itself at the bottom of the food chain this time."

A groan came from the drone's speaker. "Revenants are not my team."

"Yes yes, whatever." Digby slipped in through the building's half-open door.

He found the bodies immediately, or what was left of them, at least. They weren't so much corpses as they were pieces of corpses. He was starting to second-guess his assumption that the killings had been done by zombies. Something had certainly had a meal there, but the dead would have left only the bones that could not fit down their gullet. Whatever had been there had left more behind. Limbs lay strewn about, only partially eaten. It was as if the monster that had done the killing had gotten distracted partway through their meal and then forgot about it. Doing the math, Digby guessed that there were at least fifty bodies.

"What did this?" Alex pushed him through the entryway.

"More importantly, is it still here?" Mason followed behind him, covering his face with a cloth.

"See if you can find a skull and check its teeth." Becca piloted her drone back in and flicked on a flashlight mounted underneath.

Digby poked at some of the remains with the butt of his staff, finding a severed head in the mix. He crouched down and rolled it over. He relaxed a little when he saw a row of jagged fangs. "These are revenants."

"So whatever did this would have to be a zombie." Becca's drone swept its light across the pile, stopping at another severed head. "Wait, someone check that one."

"That's odd." Alex nudged it with his boot, revealing a jaw full of human teeth.

"Maybe whatever zombie did this killed a human too and just dragged them to the same pile." Mason turned back to keep an eye on the door.

"I don't know." Alex bent down to examine the half-eaten skull's mouth, pointing to a few broken teeth. "This damage is consistent with that of a zombie that's chewed on a few bones. Then again, they could have just been a guy with bad teeth."

"We are in Florida," Becca commented through the speaker of her drone.

"Florida isn't that bad," Mason complained.

"Yes yes, I'm sure Florida is a wonderful place." Digby stood back up. "But we have a mystery to solve here and I find it hard to believe that a zombie ate another zombie."

Digby stomped back out through the door, dragging his staff behind him. He spun as soon as he got outside, sweeping his vision across the area until he found a corpse lying near one of the buildings. The mystery grew the closer he got to it.

The corpse definitely belonged to a zombie, though it was missing a limb. From the look of it, one arm had been torn clean off by something strong. In addition, the top of his skull was missing. At first glance, Digby assumed it had been shot, but on closer inspection, the zombie's head looked more like it had been crushed.

"I do not want to run into whatever did this." Digby turned back to the others who were standing in the middle of the throughway. "We best be getting this artifact and getting out of here."

"No argument with that." Mason glanced at Alex. "Now, where is this scrying mirror thing?"

The artificer slid his messenger bag around to his front and opened the flap to retrieve Kristin's skull. "You told me the artifact is in one of the rides here, right?"

"It is about time you remembered I was in here," the skull complained before answering the question. "And yes, though, technically the artifact is not complete. In its current state, it can't access its power. That is the reason why Autem never collected it."

"I really wish you had mentioned that before," Digby spoke through his teeth, running out of patience with the skull.

"Oh relax, the artifact is a decorative frame meant to go around a mirror. The reason it doesn't currently function is that there is no mirror in it at this time. To activate it, you just need to cut a piece of glass to fit it. I'm sure your artificers back on the ship would be happy to handle the job."

"Anything else you want to mention while you're at it?" Digby eyed the skull.

Kristin remained silent for a moment before adding, "Yes, there is an invocation phrase that must be spoken to access the artifact's scrying ability."

"What is it, 'Mirror, mirror on the wall'?" Mason chuckled.

"Actually, yes. That's exactly what it is," the skull responded, sounding completely serious.

"I guess we're going to fantasy land then." Mason started walking again only to stop and duck back against a wall. "Shit, I saw movement."

Digby crept over as well, afraid that they might run into whatever had crushed that zombie's head. He checked his mana, just in case.

MP: 524/524

"Where is it?" Alex froze, still standing out in the open.

"There." Mason pointed at something moving within one of the shops on the other side of the park's throughway.

Squinting at the window across the area, he couldn't get a good look at the monster on the other side of the glass. The only detail he could make out was that it was big. It was still roughly human-sized, just large, as if the person it had been in life had been huge.

"I'm not getting any heat signatures." Becca's drone lowered itself down a few feet away. "It's definitely a zombie."

"Good." Digby relaxed a little.

"I don't think it sees us yet." Alex crept away, only to step on an empty plastic bottle that had fallen from an overturned rubbish bin.

Of course, that was when the monster inside the building snapped its head toward them.

"Shit, it heard you." Becca's drone pulled up to stay out of the way.

Digby didn't waste time, raising his staff in the direction of the monster as it crashed through the door of the building it had inhabited. It was even larger than he'd thought it was. A torn T-shirt and ripped denim shorts strained to contain its tree-trunk-sized limbs.

Common Zombie, Hostile.

Digby cast his Control spell on the hulking monster to bring the zombie under his command. The zombie didn't even look at him. Instead, it stomped its way toward Alex.

"Why isn't it stopping?" The artificer scrambled backward.

"I don't—" Digby stopped talking as soon as he looked down at his HUD. He hoped that the Heretic Seed would be able to give him an answer. Instead, it just raised more questions.

Control common zombie, failed.
Warning: Florida Man cannot be controlled.

Digby's eyes bulged at the text. "What the devil?"

The hulking zombie kept moving, closing the gap between it and the artificer that had been caught out in the open.

"Run! I can't Control it." Digby summoned his crone's echo to buy time, sending a dozen spectral arms surging up from the ground to wrap around the oversized zombie's legs and arms.

"What went wrong?" Mason raised his rifle at the monster as it tore at the ghostly limbs that held it at bay.

"The Seed said it was a Florida Man." Digby kept his staff raised. "The human that it used to be must've had the status."

"You can't be serious. That's a thing?" Becca's drone drifted over Digby's head.

"Yes, and we best dispatch it before it breaks free." Digby summoned his wraith just as the monster tore apart the last two of the crone's spectral limbs.

The flickering image of a long-dead killer streaked toward the oversized zombie, only to slow to a casual walk before fading.

"What?" Confusion flooded Digby's mind as the Florida zombie charged straight through the crimson image of his wraith and rushed him. "Wait, wait!" He pulled his staff in front of himself for protection only for the monster to slap him aside as if he was an insect. The back of the zombie's hand impacted the side of his staff, buckling the metal shaft before slamming into Digby's chest.

The attack hit him like a tank. Something that he knew all too well since he had been hit by a tank just two weeks before.

Digby's feet left the ground as the world spun. The sky was suddenly below him. The pavement above. A moment of weightlessness seemed to last forever. It came to a stop when he smashed through a window with the words Main Street Bakery written across it. His body continued onward, crashing through a case full of month-and-a-half old pastries. He finally came to a stop behind a counter with one leg bent up around his neck and both elbows bending in the wrong direction. His staff was nowhere to be seen. Checking his mana value, he'd regained the thirty points of MP that he'd donated to imbue the weapon. That could only mean it had been destroyed.

"So much for making my staff more durable."

From where he lay, he heard Alex cry out from the street.

Digby cast Necrotic Regeneration while willing his Body Craft mutation to put himself back together. His mana dropped by twenty-five points in an instant, but his limbs snapped right back into place as he rose off the floor of the bakery. Getting to his feet, he sprinted toward his apprentice's cries. He cast Decay and Necrotic Regeneration at the same time as he leapt straight through an unbroken window to land back in the street.

"Oh, thank heavens." Digby relaxed when he found the over-sized zombie casually chewing on Alex's shoulder.

As bad as the situation looked, the blue shimmer of a Barrier spell swept across the artificer's body. As long as it didn't break, he would be fine.

"A little help here." Alex kicked his legs, trying to break free of the zombie's grip.

After a moment of frustration, the deceased Florida man simply threw the artificer aside and turned to Mason.

"No, you don't." Digby cast Emerald Flare at the space between the foe and the soldier.

Mason turned and broke into a sprint. The Florida zombie followed, passing straight through the flare spell as it detonated. The unsuspecting monster flew backward as if it had been hit by a truck. It crashed down through a store window over forty feet away.

"Okay, that was weird, right?" Alex pushed himself off the ground and jogged to catch up to Mason.

"Indeed, quite strange." Digby walked across the street to join them as he glanced at his HUD, expecting a kill notification. His body tensed a second later when none came.

The sound of thrashing came from inside the store where the monster landed. Then, the extra-large zombie smashed through a closed door as if it hadn't been there.

"It seems this foe is more resilient than most." Digby took a step back as the monster broke into a jog.

"Stand aside, a-holes." Alex pulled Dominic's pistol from its holster and raised it. "I've got this."

The gun barked, firing a plume of smoke and flame from its muzzle.

"What?" Alex's aim faltered when the enchanted bullet hit the ground a few feet behind the charging monster. "How did I miss? I called everyone a-holes and everything. Should I have said assholes? Would that have been better?"

"Just flip Dig off and try again," Becca shouted from the drone hovering overhead.

"Okay." Alex shoved a middle finger in Digby's direction and shot again.

This time the bullet hit a building nowhere near the zombie.

"Oh yes, that worked perfectly." Digby shook his head as he backed away.

"Crap, my aim-bot isn't working." Alex backed away as the Florida zombie closed the gap.

"Just shoot it normally." Mason turned and started running to put in some distance.

"Okay, fine." Alex stopped running and unloaded the gun whilst shouting.

Not one bullet hit the monster.

"Remind me why I brought you with me." Digby broke into a run.

"Sorry, I have no depth perception." Alex ran as well.

"Are we really getting our asses kicked by one zombie?" Mason ran alongside him.

Digby hung back to make sure Alex didn't trip or something. His mind raced through every option he had left that might pose a threat to the foe. He'd already used all of his strongest spells. The only thing left was to simply fight the beast himself. If he combined the extra strength granted by his Necrotic Armor and his Limitless mutation, there was a chance he could win. Then again, that was also a big risk without knowing exactly what the zombie's attributes were. He couldn't help but think of the corpse he'd found earlier with its skull crushed. He didn't want to end up the same way.

"That thing's gaining on us," Alex shouted. "I think it's getting faster the longer it runs. Like it has to pick up speed."

"We need to climb something." Mason took a left just before they reached the castle ahead of them. "That thing's strong, but it doesn't seem maneuverable. I doubt it can jump."

Becca's drone flew by overhead. "There's a sign you can get on top of just ahead."

Digby pushed on, picking up his pace. She was right. There was a bridge not far ahead with a sign with the word Adventureland stretching across the space above it. The bases on both sides were built from sturdy-looking logs and there was plenty of room to stand on top of it. He opened his maw and cast forge as soon as he was within range, sending a surge of necrotic blood up from the ground to reach the sign. It formed the rungs of a ladder just as Mason reached it.

The soldier climbed up without hesitation, turning back as soon as he reached the top to make sure the others were behind him. Digby stopped at the bottom to wait for Alex. The artificer gave him a grateful nod as he jumped up the first few rungs. As soon as he made it to the top of the sign, Digby followed, glancing back as he climbed.

The Florida zombie was nearly on top of him.

"Gah!" Digby jumped the rest of the way, using his Limitless mutation for an extra boost.

Then, he spent the extra mana needed to reform the ladder. There wasn't time to turn it into anything complicated, so he just covered the surface of each rung with spikes. The charging zombie plowed straight into it, shattering the ladder into a thousand tiny chunks of black blood. Digby stared, dumbfounded as the Florida man slowed.

The monster wasn't even damaged.

"How is that possible?"

The Florida zombie growled and groaned as it reached up, trying to grab at the sign. Fortunately, they were high enough to be out of reach. At one point, the monster tried to jump but fell short by a few inches. After that, it turned to one of the sign's support posts and started punching it.

"Alright, we need a plan." Digby held on to a log that stuck up behind the sign, feeling the vibrations of each impact of the monster's fist. "It doesn't look like that thing is going to give up anytime soon."

Alex pulled his gun again and tried aiming it at the monster now that he was closer. Then he lowered it. "This is weird. I usually feel it when the aim-bot kicks in. It tugs at my hand, and right now I'm feeling nothing." The artificer looked down at the gun, then back to the zombie, then back to the gun. "I don't think this zombie has a weak point for my Guiding Hand ability to target."

Suddenly, it made a lot more sense why Digby's wraith had stopped before attacking. The spell specifically hit weak points, and if the zombie below didn't have one, then the echo had no way of knowing what to do.

"If we can't reliably target this thing with magic, then just get a little closer." Digby pointed out the beefy zombie below. "That thing is massive and I'm willing to bet you can hit it at this range."

"That's true." The artificer took aim again, this time steadying his wrist by resting it on the top of the sign. Then, he exhaled as he squeezed the trigger.

Fire and smoke exploded from the gun as the bullet slammed straight into the zombie's face, only to ricochet off to punch a hole in the sign's support post below.

"Gah!" Digby choked out. "Don't do that."

A blue shimmer swept over the Florida zombie's body.

Everything began to make sense after that. The monster must've been granted enough additional attribute points to its defense by the territorial enchantment to give it an active barrier. Digby willed the Seed to show him the area's information again.

FLORIDA MAN
During a state of heightened stress, all persons born within this land will have a .00001% chance of becoming a representative of Florida. This may result in a permanent increase in one or more attributes. The number of additional attribute points will be distributed amongst all existing representatives from this land's common pool.

It was that last line that was the problem. It was safe to say that the majority of people living within the state of Florida had been killed during the apocalypse, meaning there were fewer to receive the boon of the land's enchantment. The result seemed to be a much higher increase in attribute points than normal, since they were being distributed between fewer people.

Digby clenched his jaw as he did the math. There was no way to know how many attribute points were in the territory's communal pool, but it was safe to say it was a lot. The barrier around the zombie trying to kill them might have been even stronger than the one produced by the Cloak of Steel that Parker had been wearing. With that in mind, there wasn't much point in attacking. Not unless they could bring some much bigger guns.

Digby stared down at the frustrating zombie for a long moment. Then, he looked back up to the others.

"Alright, we might have a problem here."

CHAPTER TWENTY-TWO

"Why are they like this?" Becca sat on the floor of the presidential limo, hunched over a laptop with a drone controller in her hands as she stared at the screen.

Through the feed, she watched as her boyfriend, Alex, and Digby clung to the top of a sign in an amusement park while a Florida man zombie tried to punch its way through the supports below them. She would not have expected a lone monster to be such a problem, but as she was learning, things were rarely as she expected. The extra-large enemy was not only immune to Digby's Control spell, but also had a defensive barrier making it nearly invulnerable.

Oh yes, it also had super strength.

In the end, all her coven could do was hurl insults down at the monster. Well, that or throw the gold-coated skull of Kristin the deceased seer at the threat. That part had been Digby's suggestion.

It had not been received well.

After about five minutes of arguing, Mason glanced up into the camera of her drone while scratching at the back of his neck sheepishly. Becca knew what he was going to ask before he even opened his mouth.

"Hey, do you think you can maybe come to rescue us?"

"Yes, good idea." Digby looked up as well. "That limousine you're in can fly, you can simply drive over here and pick us up."

Alex placed his hands together in a pleading gesture to back them up.

"Fine, I'll be there in a minute." Becca set her drone to follow Mason and crawled to the front of the limo to reach through the open partition and dropped her laptop on the passenger seat. After that, she popped the nearest door open and jumped outside. She was already feeling a little weak, but the moment she stepped into the direct light of the Florida sun, she felt ten times worse. She yanked open the driver's side door of the limo and threw herself inside to limit the exposure.

Once the door closed, Becca placed her hands on the wheel only to realize that she had never driven one of Alex's flying cars before. She glanced around at her surroundings to see if anything was drastically different from normal. It all looked familiar. All except the key, which was missing.

"Okay, how do I start this thing?" She looked at Alex through the screen of her laptop.

"That's the neat part; you don't," he responded. "It's kind of one of those always on types of magic cars. All you have to do is step on the gas and you'll feel it start to pull on your mana."

Her fingers tightened around the steering wheel. "This thing is going to drain my MP?"

Alex's mouth fell open, clearly realizing why that would be a problem for a vampire. "It won't take much. Just a slow trickle. For a normal Heretic, their absorption rate would replenish everything faster than they lost it."

"Well, I am not a normal Heretic," she snapped back.

"You should still be fine, but try to go fast just in case."

"Yes, make it quick, Becky," Digby added unhelpfully.

"Fine, but you three owe me." She gently pushed on the gas and waited to feel the vehicle pull on her mana.

Nothing happened.

She looked back to her laptop. "I think something's wrong. It's not moving."

"It should." A confused expression fell across Alex's face only to be replaced a moment later by one of surprised recognition. "Oh."

"Oh, what?" She glowered at him as hard as she could despite the fact that he couldn't see her through the drone's camera.

"Small problem. The same thing that stops a vampire from using magic during the day might be stopping you from being able to operate the car." Alex shook his head.

Becca leaned forward to rest her forehead on the steering wheel as she filled in the blanks. The life essence that was disrupting her mana system was also disrupting her ability to feed mana into the car's propulsion enchantments.

She raised her head back up. "Okay, what now?"

An awkward silence fell, calling attention to the fact that no one had a clue what to do. Then, Digby decided to speak up.

"You could just push the car over to us."

"What?" She snapped her head back toward the laptop.

"Well, the car is floating above the ground. It's not so hard to push. All you would have to do is get it close enough so that one of us," he gestured to Mason, "would be able to make a break for it. I can hold this foe for at least a few seconds to give him a head start."

"Are you forgetting the part where the Florida sun will wreck me? I'll have less strength than a small child out there."

Alex leaned in beside Digby. "To be fair, a small child could probably push that car without too much problem."

She glowered at him even harder than she had before.

"Becca?" Mason stared up at the drone when she failed to respond for several seconds. "Is this a bad time to remind you that I love you and I don't want to be eaten by a Florida man zombie?"

"Yeah, I know." She groaned before adding an annoyed, "Love you too."

In truth, she didn't want him to be eaten by a Florida man zombie either.

It was a little funny. Ever since she'd returned from the dead, Mason had been trying to be as protective as he could. Yet, every time they got into trouble, he'd ended up being the one in need of rescue.

Becca sighed and popped the door of the limo open. The sun beat down on her the moment she stepped outside. It wasn't too hot, but the flood of life essence into her system made her feel like she was walking through cement. She forced her way through it regardless, dragging her feet as she made her way to the back of the limousine.

"Okay, here goes nothing."

Becca leaned into the trunk of the armored car. Alex was right, it moved easily. Similar to a shopping cart half full of groceries. The only problem was keeping it going in the right direction. With only one person, she kept having to readjust her positioning to keep the car moving in a straight line. After pushing for a few minutes, she reached the turnstiles at the entrance of the park. She glanced back to see how far she'd pushed it. It had only been about a hundred feet, and she was already out of breath.

"This sucks," Becca grumbled to herself as she walked to a gate next to the turnstiles and dragged it open wide enough for the vehicle to get through.

Returning to the back of the limo, she pushed for another couple of minutes until she reached the entrance tunnels that Digby and the others had passed through earlier. Of course, that was where the car decided to veer off to one side and bump into the corner of one of the openings. The vehicle stopped in an instant. If it hadn't been for the Florida sun, she wouldn't have skipped a beat. Instead, she fell forward and banged her head into the trunk of the car. The impact made a hollow metallic sound as she stumbled and fell to the bricks below.

"This isn't working." Her arms shook as she pushed herself up.

She was getting weaker by the minute.

Becca glanced back to the limo, wishing they had thought to cut a hole in the bottom so she could push it with her feet from inside, Flintstone style. Staggering, she forced her body to move through the oppressive light to reach the darkened area within the entrance tunnels.

"Thank god."

The difference was immediately noticeable. She was still

severely weakened, but the weight that had been crushing her was gone.

"Too bad there isn't a way to do this and stay out of direct sunlight." The thought gave her an idea. "Maybe there is."

Becca walked forward to the other side of the entrance tunnels and looked around at the shops. There were bound to be umbrellas and things like that available to sell to the park visitors in the event of rain. She returned to the car and climbed back into the driver's seat to grab her laptop. Digby complained that she was taking too long the moment she took control of her drone again. She responded by telling Alex to flip the necromancer off again, which he did.

Letting the sound of an argument that she'd started fade, she piloted the drone back to her location and used it to search some of the stores. It was unlikely that there was more than one Florida man zombie in the same area, but she knew better than to tempt fate.

Becca flew the drone into the nearest shop through a broken window. It didn't take long to find an umbrella. She made an extra pass around the sales floor to ensure there was nothing to worry about. For a moment, she thought she'd found an oversized corpse lying on the floor half behind the register. It turned out to be one of those bulky character costumes. A chipmunk wearing a Hawaiian shirt. The head was sitting on top of the sales counter, as if somebody had discarded it in favor of something less bulky. Her imagination produced an image of one of the park's unfortunate employees struggling to escape from the undead while dressed as a chipmunk.

It was likely that the tourist attraction had been one of the locations that Autem had seeded with zombies on the first night that the curse had returned. After all, it would be the perfect place to start the spread. Most of the guests would flee and try to return home to help the curse travel further.

She decided not to think about it.

After making sure that the store was safe, she pushed her way back out into the sunlight and forced her weakened body across the pavement. She practically fell into the doorway of the shop when she reached it.

"Why did it have to be Florida?" Becca panted as she supported herself by leaning on the sales counter at the front.

Once she'd caught her breath, she grabbed the largest umbrella she could find off the display and headed back out the door to test her theory. Popping it open, she noticed a mild sense of relief but not much more than that. The umbrella was helping to shift the balance of life essence in the ambient mana around her, but there was still too much flooding in from the sides.

"I'm going to need more barriers." Becca dropped the umbrella and turned back into the store to find something better.

Trying a rain poncho next, she found it had the same problem. There just wasn't enough to it. To compensate, she layered on another five ponchos as an experiment. The result paid off to a degree. It was better than the umbrella, at least. Following that line of logic, Becca added another five ponchos on top of the ones she was already wearing. Strangely, wearing twice as many didn't feel much different.

"Hmm." She stared down at herself. "It's like I've already reached the limit of what the material can keep out so adding more does nothing."

Becca grabbed the umbrella off the ground and held it above her head. The combination of layered plastic and shade did improve the situation. Though, it still wasn't enough. If she was going to keep out the life essence, she needed a more complete barrier. Preferably, something thicker that could cover her entire body.

"Shit," she said to herself the moment she realized there was already something readily available that would fulfill both of those requirements.

"I'm going to have to put on that chipmunk costume, aren't I?"

She blew out a defeated sigh before answering her own question.

"Yeah, it's time to suit up."

Becca yanked off all ten layers of ponchos and threw the umbrella to the side as she reentered the shop to get the bulky outfit. It took a solid ten minutes to figure out how to get into the thing. To her surprise, there was no internal fan or cooling system. She'd always assumed that there was a safety regulation or something that required one since employees of the park would be wearing the heavy costumes all year round. Employee comfort must not have been a high priority.

After getting herself put together, Becca stepped to the door with her chipmunk head under her arm and stepped outside. Even without the mask on, she could feel the difference. The suit was working. It felt similar to when she'd been hiding in the limo. Better even.

Shoving the head on, a wave of relief swept through her. A second later, she recognized the sensation as her body purging itself of life essence the way it usually did at night. There was still a hint of weakness, but nothing like it had been before. In fact, her mana system had nearly returned to normal.

It was hard to see or hear through the giant furry head, but after wearing the suit for a minute or so, her senses grew stronger to match the stats she had as a Heretic.

"I wonder if I can use my magic or vampire abilities?"

Becca held out a furry hand toward her shadow and willed her Shadecraft to produce a single bat. The power flowed as a winged form puffed out of the silhouette she cast on the ground. It vanished as soon as it reached the edge of her shadow.

"Interesting. Good to know there are limits."

She followed her first experiment with another, flicking a few points of mana into her agility and tapping her strength for an instant. With that, she jumped straight up into the air, chipmunk suit and all. Her vampiric prowess answered as she pulled off a successful backflip. The head didn't even fall off her costume when she landed.

"That's better. I don't know how people were able to move easily in these things before, but I'd say being a vampire helps quite a bit." She stood with her hands on her hips, feeling proud.

Then she caught her reflection in an unbroken window and deflated. The only person she knew that could pull off a look like that without embarrassment was Parker. Despite that, she spun on her fluffy heel and walked back to the entrance tunnels where she'd left the limo. To make things easier on herself, she scavenged the chains that made up the queue line in the ticket area and hooked them to the front of the limo. That way she could pull the car instead of pushing and avoid having to readjust its direction constantly.

"Okay, chipmunk Becca, you're going to be laughed at and probably never live this down, but you have a boyfriend to save from a jacked-up Florida zombie." She started pulling. "My life just keeps getting weirder."

It only took her another ten minutes to get the limo all the way to the Adventureland sign where her friends were still shouting insults at the monster below them. The Florida man had done a considerable amount of damage to the sign's support posts. If she had taken another twenty minutes, the zombie might have had a chance of getting to them.

The laughter started the moment they noticed her.

"Becca?" Mason squinted, clearly unsure if it was her inside the chipmunk. "What are you wearing?"

"Oh, that is amazing." Alex clapped his hands.

"Never mind what she's wearing, it is about time rescue arrived." Digby stood with his arms folded only to nearly fall a second later when the zombie beneath them broke through one of the supports causing the sign to wobble.

"I'd say I'm just in time," Becca commented back through a layer of sarcasm.

"What?" Digby stared at her.

"I said, I think I'm just in time," she repeated.

"What?" Digby repeated, this time louder. "Take off the bloody mask, Becky, nobody can hear you in that thing."

By then, the Florida zombie had turned around to face her, its head cocked to one side, looking confused.

Becca pulled her chipmunk head off just long enough to say, "Never mind, just get to the car. I'm going to lead that thing away. Come and get me once you're in the air."

With that, she shoved the costume's head back on and prepared to dodge the hulking zombie that was now stomping toward her. Hopping backward, she stayed out of reach as the monster swiped its meaty hands through the space that she had been. As long as she dropped a couple of points into her agility every few seconds and avoided moving in a straight line, staying away from the Florida man wasn't a challenge. The zombie was strong but it lacked the ability to make quick corrections to its movements.

Mason climbed down from the sign and made a break for the limo the moment she got the threat far enough away. The car lifted off the ground a few seconds later, spinning around before flying straight for her.

Becca didn't take any chances. When the vehicle got close enough, she jumped. She landed on all fours on the hood, staring into the windshield at her boyfriend as he struggled not to laugh.

Obviously, he couldn't hear her, but she yelled regardless.

"Not one word, you hear me! Or I will end you."

She turned to Digby and Alex as Mason brought the car around.

"I will end all of you!"

CHAPTER TWENTY-THREE

Silence filled the rear compartment of the presidential limo as it lifted off the ground. Digby opened his mouth for an instant only to close it again when an angry vampire dressed as a chipmunk glared in his direction.

Dealing with the Florida man zombie that had caused so much trouble ended up being a simple matter. Once they had the car, they were able to fly just over its head with Alex hanging out of the trunk as bait. There was no point in killing the foe since it was only a common zombie and wouldn't even reward them with experience, despite its unique status. Instead, they just led the monster a few miles away and left it there. It might find its way back later, but they had plenty of time to retrieve the artifact they had come for before then.

The scrying mirror, or at least the frame that held the enchantment, was exactly where Kristin the skull had said it was. With the Florida zombie gone, they were able to walk right into one of the theme park's attractions to pry the artifact off the wall. Digby understood why Autem had never retrieved it the moment he saw it. The frame was simple enough, just an oval cut into a section of wall and painted gold. Instead of a reflective surface, it held a transparent piece of plastic. Figures were positioned on both sides to give the illusion that there was still a reflection. One was of a woman wearing a crown while the other was of an old crone.

The overall attraction was quite interesting. Digby made a point to walk through the entire place. It was like strolling through a storybook while events played out around him. There wasn't time to investigate any of the other locations in the park, but he filed the place away for later. As much as he disliked the land of Florida and its enchantments, he still wanted to come back to explore at some point after they had less to fear.

Getting the scrying mirror turned out to be a little more difficult than he'd assumed. The frame was not simply hung on the wall. No, it was fully integrated into it. To avoid any kind of damage that could impact the artifact's enchantment, they simply cut through the fake stone around it. Once it was free, Digby double-checked that its power was intact, then they carried it back out to the car and tied it down to the roof.

All that was left to do after that was to jam Becca and her over-sized costume in through the door of the back seat. It was around then that the vampire had forbidden everyone in the vehicle from making comments.

"You know, you can probably take off that chipmunk suit now that you're in the car." Digby winced, hoping the comment would be taken as a helpful suggestion.

"You're probably right." Becca lay on the floor of the car since it was difficult to position herself on one of the seats. "I was just enjoying a few more moments without the sun messing me up." The vampire gestured to the windows that lined the passenger compartment. They may have been tinted, but they still allowed enough light through to alter the balance of ambient mana within the vehicle. "I know I look ridiculous in this, but being able to feel a little more normal is nice." She began wriggling around in an attempt to escape from the chipmunk body she inhabited.

"You know, if all it takes to insulate you from life essence during the day is layers of material, there are better options available than that costume you found." Alex picked up the chipmunk head and examined it. "I mean, I've been through all of the hotels back in Vegas and there was a pretty big furry convention going on when the world ended. So I'm sure there's a bunch of high-end fursuits that you could choose from."

"The apocalypse is not turning me into a furry, Alex." The vampire narrowed her eyes at him.

"Beggars can't be choosers, Becca," Mason added from the front seat. "I'm sure we can find you a bat costume or something. That would at least be thematic."

"You are not helping." She squirmed herself the rest of the way out of the chipmunk and threw herself into one of the seats at the back of the car. It wasn't long before Mason brought the vehicle up over the side of the Queen Mary's rail to land on the deck. Captain Jameson was waiting for them when Digby stepped out of the car.

"Welcome back." He gestured to the section of wall strapped to the top of the vehicle. "I see the trip was successful."

"Indeed." Digby glanced back and forth, remembering what Kristin's skull had said before about the empire having scrying mirrors of their own. "We best get the artifact inside." He turned back to Alex. "And get this place warded against scrying magic immediately."

"We are on it." The artificer pulled the seer's skull from his messenger bag.

"He could at least say please," Kristin added as they walked away.

Digby ignored them and stepped aside as Jameson waved in some of the cruise ship's artificers to help offload the artifact from the roof of the limo.

"I think there's a full-size mirror in one of the first-class bathrooms that we can cut down to fit that thing." Jameson followed his artificers as they turned the section of wall they carried sideways to fit through a hatch. "We'll have that artifact up and running in no time. We've been working on a few projects in the ballroom, so we'll bring the mirror there when we're ready."

Digby nodded and headed inside.

Becca gave him one more reminder not to tell anyone about anything that happened back on the ground before heading back to her room to sleep until nightfall. From there, Digby headed straight for the ballroom to check on Jameson's other projects.

He was struck speechless the moment he arrived.

The space had been completely transformed. The pillars that surrounded the dance floor had been wrapped in some form of cord made of artificial pine branches, complete with twinkling lights embedded at regular intervals. The back of the room was lined with numerous evergreen trees of varying sizes, including one that was nearly two floors tall. Two-thirds of them were covered in a white paint-like substance to suggest snow. Tiny decorations had been hung throughout their branches.

Looking up, he found large bows of red and green ribbon hung from the ceiling. Digby dropped his vision back down to the center of the room where an object sat beneath a tarp, surrounded by a few covered tables.

It looked like one of the holiday movies that he'd watched a few nights before had simply vomited its contents onto the room's walls.

"What is going on here?"

Asher cawed unhelpfully from atop the tallest tree in the room.

"Parker found the Queen Mary's holiday decorations." Hawk appeared out of thin air as a Conceal spell faded. "The captain's guys were looking for a good example of a sleigh to base their designs on. This place used to be a fancy hotel, so I guess they had a lot of Christmas shit. Parker's been putting it all up since you guys left earlier."

Digby stared at the room for another few seconds, then he shrugged. "Well, at least she is keeping busy."

"You know I am." The messenger appeared in the doorway behind him holding a pair of candlesticks in her hands, each with room for nine candles. A red hat sat on her head with a fringe of white fur and a ball of fluff hanging to one side. Below that, she wore a matching red coat lined with more fur. A canvas bag hung from one arm, full to the brim with more ridiculousness. "I figured if we're doing this whole holiday con job, this place should look the part. You know, to help everybody get into the spirit of things." She placed a candlestick down on one of the tables. "I found the

Hanukkah stuff too. I don't know what everybody here follows, but I figured let's just do it all."

"Yes, yes." Digby shook his head. "But I'm not sure all of this is necessary."

"That's what I said." Hawk shoved his hands into his pockets to make it clear that he had no part in the redecorating.

"And I said that's too bad." The messenger passed by him, depositing a hat that matched hers on his head.

The young rogue snatched it off a moment later and tossed it aside.

Digby opened his mouth to argue but closed it again after getting a good look at her face. Parker still looked exhausted, but some of her color had returned and she was clearly enjoying herself. It might have just been the fact that she hadn't cast any spells, but if decorating the place was having any kind of positive effect on her condition, then he wasn't going to put up a fight. Besides, it wasn't like any of it was in the way.

"It gets better too." She rushed over to one of the tables that was covered by a cloth and pulled it off to reveal a full outfit that matched her coat, complete with a thick, black leather belt with a decorative buckle and a pair of boots. It looked a little big, but for the most part, it resembled the costumes that had been worn by the various incarnations of the Santa Claus figure that he'd seen in the movies. Parker pulled the coat off the table and draped it over Digby's shoulders. "See, we don't even have to go looking for a costume for you."

"Disguise," he corrected.

"Whatever." She waved away the comment as she casually slipped a headband resembling a deer's antlers onto Hawks's head.

"Cut that out." He pulled them off in protest.

"You can fight me all you want, but I will only grow stronger." Parker tugged off her own hat and dropped it onto the rogue's head before he could stop her.

Digby left her to torment the teenager and turned toward the object beneath the tarp. "What is all this?"

"That's your new transport," Jameson answered as he walked in through the doorway.

The burly old man headed straight for him and pulled away the tarp to reveal a red and white sleigh large enough for one person. He pulled the tarps off some of the tables around them as well. Underneath lay a series of metal panels, along with several rods, all covered in engravings. Some looked to be made of iron, while others were gold and steel. None of them looked like anything on their own.

"Alright, what am I looking at?" Digby picked up the nearest piece of the puzzle.

"I know it doesn't look like much now, but when my team is done installing everything into this here sleigh, we should be able to get it flying on its own." Jameson picked up one of the engraved plates and held it up to the sleigh to show that it had been cut to shape.

Digby frowned. The sleigh was about the size of a child's crib. For what they had planned, they were going to need something that could carry both him and Becca, as well as some equipment.

"I'm not sure this is going to be large enough."

"Of course not." Jameson waved a hand in front of the tiny sleigh. "This is just a prototype. Once we get this flying, we'll use what we've learned to build something more functional. This isn't exactly a normal project, so there's going to be a fair amount of experimentation. But don't you worry, no one will know the difference between you and the real thing when we're through. Though it would be good if you could grow a beard or something. You know, to look the part." Jameson stroked his own beard as if to illustrate the point.

"Yes, well, we shall see." Digby considered the possibility of using his Body Craft mutation to grow facial hair. He pushed the question aside a moment later when four of the ship's crew members entered through the doors in the back, carrying the section of wall that held the frame he'd retrieved from Florida. A large oval mirror had been inserted into its center.

"Where do you want this?"

Digby glanced around the room for a space that was not inhabited by several imitation trees. He pointed in the direction of one of the side walls. "Right over there is fine."

Alex wandered in, carrying Kristin's skull while Digby waited for the mirror's installation. They were just in time too. Something told him that using the artifact was not going to be as simple as it seemed. He approached the mirror as soon as Jameson's artificers had it secured to the wall and placed his hand against it.

MAGIC MIRROR
Any reflective surface within this frame will attempt to show its viewer anything they ask to see.

"So this thing will really let me see anyone?" he asked, glancing down at the deceased seer's skull.

"Yes, but you will need to be specific."

"Can I spy on Henwick?" Digby arched an eyebrow.

"I doubt it." Alex stared at the mirror. "If there are ways to block scrying magic, I'm sure Henwick would have done so long before we were ever his problem."

"It would also be a considerably bad idea to try. Honestly, scrying mirrors should all come with a warning. Use at your own risk," Kristin added. "For anyone with a heightened perception, it is possible that they may sense that they are being watched. I myself would have been capable of as much back when I was alive. If you were to succeed in spying on Henwick, you would almost certainly be notifying him that you have the ability to do so at the same time."

Digby frowned. "Alright, no watching Henwick."

"How do we use the mirror to locate someone if we don't know their name?" Parker leaned in to place a headband of antlers on Kristin's skull.

She had a point.

The entire purpose of retrieving the artifact was to locate children that they could trick into believing he was this Santa Claus person. But if he didn't know any of their names, how would that be possible?

"That is where things get a little tricky." Kristin started to sound less confident. "It is still possible, but you will need to be specific to narrow things down to an individual."

"Very well." Digby turned to the mirror. "Show me the youngest person in the world."

Nothing happened.

The skull clicked a nonexistent tongue. "You forgot the invocation phrase."

"Ah yes, I remember. Mirror, mirror, on the wall, show me the youngest person in the world." A part of him felt a little silly saying a bunch of magic words, but the result was worth a little embarrassment.

Almost as soon as he finished speaking, his reflection began to fade into a blurry green. The image coalesced back into a scene that he recognized. The infirmary back in the casino came into view. A woman lay in one of the hospital beds with a baby in her arms.

Digby shot Alex a look, questioning if what they were seeing was real.

"We did have a couple of pregnant residents back in Vegas, one of them must've given birth in the last few hours." The artificer stared at the image as if in disbelief.

"Wow." Parker teared up a little. "The youngest person in the world is right there in Vegas."

An ache echoed through Digby's unbeating heart. The world may have been filled with the dead, but it was not dying. It was as if he was looking directly at the future that he was struggling to protect. He shook off the thought as soon as he had it, not liking the pressure that came along with it. Then he repeated the mirror's invocation phrase, followed by, "Show me the second youngest person in the world."

Parker let out a laugh as the scene shown in the glass faded. "Is that really the plan, you're just going to brute force this thing?"

"Do you have a better idea?" Digby glowered back at her.

"It's not actually a bad strategy," Alex commented. "As sad as it is to think about, there probably aren't that many children in the world. Maybe just a few thousand. It's not unreasonable to locate them all. If we find any that are close enough to Vegas, then we can send out a rescue team. There's a limit to how many we can get to, but every kid we relocate back to Vegas will be one more that can count toward bestowing a mass enchantment on you. We should probably make a note of any settlements we find out in the rest of the world as well, for future reference."

"Indeed."

The image in the mirror coalesced to show another, slightly larger baby. This one, however, was lying in a clear, plastic cradle in a well-lit room. It was hard to tell from the angle, but it looked like a second infant lay in an identical cradle near the edge of the frame. Autem's crest was clearly visible on the child's blanket.

"And that appears to be a medical facility within the empire's capital." Kristin stated the obvious. "They have been prioritizing the acquisition of children for weeks since they are so easy to manipulate. It makes sense that many of our targets will be there."

Digby laughed. "It seems they have done us all a favor. It would be impossible for us to reach every child that is out there by the deadline required, but with Autem grabbing up the world's youth, they have brought many to one location. It's only because of them that this con might work."

That was when Hawk scoffed. "Yeah, but I don't think Autem has been rescuing many of those kid's parents along with them."

"That is true," Kristin confirmed, a hint of guilt entering into her voice. "It is the empire's policy to leave family behind unless they seem eager to join them. Especially if any of the children are young enough that they won't remember anything. I'd say that at least one out of every three families is separated. The orphans are then placed into the homes of loyalists. Or enter directly into the Guardian program if they are old enough."

"That's horrible. All those families torn apart." Parker winced and rubbed at the sides of her head before sniffing.

Digby lowered his head. He'd been thinking of their mission as a con. Just a way to trick the world's children into handing him the power needed to defeat Henwick once and for all. Many of them had lost everything, and he was going to lie to them. A moment passed when he was glad that his deceased body couldn't shed a tear. Then he swallowed his guilt.

Sometimes lies were necessary.

Not everyone had the luxury of seeking the truth that Dominic had.

Eventually, he nodded and turned away from the mirror.

"We're one step further to pulling off this con."

He rubbed his hands together.

"Now, what's next?"

CHAPTER TWENTY-FOUR

"Well, this is not the kind of gift that I expected." Digby approached the doorway of an enormous store on the outskirts of Las Vegas as a swarm of twenty revenants gathered before him.

The sun poured in behind him to keep them at bay.

Holding his ground, he waited as a few pale forms worked their way through the crowd toward the front, moving with the steadiness of a creature unafraid of the light. The Seed's HUD marked them for what they were.

7 Revenant Lightbreakers

Digby let a grin creep across his face as he raised both hands out to his sides. The sound of hungry moans came from above. The revenant lightbreakers broke into a sprint, darting toward him. They slid to a stop a second later when two lifeboats—each carrying a dozen zombies—lowered to the ground behind him, their descent slowing to a stop just as they touched down.

After the trouble he'd run into in the Vatican, followed by the irritation he suffered in Florida, he vowed not to walk into an unknown situation without a horde to back him up ever again.

"To me," Digby commanded as every member of his horde climbed out of their boats.

Taking a cue from that vampire Durand back in Italy, he'd outfitted each zombie in full armor and armed each with a sword. After enhancing them all with his Body Craft mutation, every walking corpse had regained the strength and agility they'd possessed while alive. Digby didn't hesitate before thrusting both hands out toward the revenant lightbreakers and shouting another command.

"Rend!"

The horde rushed forward, a Control spell granting them the intelligence to wield their weapons. Swords were drawn from sheaths, their blades biting into the creatures ahead of them. Digby walked forward as the horde cut a path through the swarm. His HUD flooded with kill notifications with each step.

Revenant lightbreaker defeated. 636 experience awarded.
Revenant lightbreaker defeated. 636 experience awarded.
Revenant lightbreaker defeated. 636 experience awarded.

He barely looked at the messages, continuing past the sales counters of the enormous, warehouse-like store.

"The rest of the place is clear." A surveillance drone met him at a display filled with bags of sweets.

The screech of another revenant lightbreaker rushed toward him from one of the aisles nearby. Digby merely waved a hand in its direction to send his wraith to handle the threat.

"The place is clear, is it?" He arched an eyebrow at the camera of the drone beside him.

Becca's voice came from the speaker. "Sorry, I must've missed that one."

"No matter, my horde will make a sweep of the building and then stand guard when they're through." Digby continued walking toward the items that he sought. "Once the place is secure, I'll need all hands down here to help with the looting."

He stopped as one of his zombies burst into the space between the aisles, driving their sword through the chest of a dormant revenant. They stopped only when they had pinned it to one of the store's display end caps. Blood sprayed across a shelf of furry red figures with wide mouths and plastic eyes. The revenant flailed their arms, hitting the items behind it to set off some form of trigger within to unleash a few strange words.

"Hee-hee, that tickles."

Digby looked down at one of the children's toys that had fallen to the floor near his boot as more of the furry things spoke in an unnerving, high-pitched tone.

"Terrifying." He looked back up to the drone beside him. "And you say children like these things?"

"I don't get it either," Becca commented with little enthusiasm.

Digby frowned and stepped around the revenant's corpse as his zombie began to eat it. Glancing back, he reminded his minion to save some for him. Then, he turned down an aisle filled with children's playthings. Many of the food items in the store had already been looted, but no one had touched the toys. Why would they? Up until now, survival was the main concern. There was no place for such things. At least, not until now.

Digby stopped in the middle of the aisle, sweeping his eyes across the shelves as a wave of confusion filled him. If he was going to have a chance at success, it wasn't enough to just give gifts. No, he was going to have to give gifts that children actually wanted. That part presented a new problem for him. How was he supposed to know what they would want?

A moment later, he turned back to the drone floating at the end of the aisle, realizing that he didn't have to know. Not when all he needed to do was simply ask a child, or at least, someone that had been one not long ago.

"Tell Hawk I have a job for him."

CHAPTER TWENTY-FIVE

"What did Dig say he wanted?" Hawk leaned toward the open partition at the front of the president's car.

"I don't know." Mason slid into the driver's seat. "Becca just said he wanted to ask your advice on something."

He furrowed his brow, unsure if he wanted anyone asking for his advice or not.

"He's probably just trying to give you something to do." Parker slouched into the seat beside him. She was still wearing the same stupid Santa hat and coat she'd found in the airship's storage.

At least she'd finally stopped trying to put antlers on his head. It seemed like she had an infinite number of the things stuffed in her pocket. Honestly, her holiday spirit was really getting annoying. A good part of him just wanted to tell her that he hated Christmas altogether. The only reason he hadn't was because he knew he would feel like shit if he ruined something she liked.

He wasn't even sure why the holiday bothered him so much. A few of the foster homes he'd passed through celebrated it, but something about the way everyone acted reminded him that he wasn't really part of the family. Either there was too much effort in trying to make him feel like he belonged, or there was none. He was always treated a little differently.

Well, that wasn't completely true.

There was one Christmas that Hawk had felt at home. It had been the year before. The last one before the world ended. He hadn't been adopted officially yet, but paperwork had been filed. He was pretty sure Becca's parents were at least somewhat Catholic, judging from the Virgin Mary statue that they kept on a bookshelf. He'd asked Maria about it once, and she'd said that it was a gift from her abuela. Apparently, the rest of the family was very traditional. They never brought any of that God stuff up, though. Hawk had appreciated that. He'd had foster parents try to push all that on him. There wasn't much difference between that and what Autem had tried to do when he'd spent time on their base. They just wanted to take away his choices.

The time he'd spent with Becca's parents had been different.

Despite all the crappy feelings he had about the holidays, he'd actually had a good time that year. They hadn't made a big deal out of things. They just watched stupid movies, drank hot chocolate, and opened presents. It was nice.

Then the world died.

Hawk popped the door of the car open as it landed and stepped out. The building in front of him was one of those big stores. The kind that messed up things for smaller shops and paid everyone who worked there crap. He didn't know much about any of that, but he'd heard enough complaints to understand that most people hated the place. Granted, everyone shopped there anyway since there wasn't anywhere else.

At the entrance, six zombies, dressed in armor, stood in front of the door, three on each side. They looked like soldiers guarding an important person's home. In the middle of the walking corpses, a drone floated in the air as if waiting for him. Becca was still up on the airship, operating the surveillance unit from an office that she'd claimed.

"Hey." His sister's voice came from the speaker as it drifted toward him and dropped down to his height. "You glad to be off the ship, for once?"

"Yeah, it's fine." He glanced around, trying to act like he didn't really care.

The drone suddenly moved closer, putting its camera in his face. "You're damn right it's fine. I've been cooped up in my office all day to stay out of the sunlight. Someone should at least be running free down here." Becca moved the drone from side to side as if looking around. "Digby and I have already scouted the place and there are plenty of zombies standing guard. There's nothing to worry about. I know you're trying to be all grown up, but as your sister I'm telling you to relax and have a little fun, okay?"

"Okay." His voice came out annoyed but he felt the corner of his mouth tug up in disagreement with his tone.

She sounded so much like her mother. He couldn't believe he hadn't noticed it earlier.

"Why don't you just come down here too?" Parker got out of the limo behind him and leaned down to look into the drone's camera. "It's not like you have to stay on the ship. Just go put on the chipmunk costume and come hang out with us day walkers."

"Chipmunk suit?" Hawk asked.

"Don't worry about it." The drone spun around and headed into the store. "Let's go."

Hawk shrugged and followed, glancing back at Parker. "Aren't you supposed to be resting back up on the ship?"

"Eh, I've been stuck up there for days. I've rested enough and I've decorated pretty much everything I can."

Hawk didn't argue. Instead, he just grumbled and shoved his hands into his pockets.

"Oh good, you're here." Digby walked out of one of the aisles as Becca's drone led him toward the toy section of the store.

Smears of blood covered the floor, along with several Tickle Me Elmos and a few scraps of corpse. From the look of the body parts, they had belonged to a revenant.

"Did you have a snack while you were waiting?" He glanced down at a pointy ear that lay on the tile.

"Gross." Parker took a step back.

"Yes, I might have replenished some of my resources. I am a zombie, it is what I do. And I did share with my horde."

"Well, at least you shared." Parker nodded.

"Never mind that. We have more important things to discuss."

Digby bent down and snatched up one of the Elmos that littered the floor only to shove it in Hawk's face. "Do you like this?"

Hawk hesitated for a long moment, having trouble processing the randomness of the question. Then he shook his head. "Why would I?"

Digby lowered the toy, letting it dangle at his side. "Honestly, I don't know. It seems rather stupid to me. But I am an eight-hundred-year-old zombie, I can't pretend to know what children would like nowadays." He turned and walked into the next aisle. "The only toy I ever had growing up was a rock with a rope tied around it. I named it Ropey." He slowed his pace. "Now that I'm thinking about it, Rocky probably would've been a better name."

Parker cleared her throat. "Wow, that is a low bar, Dig."

"Yes, I had a bad childhood. I am well aware."

"Wait, wait, wait." Hawk followed after the zombie. "Is that why you called me down here? To ask me what toys kids like?"

"Indeed." Digby spun and placed both hands on his hips. "And before you get all bent out of shape about me treating you like a child, I'll have you know that is exactly the opposite of what I am doing." He stood tall with his nose in the air. "What I require is the expertise of a trusted ally. And the fact is, whether you have grown up or not, you were a child more recently than any of us, especially me. That makes you the resident expert. In this case, for you to fulfill your responsibilities as an adult, you need to pretend that you are not."

Hawk rubbed his eyes, trying to push his mind around the circular logic that Digby was using. "I guess that makes sense, sort of…"

"Of course it does. Now, which of these items do you think would make children believe I am this Santa person more?"

Hawk took a moment to look over the shelves. The aisle the zombie had wandered into was mostly full of toys for younger children. Some had bright colors, some made noise, and some had blocks with little pictures of animals on them. It was all educational stuff that parents gave to push kids to learn faster. Probably because kids were annoying and raising them got easier when they understood more.

He frowned. It didn't matter what you gave kids when they were that little. They would pretty much play with anything. An empty cardboard box would be fun for an afternoon. Maybe that was just him. He'd never had many toys growing up. Sure, the homes he'd been placed in had stuff to play with, but none of it came with him when he moved on. None of it was his, so none of it stood out as special.

Hawk walked on only to stop a second later at a shelf of stuffed animals, a memory of something soft floating to the front of his mind. There had been one toy that he'd owned. He just hadn't thought about it until now. It hadn't been given to him by any of his foster parents. No, it had been from the state of California, before anyone had taken him in.

What was it?

He struggled to remember. It was a stuffed animal of some kind. A bear? His chest tightened as frustration began to take over. He couldn't remember. Whatever it was, it had been left behind at some point when he moved from one home to another. The only thing he could be sure of was that he'd cried for hours when he'd realized he'd lost it.

Hawk looked away from the shelf of stuffed animals, realizing he'd been staring at it for too long. Glancing to the side, he noticed Becca's drone floating beside him, her camera pointing at the shelves as well. The little surveillance unit turned away the instant he looked in its direction.

"What?" He eyed the drone.

"Nothing." His sister responded in an obvious attempt to sound casual.

A prickling wave of heat crept up the back of Hawk's neck to his scalp. He said the first thing that came into his head as a distraction. "I don't know what kids would want. I barely had any toys."

Digby didn't say anything. Instead, he just deflated.

"But," Hawk continued, not wanting to mess anything up. "I'd probably try to keep things simple. Stuffed animals are good for kids. And we should probably stay away from anything with a lot of pieces. You know, because they could get lost. Oh, and nothing that makes noise, because this is the apocalypse."

"Those are all good points," Becca backed him up through the drone's speaker. "Depending on the timing, a noisy toy could get someone killed. And with everybody's living situation being so up in the air right now, things could get lost easily. Plush toys are at least easy to keep track of."

"Are you sure?" Digby ran a clawed finger along one of the shelves on the other side of the aisle. "There are a lot more options here, and judging by the quantity that this shop has chosen to stock, it would indicate that some items were more popular than others."

"Nah, that's just 'cause parents are always reading crap about what's best. It's all trends and shit. Nobody cares what kids actually like," Hawk answered, standing a little taller.

"Alright." Digby gave him a nod. "Plush toys will do for the majority of the children."

"Hey, what are we going to do for kids that don't do Christmas?" Hawk threw a new question into the plan, thinking back to the foster homes that hadn't given him a choice of what to celebrate.

"What do you mean?" Digby stopped and turned back.

"I mean, there's a lot of holidays this time of year, and not everybody celebrates them all. I don't know what I believe, but I didn't like being forced to be a part of things just because it was what other people did."

"I suppose that's fair. Actually, I was wondering about a few things." Digby tapped a claw on one of the shelves. "Back in my time, Christmas didn't resemble anything like what your movies portrayed it as."

"Supposedly it evolved over time," Becca added. "Christmas sort of absorbed other holidays to make it more familiar and to carry some old traditions into a new holiday. I don't know how true that is, though. Either way, religion was probably handled a lot differently back then, right?"

"I'll say." The zombie frowned. "I never had much faith in

God, but I had the sense to keep that to myself. Didn't want to be viewed as an outcast."

"I think people got a little more accepting of things in the last eight hundred years." Parker hesitated before adding, "Okay, that might not be completely true. But there's definitely more options now."

"I don't see why something as simple as giving gifts has to be tied to anything like religion," Digby grumbled. "Can't we just leave a present, offer a happy holiday, and be done with it? Isn't it enough to simply wish each other well?"

"You would think so," Becca added, sounding a little sad. "But it's gotten a little complicated."

"That's ridiculous. Traditions evolve, this is no different. We are living in the apocalypse, for crying out loud. I say if a child has survived this long, then they deserve a present no matter what their family has decided they will believe in."

"So, we're doing a secular Christmas episode," Parker added.

"That's actually pretty common in some other countries." Becca's drone moved its camera in an up-and-down motion, suggesting a nod. "Santa is still a thing, but it's mostly just about giving gifts and spending time with people. The religious aspect hasn't always carried over."

"It would be good if we could still pay respects to other beliefs, though. Just to make sure people don't feel like their identity is being erased," Parker added.

Hawk listened along, unsure what to say. Obviously, he knew that things like religion mattered to people, but it was a little too big of a subject for him to think about. He hadn't liked the way that Autem had told him what to believe, but would he feel the same way about being given presents that he didn't ask for? Maybe.

"Could we print some wrapping paper or something? A design that had stuff for everyone on it?" He felt stupid as soon as he said it. "Sorry, that's a dumb idea."

"No, I love that." Parker stopped short. "It would be like Santa is just filling in because the world ended."

"Printing wrapping paper wouldn't be that hard." Becca

started planning. "I bet Alex could set up a design file and we could run the prints on any copy shop equipment. Most should be able to output prints the size of architectural drawings, and that would be big enough to wrap a gift with."

"Seriously?" Hawk asked in disbelief.

"Yeah, it's a good idea." Becca tilted her drone in his direction.

"Indeed." Digby continued, clearly glad to have settled the subject. Reaching the end of the aisle, the zombie marched straight into the next one. "Alright, what about the older children?"

"Video games?" Parker suggested.

"Probably not." Hawk shot her down.

Before the world ended, all the kids at school had been obsessed with the most recent game system that had come out. Hawk had only played some of the older systems that were a little cheaper. Videogames were fun, but they weren't even an option anymore.

"Game systems need the internet to work." He shoved his hands in his pockets and walked straight past the game aisle.

"That's true, they need constant updates and support. Without it, the games stop working," Becca added.

That was when Parker scoffed. "If the game doesn't work, just pull the cartridge out, blow on it, and put it back in."

"Wait, what system did you have?" Hawk stopped and turned to look at her. Becca's drone spun to do the same.

Parker looked up and to the side as if thinking. She rubbed her head for a moment before answering, "I had a Nintendo when I was little, and my aunt and uncle bought me a Sega when I lived with them."

Becca laughed through the speaker of her drone. "Geez, Parker, did you grow up in the nineties or something?"

Hawk got stuck on a different detail. "Why didn't you live with your parents?"

The pink-haired woman pinched at the bridge of her nose another few seconds before answering with a blunt, "Because they were dead."

Hawk stopped short, her words hitting him like a slap in the face. "Oh shit, I'm sorry."

"Don't be." She shrugged. "It was a car accident. I don't know how I survived, but the paramedics found me fifty feet away. Things sucked for a while after that, but I'm okay."

"Still, sorry." Hawk cringed, remembering how annoyed he'd been with all of her holiday spirit. He'd assumed Parker was just another person who had grown up in a perfect house with a perfect family. That she was another person who didn't understand him.

Maybe it was the other way around.

He forced himself to speak. "How can you still like holidays and stuff after, you know…?"

Parker went quiet and closed her eyes for a long moment, wincing as if it hurt to think about the question. Then she snapped them open again. "I never cared about the holidays. Not really. Not before the accident. But after, it was different. It didn't matter what day it was. It could have been Thanksgiving, Halloween, the Fourth of July, or whatever. It's all just an excuse. I know that. But people still gathered together with everyone they cared about. I had lost the people I loved most, but I still had friends and relatives, and I didn't feel so alone." She lowered her head to the floor. "I know I'm annoying everybody now, but we've all lost so much." She looked back up. "It's important to remember that we aren't alone."

Hawk struggled not to tear up as silence fell across the store.

Then Parker threw an arm around his shoulder and dragged him toward Digby to glom onto him as well. "See, we're all together and having a fun time."

Digby squirmed a little, attempting to escape. "Parker, you're hugging a corpse."

"I know. Plus, you broke my finger a couple of weeks ago. But I'm choosing to forget about all that and appreciate what I have."

"You know, you all are still technically on a mission here." Becca's drone swayed its camera back and forth as if shaking its head.

"Oh, don't think you're not a part of this." Parker grabbed at the lens, ready to pull the drone into the hug as well.

"Hey, watch the propellers. I don't have many of these things." Becca pulled the surveillance unit away.

"Fine." Parker let go of Hawk and Digby only to point a finger at the drone's camera. "But I'm coming for you as soon as I get back up to the ship. There is no escape, not even for vampires."

Hawk couldn't help but smirk at the idea of the pink-haired woman hunting down his sister for a hug. He groaned a second later when Parker produced yet another Santa hat and dropped it on his head.

This time, he didn't take it off.

CHAPTER TWENTY-SIX

"Just one more stop for the day." Mason walked across the deck of the airship toward the limo.

Digby's insane plan was in full swing. They'd already gotten the costumes, the sleigh was half-finished, Jameson had a containment system in the works for Digby's void, and Easton was working on completing a list of the world's remaining kids.

It had been Mason's job to transport load after load of toys back to the airship. Digby and his horde would secure a store, then move on to the next. Mason would swing by after that and pack up each location's stuffed animals and shove them in the back of the limo.

The task was straightforward but had taken a lot longer than he'd expected. Stores didn't stock that many plush toys, forcing him to make a lot of stops. According to Easton—who had been spending just as long using the magic mirror to track down the world's kids—about a third of them were located in the U.S., mostly in Autem's capital, but Vegas held around five hundred. The rest were scattered throughout the world across hundreds of settlements and survivor groups. There were only a few thousand left in total.

That part was a sobering thought.

He'd always known that most of the global population had died in the apocalypse, but having an actual number was almost too much to bear. Judging by the statistics, it was clear that kids had an especially low survival rate.

Vegas had begun sending out rescue teams to try to find as many as possible, but the empire had a significant head start since they'd had access to scrying magic from the beginning. Not to mention multiple aircraft bases throughout the world.

Trying not to think about it, he took his hat off and dropped into the limo's driver's seat.

"Hey." Becca was already sitting on the passenger side, as if waiting for him.

"Jesus." Mason jumped, hitting the car's horn by accident, not expecting the sudden vampire jump-scare.

"Shit, sorry." She leaned across the center console to place a hand on his leg. "I wasn't even doing anything spooky."

Mason took a few deep breaths to recover. "I thought you were with Graves."

"Nope. We finished up for the day." She leaned back into her seat. "I figured you might want some company."

"You sure? I thought you were trying to avoid missions?" he asked, unsure how he felt about taking her with him after she'd decided to live a normal life.

She shrugged. "I wouldn't call this a mission. Besides, there's still a couple of hours of daylight and I gained enough mana last night to get me close to full. So I should be safe to be around right now. And I've been cooped up too much lately. I'm about to go crazy if I don't get out."

"Okay." He let out a long sigh and pulled the lever that raised the limo off the deck.

"That was a heavy sigh." Becca eyed him sideways.

"What? Sorry." He stepped on the floor pedal, feeling the car tug on his mana as it began to move. "I just have a lot on my mind."

"You want to talk about it?" Her tone grew sympathetic.

"No, it's okay." He brought the car around to head toward their destination.

The store in question was a little over twenty minutes away from the ship. The rest of the descent was spent in awkward silence.

If he was being honest, he didn't know what was bothering him. A part of him was glad that Becca had come, but he hadn't been doing a very good job of keeping her safe of late. She'd been rescuing him a lot ever since their time in the Vatican. On top of that, she had been starting to take more risks. He wasn't sure if he had a valid concern or if it was just his pride.

Bringing the limo down to land in front of an IKEA, he grabbed his hat off the dash and got out. "Why did Graves hit a furniture store?"

"They have a couple of bins full of stuffed animals in there. We can get a lot." Becca shielded her eyes from the sun as she got out.

"You sure you don't want to wait in the car?"

"I'm fine. After experiencing the hell that is the Florida sun, everywhere else doesn't bother me nearly as much." She lowered her hand to her side.

"It would be safer in the car, though." He put on his hat and tried not to make the offer sound like anything more than it was.

"No, I already scouted this whole place and Dig secured it. There's nothing to worry about. Plus, I wouldn't get to see my courageous cowboy boyfriend in action." She chuckled.

"Yeah, courageous, that's me." He let out another sigh only to immediately regret it.

"There's that sigh again." She slapped the roof of the car.

"I, ah." Mason tried to hide under the brim of his hat and headed for the store.

"I think I've passed my perception check here, so spit it out. What's bothering you?" The vampire followed him to the entrance.

"I'm not sure that's the best question to ask right now." He hesitated at the door. "We are about to walk into an IKEA and no couple gets out of there without getting in a fight."

Her face fell. "Wait, are we going to fight?"

"No." He walked in to escape the conversation.

It was hard enough to get oriented in an IKEA as it was. Now, with the lights off, the place was even more confusing. He pulled a headlamp attached to a strap and looped it around his hat to shed a little light on the situation.

"We're not in a fight, right?" Becca caught up to him.

"No, it was a joke." He looked in her direction, inadvertently shining his light in her eyes.

Becca hissed before covering her mouth and adding a quiet, "Sorry."

"It's okay. You can't help it."

She removed her hand from her mouth. "I know, but I'm trying."

"Are you though?" he asked without meaning for it to sound like an accusation.

"What's that supposed to mean?" Becca snatched a hand lantern from one of the store's checkout displays and ripped it open to install the batteries that came with it.

"It's not like that." Mason started walking in the direction that the arrows on the floor pointed. "I'm just worried about you. You've been getting caught in bad situations of late, and I just want to make sure you're safe."

"But in half of those situations, you needed help." She stared at him in confusion.

"I…" He trailed off.

She wasn't wrong. Hell, he'd practically begged her to save him in Florida. Granted, that wasn't that big of a threat. The only serious situation had been in the Vatican where she'd run off on her own and gotten herself involved with that Durand guy. She could have gotten herself killed and he wouldn't have known.

"Look, I'm just concerned that a lot of these things happen because you put yourself in danger just by going out in the field." He kept walking.

"It's not like I wanted to." She put her foot down. "And why are you following the arrows on the floor? The toy bins are at the end of the store's loop. It's not like there are other shoppers. No one is going to care if we go backward."

Mason looked down at one of the arrows on the floor, realizing how well society had trained him. "You're right. And let's just not talk about things now. I don't know why, but I'm having trouble putting my thoughts into words."

"I don't think so. We're in a fight now, buddy." The vampire stomped in the opposite direction of the arrows.

Mason let out another sigh and followed.

"And quit sighing," she shouted back.

It wasn't until they reached the lighting and wall art section of the store that the fight finally found a lull, and that was only because one of the displays had been thoroughly destroyed. A section of shelving lay in ruins, with picture frames and art prints of animals dressed in steampunk costumes littered the floor.

"Was the place like this when you and Graves were here before?" Mason held perfectly still.

Becca shook her head.

He immediately switched off his headlamp in case there was something in there with them. The store went dark again, the only light coming from the entrance in the distance.

"Can you see anything with your vampire senses?"

"Oh, so now you want me to use my abilities?" she hissed back. "And no, I can't. The sun is still up. I can't see shit."

"Jeez, what is going on with you?" Mason crept forward, finding another destroyed display and some knocked-over shelves.

"What do you mean, what's going on with me? What kind of question is that?" The vampire looked at him like he had three heads. "Are you trying to make things worse?"

He hesitated, wondering why he had asked the question. Even he knew it wasn't helping.

Mason shook his head. "You're right. That was a crappy thing to say."

"Fine," she huffed as she changed the subject. "Whatever came through here is big, and I don't want to run into it right now."

"Why don't you head back to the car? I'll check it out." Mason continued deeper into the store.

"Are you insane? You're only level twenty-five, that's nowhere near high enough to handle something big on your own."

"I don't intend to fight it." He didn't stop. "I just want to see what it is."

That was when he noticed something moving further away. He squinted, unable to make out the details in the dark. From what he could tell, it was lying across the top of a shelf. The dark shape swelled up and down as if breathing. Beyond that, it didn't move an inch.

"I think it's sleeping."

"How could it be? Neither revenants nor zombies sleep," Becca argued.

"Maybe it's just dormant then?" Mason checked his mana.

"Give me your gun," Becca whispered, holding out a hand. "I can't use magic right now."

Mason glanced down at the pistol holstered at his side, wishing he'd brought a rifle too. He had magic, but he still fell back on his firearms training more often than not. Spells still didn't feel natural to him and as a result, his were still underpowered. The only reason he'd reached level twenty-five had been because he'd been in covens with Becca and Graves.

To make matters worse, the Heretic Seed hadn't offered him a new class at level fifteen as it had for most people. He was pretty sure it was because he hadn't ranked up his spells enough to access a more specialized class. Instead, the Seed had unlocked the rest of the mage class's starting spells, as if trying to give an option that he felt more comfortable with.

He hadn't gotten any of them past rank C. Most of his spells were still stuck at D.

Despite that, he pulled his pistol from his holster and handed it over. He felt exposed as soon as he did.

"You really need to start using magic more," Becca commented, picking up on his apprehension.

"I know, I'm still getting used to it." He checked his mana.

MP: 283/283

Hopefully, it was enough.

"We should head back and return with a full coven." Becca stepped away.

"It doesn't look that big," Mason said, surprising himself.

He wasn't a coward, but he wasn't stupid either. He knew better than to try to approach the creature. That was the wrong move from a tactical standpoint. Despite that, every instinct he had was telling him to get closer.

"Big or not, we don't know what that is," Becca hissed back in the dark.

The urge to turn his headlamp back on in defiance passed through his head. He shook it off as soon as he had it. He wasn't even sure why he was mad, but it seemed like his every impulse was dead set on aggravating the vampire beside him. Was he really that upset with the risks she'd been taking, or was it something else? Either way, he couldn't let his emotions put them both at risk.

Stamping down the urge to antagonize his girlfriend, he nodded. "You're right, let's sneak out of here."

"Finally." Becca took a step back just as a crunching sound came from under her boot.

"What?" Mason looked down to find glass glinting on the tile floor.

A nearby display of lamps had been knocked over.

"Damn, I think you stepped on a light bulb." Mason cringed.

Then he stepped on another.

"Shit, stop walking." Becca snapped her head back to the creature on top of the shelf.

It hadn't seemed to notice them.

"Okay, new plan." Mason slid his feet along the floor without picking them up. "We shuffle our way out."

"Are you serious?" Becca started to argue, only to flinch when the creature in the dark let out a heavy huff.

"Okay fine, we shuffle." The vampire slid herself around and started dragging her boots through the broken glass.

They both froze as the sound of something moving came from behind. Mason ducked his head, realizing that it sounded much larger than he'd thought it was. Turning back to see, he found that the shelf that the monster had been lying on was no shelf at all. No, the entire thing was the monster.

"I'm going to regret this." He flipped on his headlamp.

The creature knew they were there, so why not shed a little light on the situation?

Mason's bladder threatened to release as a beast larger than any he'd ever seen stretched out across the furniture store. At first glance, it had traits of a revenant bloodstalker, but somehow it was even larger. Its body was thicker and longer, with a tail extending from the back.

The thing must have been over fifty feet long.

The rest of the creature appeared mismatched. Its body might have been massive, but its limbs were still the same size as a regular bloodstalker. A pair of small wings sat atop its back, clearly unable to carry the weight of the beast below them. If anything, the thing looked half-formed.

Then it turned to face them.

A ten-foot-long neck dragged its head around as if having trouble holding it up. Its nose resembled the same bat-like snout as any other revenant, but that was where the similarities ended. Instead, it was elongated, like the face of a T-Rex.

"What the hell is that?" Becca's eyes widened.

The Heretic Seed tried to answer the question.

Revenant ??????, Dormant, Hostile

The beast opened its mouth, revealing a set of jaws large enough to chomp down someone as large as Jameson in one bite. Mason braced himself as the unknown revenant roared. A blast of hot breath slammed into him, nearly knocking him over. Both ears rang like a bomb had gone off.

Becca raised her pistol and fired a few rounds straight into the soft tissue of the beast's mouth.

It reeled back, dragging its massive head across the floor and destroying several displays with its tail. Cheap lamps flew through the air, crashing to the floor in a shower of inexpensive decor.

"Come on!" Becca grabbed his shoulder.

Mason could hardly hear her over the ringing in his ears. She didn't need to tell him twice. He started running, casting two Icicles behind him followed by a Lightning Bolt. He wasn't sure if any of his spells would hurt the thing, but it was worth a try.

Glancing back, the beast thrashed like a crocodile before dragging its head back around to lock its eyes on them. It crouched down close to the floor and shoved off all at once to launch its serpent-like body. From there, it slithered toward them while occasionally kicking with its undersized limbs to maintain speed.

"It's gaining on us." Mason snapped his head forward, the light of the store's entrance shining in the distance.

Becca looked as well. "We're not going to make it."

The sound of shelves and affordable furniture splintering grew louder from behind, the floor vibrating with every stomp of the beast's feet. Running in a straight line wasn't going to work. Not unless they wanted to get trampled.

Mason reached out and grabbed Becca's shoulder to pull her to the side. She didn't fight him. They may have been in the middle of an argument, but they still knew how to work together in a crisis.

They veered to the left, away from the entrance.

The enormous revenant plowed through the space where they'd been, pushing its head forward as it chomped at the air. When it realized it had missed them, it simply stopped running, its momentum forcing it into a slide as it turned sideways. Its tail took out half the tables in the cafeteria before rolling into a wall. The entire store shook from the impact, the ceiling fixtures rattling overhead.

The creature may have been dormant, but it was still unbelievably strong. The thought of what would have happened had they stumbled across it at night sent a wave of terror down Mason's spine.

"We need a plan." He let go of Becca's shoulder.

"We've got to get off the floor," she suggested.

The sound of furniture and debris crashing from behind told him that the revenant was getting ready to start the chase again. Mason looked back just as it launched itself after them.

"We need to find a back door. There should be a ton of fire exits. I don't think that thing will follow us outside."

"Good luck finding one. There's so many shelves and fake rooms in here that I don't even know where the outer wall is." Becca was beginning to gasp for air.

It may have been dark in the store, but the sun was still up outside, flooding the place with plenty of life essence to disrupt her body's systems.

"I'm starting to wish you brought the chipmunk costume," Mason joked as he ran.

"That's not funny," Becca snapped back before thrusting a finger out at a sign that read, restroom. "What about a bathroom? The outer walls are cement, I doubt that thing can get us in there."

"And get trapped? No way." Mason passed right by.

They continued, falling into the path that had been laid out by the store's designers. The arrows on the floor pointed them further into the labyrinth. Looping around the bedroom section, they put a wall of tiny yet efficient mocked-up rooms between them and the creature. Mason started to relax as soon as it was out of sight.

The beast simply burst through the display, crushing particle board in its teeth.

"Holy hell!" Mason quoted Digby as they ran faster.

He held out a hand to help keep the exhausted vampire from falling behind. Becca took it, but it was clear she couldn't keep up the pace. Even he was gasping for breath. To make matters worse, he hadn't seen a back door anywhere.

Passing another restroom sign, he gave in. "Fine, the bathroom it is."

Veering to the right, he headed for a narrow hallway hidden between two kitchen displays. The familiar pattern of cinderblocks covered the walls around it. Hopefully, it would be enough to hold the revenant at bay.

Becca fell as soon as they made it inside, landing on her knees a dozen feet from the hallway's entryway. Mason kept hold of her hand and dropped down beside her. They both slid straight past the men's room door to stop just before reaching the women's restroom.

Letting go of the vampire's hand, he spun on his rear and prepared to launch a spell. The enormous revenant's head crashed into the hall, its jaws snapping at everything in its path. Mason raised his feet just in time to plant his boots on the creature's snout. He kicked himself away another few feet just as the beast's shoulders hit the sides of the narrow hall. Its progress halted in an instant, leaving it snapping at the five feet of space between them.

"Leave us alone!" Becca shoved Mason's pistol in the thing's face.

The revenant chomped its jaws shut just as she fired, the bullets slamming into its hide. The creature didn't even react. Its skin might as well have been made of Kevlar. Becca pumped off another two rounds before the gun's slide locked back, empty.

Mason tensed his jaw trying to combat the ringing in his ears as the gunshots reverberated off the cement walls. All he could smell was smoke. With few options available, he raised a hand and cast Icicle, sending a frozen spike into the revenant's jaws. It chomped it to pieces before it had a chance to pierce anything. He cast a Lightning Bolt next.

This time, the beast recoiled.

"Come on!" Becca was already pulling open the door of the lady's room. She flattened up against the wall as soon as she was inside.

Mason slipped in past her, leaving the roaring behemoth behind. "That thing's not giving up."

"Give me another clip." Becca ejected the pistol's spent magazine and held out a hand to him.

He reached for the ammo pouches on his belt and pulled out a fresh one. "Actually, clip is the wrong word."

"What?" She angled her head to the side and narrowed her eyes.

"I just mean that magazine is the right term. If it didn't have a spring in there, then clip would be right, but it does, so..." He trailed off, unsure why he had even said the useless fact in the first place.

"Did you seriously just umm, actually, me? Now of all times?" The vampire snatched the magazine from his hand and reloaded the gun. "You sound like one of those gun bros that correct people on the internet whenever they say anything slightly inaccurate. No one cares what it's called. There's plenty of words that are used wrong because everyone knows what they mean." She leaned out the door and unloaded the gun into the creature's face, this time landing a few into the inside of its mouth.

After that, it pulled its head out of the hallway and resorted to clawing at the cinderblocks beyond it. Becca stood in the doorway panting, a combination of stress, exhaustion, and anger showing on her face.

Mason took a step back from the door, unsure what was happening. He'd meant the comment as a joke, but couldn't believe he'd thought it was a good idea in the current situation. It was like something was clouding his judgment.

"What is that monster?" Becca brought things back to the problem at hand.

"I don't know." Mason took off his hat and set it down on one of the bathroom sinks so that the headlamp didn't shine in Becca's eyes. She'd dropped her light during the chase. "The Seed didn't know what the thing was either."

"I know." She stomped across the room. "How could the Seed not know?"

"Maybe we didn't get a good enough look."

"Obviously we did, or it wouldn't have even tried labeling it," she snapped back.

Mason flinched but passed off the hostility to the stress of the situation. "Maybe the Seed doesn't know because that revenant hasn't finished evolving."

"What the hell does that mean?" She glared at him for a second before her expression shifted into one of recognition. "That's it. There must be a higher tier than bloodstalker. That rev must have come in here to hide while it changed. We just walked in on it before it was done."

"That's what I was saying. The Seed probably can't tell what that rev is going to become yet." Mason's mouth fell open as soon as the words left his mouth. "Wait, if that thing is still evolving, what the hell is it going to be when it's finished?"

"Don't look at me." Becca threw up her arms. "It looked like a bloodstalker that someone stretched out."

"Shit, I knew we shouldn't have hid in a bathroom." Mason leaned against the wall and placed the back of his head against the tile. "We're going to be trapped in here until that thing finishes changing."

"Oh, don't start blaming me. It was hide in the bathroom or get eaten." She punctuated her argument with a vampiric hiss.

This time, he was pretty sure it had been on purpose.

"Are you going to do that every time we get in a fight now?" Mason held both hands up in a mock impression of Nosferatu.

"Oh, I'm sorry, I wouldn't want to make you uncomfortable." She folded her arms and turned around. "Sorry I had to go and die and fuck everything up."

"You didn't fuck anything up…" Mason let the sentence fade, unsure what to say to her.

He wasn't even sure why they were fighting. So many emotions were swirling around inside him. There was so much guilt and frustration, all of it bubbling over to make things worse.

Then it hit him.

Without hesitation, he crossed the room to throw his arms around her.

"Hey? What are you—" Becca started to squirm.

"Stop talking." He squeezed her tighter.

She was so tense. The muscles in her back were stretched taut like a rubber band about to snap. Letting his head rest against her shoulder, he could hear her heart racing.

She stopped struggling. "If you think a hug is going to fix things, you—"

"Shh. Just take a moment." He held her until she began to relax, only speaking when her heart rate fell back to normal. "None of this is our fault."

Becca scoffed. "Well, it's sure as hell someone's fault."

He let her go. "No, it's not."

She turned back around but kept her arms folded tight. "What are you even talking about?"

Mason could see the flicker of annoyance in her eyes just as he could feel the frustration burning in his chest. They'd calmed down, but it wouldn't last. He had to explain things quickly.

"I know everything seems bad, and we're both mad at each other right now." Mason raised both hands between them. "But we're not really. And we don't want to fight."

"No shit. No one wants to fight." Becca groaned back. "Can you at least try to make sense?"

"I know how this sounds, but it isn't us causing this." He struggled to find the right words.

"Then who is it?" She stared at him expectantly.

Mason held one hand out toward the wall and uttered the craziest accusation of his life. "It's IKEA."

CHAPTER TWENTY-SEVEN

"What do you mean, it's IKEA's fault?" Becca stared at her frustrating boyfriend in complete and total confusion.

Mason's eyes darted around wildly. "Think about it. We have been at each other's throats ever since we set foot in this building, and it's been getting worse by the second."

He wasn't wrong, but that had been because he kept sighing and saying dumb shit.

"You can't just blame us fighting on IKEA."

"Of course I can." He threw both hands up. "If the state of Florida can have its own enchantments, then why not IKEA? Hell, you are planning to dress up like an elf to help Graves gain the powers of Santa Claus. We live in a crazy ass world, and everyone knows IKEA is a relationship deathtrap. What if that belief is powerful enough to manifest an enchantment, and that is the reason we're fighting? This place just takes whatever problems we have and blows them way out of proportion."

Becca opened her mouth to argue, but he placed a finger over her lips.

"Just think about it before getting mad." He immediately removed his finger, clearly realizing that he was only making things worse. "We can't let IKEA win."

Becca felt like she might explode at any second. Then, she tensed and swallowed the hostility back down. "Fine, I suppose that's a possibility."

"Good." Mason exhaled. "I think we need to think really hard about how we react. Okay?"

"And what we say." She eyed him, implying that he'd not chosen his words well before.

Mason looked like he might argue but seemed to stop himself. "Okay. We can do this."

Less than ten seconds went by before things got started again.

"So what's your problem?" Becca asked, unable to forget about a detail he'd mentioned. "You said this enchantment might be blowing our problems out of proportion." She gritted her teeth and decided to be honest. "I know what my problem is. I'm afraid that my becoming a vampire is too big of a change to make things work between us. But what's the issue that you're dealing with?"

"I don't think now is the time to talk about it." He seemed to be trying his best to table the conversation.

Becca couldn't accept that. "I don't think I can let this go."

"That's IKEA talking."

"No, it's not." She rolled her eyes. "And even if it was, wouldn't it be best to get this out of the way so that there will be nothing left to fight about?"

"Alright, fine." Mason let out a frustrated growl. "I feel like I can't protect you."

Becca frowned at the ridiculous concern. "You don't have to protect me."

"I know, I know. But I want to be there for you." He let his eyes fall to the floor. "I just keep thinking back to when you came back from the dead. You were stuck all by yourself with no backup in D.C. And I did nothing. I didn't even try to get to you. I just followed orders and helped Graves with his airship fleet."

"That's stupid." Becca huffed. "Staying was the right choice. If you had come after me alone, you probably would have died or been captured. Even if you had brought a coven, you would have put them in danger. Even worse, coming after me would have put everyone back in Vegas at risk, because it would have increased the chances of Autem finding out where the Heretics were hiding. You followed orders because you're a good soldier and you understood what was best."

"I was in the army for less than a year. I'm no soldier."

"I don't care how long it was." She threw up her hands. "You have always been able to look at the larger picture and put your emotions aside to make the right decision. That's one of the things I love about you. You're reliable, and I know I can trust you. More often than not, you're a voice of reason. Which is something we desperately need with Digby in charge. So stop feeling shitty about all that. There's no reason for it."

"I know." He sighed.

"There's that sigh again."

"I was sort of happy when you said you wanted to try to live a normal life. I thought maybe that would be a new chapter for us where I didn't have to worry about you." He glanced up at her. "It doesn't look like that's going to happen though."

"Yeah, I know." Becca deflated. "I thought that was what I wanted, but now I'm not sure. I think I was just afraid of what I'd become. I thought that if I could pretend I wasn't a monster, I could be happy."

"And are you happy?" He looked like he was bracing for impact.

"I don't know. Being cooped up in the ship isn't great, and I miss being out at night." She stared up at the ceiling. "I think Dig might have been right." She snapped her gaze back down to him. "And don't you dare tell him I said that."

Mason held up a hand in defense. "I won't."

Becca settled down. "I lived for years, content to be locked in a room, to see the world through a monitor, and even when I was free, I hid in closets and put up walls around myself. Now that I'm strong enough to go where I want, I don't want to go back. I don't want to hide in closets anymore."

It was something she'd been thinking about ever since the Vatican. She had been tested then. She'd even hit rock bottom, forced to lick blood off the floor of the Pope-mobile for a few points of mana. The crazy thing was, that was when things started to change for her. As a human, she should have been ashamed of herself. Yet, she wasn't. Instead, she felt free. Like she'd finally shrugged off a weight that had been threatening to drag her down.

Becca ran her tongue across her fangs, surprised at how comfortable they felt in her mouth even with the slight lisp they caused. "I still don't know how to deal with my mana problems, but I think I might actually be happier as a monster."

"That's where you're wrong." Mason took a step closer.

"I thought we were going to think before speaking." She barely looked at him.

"What I mean is, you aren't a monster."

"I rip people's throats open with my teeth and eat their souls." She bared her fangs.

"That might be, but that's just the world we live in now." He placed his hands on her shoulders. "People and monsters aren't really that different. And there's no reason why they can't live together."

"I know. And I think I've come to terms with that. I won't go out on missions when I'm low on mana, but if I have enough, then I want to use it." She looked down at her hands, feeling her conflicted mana system flowing through her body. "I know it's not what you want to hear, but there will be times when what I need most is for you to stay home."

"Alright," he grunted. "I hate it. But I can deal with it."

All Becca wanted to do was to tell him to shut up and stop being such a guy about it. She was pretty sure that was IKEA talking. Instead, all she said was, "I'm sorry."

"Me too." He forced a smile. "I think I just feel a little left behind. It's like you said. When we met, you were hiding in closets. Now you're the most lethal person I know."

"Yeah, that part's hard to get used to." She let a chuckle slip out.

He laughed as well. "I guess you could always turn me into a vampire and we could be dangerous together."

"That's not even funny." She swiped a hand through the air, clawing back some of the hostility.

"I just mean you wouldn't have to worry about attacking me if I was like you."

"I can't just start turning everyone that I'm close to into vampires because I'm afraid of attacking them. I have to learn to control myself. I know I'm not there yet, but I can get there." Becca folded her arms.

"Alright, I get it." He stepped away. "Making me a vampire is a bad idea. I was mostly joking anyway."

"Well, stop joking. It keeps getting you in trouble." She held a hand out toward him. "And what makes you think you could handle being a vampire when you're still afraid of using your own magic?"

Mason sucked air through his teeth as if he'd just been kicked in the shin. "Ouch. But that is a fair point."

"You know what?" Becca held out a hand. "Give me the rest of your magazines. No more guns for you. I'm throwing you in the deep end so you can swim your way out."

"Don't you mean clips?" He smirked.

"Do you really want to make that comment?"

His smirk fell. "No. That was IKEA talking."

"I bet." Becca narrowed her eyes.

"Either way, we're going to need to find a way out of here." Mason headed to the door and leaned out.

Becca hung her head out beside him. "That's one thing we don't have to argue about."

The half-formed beast was still wandering around just beyond the hall.

She leaned back in. "It's no good. I'll never make it past that thing during the day."

"Alright." Mason stepped away from the door, suddenly looking serious. "If you can't make it, I'll have to come back with help."

"Wait, what? You're not going out there alone," Becca argued.

"That's our only option. You could barely keep up with me out there. The best choice is for you to stay here while I make a run for the car. I think I can make it without—"

"Without me slowing you down." Becca finished his sentence for him.

"Don't make it sound like that. We have to be realistic. You might be unstoppable at night, but you need to take a step back during the day."

"I am being realistic." A sudden urge to shout swelled, but Becca swallowed it down. "With or without me slowing you down, that thing will still catch you. Making a run is suicide."

"I know it's a bad option, but it's the only one we have. Hopefully, I can sneak past it while its back is turned."

"And if you can't?"

"Then we hope for the best." He shrugged.

"That's stupid," she spat back.

"If you have a better idea, I'm listening."

"Of course, I have a better idea." She swiped a hand through the space between them, before letting a lengthy pause pass.

"And that is?"

"I'm thinking." Becca glanced around the room before defaulting to the only option she had. "We wait until nightfall when I'm stronger. Shit, I could probably carry you out of here if I have to."

"No way." Mason shook his head. "That thing might finish evolving by then and become something much worse. Even if it doesn't, it'll still be faster at night. Without me there to slow you down, I'd say you'd make it. But together nothing is certain."

"Then I'll use my shadows to distract the rev while we make a break for it." She tried again.

Mason seemed to consider it for a second. "It's still too big of a risk."

"So is going out there now."

"I know." He turned toward the door. "But if we wait for nightfall, it will be too late. If I try now and don't make it, you can still wait for dark and escape on your own." A somber tone entered his voice. "This is something I have to do. I have to make sure you can escape."

"No, you don't." Becca grabbed hold of his coat. "We just talked about this. You don't need to save me."

"I know what I said." He didn't turn to look at her. "But that doesn't change the fact that I want to save you."

"I won't let you go." Becca shook her head frantically.

He didn't stand a chance out there.

He had to know that.

Mason gently placed his hand on hers before prying her fingers loose. "The sun is still up, so you can't actually stop me."

Her heart ached as he stepped toward the door again. Everything she said pushed him further away. She wasn't sure if the store's enchantment was the problem or she just couldn't find the right words. Hell, she wasn't even sure if there was an enchantment. In the end, all she could do was throw her arms around him.

"Hey." Mason tensed as she held him.

She whispered in his ear, "I trust you to make the right decision. All I ask is that you believe in me in return."

"I…" He started to argue.

"If you go alone, my safety will be secure, but you'll probably die. If we wait and go together, neither of us will be safe, but we both have a chance of getting out. Given those options, I want to choose the one that has a better chance of us staying together." She squeezed him tighter. "So stay with me."

Mason remained where he was for a long moment as if debating the choice.

Eventually, the tension melted from his body.

"Damn. You're right." He rubbed at his eyes. "I swear, this enchantment is messing with me. Everything you say makes me want to do the opposite."

Becca finally let him go. "You know, we don't really know if there is an enchantment in play."

Mason turned to glower at her. "There has to be. Neither of us is this bad at communicating. And we both have better judgment."

"Either way, we can get through this." Becca checked the time on her phone. "We just have to wait an hour and a half."

"What do you want to do until then?"

"Anything that doesn't involve us fighting." She stared up at the ceiling before letting her gaze fall back to him.

"I can think of something." He pumped his eyebrows just in case he wasn't being obvious enough.

Becca rolled her eyes. "We're not having sex in an IKEA bathroom, Mason."

A sheepish expression took over his face. "Ah yeah, I realized that was the wrong suggestion as soon as I said it."

Becca eyed him for a few seconds. "Okay, I'm going to blame IKEA for that one."

"Thanks." Mason chuckled. "I guess we can just play the quiet game. Can't fight if we don't talk, right?"

"Good point." Becca nodded, finally finding something they could agree on.

Only five minutes of silence passed before she yelled at him for breathing too loud. He immediately criticized her for biting her nails in return. After that, they resigned to hiding in the bathroom stalls to keep out of each other's way. Becca remained there until she felt her body begin to purge itself of life essence. Her magic and abilities returned soon after.

"Okay, it's now or never." She stepped out of her stall.

"What's the plan?" Mason emerged from his as well, buckling his belt.

"Did you just use the bathroom in there?"

He looked back at the stall. "It's a toilet. And we've been here a while."

Becca immediately cursed her returning vampiric senses. "You couldn't have waited until we returned to the airship?"

"Not when I might have to run from that revenant out there." He did a little jig. "This way I'm in better shape to maneuver."

"I don't suppose you're planning on washing your hands?" She arched an eyebrow.

"Oh..." He trailed off, pointing to the row of sinks. "The water doesn't work."

Becca pulled a bottle of water from a pocket in the hoodie she wore. With that, he was able to lather and rinse using the soap dispenser.

"Happy, now?" He dried his hands on his pants.

"Thrilled." Becca shook her head.

"Great, now what's the plan?"

"First I have to scout." Becca braced for the inevitable and cast Shade Projection.

Mason stood unsuspecting as the headlamp illuminating the space began to flicker and an inky darkness gathered behind him to form the shape of a woman. The shade's hair drifted up, as if burning with a black flame of gloom while clouds of shadow drifted around it.

"Jesus!" Mason leapt three feet in the air when he noticed the shade standing behind him. "Do you have to do that?"

"Actually, I do." Becca didn't apologize. "Most of my magic requires the intent to scare someone. And you're the only one here."

Unlike her previous projection spell, which cut off her control over her real body while active, the death mana version just created a shade that moved according to her will. She could still use it to see, hear, and speak, making it perfect for scouting an area or distracting an enemy. The fact that it still allowed her real body to move meant it could also be used on the fly in the middle of battle without leaving herself vulnerable.

Closing her eyes, her view shifted to the shade's point of view from where it stood behind Mason. She could see herself standing further away by the bathroom door. Of course, she immediately caught her boyfriend looking at the shade's chest.

Becca cracked one eye open, giving herself a view from two different angles at once. "Did you just check out my projection?"

"Maybe." He pointed to her shadow form. "Your shade's naked. You know that, right?"

Becca opened her other eye to stare at the projection. There was some resemblance to her, and occasionally the shadows drifting around it cleared enough to make out a curve here and there. She willed the projection to turn around, groaning when Mason looked at its butt.

"What? I am a simple man." He shrugged as he turned back to face her.

"That's the truth." She smirked as she willed the projection to give him a gentle pat on the ass.

"Hey now!" He jumped forward.

"Did I forget to mention that this version of the spell can touch things if I want it to?"

"Really?" He looked back to the shade, then back at her, then back at the shade again. "You know what would probably work?"

"I'm going to stop you there before you make any suggestions that might incriminate you further." She willed the shade to walk toward the door and closed her eyes to switch to its point of view.

From there, she crept out of the bathroom hallway and into the store. Her shade's eyesight was a little better than hers had been earlier. It wasn't long before she spotted the revenant. How could she not? The thing had nearly doubled in size. Despite that, it still looked awkward and partially formed. Its limbs hadn't grown much.

Becca cracked an eye open to see Mason standing in front of her in the bathroom. "We might have gotten lucky. I don't think this thing can carry its own weight. I'm terrified of what it will become later, but it shouldn't be able to maneuver well until it finishes its evolution."

"I guess it's good that we waited then," he said begrudgingly.

Becca resisted the urge to say she'd told him so and continued to scout.

The rev was still resting, probably to save its energy for the metamorphosis it was going through. Thankfully, her shade was barely noticeable in the dark of the store, allowing her to stroll past the beast to find the best path out of there. The bathroom was at the halfway point in the middle of the customer loop. That put them somewhere in the kitchen department.

Going back the way they had come was out of the question. The destruction caused by the previous chase had strewn pieces of furniture all over, making it treacherous to travel through in the dark. They wouldn't make it a dozen feet without one of them tripping over something. There was no choice but to follow the rest of the pathway to its end. With a little luck, they could grab a couple of the stuffed toys that they had come for on the way out.

The tricky part was going to be getting through the cafeteria. Their chase earlier had passed through there as well, making the terrain just as difficult as the other direction. The only advantage was that there was slightly less ground to cover. She managed to find a back door as well, but it was locked.

As soon as she was done scouting, she headed back to where the revenant was still resting and cracked an eye open to check on Mason.

"You ready?"

"As I'll ever be."

"Okay, I'm going to use my Banshee ability to get the rev's attention. Then I'm going to lead it away. Go when I say so, and move carefully. Don't run unless it starts chasing us. And be extra careful when we hit the cafe, the floor is littered with broken furniture."

"Anything else?" Mason picked his hat and headlamp up off the sink where he'd set them down earlier and put them back on his head.

"Yes. Try to grab a blahaj on the way out."

"I don't know what that is." He stared at her blankly.

"It's a stuffed shark. We're going to pass by a bin of them."

"I'll try to pick one up, then." Mason turned off his headlamp to let their eyes adjust to the dark.

Becca closed her eyes again and willed her projection to head toward the furthest point she could find from both the bathroom and the path they had to take. Then, using her shade as a source, she used her Banshee ability to let out a bloodcurdling scream,

The revenant reacted instantly, raising its awkward head and hefting its body up to investigate. She had been right. Despite no longer being dormant, its mobility was still impaired. It wasn't exactly slow, but it couldn't launch its body the way it had before. Instead, it traveled at a moderate yet unstoppable waddle, crashing straight through anything in its path.

Becca resisted the urge to cancel her projection and kept her Banshee going. Even as the beast plowed toward her, she waited. Instinctively bracing for impact, she held her ground as the revenant's jaws closed around her shade. She snapped her eyes open in the same instant.

"Let's go." Becca racked the slide of the pistol Mason had given her.

He motioned to take the lead but stopped at the door to let her go first.

Becca slipped past him, appreciating the lack of arguing. From there, they moved quickly but kept quiet. The revenant was only a hundred feet away, but it was too busy thrashing around in search of the prey that had vanished to notice them. The sound of hollow furniture splintering echoed through the store. Becca could still feel the vibrations of the creature's movements through the floor even as they approached the end of the display area.

Reaching out, she snagged a stuffed toy as she passed the bin of plush sharks. Mason grabbed one as well and tucked it under one arm. At least they weren't leaving completely empty-handed. Everything was going smoothly until they reached the cafeteria.

"Shit." She nearly lost her footing after stepping on what remained of a plastic chair. Flicking a point of mana into her agility, she was able to stop herself from falling.

"Woah." Mason struggled to find somewhere stable to put his foot down as he climbed over a broken table. When it became clear he wasn't going to make it without more light, he turned on his head lamp. Another few seconds went by before the distant thrashing behind them began to grow louder.

"It's coming, move." Becca leaned into her agility and leapt across the debris.

Mason simply launched himself forward over a downed table, using the stuffed shark he carried to cushion his fall. The entire store rumbled as the creature behind them began to catch up. An earsplitting roar announced its arrival.

Becca threw out a hand toward Mason as he lay on the ground amidst what was left of a few plastic chairs. She yanked him up to his feet the instant he grabbed hold. They made a break for the warehouse near the exit just as the beast plowed into the cafeteria behind them. Turning briefly, Becca flicked her pistol in its direction to fire half a magazine.

Mason fired bolt after bolt of lightning at the same time.

Bullets thumped into the beast's hide as electricity arced across its body.

It flinched but didn't slow down.

Giving up on hurting the monstrosity, Becca used her Banshee to let out another scream from someplace behind it. The revenant turned for a few seconds, but quickly returned its attention to them.

It was enough time to sprint through the checkout area and into the warehouse.

Becca slowed as the size of the place gave her reason to pause. She had never gone furniture shopping before, so she'd never realized there was so much to choose from. Before her, rows of shelves stretched out from a center aisle like the ribs of a skeleton, standing over twenty feet tall.

"We're almost there!" Mason shouted as the exit came into view at the other end.

"I swear I am never going furniture shopping again." Becca held the stuffed shark under her arm tight as she ran into the center aisle.

The half-formed revenant crashed through the registers behind them, sending coins sprinkling to the cement floor of the warehouse. Next, it rammed its massive body straight into the open pathway down the middle. The beast came to a stop immediately when its shoulders got stuck. Still, it thrashed and roared, unwilling to give up. The sound of creaking metal followed.

Becca looked back in horror as the shelves beside the beast began to buckle. They were coming down. At first, they fell slowly, tipping over to rest against the next aisle. Then those shelves began to give way as well. Another row crashed into the next, then another. A chorus of creaking steel merged with the furious roar of the revenant that had wedged itself in the middle.

"Holy shit, run for your life!" Becca shouted as the shelves came down behind them in a tsunami of affordable furniture.

She unloaded her pistol into the glass doors ahead just before jumping through them. Mason followed just as the final aisle collapsed. Boxes of hollow desktops and particle board rained down like a cave-in. Becca kept running straight for the limo only to realize that no one was behind her. Spinning back around, she found Mason standing by the exit doors that they had just jumped through.

"What are you doing?" she called to him in astonishment.

"I have to check something." He raised his hand to the building's threshold.

"That revenant is coming," she argued back.

Mason leaned to the side to look in through the door. "I don't think so. It looks like it's trapped under the shelving."

Becca slowed to a stop. "Okay, but hurry up, now is not the time to get cocky."

Mason didn't answer. Instead, he just stood there, staring blankly at the empty space in front of him with his hand on the store's entrance. "You're going to want to see this."

Becca hesitated, still afraid that the beast inside might come crashing through the broken doors at any second. When it didn't, she loosened her grip on the stuffed shark under her arm and crept back toward her boyfriend. The beast continued to roar from within as the sound of thrashing rumbled through the warehouse. Despite its fury, it didn't seem to be getting closer.

Stepping beside Mason, she raised her hand to the threshold. Her mouth fell open a moment later.

MASS ENCHANTMENT
Due to widely known beliefs or reputation, this land has gained a power of its own.
Occupant Requirement: This structure must be occupied by at least two or more conscious beings currently in a partnered relationship.
Area of Effect: All space within this structure's walls.

ENCHANTMENT EFFECTS:
THE TEST
Any conflict between a partnered couple will be subject to increased levels of hostility. This enchantment ends when the affected couple either resolves the original conflict, has

their bond damaged beyond repair, or escapes the area of effect. Few will survive this enchantment unscathed.

Good luck, you're going to need it.

"That's just wrong." Becca dropped her hand from the door, realizing that the anger she had been feeling was gone.

"True." Mason lowered his hand as well before turning to her. "But do you know what this means?"

"What?" She eyed him suspiciously.

"We beat IKEA." A smile spread across his face.

Becca couldn't help but smile back. "I guess we did."

Mason immediately threw his arms around her to pick her up off her feet and spin her around. "We won. We can survive anything!"

Becca laughed as the tension between them melted away. Then, she noticed something glowing from within the store over Mason's shoulder. Flicking a few points of mana into her vision, the glow focused into a burst of flame. She slapped him on the back when she realized it was getting closer. "Shit! Put me down."

"What?" He set her feet back on the pavement and turned.

"Run!" Becca was moving as soon as her boots touched the ground.

Mason scrambled to catch up just before a jet of flame sprayed from the store's exit, nearly consuming them both. It poured forth like the breath of a dragon as they dove into the limo's front seat and closed the doors.

"Where the hell did that fire come from?" Mason launched the car without hesitation.

"I think it came from the rev." Becca watched as the ground fell away, a jet of flame still pouring from the doors below. Seconds later, the entire front of the building was burning.

"Jesus, since when do they breathe fire?" Mason pulled the limo away and headed back for the airship.

"Since now?" Becca tore her attention away from the window.

"I don't want to run into that thing when it finishes evolving." Mason held tight to the steering wheel.

"Me either." Becca shoved the stuffed toy she'd escaped with through the open partition behind her.

Mason did the same. "This is going to be one hell of a story when Graves asks us why we only got two toys."

"True." Becca settled into her seat. "But there's something more important right now."

Mason calmed down a little. "And what's that?"

Becca turned her head to give him a smile, letting her fangs peek out. She wasn't sure if it was the relief at having escaped the store's enchantment or the knowledge that even under all that pressure, Mason had remained on her side. After everything that they had been through and how much things had changed, she could still count on him.

"What?" He looked to the side awkwardly when she didn't answer him right away.

"That was the worst fight we've had. And despite IKEA's best efforts, we survived it." Becca placed a hand on his leg. "I'm pretty sure the right thing to do now is make up."

He furrowed his brow. "What do you mean?"

She gave his leg a squeeze to explain.

Mason slowly turned to look at her before adding a quiet, "Oh."

CHAPTER TWENTY-EIGHT

"Let's see now."

Digby sat on a bench in the town of Jefferson, New Hampshire, surrounded by two dozen of his enhanced zombies, and pulled his phone from his pocket to look over his shopping list.

"Disguises. Done." He crossed the first item off with a stylus.

"Sleigh. In progress."

"List of the world's children. Also in progress."

"A containment system for toys. Again, in progress."

"Toys." He glanced over to the limo, sitting not far away with a stuffed shark sitting on the dash. "In progress."

Finally, he came to the last line.

"Reindeer." He raised his gaze to a sign in front of him. The words Santa's Village Reindeer Rendezvous were written across it. He grinned. "Soon."

Shockingly, finding animals to pull his sleigh had proven to be more difficult than he had thought. The first place they checked was a zoo in San Diego. Unfortunately, all of the animals there had been set free from their enclosures out of concern for their well-being. Once it had become clear that no one would be left to care for them in the apocalypse, an employee named Mitch had decided to release the animals to give them a fighting chance in the wild. Digby understood this because he had found Mitch's corpse, or at least, his name tag and a few scraps of uniform outside the lion's cage. It appeared he'd become a first meal to celebrate some of the zoo's inhabitants' newfound freedom.

During the search, they had nearly lost Alex when he stumbled upon a boa constrictor that was still living in the zoo's facilities. Digby had been there to pry the animal off the artificer, before dropping the extra-large snake into his void. It didn't make sense to waste the resources and he could always use new body configurations for his Body Craft. After that, they traveled to several more zoos throughout the country.

All came up empty.

Digby was starting to think he was going to have to get creative. Finding some ordinary deer probably wouldn't be too difficult. Perhaps that would be good enough, provided they didn't let anyone see them up close.

Hopefully, it wouldn't come to that.

Digby closed the notes application on his phone and shoved it back in his pocket before getting up off the bench. From there, he left his horde to stand guard while he followed the sign he'd been sitting by toward a barn.

Mason and Alex waited in front of the doors; one of Becca's drones hovered between them.

Digby clapped his hands to announce himself. "Alright, this is the last place that might have what we need. If we don't find some reindeer here, I'm going to have to start improvising."

"I'll just be happy as long as we don't run into any more snakes. That boa constrictor in San Diego almost squeezed me to death." Alex placed a hand around his throat as if reliving the memory.

"I don't think that will be a problem," Mason commented. "Not the right climate here. Besides, there are worse things than snakes."

"Indeed, and we shan't run afoul of any Florida zombies either." Digby waved away the conversation. "Now let's get inside, we don't have all day. Need I remind you we are currently on the continent's east coast along with Autem's capital? We don't want one of their patrols showing up to question what we are doing here."

"The door's locked." Becca's drone rotated to point its camera at a secured bolt. "We thought you could Decay your way through it."

"Why didn't you say so sooner?" He shoved his way past Alex and wrapped his hand around the bolt's lock. One Decay spell later, he tore it right off the doors.

Mason pulled them open after that.

Digby hesitated before going in.

It was too quiet.

The space inside was dark. The only light was the sun shining in behind him to cast his silhouette across the floor. Dead silence filled the barn. Then, a figure shuffled out from the shadows. They looked starving.

Common Zombie, Hostile

Digby cast Control without hesitation to calm the monster down. It must have been locked inside since the world ended. Mason and Alex were probably the first edible humans that it had seen. Digby ordered his new minion to go wait with the rest of his horde outside. Then he deflated.

There was no sign of the animals he required. If that barn had been sealed all month, the zombie inside would have gotten desperate and eaten the reindeer. Even if it hadn't, anything living would have starved to death weeks ago.

"Let's go." He turned around. "We're going to need a plan B."

He started to walk away, but Becca called out to stop him.

"Wait. There's something else in there."

Digby spun back around as the nose of an animal poked out from one of the barn's stalls to sniff around. The space was still dark, but after all the holiday movies he'd watched, he would have recognized a reindeer anywhere. Another nose appeared from a stall on the other side of the barn. Then another, and another.

"They're still alive," Mason said in disbelief.

"The zombie must not have touched them since they aren't human." Alex started walking in.

"Indeed, but how did they survive without anyone feeding them?" Digby followed him.

"Maybe someone put enough food in their stalls before locking the doors?" Alex stepped toward a stall with the name Dasher on it and held out a hand.

"Don't touch it!" Becca shouted from the speaker of her drone just as the reindeer tried to bite the artificer's fingers off.

"Wha!" Alex yanked his hand back.

That was when all of the animals started stamping at the walls. It sounded like a stampede of hooves, running up and down the sides of the building.

Digby cast Control along with Zombie Whisperer to quiet them down, understanding what they were from the milky white eyes in their heads.

"The hell was that about?" Mason remained in the doorway.

"They're all dead," Becca answered. "I turned on the drone's heat vision and they're all cold."

"Damn, zombie reindeer," Mason added.

"Ouch, right in my childhood." Alex placed a hand over his heart.

"I can't say I'm surprised." Digby strode into the barn. "Zombified animals are rare but we have seen them before."

Each stall was comprised of half walls that allowed for the animals to lean over. The zombie that had been locked inside with them must have bit one or more out of desperation. Yet, they had been unable to climb over the stall doors to finish the job. From there, the cursed reindeer reached over and bit their neighbors.

"I'd say this works out quite well for us." Digby ignored the looks of horror on the faces of his accomplices. "It is much easier to handle dead animals than live ones. I will just need to cast Control on them every hour to keep them from eating Alex."

"That's grim." Mason seemed to disapprove.

"So is this." Alex stood on his toes to look over the half door of the stall at the far end of the barn.

Digby joined him to find one of the animals lying dead on the floor. "It must have stayed far enough away from the others to not get bitten."

"We have another dead one here." Becca's drone floated into one of the stalls.

"Damn, there's one down here too." Mason peeked over one of the half walls near the entrance.

"No matter." Digby waved away their concern. "One of the advantages of being a necromancer is that death is not as big of a problem as it is for most."

Opening one of the stalls, he crouched down to inspect one of the corpses. It was in good shape. The Heretic Seed took things from there.

Corpse, quadruped. Cost to animate, 25 MP.
Animate corpse?

He shook his head, causing the question on his HUD to fade away. Then he opened his maw and swallowed the reindeer whole. It had been dead too long to be used as a resource, but it would be enough to teach him how the animals were built. Of course, there was a limit to how much inedible material he could take into his void, so he would have to spit the corpse back out later.

"What are you doing?" Mason leaned over him. "I thought you were going to animate them."

"I will for the other two. But I need to eat a regular corpse to understand their anatomy first. That way I can gain the knowledge to restore the rest of them to their peak physical condition." Digby turned to the other two corpses, this time accepting the animate messages that appeared across his vision. Both of the deceased reindeer began to twitch.

"Oh wow, this feels so wrong." Alex shuddered.

"Bah! Don't be so sentimental." Digby split his bond points across perception and intelligence for both of his new minions. Checking the names written on their stall doors he found one was called Comet and the other Vixen. "A pleasure to meet you both."

The reanimated reindeer both stomped one hoof on the floor

and lowered their heads as a feeling of hunger drifted across his bond along with a word.

Carrot?

"I'm afraid you don't eat those anymore, but we will get you some nice tasty revenants to eat as soon as we can." Digby patted Vixen on the head, receiving a feeling of gratitude from the monster.

"I hope Asher doesn't get jealous of your new pets." Alex chuckled.

"Of course not," Digby snapped back. "She knows her place will always be at my side. Though I do sort of regret leaving her up on the airship now."

Before anyone had a chance to say anything else, Becca's drone darted into the center of the barn.

"We have problems. There's five aircraft coming our way."

"Kestrels?" Mason rushed back to the door to look up at the sky.

The drone shook its camera back and forth. "No, they're owls, the mana-powered ones that they tried to attack Vegas with a couple of weeks ago. Jameson caught sight of them from up on the airship's deck. We have about a minute or two before they land."

Digby snapped his head back toward the door. "Damn, why would they be here? We haven't caused them any problems."

"It could be a patrol, like you said. Or they might have caught the airship on their satellite feeds," she guessed.

"That's not so bad." Alex joined Mason at the door. "We knew they'd see the ship eventually, and we haven't breached any of the treaty's agreements. They're probably just here to see what we're up to."

"How is that better?" Digby threw both arms out to the eight zombified reindeer. "Because we can't let them see this. For one, I have no idea whether or not they will consider what we're doing as hostile. And two, they are bound to have some questions that we can't answer right now without incriminating ourselves."

"Good point." Alex nodded. "We don't have a good reason to be making zombie reindeer. If they find out, it could tip off Henwick that we are setting up a mass enchantment."

"Okay, everything is going wrong. That much is obvious. But we need a plan, right now." Becca flicked her drone's camera back to Digby.

"I've got it." He rushed to the barn's doors and pulled them closed. Then he relaxed. "There, problem solved. We just wait until they leave." He stood still for a moment before remembering he'd left a horde of zombies standing guard outside. "No, that's a stupid idea."

"It's not your best." Becca's drone flew toward him. "They're not going to leave until they talk to someone, and they're probably going to watch us the entire time we're here. So we're going to have to do a lot more than just hide."

"I know I know, don't rush me." Digby swatted at the drone. "I just need time to think."

The otherworldly hum of mana-fueled aircraft came from the sky above to inform him that there wasn't any time left.

With that, Digby pulled the door back open and enacted the only plan he could. He stepped outside and glanced back to Mason, Alex, and the drone. "I will try to stall them. The rest of you, figure something out."

All three of them began arguing at once, but he closed the door before any of them could get more than a few words out. He might not have been able to come up with a way to hide the reindeer before Autem's aircraft landed, but between the three of them, he was pretty sure they could handle the task. If there was one thing he learned in the time since his death, sometimes the best option was to put his trust in others.

Clapping his hands, he drew the attention of his horde that stood waiting. Unfortunately, he didn't have time to do much else. The owls were already descending. Each of the aircraft rotated to face him, as if making sure to keep him in their sights. Thinking fast, he gestured to his zombies, telling them to line up facing the direction of the barn. He took a position in front of them facing the same way, hoping that by doing so, the empire's forces would follow his lead and set down in the opposite direction.

He suppressed a grin as all five of the owls landed in a semi-circle in front of him. None landed behind him. Probably because they didn't want to risk friendly fire if they decided to shoot. The result left his enemies focused on him with their backs to the barn where the rest of his coven was sure to be coming up with a plan.

He just hoped it was a good one.

Digby gave a polite bow as the aircraft in the middle lowered its ramp to let out a squad of Guardians. From the look of their medieval-style armor, he assumed that they were some of Henwick's elite forces. He swept his eyes across the group to let the Seed confirm it.

He swallowed with an audible gulp.

They were all close to level fifty. He may have been a few above them, but he didn't like his chances against six. Not to mention there were four more aircraft with guns trained on him. Each was sure to hold a squad of Guardians of their own as well. He doubted they were elites, but either way, the math was not kind.

If things came down to fighting, he was done for.

"Hello there." He spoke first, trying his best to act friendly to set the tone.

None of the Guardians spoke, their faces covered by engraved helmets made of silver with gold accents. They walked toward him in two lines of three, the two in the back carrying something between them.

Digby leaned to the side to try to get a better view.

It looked like a mirror with handles attached to the frame. When the first two Guardians reached him, they parted to walk in opposite directions. As did the two behind. The final pair stopped directly in front of him, the squad now standing in a line parallel to him and his horde.

Raising the mirror, they held it so that he could see his reflection. His image faded from the glass a second later, only to be replaced by one of Henwick standing in front of a mural of angels.

"To what do I owe the pleasure, now that we are no longer enemies?" Digby tried to proceed with caution, making it clear that he had no intent on fighting.

"Graves." Henwick stared at him with disdain. "As per our arrangement, I am informing you that you have trespassed into the empire's territory."

"I see that." Digby opened his mouth to say more but found the words missing when he noticed Alex and Mason peeking out from the back side of the barn behind the row of Guardians.

The pair ducked back into hiding as soon as they saw what was happening outside.

Digby ignored them and kept his attention on Henwick as he began to speak again.

"As I said, you are trespassing—"

"Hold on." Digby didn't let him finish. It was clear that Henwick didn't want to be talking to him so if he was going to stall, he was going to need help. "I'll be right with you. I just want my negotiator here with me if we are going to discuss anything important."

"That is unnecessary, Graves. You are to cease—"

"I know I know, one second." Digby held a hand out over the ground and opened his maw to call forth the bones of one of several skeletons that he'd swallowed for just such an occasion. At the same time, he called Union back to the gemstone he carried and cast Animate Skeleton.

The squad of Guardians in front of him all reached for their swords as his maw widened.

Digby glanced up at the armored men before flicking his eyes to Henwick. "Easy now, I have no interest in breaking our treaty."

"Stand down." Henwick let out an annoyed sigh.

"We have arrived." Union rose from the shadowy black opening of his maw, their hands reaching out to pull the rest of the skeleton out. Necrotic blood dripped from their bones as they took a position in front of the mirror.

"Good, now we may begin talks." Digby held a hand open to Henwick. "Now, what was it you were saying about—" He nearly choked mid-question when he caught Alex and Mason again, sneaking out from behind the barn.

They both seemed to be beckoning to something behind them. Digby tensed every necrotic muscle in his neck when a pair of deceased reindeer followed the pair out into the open. Digby snapped his attention back to Henwick.

"Yes!" He practically shouted the word.

"Yes, what?" Henwick eyed him suspiciously. Well, technically he already was eyeing him with suspicion, but the degree of intensity had increased.

"Yes…" Digby thought back, realizing that he had no idea what they had been talking about. "Yes, back to what you were saying."

"I was saying that you are to return to that airship of yours and remove it from the empire's territory."

Digby glanced past the mirror, relaxing when he saw that his coven had led his zombified reindeer away. He wasn't sure where they had gone, but they were no longer out in the open. Putting the concern aside, he gestured to Union. "Does that request sound reasonable to you?"

"No." The skeleton stood tall. "As per our agreement, we will not interfere with imperial activities, or take hostile actions."

"See." Digby gestured to the skeleton. "We are minding our business. So there's no need for us to leave."

"That may be, but there is no reason for you to be here." Henwick locked eyes with him. "And if you intend on taking anything while you are here, I must remind you that this is our territory. Any looting done here would be considered both hostile and interfering with our operations."

"Oh, haha." Digby tried to laugh off the thinly veiled accusation. "Looting? I would never."

"I'm sure." Henwick didn't take his eyes off him. "Which is why I must ask you to leave so that you are not tempted to do anything that you would regret."

That was when Union stepped in again. "Very well. We will leave."

Digby turned toward the skeleton. "We will?"

"Good." Henwick looked just as surprised at the sudden agreement.

Union opened their bony jaws again to clarify. "We will remove ourselves, but you must inform us of which borders we have crossed."

"Ah, yes." Digby nodded along as Union continued to go over the details. He may not have instructed Union to stall, but the very nature of the infernal spirit was to be thorough. Not only that, but the annoyance on Henwick's face was a bit of a bonus.

Digby stopped nodding a moment later when the two undead reindeer that had been following Alex ran out into the open again. It looked like Comet and Vixen, the pair he'd animated.

They both stopped as soon as they saw him.

Then they started walking toward him, their voices traveling across his bond.

Carrot?

Carrot?

Wait! he shouted back with his mind, not specifying who or what he was talking to. This, of course, caused Union to stop speaking mid-sentence.

Digby froze for an instant as Henwick glanced to him.

Not you, Union, he added over his bond.

The skeleton began again.

Digby flicked his attention back to the reindeer. *You there, get back in the barn!*

Vixen tilted her head to the side. *Carrot?*

No carrot, Digby responded.

Carrot? Comet stepped forward.

No carrot! Digby shook his head. *I will feed you as soon as I can.*

The deceased animals lowered their heads and walked toward the back of the building just as Alex rushed out into the open after them, looking confused, as if he had only now realized where they were.

Digby glowered at him as hard as he could.

The artificer took a moment to cringe before following the reindeer back to the barn.

Digby relaxed.

Then he tensed back up when Alex rushed back out, somehow sprinting and tiptoeing at the same time. He'd almost made it to another building not far from the barn before he tripped over himself and fell.

Digby cleared his throat as loud as he could to cover the sound, dragging it out as he pounded a fist against his chest.

"What is wrong now, Graves?" Henwick grew even more annoyed.

"Erhem!" Digby rubbed his neck. "Sometimes a finger gets stuck in my throat, you know how it is."

"Unfortunately, that won't kill you, so you can deal with it later."

"Yes, yes, where were we?" Digby coughed once more for good measure, making sure that Alex had removed himself from view.

Henwick stared at him for a moment, as if trying to figure out if he was up to something or not by his expressions alone.

Digby let his face go slack. If there was one thing he could do, it was sell a lie.

Henwick frowned, clearly unable to find a reason to call him out. "As I was saying, we do not have an official map drawn up at this time."

"Well, you best have one made then." Digby shoved his hands in his pockets as if there was nothing left to discuss.

"Yes, however, for now, the simplest guideline is the Mississippi."

"I don't know what that is."

"It's a river, Graves." Henwick sighed. "You should consider everything to the east as imperial territory." He gestured to one of the men holding the mirror up. "Someone show him a map."

Just as one of the Guardians started to turn around, Mason crept out into the open behind them, heading back toward the barn. He carried a bucket in each hand.

"No need for a map." Digby held up a hand. "I think I know the river you mean," he said, having no idea where the Mississippi was. "We will be sure not to loot anything from your territory."

I hope that wasn't a mistake. Digby shoved the question out of his mind before glancing to where Mason had been a moment before. The soldier and his buckets were gone. He relaxed yet again.

"What are you looking at, Graves?"

He glanced back to the mirror, finding Henwick staring at him. "I'm looking at you, who else would I be looking at?"

"You were looking off to the side." Henwick's eyes swept the area behind him. "You have been looking all over the place this entire time." He let out a frustrated growl and gestured to the men holding the mirror. "Turn me around."

"Wait, I'm not so sure—" Digby reached out as if to stop him, but it was too late. The Guardians were already turning.

"There." Henwick's voice came from the mirror that was now facing in the opposite direction. "That barn. Take me in there."

"Now you wait just a second, we aren't done here." Digby stomped after him. "We were in the middle of a discussion."

"Now I know I want to see what's in there." Henwick chuckled.

"We must negotiate." Union tried to help.

The Guardians ignored them both and kept marching toward the barn.

Digby reached out a clawed hand, half debating on casting a spell. *No, that wouldn't help. Attacking would ruin everything.* This had to be resolved peacefully.

"On second thought, go ahead. I have nothing to hide." Digby rushed forward as if attempting to lead the way. "We acquired one of your drones weeks ago before the truce, and I figured you would demand we return it if you saw it. So I left it in that barn where it was out of view."

He clenched his jaw. That explained his hesitation, but he still had no idea how he was going to get the man to ignore the eight zombified reindeer that were hiding with the drone. Digby pushed past the Guardians and threw himself against the barn's sliding doors.

"Let me just get this open for you." Digby reached for the latch, hoping that Alex and Mason had come up with some way of hiding things during the time he'd bought them.

He made sure to move at a snail's pace. Every second that passed brought him closer to the inevitable, leaving him with nothing left to do but open the door and accept his fate.

He pulled.

"What's going on here?" Henwick shouted as soon as the door opened.

Digby nearly collapsed in shock as Becca's drone floated in the middle of the barn.

Alone.

"Huh?" She rotated the surveillance unit to face them.

Digby's eyes darted around the barn, yet there was no sign of Alex, Mason, or any of the undead animals that had once inhabited the building.

"Like I said," he tried to recover as naturally as he could, "just a drone."

He stepped into the middle of the barn, half expecting to find Alex and Mason hiding inside one of the animal stalls. They were gone. The only thing he noticed was that there was now a layer of damp hay covering the floor.

Digby struggled not to let his surprise show. "Now if that is all, I will be on my way." He walked back out of the barn, briskly passing by Henwick's mirror. "Come along, Becky."

The drone followed him.

"Graves?" Henwick called after him as his men turned the mirror.

"Yes?" He looked back.

"Leave the drone."

Digby forced out a sigh and waved a claw through the air. "Fine."

With that, Becca set the unit down and Digby beckoned to his horde. The zombies followed him back to the area where they had originally been lowered to the ground in one of the airship's lifeboats. To his surprise, Mason was already waiting for him.

The soldier leaned on the edge of one of the hanging boats as it hung just above the ground. He hopped out so that the horde could climb aboard. Then he headed to the presidential limo that was still sitting where Digby had last seen it.

"What happened?" he asked as soon as he entered the vehicle and closed the door behind him.

"You have no idea how close that was," Mason commented as he slid into the limo's driver's seat and passed a mirror compact through the open partition.

Alex's face looked back from the glass.

Digby pulled the compact close. "Where are the reindeer?"

"We got 'em." Parker leaned into the frame from the side of the mirror as it shifted to show the ballroom aboard the airship, now with eight new undead passengers. The reindeer looked a little confused now that they had been separated from their master.

"How?" Digby's mouth hung open.

Mason lifted the car off the ground. "We had Becca run and get Parker as soon as you left. I know we aren't supposed to be using her magic, but given the situation, it was all we could think of."

"I see." Digby tried to work out what had happened before shaking his head. "Why were you running around down there?"

"We tried to sneak the reindeer away to one of the other buildings that had a window large enough to use for a passage. It almost worked too," the soldier answered.

"What went wrong?" Digby arched an eyebrow.

"The windows were a few feet off the ground and the reindeer couldn't jump high enough without being enhanced. Then they just kind of got confused and tried to go back to you. We ran out of options after that, so I filled a couple of buckets with water and dumped them on the floor of the barn."

"It wasn't an ideal surface for a passage but I made it work," Parker added from the mirror in Digby's hand.

"Once the deer were through, we tossed hay up in the air and jumped in behind them. Hopefully, the hay was able to hide the water somewhat." Alex finished the explanation.

Digby just let himself slide back into his seat in disbelief that their plan had worked. He suppressed the urge to criticize the chaos of what had just happened. Instead, he laughed.

"Well done."

He let a grin slide across his face.

"It's going to take a lot more quick thinking like that to pull this con off."

"Let's try not to put ourselves in any more tight spots if we can help it." Becca pulled the mirror out of Alex's hands to glower at Digby from the other side, as if the whole thing had been his fault.

"Don't worry, Becky. That was the last item on our list." He grinned back at her. "All we must do now is to get prepared."

CHAPTER TWENTY-NINE

The next two weeks passed by in a blur, the days of the calendar falling away one after another until only five remained before the final night.

Five days left to prepare for the con.

Everyone had a job to do.

For Digby, he spent the time sweeping every toy store in the entire state of Nevada. In the process, he gained two levels and ate over three hundred revenants. With that many corpses filling his void, he felt about ready to take on the world. Unfortunately, not everyone was feeling as confident.

"We have a problem." Easton was waiting for him the moment he entered the airship's ballroom.

Digby stopped in the doorway. "And that is?"

"We found a town."

"A town?" Digby stared at him blankly.

"A TOWN!" Asher cawed from where she perched at the top of the imitation trees that lined the room.

Easton turned and walked back toward the mirror that was mounted on the wall. "From what I've found, over a third of the world's children already reside either in Vegas or in the empire's capital. Most of which are in the latter, on account of Autem's recruitment slash kidnapping efforts. I wasn't able to see any of them since the empire's training facility is warded, but I was able to narrow down what building they are in. I've also gathered some intel on the facility to help you infiltrate it when the time comes. Overall, this mirror has been a game changer."

"Good, good." Digby nodded along.

"However," Easton continued. "I have also located hundreds of small groups that have been on the move. Once found, I've sent covens out to rescue them whenever possible. Our range is limited, but we've at least gotten to the closest survivors. The furthest we've been able to reach were in Canada and Mexico. Figured if the empire wasn't going to stop grabbing kids, then the least we could do was show up and offer them an alternative. That way their families get to stay together. So far, Vegas has gained a couple hundred more inhabitants through this process. A quarter of which have been kids."

"That sounds like a good thing." Digby nodded. "So what's the problem? And what town are you talking about?"

"It's a small campground in the Colorado mountains." Easton turned to the mirror and rattled off the artifact's invocation phrase. A moment later an image of a quaint village covered in snow appeared. "To make sure I didn't miss anything, I checked over my list a second time. And strangely, the mirror found a dozen more kids that the scrying magic couldn't find before."

Digby leaned toward the glass, noting puffs of smoke coming from the chimneys of a couple of cabins. "Looks rather cozy."

"Yes, it does. That's part of the problem." He threw a hand out toward the glass. "I sent a coven out there already. They found a community of over thirty people. But when we offered to take them back to Vegas, their leadership refused."

"What? Why would they refuse?"

"It's like you said, it's cozy there." He dropped his hand to his side. "They've built their own town and have plenty of supplies. Plus, they haven't had to worry about threats thanks to the cold. Once the frost set in, the revenants migrated to warmer temperatures. And the zombies, well, they just froze. The settlers there have been handling any of your kind just by poking them in the brain with something pointy."

"Ouch." Digby rubbed at the side of his head.

"The reason that I couldn't find the kids before was because a heavy snowstorm had just passed through the area. Everyone had gathered together in one of the larger buildings that had been used as an infirmary. As I understand these mass enchantments, the building was enough to block the mirror's scrying magic. Doctor-patient confidentiality was still in effect somehow. Once the storm passed and everyone returned to their cabins, I was able to get a lock on the children's location." Easton mumbled a few words at the mirror, causing the image to fade, replaced by a reflection of him and Digby. "Whatever the reason, the people there were adamant. They are staying where they are. They think it's safe and they don't trust us. Our coven didn't tell them about magic, and I'm not sure that will help or hurt our situation."

"It may be wise not to. Magic is a difficult truth to accept. Many would consider it a lie or assume we've gone mad. Even worse, they may come to fear us if we show them proof." Digby stood quietly with his hands in his pockets for a moment before speaking again. "You said that these people are not currently in any danger?"

"As long as the weather doesn't suddenly become unseasonably warm, the cold should keep any monsters away. And this is Colorado we're talking about. It's unlikely to warm up anytime soon."

"Very well. Keep an eye on them." Digby stepped away from his reflection. "If I remember correctly, this territory is one over from Nevada. As long as we get an early start delivering presents to the children in Vegas, we can take the airship to this village. Then I'll just pop down in the sleigh that Jameson and his artificers are working on, give out a few gifts, and come right back. From there, we will just use Parker's magic to get us to the empire's territory."

"That should work." He eyed him skeptically. "Out of curiosity, what is the plan for the empire? I mean, it's not like they are going to let you run around their refugee camp pretending to be Santa."

Digby's jaw tightened at the question. "As long as we travel by Mirror Passage whenever possible and only fly the sleigh out in the open when we're finished, they shouldn't figure out what we've done until we are already making our escape."

"But won't they consider that a breach of the treaty?"

"Why should they?" Digby scoffed. "I'm sure Henwick will have some choice words about it, but the agreement stated that we would do nothing hostile within their territory. And we shall not steal anything while we are there. So as long as I don't eat anyone or do anything else that could be considered combative, then they will have no choice but to uphold the treaty. We should be able to smooth things over after that. Besides, what can they accuse us of? Brightening their lives?"

"If you say so." Easton turned to the mirror only to glance back over his shoulder. "Oh, you should probably look in on your little helper down the hall. Parker went in a few minutes before you arrived and I heard quite a bit of yelling."

"Yelling?" Digby turned toward the door in the hallway beyond.

The last he'd seen of Becca, the vampire had been buried in a pile of gifts and tasked with the job of wrapping them. She'd argued, of course, but since they were sticking as close to the legends as possible, all present preparation needed to be completed by one of Santa's helpers. Unfortunately for her, everyone agreed that she was the only one who could pass as an elf.

"Alright, no sense putting this off then." Digby gave Easton an appreciative nod before heading back out into the hall.

On his way out the door, he patted his shoulder to call to Asher. The zombified raven flapped down to land on his pauldron with a happy caw. He slowed to a stop as he reached one of the airship's other function halls. Someone, most likely Parker, had taped a handwritten sign on the door that read Santa's Workshop. His senses weren't nearly as strong as a vampire's, but he still leaned in to listen, hoping to avoid walking into any uncomfortable situations.

Only silence answered.

"It sounds safe enough." He patted Asher's wing, and he opened the door.

The room was filled with wrapping supplies and presents. On one side, a pile of several hundred gifts covered in red paper had been stacked. On the other, a mound of around five hundred stuffed animals sat on the floor. At the center of the space, a few tables had been set up. A thoroughly annoyed vampire sat in an office chair between them. "Finally!" Becca jumped up with inhuman speed the instant he stepped inside.

The sound of bells ringing accompanied her every movement, informing him of the reason why she might be angry. The blood-thirsty monster was dressed in a green velvet coat that came down to her waist. A trim of white fur lined the collar, similar to the coat that he intended to wear on the night of the mission to come. A pair of red and white striped tights covered her legs. Finally, the toes of her shoes terminated in an impractical curl, a bell hanging from the tip of each.

A voice came from the other side of the room. "She doesn't like her outfit."

Digby furrowed his brow as he swept his vision to the side, looking for the source. He rolled his eyes when he noticed Parker lying in the pile of plush toys. She was still wearing the red coat she'd found in the airship storage and was holding a stuffed shark to her chest. The messenger looked as if she was already halfway into a nap.

"What seems to be the problem?" Digby prepared for the worst.

Becca took a deep breath before speaking. "If it's not bad enough that you are making me wrap two thousand some odd presents by myself, I am also saddled with the fashion police over there." She threw her hand out toward Parker. "Who won't even let me take off my shoes."

"I didn't make the rules." The messenger shrugged, half-buried in a pile of children's toys. "We have to stick as close as we can to the legends. Every little bit counts. And you should put your hat back on."

"I have bells on my shoes, Dig." Becca ignored her and placed both hands on the table in front of her, leaning all her weight on it until it creaked. "You can't expect me to wear these behind enemy lines when we go into the empire's refugee camps."

"I admit that it is not the best outfit for stealth." Digby chuckled. "But the legends do mention the sound of bells."

"That's what I said." A voice came from behind him as Hawk entered the room carrying an armload of folded cardboard boxes. He dropped them on the floor over by the tables before turning to his sister. "Oh no, you're not wearing your hat." The young rogue grinned as he picked up a green stocking cap, complete with a bell on the end from where it hung on the back of her chair, and gently placed it on her head so that her pointy ears stuck out at the bottom. "There, can't forget that."

"You're all enjoying this entirely too much." Becca blew the end of the hat out of her face, its bell jingling as it flipped back over her head. "I swear, I would rather have the chipmunk suit."

"Nonsense, you look fine." Digby waved away her concerns before gesturing to the stack of perfectly wrapped presents. "You're getting pretty good at that. At least, they look much better than your first few."

"That's true, the ones you wrapped a few days ago looked like crap," Hawk added.

"LIKE CRAP!" Asher cawed to help out.

Becca bared her fangs. "I'm gonna need you all to leave before I decide to juice box the first person within reach."

Hawk took a step away from her to keep out of grabbing range.

"Indeed, I must check on the rest of the preparations anyway." Digby began slowly backing out of the room only to stop when Becca spoke up again.

"Wait. There's something else." The vampire hopped over the table in front of her before snatching a sheet of wrapping paper up and marching toward him. Her shoes jingled angrily the entire way. "I've already wrapped a thousand presents and I just noticed this." She jabbed a finger at the paper.

Digby lowered his eyes to the material. It was red and had several drawings of items and characters rendered in a rather cute style. Each was meant to represent a different set of beliefs to ensure no child receiving a gift would feel slighted or un-included. Most had been drawn by an artist back in Vegas under the instruction of Alex.

"I just wanted to point out what your apprentice has decided to represent, here." She tapped at the paper.

Digby grabbed the material from her and held it up. She had been pointing to a little illustration of a figure sitting in a chair. It looked happy and festive. However, upon closer inspection, it had a pair of cloven hooves and the head of a goat.

"Is that—"

"The devil?" Becca finished his question. "Yeah, it is."

"You said you wanted all belief systems covered." Parker defended the illustration from her throne of stuffed animals.

Digby hesitated. "I did say that, didn't I?"

"What I don't understand is that when you already have the word Santa available, why couldn't he just have rearranged the letters in a couple of places so it would be less noticeable." Becca dropped her arms to her sides and walked back to her worktable, dragging her feet so that the bells made less noise.

Digby stared at the little drawing of the devil. "Well, at least it's friendly looking. It could be worse." He looked over the rest of the paper at the various characters. Some were simply drawn looking festive, while others were collected in little scenes celebrating various traditions. "All things considered, this does show everyone gathering together and appreciating what they have. That's what this is all about."

"I think it's fine," Hawk commented.

"Indeed." Digby put an end to the conversation. "I doubt anyone will notice the devil anyway."

"Fine, if you're okay with it, I'm okay with it." Becca dropped back into her chair. "I just wanted to call it out now before I finish wrapping all the rest of these presents."

A final nail was driven into the subject's coffin when the doors at the far end of the room swung open with Jameson standing in the entryway. "There you are, Graves."

"Let me guess, you have a problem?"

"No."

"Oh, good."

"I have two problems."

"Oh." Digby deflated.

The old soldier-turned-airship captain walked back out the way he came.

With a shrug, Digby followed him down the hall, eventually coming to what had become known as the hangar. Three of Jameson's artificers sat in the corner, taking a break. The room itself had been chosen because it had a set of double doors that opened onto the ship's deck. That way, they would have a way to launch the sleigh without having to work on it outside.

A third of the room was taken up by eight makeshift stalls containing Digby's reanimated reindeer. Comet and Vixen both picked up their heads when they saw him.

Carrot?

"Not now!" Digby rubbed at the bridge of his nose.

He was going to need to find some kind of treat to feed them if he was going to carry out his plan and keep them happy at the same time. The rest of the deceased animals stood, side-by-side, waiting patiently until they were needed.

The rest of the room was filled with tables and equipment. Most of it was covered by tarps, making it hard to tell what Jameson's team had been working on. The only thing he recognized was the tiny prototype sleigh that he'd been shown before.

Digby followed Jameson over to a pair of long, covered objects.

"The first problem we have is with the silos." The burly man pulled the tarp from a strange contraption.

It looked like some kind of hexagonal pillar, lying on its side with wheeled carts supporting it. One end terminated in a pointed section that resembled a six-sided pyramid. The other end was flat. The whole thing was metal and welded together thoroughly.

"What is a silo?" Digby reached forward and knocked on the surface, getting a hollow sound in response.

"It's what we're calling these storage units." Jameson walked toward the pointed end. "It's the best solution we could come up with to solve the problem of putting gifts in your void."

"I see." Digby followed him. "So I can place all the presents I have to deliver inside this chamber to keep the necrotic blood of my void from getting all over everything."

"Yes." Jameson reached into his pocket and pulled out a small remote control before holding it toward the tip of the silo. As soon as he did, the pointed section split open into six triangular doors that came together to seal the container shut.

Digby bent down to look inside, finding a second barrier unlike anything he'd seen. It was metal and made up of multiple segments that spiraled toward the center. A pair of buttons were mounted on the rim beside it, one red and one green. "Interesting."

"Press the green one." Jameson gestured to the button.

Digby nodded and tapped it. As soon as he did, the center of the second barrier opened, the layers of metal sliding into each other as the hole in the middle widened. Inside, a dark, circular tube stretched to the other end of the silo. "Very interesting."

"We figured there should be an airlock to make sure none of that black goo from that dimensional space of yours gets on any of the packages inside," Jameson explained. "The intent is to take this whole thing into your void." He turned around and grabbed one of several large red velvet sacks from behind him. At the bottom of the sack was a flat portion that matched the width of the silo. "You just have to open your maw inside this bag and raise the container enough for the top to emerge. The first door opens by remote. The second is with the button inside. It's not quite the same thing as a bag of holding, but it should give the illusion that you're pulling presents from the sack itself."

Digby squinted into the dark space inside. It had to be at least thirty feet deep. "How am I going to get the packages on the bottom out?"

"That's what the red button is for." Jameson crouched down and pointed to the chamber inside. "There's a panel in the bottom of the silo that will rise to the top and push its entire contents up toward the opening. You just have to grab the package on top and then hold the button down until the next gift moves into place. We made sure to install all the motors and electronics up here on the opening since we don't know how your void will affect any of that stuff. My guess is an electronic signal won't travel past the opening, so the only moving parts inside are just a series of chains connected to the sides of the platform."

"That's true, I have no idea how my void would react. Best to err on the side of caution." Digby stood back up. "What is the problem that you're having?"

"The issue is that you have a lot of presents to give out. Now that we've got a working prototype for the silo, we can make more. But you mentioned that there is a limit to how much foreign material you can take into your void without it messing up your mana system. We've been doing the math and we think we're going to need close to twenty silos, and that might cross the threshold."

"I see." Digby tapped a claw on the surface of the silo. "One or two should be fine, but all twenty is certainly out of the question. I will just have to take them a couple at a time and return to the ship whenever I run low. It's not ideal, but it should be alright as long as we move fast."

"Good, we will continue production then." Jameson nodded.

"Excellent." Digby turned away and wandered over to an object the size of a car and lifted the corner of the tarp that covered it. "And what is your second problem?"

"You're looking at it."

Digby pulled the tarp off to find a large sleigh. It was made of wood, with several metal plates installed along the inside. It still needed a coat of paint but it was still a far cry better than the miniature prototype. "Now this is more like it."

"Yes, but we ran into an issue with the propulsion system. For the prototype, we installed the same one as the limousine you have been using. It works, but it might not be a good idea to use a system that draws mana directly from the sleigh's driver. The way I see it, you are going to need every point of MP you can get out there. And letting Becca drive is obviously out of the question."

"Indeed, she'd be likely to rampage her way through a house of civilians if her mana gets too low." Digby leaned on the sleigh for a moment before glancing to the side at his undead reindeer. "Can we pull mana from my minions?"

"We thought of that as well and ran the numbers." Jameson's tone didn't sound confident.

"Not enough power?"

"Not for prolonged use." Jameson walked over to the deceased animals.

After being enhanced with his Body Craft mutation, they didn't look any different from when they were alive. The only giveaway was the pale white color of their eyes. The problem with zombies was that their mana supply was still limited even after regaining their physical attributes. Comet and Vixen had larger mana pools, but still nowhere near that of a Heretic.

"Your new friends here can certainly pull the sleigh, but the amount of mana it takes to do so is nearly the same as the amount they absorb. The fact that they're dead and can only take in death essence is what's slowing it down. If they were alive, we wouldn't have a problem. As it is, there's a chance that the demand on them could destabilize their mana system. And that could leave you dead in the water with a bunch of reindeer corpses hanging from your sleigh. Probably not a good look for Santa."

"Probably not."

"What you need is one more to make sure you don't run into a problem." Jameson chuckled. "So unless there's a Rudolph that you can ask to guide your sleigh, you're going to have to go out there and find another reindeer."

"I don't know who that is." Digby folded his arms.

"I guess you skipped all the claymation movies, then."

"I don't know what claymation is either."

"That tracks." Jameson let out a heavy sigh. "I guess that adds another item to your shopping list."

Digby started to nod only to stop and turn his head to the side where Asher was still perched on his shoulder. The raven was picking at her feathers with her beak and minding her own business.

Maybe I don't need another reindeer after all.

With his Body Craft mutation, he could technically convert any zombie into another form. He had already been debating on using it to grant Asher a more durable body, but had been putting it off until he had more practice.

Perhaps now is the time?

"Asher?" Digby held a hand up to the raven so that she could hop down to one of his claws.

The deceased bird looked at him, cocking her head from one side to another.

Digby found an open space on the floor and carried her over to it. Then he placed her down and gave her a pat on the head. "What do you say? Do you want to lead my sleigh?"

Asher stared at him for a moment, then nodded her beak. A wave of excitement floated across their bond.

"I'll have to change you." Digby sat on the floor in front of her. "You'll be stronger and harder to hurt. But you won't be a bird anymore."

The excitement he felt a moment before was replaced with a sudden unease along with one word.

Wings?

Digby thought for a second. Technically, Asher wouldn't need wings once she was hooked up to the sleigh, but it seemed cruel to take them away. Perhaps there was a way to combine animals to retain some of the features that were important to her. He was going to have to make sure nobody got a good look at the rest of his reindeer anyway, so what would be the harm in allowing his minion some comfort? She had been there for him from the beginning. He owed her that much.

"I think I can find a way to keep your wings."

Asher nodded again, the unease fading into a feeling of trust.

"Alright." He got up from the floor and held a hand out toward her. "This won't hurt, but it will feel a bit weird."

Digby let his thoughts wash over the memories of all of the corpses that he'd eaten so far. He'd never tried to craft something specific before, other than enhancing the dead back to the condition of the living. Mostly he'd only used the mutation to create minions with random limbs, tentacles, and other strange formations. He closed his eyes as a shape began to coalesce in his mind's eye. Then, he snapped them open and let his resources flow.

At first, Asher began to swell. Her wings flapped as her body bulged, suddenly too small to fly. Then her neck twisted and stretched along with a series of popping sounds.

Jameson took a step back to make room.

Her legs grew, snapping back and forth to reorient themselves as new muscles and tendons connected the pieces. For a brief moment, she resembled an ostrich. The metamorphosis continued as two new limbs poked through the feathers that covered her front to reach toward the floor. The Raven's head grew and her beak elongated until it was roughly the same size as the heads of the undead reindeer across the room. Growths of bone extended from her forehead in place of antlers. Narrow tendrils flowed from her rear to create a fan of wide tail feathers. Then, finally, she spread her tiny wings. They surged outward with a series of snaps and cracks until they stretched out for several feet. She flapped them momentarily before tucking them in close to her new body when she began to stumble.

Digby slowed the flow of resources as a transformation finished, leaving an entirely new animal in the raven's place.

Asher stood stock-still, only her eyes glancing around, as if unsure how to move in her new form.

"Good god." A stunned expression consumed Jameson's face. "She's beautiful."

The raven that was no longer a raven raised her head cautiously. She was the same size as a reindeer and her overall shape was similar, but that was about all they had in common. Feathers still covered her body, her feet still had talons, and her beak was still right where it had been. She was just bigger. Sure, her neck was longer and she now had four legs, but she was still the same Asher that had been there before.

Digby placed a hand on her forehead, running his fingers up one of her new horns. There were two sets. One that curled back like a ram's, and another twisted upward like a goat's. They weren't quite the same as antlers but from far away, it was enough to blend in with the rest of the animals. As long as she didn't spread her wings, her silhouette was close enough as well.

"Well, what do you think?" Digby lowered his hand from her horns.

Asher held perfectly still, only moving her head. She cocked it from side to side for a few seconds, then she twisted her neck back, clearly surprised at how far she could turn now that she had several extra vertebrae. Spreading her wings, she ran her beak through her feathers. After a few cautious tests, she flapped twice, lifting her new body.

Tarps blew from tables around her as random items fell to the floor, knocked over by the sudden draft. Asher immediately tucked her wings back in, startled by the noise. She dropped back to the floor, her legs struggling to catch her, leaving her crouched with her head close to the carpet. Her knees shook as she raised herself back up. Then, she carefully tried walking.

That proved to be the tricky part.

Digby arched an eyebrow. Clearly, four legs were very different from two.

Asher stumbled forward like a newborn deer. After a minute of practice and using her wings for balance, she began to get the hang of it. For birds, walking was impractical. Why bother when they could just fly? Eventually, she managed to figure out her own unique way to move. Instead of simply putting one foot in front of the other, she appeared to find it easier to prance in a way that resembled a bird hopping.

Jameson thought it was cute.

Digby would have preferred something more intimidating, but he wasn't about to argue.

Nevertheless, he willed the Seed to show him her attributes.

ATTRIBUTES
Constitution: 0
Defense: 22
Strength: 27
Dexterity: 14
Agility: 18
Intelligence: 15
Perception: 12

Will: 7

The change had completely upended her values, putting strength at the top. Not only that, but she was far more durable than she had been. Digby nodded to himself. His biggest fear had always been that she would get hurt, and considering how important she was as a zombie master, a higher defense was a big improvement.

He led Asher outside to the deck where she could run free once she grew more confident. Thanks to Jameson's insistence, the ship was traveling at a safe speed for her to move about the deck. The next hour was spent with her prancing up and down the walkways that ran along the sides of the ship. Her talons clicked against the deck with each excited step until she decided to take flight.

"Be careful now." Digby ran to the rail as she leaped over it. His un-beating heart nearly climbed into his throat.

She swooped back up a moment later, flapping with wild abandon as a feeling of elation flowed across their bond.

"It looks like she's enjoying the changes." Jameson stared up at her. "What do we call her now, by the way? I mean, she isn't a raven anymore?"

Digby furrowed his brow. "I don't know. Asher is something new."

"Just like the rest of this world, I suppose." Jameson took a deep breath.

"What do you mean?" Digby turned to look at him as the clouds rolled by behind him.

"The world died a month ago along with everything else. From here on out, everything's new."

CHAPTER THIRTY

"So this is it." Digby stood on a balcony in the atrium of the casino, overlooking an enormous yet artificial pine tree covered in ornaments and lights.

He hadn't been down to the city in weeks.

The days of the calendar had fallen away faster than any before. Yet, as the year dwindled to a close, a feeling of excitement had begun to take hold. It wasn't just the festivities of the season. No, it was the hope that had been gained while the peace lasted.

No one in Vegas had died in weeks. Not even from an accident or stray revenant. There had been a few close calls here and there, but with nearly everyone in the city having taken on the power of a Heretic, they had learned to protect themselves. Digby wasn't sure if he would be able to beat Henwick when the time came, but if he could, the future would belong to everyone again.

While he had been traveling the country aboard an airship, preparing to con the world into handing him the power of a demigod, the lives of everyone in Vegas were returning to normal. Many had come to Elenore, asking for her to open the casino's storage areas. After that, seasonal decorations had been put up one after another. Not just for Christmas either. The apocalypse had canceled many holidays, and it was time to take them back. Digby hadn't heard of most of them but the decorations were put up regardless. They were no longer celebrating a specific day or belief. No, it was more like one enormous festival standing in defiance of the world's end to reclaim what was lost.

Now, on the twenty-fifth of December, it had all come to a head.

Everyone had come out of their rooms and ventured down to the casino floor to celebrate together. Campbell had outdone himself, preparing a feast for over a thousand. They didn't have much in the way of traditional foods, but he had done what he could with what he had. From Hawaii, they had all manner of fresh fruits as well as pork and chicken that had been obtained through trading. All of it had been loaded onto the airship and brought back to the city. There was even fresh baked bread and cakes produced by a bakery in the casino that had been reopened by some of the settlers.

The atmosphere made Digby feel out of place.

Not only was everyone enjoying food that he couldn't eat, but he'd never really been a part of celebrations before. Back in his time, there hadn't been anyone to celebrate with. It was strange how so much had changed. Walking down the stairs to the casino floor, he was greeted with a smile by nearly everyone he saw. Many wished him a happy holiday or a season's greetings.

Digby checked the time on his phone. It was still light out and there were another two hours before the con would need to be set into motion. Everything was ready to go. All he needed was to wait until nightfall. Until then, there was nothing to do but join in the festivities.

It wasn't long before he found Hawk, Becca, and Mason sitting at a table, sharing a meal. He didn't join them. Instead, he puttered around until the young rogue spotted him and waved him over. He couldn't possibly argue, so he took a seat at the end of the table.

Parker dropped into a chair to his right with a plate of food. Her hair had faded almost entirely over the last few weeks, leaving a mess of grayish locks peeking out from a stocking cap. She hadn't taken much from the buffet, which made sense since she would be using her magic heavily throughout the night. Over the last month, she had only opened one Mirror Passage, and it had taken a couple of days for her appetite to come back. Digby had asked her if she would be able to handle everything to come, not wanting to put her life at risk.

Of course, she'd assured him that she would be fine.

He wasn't so sure.

She still looked exhausted.

His thoughts were pulled away when Alex joined them, carrying a tray of food for himself with Kristen's skull sitting next to his plate. The deceased seer hadn't complained about being murdered for at least a week and had certainly earned her place at the table. Even if she couldn't eat anything.

At least, that was something they had in common.

Well, technically he could eat. There was just a limit to how much unusable material he could take into his void before it disrupted his mana system. Despite that, it didn't seem wise to add anything just because he wanted to share a meal with his friends.

That was when Campbell came by carrying a plate covered by a silver lid.

"Since this is a special occasion, I thought everybody deserved to have a decent meal." He set the plate down in front of him.

"What's this?" Digby looked up at him, confused.

Campbell picked up the silver lid to reveal a plate full of cubed meat. It hadn't been cooked, but seasonings had been sprinkled across the meal. "I wouldn't mention this to too many people," Campbell leaned down and lowered his voice, "but the last time one of those wardbreakers made it into the city, I had it kept alive for such an occasion. You know, just looking out for you."

"Wait. That's revenant?" Becca pointed at the plate of meat.

"You guessed it." Campbell chuckled. "And before you feel left out." He turned and rushed over to a counter, returning with a fancy-looking glass full of what looked like blood. "I've also prepared something special for the vampire in our little city. It's still warm too."

Becca buried her face in her hands. "You didn't have to do that. My mana is almost full."

"Oh." He pulled the glass back toward him. "I didn't realize. I'll take it back to the, um, kitchen."

"Wait." A sheepish expression fell across the vampire's face. "You don't have to. I mean, it's already here. You can't put it back in… whoever you took it from. I'm sorry, who did you take it from?"

Campbell cleared his throat. "You might say I'm running a little low."

Parker laughed at the explanation. "Is it better or worse if you know where it came from?"

"Honestly, I don't know." Becca took the glass but waited before taking a sip.

Digby assumed she didn't want to drink the blood in front of its donor.

"Well, thank you for the meal, Campbell." He reached for one of the chunks of meat on the plate in front of him with his fingers only for Alex to stop him.

"Use a fork."

"Yes, where are your manners? Were you raised by wolves?" Kristin added from the artificer's tray. "Actually, I wouldn't be surprised if you had been."

Digby rolled his eyes at the skull and grabbed a set of silverware from a container in the middle of the table. He hadn't eaten with anything but his hands since he'd become a zombie, but had no trouble spearing a chunk of meat. He shoved it in his mouth without hesitation.

"I never thought I would be eating at the same table where borderline cannibalism was going on, but whatever." Parker nibbled at a piece of bread.

"Shit's gotten weird." Hawk continued eating.

"Truer words have never been spoken." Campbell gave Becca a nod. "Enjoy my blood." Then he spun on his heel and headed back to the kitchen.

"I hope he's not preparing freshly killed revenant in the same space as he's making the rest of the food." Mason looked down at his plate.

"Don't be so squeamish." Digby pointed at him with his fork, dropping a piece of meat on the table in front of him. "Oh, whoops." He grabbed it with his fingers and popped it in his mouth, hoping he got to it before he ruined anyone else's meal.

The next hour was delightfully uneventful, but as the day drew to a close, everyone began checking their watches.

"I suppose it's time." Digby pushed himself up from the table.

The others did the same. Over a month of preparations had gone into the plan, and now it all came down to one night. Everything had to be perfect. Fortunately, everyone knew what to do.

Alex and Hawk left with Mason to head back up to the airship while Digby and Becca got to work. Passing by Elenore, who looked as busy as ever, he gave her a conspiratorial nod.

With that, the con was officially on.

Elenore checked a clipboard as the three of them boarded an elevator. "I've spoken to all the parents and guardians of every child in Vegas. I didn't tell them anything about what we're doing, but I've made it clear that they're to get the kids into bed as soon as night falls. And I have let them know to expect a delivery." She reached into her pocket and pulled out a key card. "Here, this will open every guest room in the hotel upstairs. Make sure you give it back to me when you're done. I don't want it getting lost."

"I should probably hold onto it." Becca took the key card from her before Digby had a chance to grab it.

"Oh please, I am not incompetent."

"No, but I am better with technology, so consider this a tactical decision. This plan is unlike anything we've ever done before. We're not fighting anyone. Tonight is all about speed, and we can't afford to be slowed down by anything."

The doors of the elevator opened to the third floor, putting an end to the conversation.

Elenore stepped out into the hall and headed to the right without hesitation. "Everything is ready for you in the high-roller suite. The costumes are good to go, and I loaded all of the gifts to be delivered onto carts. I've also left you a printout listing every room number that requires a delivery, along with the name and age of each recipient."

"Perfect." Digby stopped in front of the door of the suite.

"You're damn right it's perfect. I have been busting my ass keeping things running down here while you have been flying around on that airship." Elenore held her clipboard close to her chest. "Now, I am going to go put my son to bed. I'll see you when you get to my room." She started to turn.

"Wait," Digby spoke up before he fully understood why.

"Yes?" She glanced back.

He hesitated, staring awkwardly at the woman for a few seconds before finally saying anything. "Thank you, for everything. None of this would be possible without you."

"You're right." Elenore arched an eyebrow and cracked a smile. "But I know you're working hard too." She turned and continued walking away, adding a, "Good luck," without looking back.

"Did you just say thank you, unprompted?" Becca eyed him sideways.

"Oh, don't make a thing of it." He placed a hand on the door handle of the high-roller suite but hesitated before entering. "I suppose I should thank you as well."

"For what?" Becca stood, looking confused.

"For joining me tonight. I know you're only coming because you look the part, but honestly, I couldn't imagine doing this with anyone else." He avoided eye contact as he spoke. "I know I'm not the easiest person to deal with, so thank you for sticking with me."

She went silent for a moment before responding. "You know, being friends with you has changed me in more ways than I can count. I'm not sure I would have gotten through it all without you. So while I may not like wearing shoes with bells on them, I'm glad to be here with you."

"Thank you." Digby felt the corner of his mouth tug upward. "Now let's go lie to some children."

"And you ruined it." Becca deflated.

"Sorry, but we are in a hurry." He yanked the door of the high-roller suite open and rushed inside.

It was the same room where he'd killed a few men, as well as where they used to store the Heretic Seed's obelisk. Now, it was home to something else. Five carts of wrapped presents were lined up against one wall, each with a clipboard hanging from a hook on the front. It was all ready to go.

More importantly, two bags sat on the poker table in the center of the room. One was labeled Santa, and the other Santa's Little Helper.

Becca rolled her eyes and grabbed the second bag, pulling out the clothes that she had been wearing while wrapping presents before. Elenore had made a point of having both of their disguises cleaned and sprayed with a combination of perfumes that smelled like cinnamon and mint. According to her, the plan would surely fall apart if they broke into someone's home that night smelling like a sweaty vampire and a corpse.

Digby had to admit she'd had a point.

He grabbed the bag labeled Santa and dumped it out on the table. A pair of red pants, a heavy leather belt, a coat, and a hat fell out. Holding the coat out, he found a series of leather straps that had been added to connect the goblin king's pauldron to its shoulder. He smiled. The item had been with him from the beginning.

Digby quickly kicked off his shoes and changed his pants while Becca did the same with her tights. He threw on the coat next and slipped the belt through the loops on its side. Finally, he pulled the hat on. The sound of bells jingling told him Becca had finished as well.

"At least I'm not the only one who looks ridiculous this time."

"If looking ridiculous is the price we need to pay for the power of a demigod, then I'd say it's a fair trade." Digby willed his Body Craft mutation to make a small adjustment to his form, sprouting a face full of white hair.

"Nice beard."

"Thank you. I have been practicing crafting it." Digby ran a hand through his new facial hair before heading to the first of the carts.

The top sheet of paper on the clipboard hanging from the hook had third floor written across it. Beneath that, there was a list of numbers and names. He grabbed hold of the cart and pulled it away from the wall.

Becca jumped in to push from behind to make it easier to steer.

From there, they moved fast to the first room on the list and went inside using the key card Elenore had provided. There was no way to convince the adults to go to bed early along with the children, so they were met by a confused-looking man with a beard. He was sitting with a plate of cookies in front of the television.

Digby raised a finger to his lips to make sure he stayed quiet.

All of the families that had settled in the city had been assigned to the larger hotel suites since they needed more room. Conveniently, this meant that the children were housed in a separate room from the main living area. Still, Digby stayed quiet. Checking his list, he found two names written next to the room number. He grabbed two packages from the cart, carried them in, and placed them on the coffee table while Becca waited in the hallway.

The man eating cookies jumped up from the couch to meet him, brushing crumbs from his beard as he looked up and down at Digby's disguise. His expression grew more confused by the second. "Mr. Graves, sorry, I didn't realize you were coming. Elenore just said to expect a delivery."

Digby had little interaction with the man, but he did recognize him as one of the survivors that had arrived with Jameson's people from Hoover Dam. A glance told him that he was now a level seven mage.

"Indeed, this is a bit of a special circumstance." Digby set both presents down on the coffee table. "Just trying to brighten the little ones' morning."

The man looked down at the packages. "Oh my god, thank you." He gestured to a closed door behind him. "The kids weren't expecting anything, but they begged me to leave out a plate of cookies just in case Santa was still alive out there."

"Cookies?" Digby looked down at the plate. "What does that have to do with anything?"

The man stared at him blankly for a moment as if the explanation should have been obvious. "Oh yeah, you're not from here." He shook his head. "It's a tradition. Kids leave a plate of cookies out for Santa and a carrot for the reindeer. Usually, there's a glass of milk too, but I didn't have any. I don't suppose you eat people food. Do you?"

"Sadly, I do not." Digby turned back toward the entrance of the suite. "Becky, come over here and eat these cookies. We need to get the details right."

"I can't." She remained where she was.

"What do you mean, you can't?"

"I can't come in. Remember, vampire. I need an invitation."

The man with the beard cocked his head to the side, clearly trying to process how ridiculous the situation was. Then, he simply waved her in. "Well, come on in and eat these."

Becca hesitated for a second then stepped through slowly, as if expecting to be hit with a ward at any second. She let out a relieved sigh when nothing happened.

The man met her halfway and offered her the plate of baked goods; there were still two cookies left.

She grabbed them both and munched them down. "Thanks."

"Sorry, I don't have a carrot for the reindeer." The man chuckled.

"That's quite alright, the reindeer are all undead anyway," Digby explained.

"Oh, that's... kind of terrifying." The man's eyes widened.

"Indeed." Digby turned to the door. "Now I'm afraid we must leave. We have a lot of deliveries to make before this night is through."

"Hang on." The man reached out. "Thank you. The kids..." He hesitated, his eyes welling up. "I'm their uncle. Their parents didn't make it, back when this all started. It's all been... a lot... for everyone. But you're doing something good here."

An ache swelled in Digby's chest. It may have all been for a con, but it was starting to seem like his plan was having more impact on the people than he'd intended. He looked away from the man's eyes and the gratitude that filled them, unsure what to say.

"It's the least we can do," Becky answered for him, giving the man a smile that showed her fangs. She had always been better at putting up a front than he was.

"Yes." Digby nodded before continuing out to the hallway and closing the door.

Neither he nor Becca said anything about the brief interaction. Instead, a heavy silence fell, making everything they were doing feel so much more important than before. Digby couldn't help but feel like he had started something that he had to finish. Not just for the power that it could grant him, but for the people that would give him that power.

"Come on." Becca pulled on the cart. "We can't afford to let every delivery take that long."

"True." Digby pushed on the back.

From there, they continued to the rest of the rooms on Elenore's list, keeping their stays to a minimum. To Digby's surprise, and Becca's frustration, each stop had a plate of cookies waiting. Apparently, Campbell had made several batches that he'd allowed the city's children to take so that they would have an offering to make. It wasn't long before it became obvious that Becca could not eat that many. She resorted to just taking a bite and leaving the rest after reaching her limit.

Thanks to Elenore and the efficiency with which she organized her lists, the first phase of their plan was finished in under an hour. All that was left was to layer on the finishing touches before moving on to phase two.

Digby rushed for the stairwell that led to the roof, stopping now and then to wait for his little helper. The vampire's mana might have been full, but after eating an entirely unreasonable amount of sweets, her stomach was as well. Digby would have offered to carry her if it had not been for the fact that she looked like she might throw up if anyone jostled her too much.

Reaching the roof, Digby grinned to find an excited Asher waiting for him, along with eight zombified reindeer all harnessed to a large sleigh. Thanks to Alex and Mason, it had been transported from the airship down to the casino.

The sleigh was the size of the average cargo van with two rows of bench seats and a flat area in the back filled with red velvet sacks. Jameson had supplied him with multiple backups under the assumption that the necrotic blood of Digby's void would end up making a mess of things as the night progressed. Having more than one sack would make it easy to switch to a fresh one if need be.

In addition, there was also a supply trunk containing a toolbox and a fire extinguisher in case of emergency. Digby wasn't sure what part of the craft could catch fire, but he figured it was better to have it and not need it than need it and not have it.

"Hurry up and get aboard." Digby climbed up over the side and dropped into the front.

"I'm coming." Becca hoisted herself into the back, pushing aside a large plastic container that was sitting on her seat. "What's in here?" She shook it once she got settled in.

"That's for the reindeer. I thought it best to bring a few c-a-r-r-o-t-s to help them stay focused."

"But they're dead, they don't eat carrots anymore."

CARROT? Both Comet and Vixen craned their heads back and stamped their hooves.

"See what you've done." Digby grabbed the container from her. "And I know their diet has changed, but severed revenant fingers doesn't have the same ring to it." He pulled the lid off the container, revealing a couple dozen digits. "Now hop out and tend to the animals while I refamiliarize myself with the sleigh."

"Fine." Becca begrudgingly climbed back out.

Digby had already taken the sleigh for a test flight, but there were a lot of enchantments all working together. The harness of each reindeer was designed to negate the force of gravity on the animals. There was also a cylinder and adjustable ring of runes hanging between each pair, as well as one attached to the bottom of Asher's harness. A chain ran through each of them to the sleigh, where a crank-operated flight system had been built into the rear seat. From there, Becca could control their altitude.

In front of Digby, a pair of leather reins ran through a row of horizontal bars that were positioned at the back of each reindeer. Connected to that were more cylinders. Mana flowed from each of the undead animals to propel them forward. To control the direc-

345

tion, all Digby had to do was pull left or right. A mental or verbal command was all it took to get the whole thing moving.

Last, there was a pair of mirrors set into the wood in front of him for communication. Once they were on their way, Parker or Lana could cast the link spell, and Easton could guide them to each of their deliveries using the scrying mirror back on the airship. It seemed they had thought of everything, but that didn't mean things couldn't still go wrong.

"Ready?" Digby glanced back over his shoulder as his vampire helper climbed back in behind him after feeding the reindeer.

Becca gave him a weak thumbs up as she got to position beside the altitude control lever.

"We're off, then." Digby held a firm grip on the reins before giving the command to launch. "Take us up."

Asher let out a caw to back him up and the reindeer began walking forward. They picked up speed as the runecraft began to lighten their load.

"Okay, just pretend it's a drone," Becca said to herself as she gave the crank beside her a turn.

The sleigh lifted off the ground by a few inches, picking up speed with every second. Digby tensed as the roof flew by beneath them. It was so much different than riding in the limo that they had been using up until now.

"We need to go higher!" Digby shouted as they began to run out of roof, the half wall that ran around the edge coming toward them faster and faster.

"Oh shit." Becca's face went white. She gave the crank another two turns, sending the sleigh, reindeer and all, curving up toward the sky in a forty-five-degree angle climb.

"Not so high." Digby pulled the reigns to the left. "We still need to make a lasting impression."

The vampire behind him turned the altitude crank back to bring them down again.

Tugging on the reins, Digby turned the sleigh in a wide curve that took it back toward the Las Vegas strip. A hard yank brought it into a path that passed by the casino's windows in view of many of the rooms they had just made deliveries to. Lights blinked on here and there as they approached, silhouettes pressing themselves against the windows in astonishment. Digby couldn't stop himself from letting out a wild cackle as they flew by.

"It's ho ho ho, Dig! Not villainous laughter!" Becca shouted over the sound of the rushing wind.

"Oh yes, you're right." He tried his best to return to character.

With another hard yank on the reins, the sleigh turned sharply to circle the back of the casino, giving everyone a good enough look. It was sure to be enough to start the right rumors spreading.

"A little warning next time!" Becca hung halfway over the side behind him, struggling to get back into her seat after the sudden turn. "This thing doesn't have seatbelts."

"Well, it's a good thing you can fly."

"I would prefer not to need—" The vampire stopped talking abruptly, only to throw herself back over the side to throw up.

"Gross." Digby cringed. "Pull yourself together, Becky. That is not a good look for us right now. Honestly, I expect that sort of thing from Parker."

"I have a stomach full of cookies and blood, Dig." She dropped back into her seat. "I am doing the best that I can."

"Yes yes, your efforts are noted." He turned the sleigh one more time to finish the loop around the casino.

Once that was finished, Becca turned the altitude crank to climb toward the airship.

Of course, that was when one of the mirrors set into the front of Digby's seat came to life with an image of Lana standing next to Easton.

"Graves, we have a problem."

"Is it in airsick vampire?" Digby winced as Becca threw up over the side again.

"I swear, if I ever see another cookie, I will literally die." She dropped back into her seat again when she was done. "And if I hear one more complaint about me being sick, Dig, I'm going to throw up in your hat."

"Alright, not another word."

Both Easton and Lana stared at him blankly from the mirror. Then the communications specialist spoke.

"We have a problem with the town in Colorado." His tone sounded serious. "They are under attack."

"What?" Digby pulled the reins to adjust the angle of their climb. "I thought the cold was keeping them safe from any monsters."

"It's not monsters." Easton frowned. "It's people. Some kind of bandit group."

"Bandits?" Digby frowned. "I suppose I shouldn't be surprised."

A moment later, the corners of his mouth tugged back up into a grin as he remembered the requirements for his last few mutations. They all required the sparks of the living. One of the downsides of making peace with the empire, even if only temporary, was that it was significantly harder to add humans to the menu. Perhaps the kind of guilt-free dining that a group of bandits could provide was exactly what he needed. Not to mention the vampire behind him could always use a meal.

A cackle began to swell in his throat.

"It looks like someone has decided to give us a present as well, Becky."

CHAPTER THIRTY-ONE

"Heh-heh-heh!" Digby turned the sleigh around as Becca angled them down toward the village below.

"Again, it's ho ho ho, Dig. Every time you get it wrong, it sounds creepier," the vampire commented.

Digby ignored her.

It had only taken an hour for the airship to reach the mountains of Colorado. Considering the situation, Jameson had been willing to push the ship to its limits. Once within range, they launched the sleigh. Digby wasn't sure how many bandits were waiting for him below, but they were sure to have at least a few sparks to offer.

Glancing at his HUD, he brought up his available mutations.

SOUL EATER
Drag your prey into a temporary immaterial space. If
devoured within this space, you will consume their spark.
Consuming the spark of another may result in the advance-
ment of other abilities or attributes. Consuming the spark of
another may also result in the discovery of new abilities.
Consumed sparks may also be saved for use later.
Resource Requirements: 5 Still-Beating Human Hearts

SPIRIT CALLER
Draw the echoes of the lingering dead toward you across great distances. Each use will consume 100MP.
Resource Requirements: 10 Sparks

CALL OF THE CONSUMED
Reform the body of a spark you have consumed from the resources available to you. This temporary entity will fight alongside you and will be capable of most abilities that it had in life. Each use will require a temporary mana donation of 150MP as well as the resources required to restore the called echo's original body.
Resource Requirements: 25 Sparks

CURSE BLAST
Unleash a blast capable of eroding a target's natural and supernatural defense. Once a target's defenses have been negated, your curse will spread to them. This version of the curse will take effect immediately. The time it takes to negate defenses may vary. This mutation will cost 10MP per second that it is active.
Resource Requirements: 50 Sparks

The first thing he needed was the still-beating hearts to reach the Soul Eater mutation. He'd already eaten three back when he'd paid a visit to Skyline's old base. He still regretted his actions there, but he couldn't take them back. That just left two more hearts to go. Once he got past that, he would be able to create an immaterial space where he could devour a person, soul and all. After that, he just had to work toward the others. Though each mutation was so powerful, he wasn't sure which he should claim first.

He checked his mana one last time.

MP: 526/526

"What's the situation down there now?" Digby glanced down at one of the mirrors in front of him.

"I'm not sure exactly how many we're dealing with, but there's at least twenty bandits, maybe more." Easton stood with the scrying mirror behind him. "I'll update you with whatever I can learn."

"How did this start?" Becca asked from the back seat of the sleigh.

"I'm not sure when it started, but I checked in on the village one last time while you two were delivering presents to the kids in Vegas. They had already been attacked by that point. It's not surprising, sadly. There's bound to be bandit groups roaming the world out there." Easton sighed. "As for the town, it's a campground with a central road running up into a dead end. Several cabins run along the road on both sides, with a larger building at the end that seemed to be used as an infirmary and general store. From what I can tell, the area was used as a corporate retreat before the world ended."

"Have any of the villagers been killed? And more importantly, do the children still live?"

"There's a few bodies in the snow outside. There's a limit to how many angles I can see using the scrying mirror, but it looks like they attempted to defend the area when the bandits showed up and were quickly overpowered. I haven't been able to find any of the kids or other villagers."

"That isn't a good sign." Digby tightened his grip on the reins. "We may be too late."

"Maybe not." Becca leaned forward over the back of his seat so she could see Easton in the mirror. "If the people were overpowered fast, then it's unlikely that everybody died in the beginning. There's still a chance that the bandits executed everyone, but I find it hard to believe they would do that after only being there for just a few hours."

"But if the villagers still live, why can't Easton scry them?"

"The fact that I can't find them might be good. If they're alive, then there's only one place they could be held, the infirmary. Just having a medical facility in the building seems to be enough to keep me from seeing inside," the communications specialist reminded him.

"Ah yes, what was it? Doctor-patient confidentiality."

"Yeah, that explains the blind spot." Becca adjusted their altitude to bring them down low enough to get a look at the village's
layout. Digby grabbed a pair of binoculars from a box that was
secured under his seat.

The village was buried beneath two feet of snow. Smoke flowed
from several of the cabin's chimneys and a group of men stood in
the street around a large fire.

"I don't like the looks of that." Digby lowered the binoculars.
"If the villagers are still alive, they may not be much longer. I know
a pyre when I see one."

"The bandits must be planning on taking over the area and
getting rid of the people that found it before them." Becca stared
down at the fire, not needing anything more to see across the
distance with her vampiric senses. "We better get down there fast."

"I recommend setting down on the road a few hundred feet
away from the cabins," Easton commented. "That way you can
approach quietly and move from cabin to cabin to take them out a
few at a time."

Digby brought the sleigh in toward the road as Becca lowered
them down to the snow. The reindeer ran as they came into
contact with the ground, pulling the craft along. Instead of stopping, he continued onward and turned toward the road that ran
through the village.

"I can't help but notice that you're not slowing down." Becca
leaned forward, holding on to the back of his seat.

"Nothing gets past you." He chuckled. "I am a zombie lord. I
am not about to hide from a group of bandits. Besides, you are the
deadliest accomplice I have. I think we will fare well."

"Okay." She nodded.

"No arguments?" He eyed her suspiciously.

"No. This time you're right." She locked her eyes on the village
ahead. "Those kids might still be alive and there's no time to waste.
And yeah, I'm ready to scare the living hell out of these bandits."
She ran her tongue across her fangs.

Digby couldn't help but stare. Earlier, she had said that their
friendship had changed her, but he had assumed she'd been talking

about finding a way to live as a vampire. Yet, maybe it was more than that. The woman he'd met back in Seattle had been willing to use children as a means to lure him into a trap. She may have become a monster since then, but in truth, she may have grown more human as well.

"What?" She eyed him sideways.

"Nothing, it's just good to see you've stopped hiding from your-self." He flicked his eyes back to the road, not wanting to make her self-conscious. "Now let's see if we can make these grown men believe in Santa again."

Becca smiled, showing her fangs. "Just save one for me."

"Ha ha ha!" he laughed before correcting himself with his most jolly, "Ho ho ho!"

"Still a little creepy, but you're getting closer." She shook her head as the sleigh slid into the center of the village.

Digby willed his undead reindeer to slow to a stop as the men ahead standing around the fire turned in their direction. Several heads cocked to the side in confusion and jaws fell open. Digby reached for one of the sacks in the back of the sleigh and threw it over his shoulder. Then he climbed down. The snow crunched as he stepped to the ground.

"Hello there!" he called out to the bandits as he approached.

There were six of them, all standing around the pyre. From the look of the wood that had been fed into the flames, no bodies had been added to the mix yet. There was still time. Only two of the men were armed with rifles slung across their backs. The other four were holding tin cups full of some form of steaming beverage. Digby caught the scent of hot chocolate in the air. Four more rifles were leaning against one of the cabins around thirty feet away. They must have set them down for a break.

Digby grinned and checked his mana.

MP: 526/526

He'd lost a fair number of points in animating Comet and Vixen, but he still had more than enough to deal with a few bandits. Especially with a vampire at full strength there to back him up.

Becca hopped out of the sleigh behind him, leaving the firearms that Jameson had placed under her seat where they were. Monsters didn't have much use for guns, after all.

"Hold it right there." One of the two armed men pulled his rifle from his back, though he refrained from pointing at them. It was as if their disguises gave the man reason to pause. Instead, his eyes darted around, glancing from Digby to Becca, then to Asher, and back again.

"Who the fuck are you?" one of the men holding a metal cup asked as they approached.

Digby stopped, letting the sack on his back slide down his shoulder to land in the snow. Then he gestured to the sleigh and Becca before finally pointing to himself. "Is that a serious question? I should think it's obvious who I am."

"I don't think so," the man holding his rifle argued. "I don't know who you are, but you're insane if you think we're gonna fall for whatever this is."

"Of course not. I didn't walk in here, I drove a sleigh." Digby hooked a thumb over his shoulder.

"Yeah, and what the hell is that?" One of the men standing around the fire pointed his cup at Asher. "That ain't like no reindeer I've ever seen."

"Oh, that is a... I think the correct term is hippogriff?" Becca spoke up. "You know how it is with this whole apocalypse situation. Had to leave Rudolph back at the, ah, North Pole. With all those monsters running around, we needed something a little tougher to guide the sleigh."

The men stared at the two of them, dumbfounded, as they approached. It was as if their brains were sending them dozens of conflicting signals. What they were seeing was so absurd that it had to be impossible, but at the same time, the impossibility of it all created an air of credibility.

"Not one more step." The man with the rifle raised it as the others glanced toward their weapons leaning against the cabin nearby.

"There is no need to bring firearms into this." Digby stopped, holding up one hand while his other remained on the sack dragging behind him.

The distance didn't matter. He was already in range to cast several spells. However, it would still be advantageous to keep things quiet. No sense in alerting whoever was in the surrounding cabins.

"What do you want?" The second man with a rifle raised his as well.

"I have deliveries to make." Digby glanced at the largest of the buildings behind the group of men. "According to my list, there's twenty children being held up in that doctor's office in need of presents."

"Yes, and they have been very good this year," Becca added, sounding eerily cheerful.

A look of panic fell across the group of men as a few of them glanced back at the building behind them.

Digby grinned as they confirmed that the villagers were still alive and being held exactly where Easton had thought they were. As a bonus, the only way he could have known where the villagers were being held was if he was the man he was impersonating. From the fear on their faces, he could tell they were beginning to believe it too.

"I don't care why you're here. Just turn around and go back the way you came. If you think we won't shoot a man dressed as Santa on Christmas Eve, you have another thing coming. It wouldn't be the worst thing we've done in the last month."

Digby frowned as he leaned toward Becca. "That's a pity, isn't it?"

She folded her arms. "Yes, it is. We still have a lot of deliveries to make and we really can't afford to be slowed down here."

He nodded. She made a good point. As much fun as he was having with the ruse, time was a factor.

"No time to waste, indeed."

With that, he opened his maw between the two men holding rifles and fed in the additional mana to widen it enough to swallow them whole. A low cackle rumbled through his chest as the ground fell out from underneath them. They didn't even get a chance to fire a shot. Instead, they flailed, dropping their guns altogether as they scrambled to find purchase. They vanished into the pool of darkness a second later.

A message appeared on Digby's HUD the instant they did.

New mutation available, Soul Eater.
Accept?

Digby didn't even think about it. He just nodded his head and waited for something to change. The other four men threw their cups aside, still struggling to comprehend what they had just seen. Three of them turned and ran for their weapons leaning by the cabin while one dove for one of the guns that had been dropped by the men that Digby had just eaten.

Becca casually walked in the direction of the three men running for their weapons. She closed her eyes as shadows grew between the bandits and their guns. All three of them stopped dead in their tracks when a figure of pure darkness coalesced in a twisting form of horror, burning like black fire. The monstrous form grew to twice the height of the bandits, bat wings spreading wide to block out the view beyond. One of the men slipped in the snow as the projected shade fell upon them. The darkness dispersed on contact, leaving the three bandits terrified.

Becca simply launched a foot into the face of the closest target before throwing her body into a spiral that brought her other foot down on top of the head of another. She landed in a crouch before diving for the third man lying on the ground.

Digby let her have them, staying focused on the one in front of him as he crawled through the snow to grab one of the rifles.

"I wouldn't do that." Digby raised a hand and cast Decay on the rifle the moment the man raised it.

A layer of rust and corrosion formed around the barrel, spreading down the weapon's length. The trigger snapped off in the man's hand when he tried to pull it.

Another message appeared on Digby's HUD.

Decay has reached rank A.
New spell discovered
WITHER
Description: similar to the spell Decay, Wither will unleash
the ravages of time upon a target, but to a greater extent.
Crumble buildings, rot flesh from bone, or blight the land.
Death finds all in the end. This spell is capable of eroding a
target's natural and supernatural defenses. The time required
to negate a target's defenses may vary. *Best not to go over-*
board. No sense in ruining a meal.
Rank: D
Cost: Variable, 10 MP per second (-50% due to mana
balance, total 5 MP per second)
Range: 25 ft

For the sake of experimentation, Digby raised his hand toward the man and cast Wither. The bandit immediately clutched his head in panic from the assault on his will. Within seconds, the spell had ripped through his defenses. He gasped in pain as his skin began to turn an ashen gray, black spots spreading from his hands up toward his body. His fingers shriveled before crumbling away altogether.

"Holy hell!" Digby stopped the spell, realizing how powerful it was, inadvertently leaving the man staring in horror at his ruined hands.

A pang of guilt reminded him to put an end to the bandit quickly. Digby reached for his mutations, calling to his Soul Eater. The instant he did, his mana value dropped by fifty and the world went silent. A circle of red light swept outward from his feet to spread out twenty-five feet in all directions. Inside the edges of the glow was nothing but darkness. Just an inky expanse of black liquid.

The terrified bandit didn't seem to notice. He simply knelt there in the pool of nothingness, his reflection rippling below him. It was as if he couldn't see any of it. Digby looked down, finding his own reflection connected to his feet. Looking around, his surroundings were visible in the pool he stood in as well. The snow, the cabins, and the pyre. They were all there beneath him, as if he were looking at the world through a pane of dark glass. He moved a hand, watching his reflection do the same.

That was when he realized that everything below him was real. He was in two places at once. The mutation had created a new space that held only his soul and that of his prey. Then, just like that, the world snapped back to normal around him. He was back in the village, standing in the snow. The pool of darkness was gone.

Or was it?

Digby glanced down, furrowing his brow. He could still feel it. The duality of his existence. Physical and spiritual. He blinked, and suddenly he was back in that temporary space. It was bizarre.

Flicking his eyes back to the man kneeling in front of him, still too scared to move, Digby noticed something behind him. A figure. No, a spirit of a man, floating around the bandit. Digby didn't recognize him, yet he was still familiar, as if they had met in passing. Then he realized why. The same man lay dead in the snow someplace over by the sleigh. He had been one of the villagers that had tried to defend their home. One of the villagers killed by the bandits when they arrived. No, it was more personal than that. He had been killed by this specific bandit.

Another figure faded into existence behind the kneeling man, then another and another. None of them were a complete soul. Those would have passed on to whatever world awaited the dead. No, these were mere echoes. The lingering traces of the dead. Fragments of everyone he killed. They drifted through the ambient mana around the bandit as if clinging to him. Most were men, though there were a few women and two children.

Digby blinked, returning himself to the physical world, not wanting to see any more. Without hesitation, he opened his maw beneath the man. Beneath the monster. Then he swallowed him whole.

His resources ticked up by one spark.

"Did you get your mutation?" Becca stood over the other three men, holding a bloody knife that she must have pulled from one of their belts. Blood pooled in the snow around them but they were still alive. One was clutching at a dozen wounds to his abdomen while another was desperately trying to put pressure on a slash to his throat. The third was dragging himself toward the guns with his jaw hanging at an unnatural angle.

"Yes." Digby arched an eyebrow. "You didn't kill any of them?"

"I do have at least some self-control." She tossed the knife in her hand over her shoulder, hitting the man who was still going for the guns on the head. "You need the sparks, right? I figured it would be more productive if you ate them. Plus, we're here to save a bunch of kids and I probably shouldn't walk in there drenched in blood. I'll pick off one of the others before we leave to top myself off."

"That's actually very thoughtful of you."

"Yes, I'm pretty much a saint." She gestured to the men on the ground. "Now hurry up and eat these guys. They're bleeding out fast."

"Wait…" The man clutching his throat choked out a word.

"Yes?" Digby hesitated, feeling a little uncomfortable killing someone who had already been beaten. The least he could do was to hear out a final wish.

"We… have… hostages." The man gurgled. "Kids."

The implication was clear. Let the man live and they might not kill the children being held by the rest of their group.

Digby rolled his eyes and opened his maw wide enough to take all three of the dying bandits. Attempting to activate his Soul Eater mutation again, he instantly flipped back into the temporary space from before. Somehow it was still active. That was when he realized the ability didn't pull people in one at a time. No, he'd pulled in every soul within its radius at the time he'd activated it, including Becca.

Not wanting to waste precious seconds, he swallowed the dying bandits and watched as the fragments of those they'd killed disappeared as the men sank into his maw. It was as if they had been set free, allowed to return to the world's essence that had formed them. He closed his maw, leaving only Becca within the space once they were gone.

The vampire's soul looked the same as the woman he knew but was surrounded by a swirling darkness. Like the bandits, she was joined by the traces of everyone she'd killed. There were dozens of them. Not just Autem's Guardians, either. She seemed to be carrying more, probably from the time she'd spent working for Skyline as a drone operator. Her actions must have caused the deaths of many. Now, they clung to her. Digby shuddered, not wanting to think about how many lingering traces collected around him.

"What?" Becca stared at him.

His mind instantly blinked back to the physical world. "Nothing."

Digby pushed the thought out of his mind.

Of course, that was when the door of a cabin not far away opened.

"What the fuck?" A man rushed out into the snow, raising a rifle as another two emerged from the cabin behind him, both armed.

"Damn." Digby spun, summoning two echoes at once, his crone to stop them in their tracks and his wraith to dispatch them before they had time to fire.

An emerald glow shined as the spectral hands of the crone reached up from the ground to grab hold of the threats. Terror and confusion flooded their faces as they struggled to decide whether they should shoot at the man dressed as Santa or the ghostly limbs wrapping around their legs. A crimson light flickered into existence as the echo of a long-dead killer streaked past the first one, barely making contact. Blood sprayed from his neck to stain the snow with a field of red splotches. One of the two men behind him started to scream as the flickering image of Digby's wraith reached him. The other beside him squeezed off one bullet. It passed right through the echo to punch into the frozen ground. They fell a moment later.

Digby rushed toward them, opening his maw and activating his Soul Eater again with the hope of claiming the bodies before they died. Two souls were pulled in time, but the first had already passed on. He was going to have to be faster in the future, or use a less destructive spell, at least.

There wasn't time to dwell on it.

The rest of the bandits must've heard that gunshot. It was only a matter of time before they either rushed out of every cabin in the village or killed their hostages. Digby glanced at his mana, finding only one hundred and ninety-six points remaining. He'd used a lot of power to activate his new mutation. He didn't dare Leach any from his reindeer or Becca. The best he could do was take fifty points from Asher.

With that, he turned toward the largest building in the village where the children were being held and started walking.

Becca kept pace beside him as the doors of several cabins opened around them. "You may not be able to keep up the Santa act here."

Men called out after them as Digby set foot on the steps of their destination.

He ignored them.

"We shall see."

CHAPTER THIRTY-TWO

Dr. Bill Aman was not a doctor.

Sure, he had started medical school, but the thought of potentially holding a person's life in his hands had freaked him out. That was why he'd backed out and become a veterinarian instead. There was a little less pressure in treating animals. Plus, he liked them better.

Heading to the campground had been his brother's idea. It was one of those corporate retreat-type places where office workers went for team-building exercises. Sort of like summer camp for adults. His brother had spent a week there the year before. It may have been in its off-season, but it was miles away from the nearest city and had plenty of room. When the world ended, they had headed straight there.

Along the way, they picked up a few more survivors.

Then, a few more.

After two weeks of traveling on foot through the woods and up the mountains to avoid running into any of those monsters, their group swelled. It had become less of a group and more of a tiny town. There were over thirty adults and twenty children. Everyone had been lucky. Well, almost everyone.

His brother didn't make it.

Reaching the campground, he found a storage building filled with enough canned goods for months. It was plenty to ride out the winter. Bill never had any ambition to be in charge of anything, but since he had inherited his brother's plan of going to the campground, everyone just kept looking to him. They knew he wasn't a real doctor, but he had the most medical knowledge out of anyone in the group. He was pretty sure the title just made people more comfortable.

Everything had gone well in the month after they reached the campground.

Until now.

Christmas Eve, of all nights.

The bandits showed up over an hour ago.

Bill cringed at the word the first time he'd thought it.

Bandits.

Was that really what the world had become?

They must've seen the smoke coming from some of the cabin's chimneys and come to investigate. The group of over thirty men were all armed with assault rifles and tactical gear. Some even carried a second weapon on their back, as if they'd picked it up along the way. A few basic hunting rifles were all Bill and the rest of his group had between them. The fight had been over in minutes, leaving five dead.

On top of being well-armed, the bandits had a look of desperation about them that was impossible to miss. In the last hour, Bill had noticed a few of them arguing with each other. They may have been well-armed, but guns didn't help in the cities or towns where those monsters had taken over. They must have fled to the mountains to escape but realized they weren't prepared for survival in the wilderness. There was less food available and fewer people to exploit. Now, they were wearing thin.

Bill swallowed hard.

Desperation only served to make the bandits more dangerous. They wanted the same things that everyone wanted, safety and supplies. They had already made it clear that they had no problem killing to make sure they came out on top.

"You can't be serious." Bill knelt on the floor in front of his people who had been gathered in the campground's infirmary.

"I think we're being pretty reasonable." A guy named John stood with one hand resting on the butt of a pistol on his belt. "No one else has to die today. We secured this area, and we will let you leave without incident."

Another six men, each holding an assault rifle, stood behind him. They must have been his most loyal.

"What kind of option is that?" Bill gestured to everyone behind him. "You want fifty people, nearly half of which are children, to go out there in the middle of the night, in the snow, with nothing but the clothes on our backs? We won't even live long enough to be killed by the monsters. We'll just freeze or starve before we get off the mountain. All so, what? You guys can just move into the campgrounds?"

"The survival of your people isn't our problem." John stared down at him, clearly feeling superior.

Several of the children cried, terrified of the men, the guns, and the cold waiting for them outside.

"You can't do this." Bill stood up, letting his frustration get the better of him.

"Of course we can. It's our right." John held both hands out wide. "These campgrounds don't belong to you, neither do the supplies. You just found them."

"First," Bill added. "We found them first."

"It doesn't matter who was first. Just who is more capable and better prepared. While you were blindly going about your life before the world ended, me and my guys were already getting back to our roots. We saw the writing on the wall. It was going to take work to survive. Grasshopper and the ant and all that. We put in the work, you didn't." He turned for a moment only to spin back around, pulling his gun from its holster and cracking it into the side of Bill's head.

He hit the floor hard, his skull throbbing as blood ran down the side of his face. Before he could try to sit back up, John placed the boot on his chest and aimed his pistol down at his head.

"No, don't get up." The man looked out across the room of

cowering people. "Okay, now I am going to need everyone here to go outside and head down the road, or I will start shooting. It's up to you whichever happens first."

Bill blinked, still trying to see straight. "No."

He didn't fully understand what he was saying until the word had already left his mouth, but he didn't stop there. "Everyone listen up, there's only seven of them in here, keep the kids back and rush them. Get the guns. Now go!"

That was the only way. Nothing but death waited for them outside. At least if they tried to fight, they would have a chance. If they could get the weapons away from John and the rest of the men in the room, they could move on from there. Bill closed his eyes, expecting to be shot the moment anyone moved. Then he opened them again.

Everyone was still right where they were.

No one had even tried to stand up.

"Did you really think anyone was going to fight?" John waved his gun across the room, grinning as people ducked. "That's the problem with everyone nowadays. They just sit by waiting for someone else to save them. And I'm sorry to break it to them, but there's no one left out there." He lowered his pistol to aim it at Bill's head again.

Bill gritted his teeth and stared back at the man in defiance. He was as good as dead.

That was when a green glow shined in through the front windows from someplace outside. A flash of red followed. Then, a single gunshot.

John hesitated, looking up to the side. "What the hell is going on out there?"

One of his men reached for a radio and repeated the question.

A voice crackled back from the speaker. "You're not going to believe who just showed up."

A knock came at the door a second later.

John glanced back at the entrance as one of his men tried to look out the window.

He shook his head. "Someone's out there, but I can't see from here."

"What about Mike and the guys building the fire?" John sounded frustrated.

The bandit at the window looked outside again. "I don't see them."

Again, a knock came at the door. This time accompanied by muffled talking.

"Do you think they're going to open it?" a feminine voice asked from the other side of the door.

"I don't know, Becky, but make sure you have that list on you. I have a plan," a gravelly voice responded.

The six armed men looked to John for what to do.

"Well, open it." He aimed his pistol at the door, signaling for the rest of his guys to do the same.

Bill sat up, debating on whether or not to do anything now that John and the rest of the bandits had turned their backs on him and his people. He froze in disbelief an instant later when the door swung open.

"What the fuck?" John cocked his head to the side as his pistol's aim faltered.

It was Santa Claus.

Obviously, it wasn't really him, but it was a man dressed like him. He even carried a large sack over his shoulder. His beard was a little scraggly and his skin was ashen and gray. Though, that could have been from the cold. Beside him, a pale woman dressed in an elf costume stood, holding a folded sheet of paper in her hand. Bells on her shoes jingled as she walked inside.

Bill's mind struggled to process what he was seeing.

Shit, she even had pointy ears.

Some of the children who had been crying stopped as soon as a strange pair entered the room, somehow finding an element of comfort in the costumes.

"Well now." The man dressed as Santa completely ignored the guns pointed at him as if they weren't a threat. "If you don't mind, I have a job to do."

"Of course, I mind. We're in the middle of…" John trailed off clearly struggling to find the right words to explain the situation in a way that was not damning. "What even are you supposed to be?"

The strange man in the red suit frowned. "What am I supposed to be? Didn't you have a childhood? I think it should be obvious." His demeanor was anything but jolly. "I am Santa Claus, the one and only." He continued to ignore John and his men and inclined his head toward Bill and the rest of his people kneeling on the floor behind him. Taking off his hat, he revealed a head of messy white hair before putting it back on.

"Hey! I am talking to you." John raised his gun to point at the costumed man's head.

"Yes, and I will deal with you in a moment." He simply raised a finger and placed it on the tip of John's pistol to lower it down a few inches. "First, I have deliveries to make."

John stared at him with a look of sheer bafflement as he went back to ignoring him.

"Now where was I?" The strange man dropped his sack to the floor beside him.

"The list." The woman dressed as an elf beside him offered the single sheet of paper she held. It looked like it had been folded up in her pocket until a moment before.

"Ah yes." The man in red snatched it from her and stared down at it for a few seconds before looking back up. "Is there a Robert here?" He held a hand out at about waist high. "Should be about yea tall."

Bill's eyes widened. There was a Robert. One of the kids. He glanced back to find the six-year-old being held by his mother not far behind him. Then he looked back at the man claiming to be Santa. Conflicting truths crashed together in his mind. Obviously, this man was not who he said he was. That was impossible. Yet, somehow he knew the name of one of the children there.

Somehow, he was there, on Christmas Eve.

"I'm—" Robert spoke up for a second, not fully understanding the danger that they were in.

His mother clutched him tighter to keep him quiet.

"Oh good, there he is." The woman dressed as an elf bent down and grabbed the sack from the floor before loosening the cord that held it closed. Just by looking at the bag, Bill could tell it was empty.

"Thank you, Becky." The man in red pulled something small out of his pocket and leaned over to reach into the sack. He fumbled around for around fifteen seconds. Then, he pulled out a present.

The whole room gasped, including John and his men.

Bill struggled to explain away what he'd just seen. It had to be a trick. Sleight-of-hand, or something. Any stage magician could have done the same thing.

"Alright, Robert, come on up. And if I could have the rest of the children line up as well, we can get this done quickly. I do have more stops to make tonight." The strange man held the present out.

The package was neatly wrapped in paper covered with drawings of friendly characters celebrating multiple holidays.

No one dared move.

"It's okay. I mean your village no harm." Santa smiled down at the boy as he urged him to stand. His grin was crooked, but it held a strange warmth.

From where Bill knelt, he could see clearly into the man's eyes. They were the eyes of someone who had seen more pain than most. At the same time, they held a kindness. Bill wasn't sure if it was the costume or just the desperation he felt in the moment, but a part of him wanted to trust the stranger.

"It's okay." He looked back to Robert and gave his mother a nod.

She looked uneasy but released her son from her arms.

"There you go," Santa said, as if talking to a frightened animal. "Come on now."

John waited in stunned silence, still pointing a gun at the stranger's chest and watching as the moment unfolded.

Robert took a few cautious steps forward.

The man in red walked to meet him, kneeling as he held the present out.

The child crept closer and reached out.

"There we are." He handed over the present and stood up. "You may open it now if you want. There's no harm in doing things a little early. I certainly won't tell anyone."

The kid hesitated for a moment before looking back to his mother. She shrugged before nodding. The situation was already strange enough, how could opening the gift make things any worse? Robert tore at the wrapping paper, finding a white cardboard box underneath. His eyes lit up when he opened the lid.

It was a stuffed cow. A red one. Nothing more, nothing less.

Just a toy.

Robert clutched it to his chest and squeezed it tight.

"Alright, run along back to your mother." The stranger waved the child away before turning back to the open sack where he'd gotten the present. "I have one for everyone."

Bill watched as he reached back into the empty bag to pull out another package. Then another, and another. He handed one to Bill, telling him to pass it back to make sure each of the children got one.

John and the rest of his men stared in disbelief at the process. Bill half expected them to interrupt, but it seemed even they didn't have the heart to get in the way.

The children all tore at the presents, unwrapping one toy after another. When the last gift had been handed out, the man in red nodded and turned to John.

"There. Now, I'm sure you and your men can find someplace else to stay. So I'll ask, nicely, for you to leave these people alone."

Bill tensed as the words left the stranger's mouth. It was a lost cause. No matter what tricks or illusions he had up his sleeves. John had already made it clear that he and his men weren't leaving.

"Look, I don't know what you're trying to pull here, or how you did any of that shit with the bag, but it's time you left." John kept his pistol aimed at the stranger's chest.

"No," he responded as a laugh bubbled up from his throat. It sounded more like a cackle than anything jolly. He cracked a smug grin as he added, "You will have to shoot—"

John pulled the trigger before the stranger could finish his sentence.

Most of the room cried out in horror as the gun barked.

"...Me." The man dressed as Santa simply continued his sentence. He hadn't even flinched. Looking down at the hole in his coat, he groaned. "You realize this outfit had to be custom-made, right?"

John took a step back with a mix of fear and confusion on his face. There was no blood.

He must've been wearing some kind of bulletproof vest under the costume.

Running out of options, John shifted his aim toward the woman dressed as an elf. Her coat was more form-fitting with no room for body armor.

"Hey wait!" she shouted just as he pulled the trigger.

The gun fired, blood spraying from her chest. A spatter of crimson coated the wall behind her.

"Jesus fuck." She staggered backward. "You shot me in the boob. What kind of person does that?" Reaching over her shoulder, she patted her back with her other hand. Then she turned around. "Hey, is there an exit wound?"

"Yes, Becky. You'll be fine." The man in red didn't seem concerned.

"Oh good. I didn't want to dig that one out." The elf relaxed as the bleeding stopped.

"What the fuck is—" John started to ask.

The bells of the woman's shoes jingled as she darted toward him, her hand shooting out with almost supernatural speed to snatch the pistol out of his hand. John was left staring at his empty palm.

The rest of his men all aimed their rifles at her now that she was armed.

"Yeah, I'm an elf with a gun. Fear me." She held the pistol casually at her side before hooking a thumb back at the man in red beside her. "You should probably be more worried about him, to be honest."

"Indeed."

As the word left the stranger's mouth, Bill felt a chill travel up his spine. It was like somebody had walked over his grave.

"I'm afraid you and your bandit friends have been very naughty." The man in the Santa costume waved a hand at the men pointing rifles at him. In the same instant, rust began forming on the barrels to travel up the length of each weapon. After that, he returned his attention to John. "Do you know what happens to naughty bandits?"

John tried to step away, but the man in red reached out to grab the front of his tactical vest.

He cackled as he pulled the frightened man close to answer his own question. "Naughty bandits go in the bag."

With that, he yanked John forward with one hand and held the other out toward the elf that accompanied him. She handed him the edge of the empty sack. The rest of the bandits fumbled with their rifles, unable to fire after whatever had been done to them. One of the men reached for a sidearm, but the elf was on him in seconds. The bells of her shoes jingled as she planted a foot on his chest and kicked him a solid ten feet. He crashed straight through a window.

"Everyone stay down!" Bill shouted to try to keep his people out of danger.

That was when the man dressed as Santa shoved John face-first into the red velvet sack. The man simply vanished, toppling through the opening as if the space inside was limitless.

Another of the bandits reached for a side arm.

"I have plenty of room for you in here as well." The man in red leapt toward him holding the opening of the sack wide to throw it over his head.

Again, a grown man vanished into the bag.

"We need help in here! We're under attack!" another of the bandits yelled into a radio just before disappearing into the red velvet sack as well.

The remaining three bandits scrambled for the doors, running for their lives.

The woman in the elf costume followed as they ran outside. She stopped in the doorway, firing at them with the pistol she'd taken from John. "That's right, I'm an elf on the edge! And it's already been a long night!"

"Easy, Becky." The man dressed as Santa held up a hand to his mouth and whispered a little too loudly, "Not in front of the children."

Her gun clicked empty and she tossed it aside. "Good point."
She held both hands out beside her as what looked like icicles
formed in the air. They grew into sharp spikes that floated in the
space above her palms. She glanced back to the man in red. "I'll
see you outside. We can't let any of them get away. They might
come back after we leave."

He nodded as she walked out of the infirmary, launching the
icicles in her hands at the men outside. The doors closed behind
her as gunfire erupted. Someone outside screamed only for it to be
cut off abruptly.

"What is happening?" Bill stood up, unable to process what he
was seeing.

It couldn't be a trick.

No, it was some kind of magic.

"Hold your questions for later." Santa held up a finger before
turning toward the doors. "There's plenty more men out there
with guns, so keep everyone inside with their heads down."

A moment later, he was gone, the doors closing behind him.

"Stay down." Bill threw a hand behind him as everyone
ducked close to the floor.

Children clutched their new toys tight as parents held them
close.

Bill snapped his eyes back to the doors as the world outside
exploded into chaos.

"Who the—" a man started to yell, only to be cut off by
another.

"It doesn't matter, just take them down!"

Dozens of rifles began to fire, light flashing in the windows
casting shadows across the floor for only a fraction of a second at a
time. Bill should have gotten down with everyone else, but instead,
he just stood there, transfixed by everything that had happened.
Bullets punched into the front of the building in a line of impact
that ran in vertically to the right of the doors.

Then, silence fell.

All Bill could hear was the hard-click clack of rifles being
reloaded.

That was it.

Whoever the strangers were, they couldn't have survived that. The bandits had plenty of men out there, and from the sound of it, they had given them everything they had. Still, he held onto a shred of hope that he was wrong. Seconds later, a voice confirmed the harsh truth.

"They're down!"

Bill's heart sank. He shook off his sorrow a second later. The man in the Santa costume and his elf may have died, but they'd bought him time. More importantly, they had thrown the bandits into disarray and softened them up. Bill swept his eyes across the room in search of a weapon. If he could get out there, he could pick up where they left off. He would almost certainly die as well, but if he could take a few of them down with them, the rest of his people would have a chance.

They could win.

Rushing to the floor where a few of the men's rifles had been dropped, he found them all damaged beyond repair. The man in red had merely waved his hand at them, and yet, it looked like the weapons had been left out in the elements for years. All that was left was the pistol that John had been carrying. The one that the elf woman had tossed to the floor.

It was empty.

Then Bill remembered that John had draped a coat over a chair near the door just before he began threatening everyone earlier. Fishing through the pockets, he found two full magazines.

He'd never fired a gun. Not until recently when the world ended. Before that, all he'd ever done was take care of sick animals. He certainly never raised a weapon at another person.

"What are you doing?" Robert's mother looked up at him from the floor.

"I'm going out there." He glanced around the room at the members of his group who were not protecting children. "I'm going to do what I can. I want everyone here that's able to wait until the men out there have to reload again. Then rush them. That's the only chance we have."

Bill didn't wait for them to say anything else. No, he went straight for the window and climbed through as quietly as he could. The bandits outside were all still focused on something on the ground in the middle of the road. It looked like a body, dressed in red. They all crept toward it cautiously. The woman in the elf costume lay at the bottom of the steps. Crimson stained the snow around her and bullet holes peppered her coat and tights. She must have been gunned down as soon as she went outside.

Why? Bill crouched nearby in the shadows. *Why did they throw their lives away? Who even were they?*

His attention was pulled back to the bandits closing in on the man in red's body as one of them shouted.

"Fuck, he moved!"

A rifle fired a short burst into the body's chest.

"There's no way he fucking moved. He's mostly lead at this point," another bandit commented.

That was when the corpse's hand snapped up into the air. It twitched and popped like something out of a horror movie. Then, the same thing that had happened to the weapons of the men inside happened again to each of the rifles that were pointing at him.

"What the hell?" The bandits all struggled with their guns as they fell apart in their hands.

Bill didn't dare move as a low chuckle came from the stranger's corpse. It grew into a villainous cackle as his back suddenly arched upward. One arm snapped out straight to the side while the other reached for the velvet sack that lay nearby. A moment later, he simply rose back up to his feet as if possessed. He staggered briefly as a series of pops and cracks came from his body. Straightening out, he cracked his neck before locking his eyes on the men in front of him.

"To answer your question of what the hell happened to your weapons, you all made the mistake of getting close enough that I could destroy them all at once." He grabbed onto his bag with his other hand and pulled it open. "Now, I think it's time that you all got in my sack."

With that, he leapt forward at the man at the center of the group without warning. The bandit screamed as the stranger threw the sack over his head, his voice going silent an instant later. The stranger in red kicked the bandit's legs out from under him with one foot and flipped him over as he shoved the rest of him down into the bag. The rest of the men scattered in different directions.

A cackle echoed through the campgrounds as the costumed man chased after the nearest bandit, holding the sack open like a child capturing a butterfly with a net.

Bill couldn't believe what he was seeing, his shock growing when he glanced to the bottom of the steps to find the body of the woman gone. There was no way she had been alive. There had been at least a dozen bullet holes in her coat. He shoved the thought aside. None of that changed why he'd gone out there. He still didn't know what the strangers wanted, but that didn't mean he wasn't going to help.

Bill rushed out into the fight, holding the pistol with both hands, ready to fire at the first bandit he saw. Catching movement out of the corner of his eye, he noticed one of the men run behind a cabin. He nodded to himself and gave chase, the snow crunching underfoot as he ran. Bill could still hear the man in red cackling behind him as he sprinted around the cabin. He nearly fell over when he turned the corner.

The man he had been chasing was in the middle of pulling some kind of submachine gun out of a duffel bag that had been left at the back door of the cabin.

"Shit." Bill took aim with the pistol in his hands and pulled the trigger. "Shit," he repeated when nothing happened. Bill's eyes bulged as he looked down at the gun. He'd been sure he'd checked the safety after sliding one of the magazines in.

The bandit in front of him turned toward him and raised his weapon.

Bill winced.

Then a green blur crashed into the bandit. It hissed wildly, like a stray cat fighting over a dead mouse. The sound blended with the jingling of bells.

Bill fell backward in the cold snow as the woman in the elf costume bent down over the bandit that she'd just knocked over and tore his throat open with her teeth. Arterial blood sprayed rhythmically from the wound. The woman just opened her mouth wider to cover more of the opening, the muscles in her jaw tensing, her teeth sinking deeper into his flesh.

"What are you?" Bill whispered. He didn't actually expect an answer. Hell, he half expected her to lunge at him next.

Instead, she tore her mouth away, breathing heavily for a few seconds as her eyes slowly drifted toward him. Blood covered her face and ran down the front of her coat to stain the white fur that lined the collar. That was when her expression shifted, suddenly looking sheepish. "Oh shit, you weren't supposed to see this part."

Bill froze, the icy chill of the snow beneath him seeping into his bones. An impulse to raise the pistol in his hand at the woman crossed his mind, but he ignored it. A part of him still wanted to trust the strangers. Anyone who'd gone to so much effort to give toys to children in the apocalypse couldn't be bad. He was pretty sure he couldn't stop her from killing him anyway.

"Give it here." She held a hand out toward his gun. Her other hand was still coiled through the dead bandit's hair.

Bill handed the pistol over cautiously.

"You have to rack the slide to chamber the first round." She let go of her victim and took the gun, only to pull back on the top part of the weapon. It snapped back when she released it. "There, you're good to go." She held it out with the handle facing him. "It took me a while to get used to guns too."

"Ah, thanks." Bill took it from her just as cautiously as he had given it. He did his best to ignore that the pistol's entire handle was now covered in blood.

The woman simply gave him a nod as shadows moved toward her. For an instant, the darkness formed what looked like wings. They stretched out behind her only to flap once before dispersing. She jumped at the same time, launching herself straight up to land on the roof of the cabin beside him. Then she was gone.

Bill could still hear the occasional gunshot as well as the man in red shouting at the bandits. He pushed himself up out of the snow and returned to the fight, making a point of circling around to check the backs of a few of the cabins before returning to the center of the campground. He let his gun fall limp at his side as soon as he reached it.

"Yeah, that might as well make sense." He scratched at the back of his neck as he stared at a sleigh complete with eight reindeer. At the front stood a griffin, or some other kind of mythical bird creature. He didn't have the energy to even think about it.

For an instant, he started to raise his gun again as one of the bandits ran by, fleeing for his life. The man slowed as he reached the sleigh, ducking next to one of the reindeer as if hoping he might not be spotted. He only made it a few feet before the animal bent its head toward him and excitedly bit down on his arm. The reindeer yanked him off balance, causing him to fall into the snow where he was held down with the hoof.

Bill recoiled in horror as the reindeer tore at the man's stomach until it ripped through his abdomen. The bandit screamed in terror as the animal pulled a length of intestine from his body and chewed on it as if it had been a mouthful of hay.

"Hey! Don't eat him." The man in red marched toward his sleigh. "I was going to..." He glanced to his side, noticing Bill standing there. "I was going to, ah, put him in my sack, for, um, safekeeping."

The bandit went limp a moment later.

"Alright, fine, whatever." The stranger stopped and placed one hand on his hip as he glanced around at the campgrounds. "I think that's all of them."

"I don't see any left," the blood-soaked elf added from the top of one of the cabins. "I'm not hearing any heartbeats out there other than the people in that building and that guy." She pointed down at Bill.

"Good, good. Then I would say our job here is finished." The man in red climbed up into the front of the sleigh.

"Wait." Bill forced himself forward. "I don't know what's going on, but thank you."

"Bah, it's all part of the job." The stranger waved a hand through the air as he took a seat. "Though, I'd stay back if I were you. We've had to make a few dietary changes for the reindeer, if you know what I mean." He gestured to the corpse that was now being torn apart by the two animals closest to it.

"Oh, yeah." Bill kept his distance.

"Come on now, Becky. We have a couple thousand more stops to make tonight and we are late enough as it is." Santa beckoned to his elf.

"Coming." She stepped off the roof she was standing on as darkness gathered around her again. She seemed to glide the rest of the way toward the sleigh, landing in the back seat. Her face was still covered in partially dried blood.

Bill glanced back to the building where the rest of his people were beginning to peek out from the door, their jaws dropping at the sight of the sleigh.

"Who are you?" Bill asked, hoping for an answer that he could somehow make sense of.

The stranger in red just looked at him. "I'm really getting sick of that question. It should be obvious. I am Santa Claus."

With that, he took the reins and clicked his tongue at the reindeer. The sleigh began to move forward, leaving Bill to watch as every bit of logic he had told him that they would just circle around and continue on down the road. He dropped the gun in his hand when the sleigh left the ground.

The rest of his people ran out into the center of the campground, all staring into the sky in disbelief as the insanity circled back around to pass overhead.

The man in red, claiming to be Santa, leaned over one side to look down at the crowd before shouting, "Happy holidays!"

The sleigh vanished into the night soon after.

Bill just shook his head in disbelief. Then he turned back toward his people. There were still a few bodies lying about. Though, most had been taken. Shoved into a sack. They had still lost people, but after everything that had just happened, the night didn't seem quite so dark.

Everyone started asking questions as he walked toward them. Only one mattered.

"Was that really Santa?" one of the children asked, still young enough to believe.

"Ah, yeah, kid. That was him," Bill said even though he was pretty sure it was a lie.

It wasn't that he didn't believe in magic.

He didn't really have a choice but to believe after everything he'd just seen. Yet, he still had his doubts that he had just met the real Santa Claus. He turned to look up at the sky where the sleigh had gone. So many stories and legends ran through his head to send him to the only conclusion that made any sense.

He wasn't sure what had happened to the real Santa, but he was pretty sure Krampus was doing his best to fill in.

CHAPTER THIRTY-THREE

"I need a new disguise, now!" Digby hopped out of the sleigh before it slid to a stop aboard the airship.

There wasn't time to waste.

The bullet holes in his coat were sure to hinder his ability to convince anyone that he was the actual Santa Claus. They still had over a thousand children in the empire's capital in need of presents. As soon as they were done changing, they would need to head straight out through one of Parker's passages.

"I need a new costume too!" Becca jumped out after him, leaving a trail of dried blood as it flaked off her coat.

"Jesus, Becca. You are the messiest eater I have ever dated." Mason met her at the door of the bridge as some of the airship crew wiped down the sleigh.

"Sorry, but becoming a member of the undead has done nothing for my table manners."

"You might want to change that. You don't see me wearing everyone I eat." Digby glanced back at her as he walked toward the ballroom where Parker waited.

"I don't want to hear comments from someone who routinely destroys every outfit he wears and ends up coating himself in necrotic tissue." She stripped off her coat and handed it to Mason. The shirt underneath was just as battered.

"Ah, thanks." He held the coat at arm's length. "Elenore figured you two might need more than one costume, so I have some waiting in one of the guest rooms. It will take ten minutes or so to switch the goblin king's pauldron to a new Santa suit, though. I can get it done while you two wash up." He gave Becca a look that made it clear he was mostly talking to her.

"Indeed." Digby pulled off his coat and threw it over the soldier's shoulder. "We'll be in the ballroom."

"Oh god, there's black goo all over the inside." Mason took a right toward the guestrooms while Digby and Becca continued straight toward the nearest washrooms.

Digby stopped just outside when he noticed Alex sprinting down the hall toward them.

"I'll see what he wants." He gestured for Becca to continue without him. "You get cleaned up. You need it more than I do."

The vampire glowered at him but didn't argue.

"What's the rush now?" Digby turned to his apprentice as he approached.

"Lana just sent one of the crew to get me." He kept running. "There's a problem with Parker."

"No." A wave of dread hit Digby like a truck. The messenger had spent the last few weeks resting to make sure she didn't pass out like she had back in the Vatican. Despite that, she still hadn't been looking well. If she was unconscious again, the whole night might be in jeopardy.

Digby broke into a sprint to keep pace with the artificer. The entire way to the ballroom, his imagination went wild with every worst-case scenario he could think of. By the time he got there, he had nearly worked himself up into a panic. It all faded away when he entered the room.

Parker was sitting on the floor still holding the stuffed shark that she'd claimed from the leftover toys.

"Lord! You had me worried." Digby relaxed as he walked toward her. He tensed right back up when he noticed Lana and Hawk standing behind the messenger.

The look on their faces said it all.

"I can't open a passage." Parker turned her head to look at him. "I can't cast anything."

"But you haven't even lost consciousness this time." Digby staggered as he slowed to a stop. "You must be mistaken. You just need to focus."

"I've tried." She raised her hand to the scrying mirror on the wall. "The surface began to ripple for a second, then it stopped. The magic just cuts off. It's like something is stopping me." Parker looked back to him.

"But you said you could do this." Digby shook his head. "I asked you dozens of times."

"I was sure I could." Her bottom lip began to tremble. "I fucked up. Shit, I fucked it all up. The whole plan is screwed."

Digby stood, feeling the weight of the night come crashing down. She was right. The con was ruined. No matter how well prepared they were, without her magic, the plan was out of reach. Just when he was starting to feel like he was doing something good, it was over.

"I'm sorry." Parker lowered her head. "Fuck, I'm so sorry."

That was when the last words Digby expected to say left his mouth. "It's alright."

"What?" Alex turned abruptly to stare at him.

"It's alright," Digby repeated.

Parker's condition had been deteriorating. No matter how many times she denied it, even he could see it. Guilt stabbed at his chest at the fact that he'd already pushed her as far as he had. The thought of calling the whole con off had already crossed his mind days before. He'd even debated on removing Parker's access to the Heretic Seed.

At least with her magic gone, she might recover.

"There's nothing that can be done." He crouched down beside her. "I think this might be a good thing. No matter how much we need the power that this con might grant us, it's not worth it if it costs you your life. And before you tell me that you wouldn't let things get that bad, we both know you would."

She blew out a heavy sigh. "But what about the plan? Everything we've done was all for nothing."

The events of the night played back through Digby's mind. "Nonsense. It wasn't for nothing. We made a difference. True, it may not have been in the way we intended, but I think we gave something back to the people we visited."

"What about the power?" Parker looked up. "How will we stop Henwick?"

"We'll find another way." Digby stood and held a hand out to help her up. "My only regret is that we couldn't see things through, if only to have the same impact on the lives of the people living under the empire."

"Wait," Hawk said. "Why can't we?"

"What?" Parker took Digby's hand and pulled herself up from the floor.

The young rogue held up several fingers before putting a couple down again as if doing a bit of math. "We got started early tonight. So we don't really need Parker's magic to get across the country. We could just take the airship. At full speed, we should be able to make it at least a few hours before the sun comes up over the empire's capital."

"He's right." Alex stepped in. "If we left now, you'll have just over three hours to make deliveries in Autem's territory. I don't think you can hit every household on the list, but you can get to a chunk of them. And there's always a chance that rumors could spread from there to increase the amount of people who believe our lie." He walked over to one of the tables where Kristin's skull had been minding her own business. "Do you think that's enough people to get a mass enchantment off the ground?"

"It's possible," she answered back.

"So there's a chance we could still do this." Parker's eyes lit up.

"But you wouldn't be able to travel through mirrors," Lana said, taking her place as a voice of reason. "You will have to physically land the sleigh on rooftops and then break into the buildings where people are living in Autem's refugee camps."

"That will certainly slow us down." Digby scratched his chin, considering the problem.

"I should also remind you that Henwick will take notice at some point," Kristin added, joining the side of reason. "He will try to stop you. And if you do anything, and I mean anything, that could be considered even remotely hostile, Henwick will jump at the chance to invalidate the treaty."

"So what? Dig just has to make sure not to fight back," Hawk suggested. "And we'll keep the airship out of the capital's sky. Just get it close enough to send the sleigh."

"Indeed." Digby considered the risks.

It was possible. Unlikely, sure, but possible all the same. He couldn't help but remember the face of that child that he'd handed a present to back down in the village. That was all it took to convince him. They had to finish what they started, or at least try.

"Hawk." Digby spun to face the young rogue. "I need you to run to the bridge. Tell Jameson we're going. I don't care how many lifeboats snap off in the wind, I want this airship hitting top speed."

"I'm on it." Hawk grinned as he took off in a sprint.

"You can't be serious." Kristin's skull took an incredulous tone.

"I'm afraid I am." Digby chuckled. "Deadly serious."

"What about me?" Parker stepped in front of him. "Is there something else I can do, you know, that doesn't involve using magic?"

Digby glanced to Lana, then back to Parker. "Yes, you can get yourself checked out. Magic aside, we need to make sure you're not in any danger."

"I'm not sure another checkup is going to matter." Lana shook her head. "I've already been thorough. The only thing physically wrong with her is her deteriorating health. But the cause is magical. I'm out of my depth with that part."

"Well, there must be something we can do." Digby held onto the suspenders that kept the pants of his disguise up. "We have some time now that we are traveling by airship. It'll be hours before we reach the east coast of this land." He swept his vision across the people around him. "This room holds our top minds when it comes to magic. I'm sure we can figure something out if we put our heads together."

anything happening within the mutation's temporary realm. Alex's eyes were tracking him, but he was pretty sure that was just because his soul was matching his physical body's movements.

"What do you see?" Alex asked, his words sounding distant as they were filtered through Digby's physical body down to his soul.

"I see you." He took a step toward him, his real body doing the same in the reflection below him. "And I see Kristin. She is sitting on the table."

"Obviously." Her voice drifted to him as well, retaining a healthy dose of annoyance. "I don't have a body. I'm sure I'm sitting wherever Alex left me."

"No, your soul has a body."

"What?" Her soul's mouth moved in sync with her voice, relief washing over her face. "What do I look like? Do I look like me, or something else?"

Digby shook his head. "We can talk about that later. Your soul is not the reason we're doing this."

Turning around, he found Parker standing with her back to him.

That's weird. He furrowed his brow. "Parker, are you facing me right now?"

Her voice drifted back to him. "Yeah, why?"

"Because your soul is not looking at me."

"Maybe my soul is shy?"

"Maybe." Digby clenched his jaw and walked toward her.

The first thing he noticed was that there was no sign of any lingering traces of the dead. He wasn't sure why. She had personally killed several of Autem's Guardians. They should have been there.

Next, he noticed her feet. Well, not her feet exactly, but a pair of tiny glowing wings that extended from her ankles. She truly was a messenger. As he got closer, he noticed something else.

A black wire.

He'd seen something like it before. It was the stuff that people of the modern world occasionally put at the top of fences to keep people from climbing over it. What was it called? Barbed wire? That was it. He stopped a few feet away, looking at her back. The dark strands of metal coiled around her body, biting into her arms and legs. It was even wrapped around her throat and head. Even worse, nearly every inch of her exposed skin was covered in crimson. Looking down, he realized the wire was also tangled around the wings at her feet. It was as if something was trying to hold her power as a messenger back while at the same time, her magic was fighting to be free.

That must be the problem.

Her magic wasn't causing the deterioration after all. There was something else there. Something conflicting with her power. Whatever it was, it was getting worse. Digby took a step toward her, hoping to learn more if he circled around to see her face.

That was when she turned around.

No, she hadn't merely turned around. It was faster than that. Her head snapped backward, her body spinning with it. Digby gasped. Her face was spattered with crimson, but it was her eyes that stood out more.

They were empty.

It was like staring into a dry well with nothing left to give. They were the eyes of someone who had forgotten what it meant to live. Before he could do anything else, she screamed.

The real world snapped back around him as he stumbled away to crash into one of the tables behind him.

"What happened?" Parker stood in front of him, looking the same as always.

Digby's eyes darted around. He couldn't return to his mutation's temporary space. Hell, he couldn't even feel it. Whatever he had just encountered there, it was powerful enough to cancel his Soul Eater altogether.

"I... I think you just kicked me out." His voice shook as he struggled to understand what had just happened.

"How could I kick you out of your own ability?" The worry on Parker's face grew.

"I don't know. You shouldn't have even been able to interact with me in there. One moment you were looking away, the next, you spun around and screamed in my face. My Soul Eater's temporary realm collapsed as soon as you did."

"Is it safe in there?" Lana peeked in the doorway from the hall.

"Yes, it's safe." Digby waved her in.

"Did you see any traces of the dead hanging around her? Like what you saw with Becca?" Alex leaned over him.

"No. A few are hanging around you but, strangely, there are no fragments of the dead clinging to Parker."

"Well, that's good." The messenger pantomimed wiping sweat from her forehead.

"Maybe, but I'm not sure why the dead ignored you." Digby pushed himself off the floor. "It's almost like they were too afraid to stick around. Plus, there's more. You have wings on your ankles. I think they represent your messenger ability, but there's also barbed wire coiling all over your body. I don't know what that part represents."

"What the hell? I don't want barbed wire wrapped around my soul." Parker rubbed her head. "What even is it?"

"I have no idea." Digby shook his head. "But it's clearly conflicting with your magic."

"I'm seriously regretting letting you poke around with my soul." Parker wrapped her arms around herself as if trying to chase away a chill. "I don't think I wanted to know any of this stuff."

"That's understandable, but it's better than ignoring the situation." Lana stopped beside her. "Plus, we learned something here. We've been operating under the assumption the headaches and overall deterioration of your health were due to your magic being too powerful and taking a toll on your body. But now we know there's something else there that's causing interference."

"Wait, wait, wait." Alex rushed forward into the center of the conversation. "I think I have an idea."

"It doesn't involve looking at my soul again, does it?" Parker stepped away from him.

"No, I want to try my inspection spell. It lets me examine things to see what they are made of and if they have magical properties. Maybe if I cast it on you, it will show me something that might explain some of this."

"Isn't that spell just for inanimate objects?" Lana asked.

Alex shrugged. "I won't know until I try."

Parker groaned before answering, "Sure, why not? We've already done weird stuff to my soul. Let's experiment a little with my body too."

"You don't have to make it sound like that. He is trying to help." Kristin's skull spoke up from the table to defend Alex's idea.

"I know." Parker sighed in acceptance before asking, "Where do you want me?"

Alex glanced around the room for a moment before walking over to grab a chair and dragging it over to the center of the floor. "Have a seat."

Parker dropped into the chair with a huff.

"Wait." Digby grabbed the stuffed shark toy from the floor where she'd dropped it and handed it to her. "Here. For, I don't know, support or something."

"Thank you." She took the shark from him and held it in her lap before turning to Alex. "Okay, let's get this over with."

Alex took up a position a few feet in front of her and held out a hand. "Okay, this won't hurt at—" He stopped talking mid-sentence only to open his mouth again to add, "What the hell?"

"What do you see?" Digby swatted him in the shoulder.

"Enchantments." The artificer's eyes darted around. "So many."

"Enchantments?" Digby flicked his eyes toward Parker before looking back to Alex. "Enchantments for what?"

"I'm looking. I just need to figure out which one is which."

"I strongly recommend against that." Kristin's skull spoke up. "You remember what happened last time you inspected an unfamiliar enchantment? You triggered a trap that nearly killed you."

"I know, but I'm already in here. I can do this." Alex didn't show any sign of stopping.

That was when Parker tightened her grip on the shark with one hand while raising the other to hold it against her skull. "Shit, what are you doing?"

"Does it hurt?" Digby asked.

"Hell yeah it does." She leaned over, rubbing her temples. "It feels like you're poking at something that you're not supposed to."

"I can stop." Alex glanced at her.

"No." She shook her head. "Just be fast."

"Okay, I'm checking out the bigger enchantments." He looked back to the space above her, his mouth forming the words holy shit silently.

A moment later, Parker's breathing sped up. The shark fell out of her lap, leaving her clutching her head and gasping for air. Lana rushed to her side just as the messenger passed out.

"That's enough." Digby snapped his attention to Alex only to find him staring blankly into the air with his hand outstretched. "I said that's enough."

Alex didn't answer. Instead, he just stood there with his hand shaking. A trickle of crimson ran from one nostril. Then another from his ear. The artificer fell backward, hitting the floor with a hard thud before convulsing.

"What?" Digby looked back to Parker, unconscious in Lana's arms, then back to Alex as he started coughing foam from his mouth.

"He hit a trap!" Kristin's skull shrieked, sounding desperate. "Someone heal him!"

Digby's eyes bulged as blood streamed from Alex's nose and ears. He raised his hand and summoned an echo without hesitating any further. A glowing image of Henwick flickered into existence and began to heal. It was like something inside Alex was trying to tear him apart from the inside out. The only thing holding it back was the constant healing.

Lana left Parker slumped in her chair and joined in to help keep Alex alive with a Regeneration spell.

"He's not going to make it!" Kristin shouted.

Digby summoned his echo again and again, but it only slowed the process. Still, he didn't stop. He was not about to lose another friend.

Not again.

———

Down the hall aboard the airship, Mason had just about finished attaching Digby's pauldron to a new Santa coat when a strange wave of power hit him. No, that wasn't right. It wasn't that something hit him. It was more like something had been torn away.

Staggering backward, he fell against the wall, clutching his head.

It felt like someone was unraveling a knot that had been tied in his mind. A knot that he hadn't realized was there until now. It stretched and uncoiled as pieces were snipped away and reconnected.

Then, suddenly, it all felt right again.

Mason blinked several times as he lay on the floor, slumped against the wall. A string of drool poured from his mouth to his shirt. He wiped it off, a series of memories flashing through his mind all at once to reveal a truth that had been hiding in plain sight for weeks.

Panic swelled as he pushed himself up. He left everything where it was and started running. Bursting into the hallway, he nearly slammed into the opposite wall. He shoved off it and broke into a sprint.

He had to get to the others.

He had to warn them.

They had no idea what was lurking right in front of them.

Mason's boots hit the floor one after another to carry him to the ballroom. He hit the door with his shoulder, shoving through to find Digby and Lana standing over Alex.

Blood flowed from the artificer's nose and ears.

Mason ignored him and instead swept his eyes across the room in search of Parker. He found her in a chair with her head resting to one side.

"Quick! Help me!" Mason rushed into the room toward the unconscious woman.

"What is the meaning of this?" Digby spun, still holding out a hand toward the artificer on the floor. "We just got Alex stable."

"That doesn't matter. We need to get Parker away from everyone. We need to get her to a room we can lock." Mason didn't stop.

He couldn't.

"What are you talking about?" Digby marched toward him.

Mason locked eyes with him, trying to convey how serious he was.

"Parker has been lying to everyone." He shook his head. "I have no idea who this woman is."

CHAPTER THIRTY-FOUR

"What do you mean Parker wasn't there?" Digby stood in front of Mason as he leaned against one of the tables in the ballroom.

The soldier had come across a bit scattered when he had insisted on moving the unconscious messenger to a room with a lock, but it was clear he was serious. After making sure that Parker wasn't in any danger, Digby and Lana carried her down the hall to one of the guest rooms. The cleric stayed with her to keep an eye on her condition.

By the time they got back to the ballroom, Alex was gone along with Kristin's skull. For a moment there, it had looked like he might not survive whatever trap he'd activated. They were just lucky that there had been someone to heal him. Otherwise, they might have lost him. He must have woken up and gone someplace to recover.

Becca still hadn't returned from getting cleaned up. The vampire had missed a lot.

Digby had no idea what was going on, or why everyone suddenly seemed so concerned, but he was going to get to the bottom of it.

"Spit it out, Mason, what did you mean?"

"I'm sorry." The soldier was still a little disoriented. "I don't know how to explain it. It's just that… Parker wasn't stationed on the quarantine line back in Seattle. It had been me, Sax, and another private named Cohen. The three of us the whole time. When things fell apart, we escaped together. Shit, Cohen saved my life in that first encounter we had with a revenant." He rubbed at his face. "Jesus, how could I have forgotten her?"

"Alright, if you escaped with this Cohen woman, where is she now?" Digby folded his arms, still trying to follow the soldier's story.

Mason shook his head. "She died. It was a few days after we escaped Seattle. We broke into a house to try to find some supplies and a dormant revenant got the drop on her. Cohen didn't turn or anything. The rev got at her throat. She bled to death on the floor. Sax and I buried her in the yard outside."

"But you were with Parker when I met you." Digby held out a hand. "Where did she come from?"

"Sax and I ran into her a day later. It was about a week before we came across you. Parker was just walking on the side of the road alone. She didn't act any different than how she does now, except that maybe, she was a little less chatty. But she was interested in teaming up, so we did."

"So she's what, just a stranger?" Digby asked. "Why did you tell us that she was in the army with you?"

"That's the thing." Mason pushed off of the table that he was leaning on and walked a few steps before turning around. "On the day that we met her, she was just someone we'd met on the road. We traveled for a few miles, then we found a place to hole up for the night. When we woke up in the morning, everything had changed." The soldier locked eyes with him. "It was like Cohen had never existed. I couldn't remember her. It was like someone had gone through my memory and replaced Cohen with Parker. I didn't even notice that something had changed. I don't think Sax did either."

"But she's talked about her time in the army with you. She knows you." Digby furrowed his brow. "How could she know so much?"

"I know. She knows things about me that she can't possibly

know. But…" He trailed off for a long moment. "Now that I know that something was wrong, a lot of what she talked about doesn't add up. Sometimes the stuff she said about her time in basic training was vague or missing details. And there were things about the military, that any soldier should know, that she just didn't. I chalked it up to her being flakey. She was always scattered and forgetful. I never had a reason to suspect there was something more going on."

Digby struggled to believe his words, despite the fact that Mason had no reason to lie. "How, then, is this possible?"

"It's the enchantments." Alex appeared in the doorway along with Lana and Becca.

"You're back on your feet already?" Digby stared at him in surprise.

"I'm fine now that I've had a few heals cast on me. Besides, this is too important for me to sit out."

"We've gone over some of the details, and I think we know what's happening." Becca strode past him. "It is not good news."

Lana slipped in as well and crossed the room to the scrying mirror on the wall. After saying the artifact's invocation phrase, she asked the mirror to show her Parker. A view of one of the guestrooms appeared in the glass. The messenger lay on the bed, still unconscious. "She's asleep, but it's probably a good idea to keep an eye on her."

"Yes, and I had a couple of the crew remove the mirror from the room. There's no window in there either, or any other reflective surfaces for that matter," Becky added.

"You talk as if she's dangerous." Digby glanced at the scrying mirror as Parker lay on the bed with her arms and legs stretching out in all directions.

"We just don't want to take any chances." Alex stepped in front of the mirror.

"Chances? Chances with what?" Digby asked. "And what enchantments are you talking about? Did her magic manifest some sort of mass belief in a messenger deity?"

"No, it's runecraft." He gestured to the ship around them. "It's the same stuff that is keeping the Queen Mary in the air. Except significantly more complicated."

"Runecraft?" Digby squinted at the image in the mirror. "But that would require someone to engrave symbols onto her body and imbue them with power. I certainly haven't examined her, but I would have thought someone would have noticed something like that by now."

"True, but these engravings aren't on the outside," Alex continued. "Runecraft works best when it's done in layers. For example, the rings that the empire's Guardians wear have three layers; one of iron, one of steel, and one of gold. In Parker's case, someone has made use of her entire body to create a multilayered system of intertwined enchantments."

"How can a person's body have layers?" Digby tore his attention away from the mirror to look at the artificer.

Alex held up one finger for each of the words he spoke next. "Flesh, bone, viscera, sinew, heart, and mind."

Digby froze, recognizing the components that made up the resources that filled his void. "Again, how?"

"That, I don't really know." Alex turned to the image of the sleeping woman in the mirror. "But my inspection spell shows the layers of whatever I cast it on and, in Parker's case, runes are engraved on all of it. They're on her bones, internal organs, the inside of her mouth, rear molars, and the lining of her heart. Pretty much every available space that isn't easily visible has been used. Somebody literally cut her open to do this. There are even runes etched into her memory. It's like they were burned into her brain."

"The runes were hidden well enough so that none of the doctors I brought in to examine her found anything." Lana stepped in. "But she does have some scarring. Most of it is hidden as well, like it was done by a plastic surgeon. Parker said she'd been in a car accident when she was younger, which could explain it, but now, I'm not so sure."

"Does this mean that it was these enchantments that have been causing her headaches and other symptoms?"

Lana nodded. "We've been operating under the assumption

that the Heretic Seed used some kind of loophole to artificially push her will value up high enough to give her the messenger class. That's why we thought her magic was too powerful for her to handle. Now, it seems it was the other way around. It's likely that her will stat was that high before she ever connected to the Seed. It was just a part of who she was. Her health has been in decline because each time she used her magic, her mana system put a strain on her enchantments. It was to a point where they were ready to collapse."

"One of them did collapse." Alex held a hand out toward Mason. "That's why the effect she has on others was canceled."

Mason's eyes widened. "That's why my memories suddenly reverted back to normal."

"You expect me to believe that runes were able to rewrite a person's memory?" Digby swiped a hand through the air.

"That's exactly what they do," Alex countered. "There's a ton of enchantments going on in her body, but two of them seem to be designed to affect memory. They work together and trigger whenever somebody sleeps near her to take advantage of their lack of defenses while unconscious. The first enchantment implants Parker into the memories of her targets, while the second steals memories from them and implants them into her. The result can make someone believe that they have known her for years while giving Parker the knowledge to make that story stand up to scrutiny. That's why Mason remembers her and she knows so much about him. It even helped her fake having military experience. On top of that, it seems like some of her original memories have been sealed. So she literally doesn't know about any of this. For her, the lie is the truth."

"Why would anybody want to do all this to her?" Digby took a step back, afraid of the answer.

"That part's obvious." Becca took over. "She's a spy."

"That's insane." Digby shook his head adamantly.

Becca didn't let him deny it for long. "Think about it, Digby. These enchantments make Parker the perfect sleeper agent. She is able to implant herself into a group and manipulate them into thinking she was there all along. Not only that, but her own memories have been locked away. So as far as she knows, she is on our side. She is completely loyal to us." She paused before adding, "Until she isn't."

"What?" Digby struggled to accept what she was saying.

"Parker is bound to have an activation condition, or possibly several, that when met, will reactivate her original memories."

"Bah! Impossible." Digby threw both hands in the air. "Parker has never been anything but loyal to us. She stood by each of us, even when we, well, mostly me, made her life hell."

"That's the point," Becca argued. "She's loyal until a condition is met and she activates. Once she's been triggered, she could become an enemy. The fact that her will stat is as high as it is proves it, since a normal person wouldn't have a value anywhere near it. She would've had to have gone through some kind of extreme training to get her will that high." Becca blew out a sigh. "There's no telling what she's capable of. Assassinations, sabotage, whatever. If she's been trained that extensively, she could probably take down any of us."

Digby threw a hand out toward the scrying mirror and the sloppy mess that it showed sleeping in the bed drooling on herself. "You expect me to believe that is a master spy. I mean, this is Parker we're talking about. I've seen her nearly kill herself by eating expired yogurt."

"Again, that just proves my point." Becca ignored his argument. "Parker has a personality that no one would ever suspect, and she's done such a thorough job of gaining people's trust that you're struggling to believe any of this."

"But..." Digby started running out of arguments to make. "But it's Parker."

"I know." Becca lowered her head. "I don't want to believe it either, but she may be the most dangerous threat we've ever dealt with."

Digby staggered in place before walking over to a chair and dropping into it. How could any of that be true? He had trusted her. Parker had been his conscience, for crying out loud. She had supported him throughout their entire ordeal while they were trapped within the Heretic Seed. Hell, she spent too much time napping to be a spy.

She was his friend.

Yet, the facts said otherwise.

Digby lowered his head to his hands and rubbed at his eyes for a long moment. Denial wasn't going to get him very far and there were still so many questions. The most important one was obvious.

"Who does she work for?"

"There's no way to know." Becca shrugged. "There's a chance that she could work for the Fools. At least that way, she wouldn't be an enemy. Though, if that was true, it's weird that Harlow never said anything. Obviously, there's a chance she didn't know. I mean, the Fools do operate in an intentionally disorganized manner, but still, Harlow was pretty high up. She seemed to be involved in pretty much everything."

Digby nodded, accepting the possibility. "Alright. What else is there?"

"Autem," Mason gave the obvious answer.

Digby looked up. "If she was working for the empire this whole time, wouldn't we all be dead by now?"

"What do you mean?" Mason furrowed his brow.

"I mean Parker has had ample opportunity to destroy us all. If she worked for Autem, she could have simply told them where we were hiding. Hell, she could have opened a Mirror Passage and delivered an army of Guardians directly to our door." Digby jumped up from his chair. "Damn, I just realized that she could do that at any time."

There was no mirror in her room, but if she woke up and decided to break out, there would be a problem. Digby willed the Heretic Seed to cut Parker's access to magic without a second thought. Her name disappeared from his list of magic users as soon as he did. Losing the ability to open a passage was a problem, but it wasn't worth the risk. Besides, if things changed, he could always reactivate her power later.

"Alright, that should keep us safe." He turned back to the others. "But as I was saying, if Parker was working for Henwick, then why did he try to recruit her before when we ran into him on Skyline's base? I suppose it could have been an act to keep up appearances, but it still doesn't make sense. There's no reason to recruit someone if they already work for you. And if she did work for him, I would think she would have done us all in already."

"That is a good point." Alex folded his arms and tapped one finger against his elbow. "Unless none of the conditions to activate her have been met."

"There is a third option," Becca said, her tone sounding deadly serious.

"What?" Digby eyed her, not liking the way she'd said it.

"Well, there's a detail that we need to consider. Parker was planted into Mason's group before he met any of us or had anything to do with the Heretic Seed. So the question becomes who could have known that we would meet? I mean, it's impossible to have predicted that. Unless someone had a way of knowing the future."

Digby scoffed. "That's impossible. We've seen a lot of magic in our time, but how could anyone see the future?"

"Oh no." All the color drained from Alex's face. "What was it Dominic said about the Nine back in the Vatican?"

Digby froze. "Prophecy."

That old priest had said that the Nine had gained the ability of prophecy back when they were at the height of their power. Their magic may have waned since then. Yet that didn't mean they were dead. One or more of them could still be out there. If they had glimpsed the future, they could have known exactly where to place a spy.

"Crap, that fits." Alex's eyes drifted to the view of Parker sleeping in her room. "Her will. That's where it came from. A lingering member of the Nine might be the only one that could train someone to increase a stat like that."

"I don't like where you're going with this." Digby glared at the artificer, as if stopping him from talking would somehow stop his words from being true.

"Before, when I said that Parker has several enchantments on her. Memory altering is not the only thing that they do. There's a bunch more. Most of them aren't anything major. Just stuff that regulates body chemistry, kind of like how the empire's Guardian rings do, but one of them slows the aging process."

"Why didn't you mention that sooner?" Digby snapped. "She was the one who taught us how to forge weapons. She could be thousands of years old, for all we know. Hell, she could literally be one of the Nine."

"No." Alex held up a hand. "The enchantment only slows the aging process, it doesn't stop it. I didn't mention it because the effect is weaker than the immortality that we get from the Heretic Seed. Besides, she only looks like she's around twenty-one. I don't know when she was born, but it couldn't have been thousands of years ago. Or even a hundred years ago. It would have to be some time in the last few decades for her to still look so young."

"I think I know when she grew up." Becca slapped a hand on the table beside her. "She said something recently while helping Digby pick out toys. We were talking about videogame systems and she didn't seem to know that they required an internet connection to function. Plus, she thought you could just blow into the cartridges if they stop working."

"You think she's from the Nineties?" Mason stared at her blankly.

"That would fit, considering how strong the enchantment slowing her aging is." Alex nodded along. "Her enchantment does use her real memories whenever possible. Or at least they use her actual memories as a basis for some of her manufactured ones. So it's likely that she really did work at a Renaissance Fair's forge when she was growing up."

"Alright, so she's not one of the Nine." Digby relaxed a little. "Though, she might answer to one of them. Provided there's at least one of them lurking out there."

"I hate to say it," Alex lowered his head, "but that might be the most likely scenario, considering how complicated her enchantments are and the skill that it must've taken to engrave them into her. Something like that seems far beyond the capability of a normal person."

Digby clenched his fists, feeling like a friend had been stolen from him by the sudden revelation. "If she works for one of the Nine, what could she possibly be after?"

"Your guess is as good as mine," Becca answered. "Unfortunately, we won't know until something happens to activate her."

"That's why we need to keep her locked up." Mason still looked a little uneasy. "It's too dangerous to let her roam free."

"We could tell her all of this, and see what happens." Lana offered another option. "If that triggers a change in her, then at least we'll know what we're dealing with."

"Yes, but if she changes, she won't be our friend anymore," Digby argued.

"She never was." Mason shook his head. "I know it's hard to think about it that way. You've only known Parker as an ally. Now that I've regained my memory, I can't ignore the truth. She may not be aware of what she's done right now, but she must have known what she was doing at the start. She is dangerous."

Digby turned to stare at the scrying mirror.

Parker had rolled over and curled herself into a ball. Anyway Digby looked at her, he struggled to see the enemy that Mason did. Perhaps that was proof of how much of a threat she was. Still, whoever she used to be or whoever she would become in the future was not who she was now. It felt wrong to simply imprison her without even an explanation. Despite that, it would be foolish to let her walk around free. If she really did serve one of the Nine, she was potentially as bad as Henwick.

Digby released a long, needless sigh.

"We can decide her fate tomorrow morning. For now, we keep her locked in that room. If she wakes up, tell her it's for her own safety. Tell her I took away her power because it was the only way to save her. If she argues, tell her that everything will be fine and that she needs to rest."

A foul taste crept into his mouth.

"I just hope that we're right about this."

CHAPTER THIRTY-FIVE

"Hurry up and get the next silo into position." Digby opened his maw on the floor of the ballroom as some of Jameson's artificers carried one of the large containers toward it.

They had already traveled most of the way to the empire's capital.

It would be time to set out on the final stretch of the plan.

"How many silos can you take in at once?" Jameson asked.

Digby considered it. The original plan was to take only one silo at a time and come back for more using a Mirror Passage, but with his messenger locked in one of the guest rooms, that wasn't an option. He was going to have to carry as many as possible. The largest object he'd ever taken into his void without issue had been a car. Comparing the silos to that, he assumed he could take at least three. Any more and the inedible material might disrupt his mana system enough to effectively silence him.

Digby tensed, not liking the idea of leaving so much behind. Not when every present he delivered could be the difference between fulfilling the requirements of a mass enchantment or not.

"Give me one more." Digby kept his maw open while a third was loaded into his void. Then glanced at his HUD only to gasp in horror.

It was gone.

"What?" He stared at the place where his mana should have been.

He was silenced.

Two silos must have been his limit. He swept his eyes across the room where several more of the large containers were lined up waiting for him. He was going to have to leave them behind. Not only that, but he would have to spit one silo out of his void to get his magic back. Otherwise, all he would have access to was his zombie mutations.

"Blast!" He pounded a fist on a table beside him. "I'll never make enough deliveries with so few presents."

They had worked so hard all month getting everything ready, yet it was all for naught.

"You could always take all of the silos." Jameson remained calm despite the situation.

"Are you mad?" Digby snapped his attention to the burly man.

"Not really. It just seems like there isn't much of a point in doing any of this if you can't bring enough gifts to make kids believe. So why not throw caution to the wind and bring all the silos at once. The way I see it, you're not supposed to be fighting down there anyway, so who cares if you're silenced? Besides, you'd still have your zombie mutations to work with if you get into trouble."

He had a point.

The plan was quickly falling apart and going into the empire's refugee camps without magic was the act of a desperate man. Though, who was he to deny it? He was desperate. All he could do was try to limp along and hope that his luck might turn.

"Bring me the rest of the silos. I know I'm gonna regret this, but honestly, I regret most of my decisions, so why should that stop me?"

Jameson gave him a decisive nod and ran to help the rest of his artificers move the silos into position. Digby swallowed them up one after another. His only saving grace was that after taking the last silo into his void, the material wasn't enough to disrupt his overall senses.

"Alright." Digby pulled his phone out and reset the time to account for the difference in time zones. "It's time to go."

"The sleigh is all ready." Jameson gestured to the door. "We cleaned the spatters of blood off it so it's as good as new."

"Tell Becca to meet me there in five minutes." Digby shoved his phone back in his pocket.

With that, he headed off down the hall toward the room that they had been using as a barn. Before he got halfway there, Lana caught up to him. "She's awake."

Digby slowed to a stop but didn't turn around. It was obvious who Lana was talking about.

Parker.

"Has she figured anything out?" Digby winced, afraid of the answer.

Lana shook her head. "She's just sorry about causing so much trouble for everyone. Plus, she doesn't understand why you took away her magic or why she's not allowed to leave her room. I explained that it was for her own safety, but that's not a great reason to go to such lengths." From the tone of Lana's voice, she wanted to say more.

"And?"

"She's asking for you?" The cleric's tone was somber. "She can accept that she's lost her magic, but I don't think she's willing to sit the night out. She wants to help, and the Seed still marks her as friendly."

Digby let his shoulders fall. He didn't know what he could say to Parker. Hell, he'd been hoping she'd stay unconscious for a few days like before. That would at least give him time to figure things out. Right now, he was too conflicted to speak to her.

A part of him felt horrible for locking her up. After all, she was still the same Parker for the time being. What harm would it be to let her lend a hand aboard the ship? That might even be the best way to keep her from getting suspicious. The rest of him was furious at the betrayal. He'd trusted her, and she'd manipulated him. It didn't matter if she was currently aware of it or not. Keeping her under lock and key was the only choice.

"Tell her to stay in her room for now. That's the best way for her to help. If you need any food brought to her, send Hawk in with it. I'm sure he'll figure out what's going on before the night is through, but no one has told him about her enchantments yet, so he can't let anything slip by mistake." Digby continued walking, leaving Lana behind.

Becca was ready to go when he reached the sleigh. Neither of them said much. Instead, they just climbed aboard and took off into the freezing night air. It was another half hour before the lights of the empire's capital came into view. Digby checked the time on his phone; they had a little over three hours before sunrise.

"I never thought I'd be back here." Becca stared out at a strange structure that rose above the rest of the empire's city. "It looks like they've made as much progress as we have in the last month and a half."

"Good lord." Digby's mouth fell open as the details came into view.

Becca had told him it was big, but it was so much more than he'd imagined. As they got closer, a large wall in the shape of a pentagon loomed. Each corner contained a square tower that stood a little higher than the rest. The tops resembled the battlements of the castle. At one corner, there was even the beginnings of a statue. It stood hundreds of feet tall with hands placed together in prayer. Portions of it were missing, but from the looks of one unfinished wing stretching above the wall and towers, it was meant to be an angel.

Further out, work on another wall had begun. It looked like the construction was still in its early stages, but it already stood nearly fifty feet tall in some places.

"They plan on building nine walls." Becca turned the crank in the rear of the sleigh to bring them down close to street level for the approach. "I saw a model when I was down there before. If they keep building, it will be a city with nine sections, each larger than the last. The model looked like something out of a fantasy movie. Everything outside that second wall that they're working on is the refugee camp. They converted all the buildings that used to be a part of Washington, D.C. into living spaces. They've also made a point of setting up enough churches of the Nine for every citizen to attend."

"It's an eyesore," Digby grumbled.

"At least that's something we can agree on." She tensed as some kind of perimeter checkpoint came into view. "I wish I still had my Conceal spell about now. We'll have to take the sleigh up just above some of the buildings and use them as cover. Once we're into the camps, there isn't much security more than a few patrols here and there."

"Then we stay on the rooftops and out of sight as much as possible." Digby turned the sleigh as Becca readjusted their altitude, bringing them in line with a row of buildings that bisected the perimeter fence. As long as no one looked up, they could pass right overhead without a problem.

Below the checkpoint was made up of a simple chain-link fence with Guardians stationed every few hundred feet. Digby tightened his grip on the reins as they flew over it, only relaxing once the perimeter fence was behind them.

"We're in," Becca announced as one of two mirrors set into the front of the sleigh lit up with a view of Easton's face.

Digby looked down at the other mirror as it too changed to show a view of the scrying mirror in the ballroom. Lana could be seen walking by in the background.

"You hear that? We're inside." Digby tapped on the glass before slowing the sleigh to a stop just above a building about five stories tall.

"Yes, ah." Easton reached for a clipboard that was sitting on a desk nearby. "I'll try to guide you the best I can from here." He stepped in front of the scrying mirror and spoke its invocation phrase followed by a request to show the delivery destination to the sleigh's location.

Digby watched as the artifact on the wall of the ballroom showed a building.

Becca leaned over the back of his seat to see. "Okay, that's our first stop."

Easton flipped through the pages on his clipboard. "According to the information I have, there should be five kids in that building under the age of eleven."

Digby leaned over the side of the sleigh to search for the building. It was four stories tall with relatively ornate stonework compared to what most modern structures had. He assumed finding it would be easy, but seeing the city from above made it difficult to recognize what the scrying mirror showed them. Not only that, but the glass set into the front of the sleigh was smaller, making it hard to get a good look.

"Do you see it?" Becca leaned over the other side of the sleigh.

"No." Digby squinted, noticing a pair of Guardians walking the street below. "But I do see a patrol down there." His jaw tightened. "We're going to have to be careful."

The job had sounded so simple back when he was planning everything. Yet now, it seemed much harder than it had in his head.

Digby looked out across the refugee camp as it stretched out for miles below. It was so big. Making deliveries had been fun and games back in Las Vegas. One big celebration. Even his visit to the village in Colorado had been child's play. Now, confronted by the reality in front of him, the night felt insurmountable. The weight of it nearly crushed him. He could practically feel the seconds ticking away. Dawn would be in three hours.

It wasn't enough.

He shook his head, trying to forget about the time.

Fortunately, Becca spoke up to pull him out of the downward spiral that he'd been heading for.

"There it is." The vampire pointed behind them. "The building is down there. We just need to turn and set down on the roof."

"Finally." He pulled on the reins.

For an instant, Asher almost let out a caw. She shut her beak a second later, clearly remembering that stealth was a priority. His minion glanced back in apology as an awkward sorry drifted back to Digby across their bond.

Of course, Comet and Vixen looked back as well.

Carrot?

No carrot! Digby glared at them as they drifted over their destination.

Becca brought them down on the roof near one side of the building.

"Let's make this quick. We have a lot more stops to make." Digby grabbed one of the velvet sacks from the back and climbed down from the sleigh.

The roof of the building was covered in a thin layer of snow, just enough to crunch underfoot. Beneath that, of course, was a bit of ice. His foot slid out from under him the instant he stepped on it. From there, he tumbled forward, nearly falling headfirst over the side of the building. He caught himself before going over but lost his grip on his bag in the process.

Becca caught it before it fell to the street below.

Leaning over the edge of the building, he stared down at the patrol below. If it wasn't for his vampire elf, he might have thrown his sack straight down at them.

"Are you okay?" Becca stared at him. "You're twice my level, you should have enough agility to handle some ice."

Digby furrowed his brow. She was right. He should have been able to handle it. Unless storing all those silos in his void was disrupting his senses after all. The last time he'd taken in too much material, it had given him a sense of vertigo, like being drunk. This time, it was barely noticeable, but enough to impair the advantages that he had as a Heretic. None of the points that he'd dropped into his agility mattered. He couldn't see his HUD to make sure, but if he had to guess, the impairment had reverted him down to a level close to the average human.

"This is going to be harder than I thought."

Digby moved away from the edge of the building and made his way toward the door that led down from the roof. He tried the knob. Unsurprisingly, it was locked. If he'd had access to his magic, he could form a key using Blood Forge, but like everything else, that wasn't an option. Though, he could just break the knob off using the strength of his Limitless mutation.

"Wait." Becca threw out a hand to stop him. "Santa isn't exactly known for breaking every door that stands in his way."

"Right, right. Breaking and entering would be a bad idea." Digby stared down at the lock with a frown.

The idea that a simple door stood in his way annoyed him. Especially when he could rip it off its hinges so easily.

"I don't suppose you know how to pick a modern lock." He glanced at the vampire beside him.

"Sorry, I didn't think that was a skill I would need to practice." Becca shrugged.

"Alright, I have an idea." Digby placed his hand on the doorknob and willed his Body Craft mutation into action.

In theory, it was possible to use the ability in the same way his Blood Forge spell worked. All he had to do was fill the lock with a formation of bone that could move the tumblers. A tendril of bone poked out through the palm of his hand to reach into the opening. It took a minute of poking around inside the lock to finally get something to click. Then, he reinforced the makeshift key and turned it.

The lock disengaged.

"It worked." He couldn't help but notice a note of surprise in his own voice as he pulled the door open a few inches.

"Good. You'll need to do that another thousand times tonight," Becca added.

He rolled his eyes at her reminder, then pulled his hand away from the knob.

"Uh oh."

The door moved with it. Digby wiggled his hand along with the protrusion of bone that extended from his palm. The door rattled as if it had become a part of his body as well.

"I think I'm stuck."

"You cannot be serious, right now." Becca grabbed hold of his wrist and placed her other hand against the door to hold it steady.

With a fair amount of twisting, pulling, and wiggling, Digby's improvised key pulled free. He severed it from his hand as soon as it was out. Then, he popped it in his mouth.

"Ew." Becca grimaced at him.

"Don't give me that look, Becky. I've seen you do worse. And I understand how things are made better if I eat them. I'm going to need to improve my ability to craft keys if we're going to make it through the night." He pulled the door open the rest of the way.

The stairwell inside was dark.

They probably kept the lights off to save power.

Becca pulled the phone from her pocket and activated its flashlight to light the way while Digby picked up his bag and headed down the stairs. He tried his best to move as quietly as he could. From there, they traveled to the third floor where their first stop waited. According to Easton, a child resided in apartment 302.

They reached the destination without incident.

"At least some things are starting to go right." Digby regretted his words as soon as he saw that the door had two locks instead of one.

On top, there was a deadbolt, and below, a common knob. He started with the deadbolt, repeating the same trick with his Body Craft to form a key of bone. Again, it got stuck. Though he was able to get it out a little bit easier than before. After tossing the newly formed key in his mouth and crunching it down, he moved on to the knob. It took just as much jiggling as the last to remove from the lock.

It was going to be a long night.

Digby pushed the door open a few inches as quietly as he could. Then he stopped to listen. By now, the inhabitants should have been asleep for hours. Still, the last thing he wanted to do was run into anyone. Nothing but silence came from the apartment. He nodded to Becca and opened the door the rest of the way.

She waited in the hallway, unable to cross the threshold without an invitation.

Creeping inside, he passed through a narrow kitchen before entering a modest living room. Unlike the rooms back in Las Vegas, there were no seasonal decorations. An empty bookshelf sat on the wall as if everything had been removed recently. That part made sense. With everything that the empire had done so far, and what they had planned for the future, they probably didn't want many texts around that could dispute their claims.

A doorway stood open on one wall leading into a short hallway. A pair of doors lay beyond that on either side of the space. Both had been left open a crack. Digby hesitated. Surely, that was where the apartment's inhabitants lay sleeping. All it would take was the creek of a floor, or a bump in the night to bring someone stumbling in to find him. He snuck over to the open door at the entrance to the hallway and closed it.

Then, he got to work.

In the center of the room sat a coffee table surrounded by a sofa and chair. That was as good a place as any to leave a present. Setting his bag down so that the flat section at the bottom rested evenly on the floor, he opened his maw and called forth one of the silos. He groaned when the thing emerged from his void upside down so that the flat end poked out from the inky darkness within the bag. Swallowing it back up, he tried again.

This time, the pointed top section rose. Black, necrotic blood dripped down the surface. Digby made an effort to hold the sack so that the sides didn't touch the silo while he reached for the remote that Jameson had given him to open it.

Of course, that was when he heard a toilet flush on the other side of the hallway door that he had just closed.

Digby froze as footsteps followed.

Then a voice called out. "Hello? Who's there?"

The voice was as gruff as it was unfriendly.

With eyes wide, Digby snapped his attention to the closed door. The rest of his body held deathly still.

The voice came again. "I know this door was open a minute ago, and I'm getting my…" The voice trailed off for a second before adding, "My gun."

Panic flooded Digby's mind, jumbling his thoughts. He wasn't worried about his safety, but killing some child's father was not a good way to make anyone believe in Santa. With few options, he dropped the opening of his bag and rushed to the door to grab hold of the knob. If he could keep it shut, there was a chance to get away without having to murder anyone.

Heavy footsteps came toward him from the other side. "This is your last warning."

The doorknob started to turn but Digby held firm.

"Who's there?" The voice climbed to a shout.

Digby blurted out the first response he could think of. "Santa Claus."

"That's not even funny."

"Well, it's true." Digby glanced around the room. "I'm just here to leave a gift for the little one. If you could leave me be for a minute, I will be on my way."

"Don't lie to me."

"Don't you lie to me either," Digby snapped back. "I thought you had a gun."

The voice went silent for a moment before admitting, "Okay, fine. I have a bat."

"Why would you have a flying rodent?" Digby shouted back.

"What?" Frustration entered the voice behind the door. "I have a baseball bat, you idiot."

A second, childlike, voice entered the hallway. "Dad? Who are you talking to?"

"It's Santa Claus!" Digby shouted in response.

"Santa!" Excitement filled the child's tone.

"It's not Santa," the gruff voice argued.

"Yes, it is. And I'm just trying to leave a present."

"What are you doing in there?" Becca shouted from the entryway of the apartment.

"Nothing, Becky. Everything's fine," Digby growled back as he reached for his sack with his foot.

"It doesn't sound fine," the vampire responded unhelpfully.

"Who's that?" the gruff voice on the other side of the door demanded.

"That's just one of my elves. Don't worry about it." Digby kept his back to the door while he dragged his sack closer with the tip of his boot and reached one hand into his pocket for the remote control that Jameson had given him.

"Do you have any idea how wrong it is to tell the kid that you're Santa while you're obviously trying to rob their house?" the man on the other side of the door asked as the knob twisted harder.

"I agree, it would be wrong if it wasn't true." Digby clicked the remote in his free hand to open the top of the silo while willing his Limitless mutation into action to keep the door closed.

"I swear, if there isn't a present out there waiting for my kid, I am going to beat the shit out of you." Something heavy hit the other side of the door.

"Well then, you're going to feel really bad about threatening me when you find a gift on your coffee table."

Digby struggled to reach the button just within the silo's opening to open the shutter that kept the presents within protected. His finger was just a few inches short. That was when it occurred to him that it didn't have to be. Not when he could alter his body at will. Focusing on his index finger, he elongated the bones of his knuckles and added two extra joints to extend the digit another ten inches. The shutter slid open as he pressed the button.

The man on the other side of the door hit it again before returning to his attempts to force the knob.

Digby held it firm and stretched to loop his extended index finger under the ribbon that was tied around the package at the top of the silo. He tugged upward to pull it out before tossing it to the coffee table. Poking the silo's shutter button again, it slid shut. He closed the top hatch as it sank back into his maw. The side of the silo smeared necrotic blood all over the inside of his bag as it vanished.

"Alright, I'm finished." Digby picked up the sack and got ready to run. "I'm going to let go and then I'm going to leave."

Silence answered back from the other side of the door. For that matter, it had been a few seconds since anyone had tried to turn the knob. A moment later, Digby heard the unmistakable creak of a window sliding open.

The man's voice began again, this time from further away as if leaning out said window. "Help! There's a man in my apartment."

Digby jumped away from the door he was still holding shut. The man on the other side must've gone to one of the bedrooms to shout from the window at the Guardians that patrolled the street below.

"Blast!" Digby started running, nearly crashing into Becca who was still waiting at the entrance. "We must flee!"

The vampire didn't argue, following him as he sprinted back toward the stairwell.

He shoved through the door and scrambled up the steps, taking them two or three at a time. Moments later, he burst back out onto the rooftop. Digby rushed to the edge and peeked over the side in search of the patrol that had been walking the street before. They were nowhere to be found. Becca did the same on the other side of the roof. Once he was sure that there was no one down there who might look up at the wrong time, he threw his bag into the back of the sleigh and climbed into his seat.

Launching the unconventional aircraft, Digby put in some distance before slowing to a stop just above another rooftop.

He was a fool to think that the plan was salvageable. They'd only made one delivery and it had taken over ten minutes.

"How did it go?" Easton asked from the mirror in front of him.

Digby merely looked at the man and let his expression say the rest.

"That bad, huh?"

"We'll have to skip the rest of the kids in that building for now. We can head back when the heat dies down." Becca leaned against the side of the sleigh staring out across the city.

"Are you ready for the next one?" Easton asked.

Digby didn't answer.

"Everything okay?" Easton leaned closer, his face filling most of the mirror.

"No, everything is not okay. This isn't going to work." Digby responded by forcing out a needless sigh. "We're heading back to the ship. I'm calling off the con."

"Are you sure?" Becca slouched into her seat. "We could try another building. Maybe it will go better."

"No." Digby pulled on the reins to turn the sleigh around. "There's too many stops to make and the area is unfamiliar. Hell, I don't even know how much mana I have. We can't continue like this." Digby's mind drifted back to Parker, locked in her room. "Especially when we have a spy to deal with."

"True." Becca shifted in her seat and grabbed hold of the crank to take them back up to the airship.

"Indeed." Digby took one last look at the refugee camp below, then he raised his head to the sky. "I suppose I was destined to come up with a bad plan at some point. I only wish we hadn't wasted so much time on it."

CHAPTER THIRTY-SIX

"Shut up." Hawk's voice came from the mirror set into the front of the sleigh as Digby turned it to leave Autem's territory.

"What was that now?" Digby narrowed his eyes as the young rogue pushed Easton out of the Mirror Link's view and leaned in close enough for his face to fill the glass.

"I said shut up." Hawk looked serious. "After everything we've done all month, you're just going to give up?"

Digby deflated. "It can't be helped. Things just didn't go our way this time."

"Yeah, they did." Hawk shook his head. "You got Vegas taken care of early, and you saved a bunch of people at that camp in the mountains. Plus, you've still got three hours to go."

"Yes, however, you weren't here for the nightmare that the last delivery was." Digby grimaced, wishing he could forget the last ten minutes. "We nearly got caught."

"You can't just give up."

"I can, and I will." Digby looked away from the young rogue. "I can't even see how much mana I have. What am I supposed to do if we get backed into a corner?" He shook his head. "No, the safest thing to do is to head back and try to come up with a new plan. It may have been fun while it lasted, but this is too much."

"But…" Hawk blew out a sigh. "I don't want to stop."

Digby looked back to the mirror as the boy's tone fell. "What's that?"

"I don't want you to stop." Hawk looked up at him. "I've always hated the holidays. But, I don't know, this year was different. It felt like just after I was adopted. Not just tonight, but this whole month. Everyone worked together. I don't know when, but at some point, it all started to feel like we were family. You, me, Becca, Alex, Parker, and everybody else on the airship. I still think I hate Christmas, but I'm happy you all are here."

"You do realize that Parker is a spy, right?" Digby arched an eyebrow.

"Yeah, I was snooping and overheard. But she doesn't know what she is and still cares about us for now." Hawk sounded hopeful.

Digby slowed the sleigh but didn't stop. "I'm glad that this month has meant something more to you, but none of that will change just because we've ended things here. All of us will still be here with you."

"I know." Hawk shook his head. "But that's not why you need to finish this. I'm not a kid anymore, I'll be fine either way. But there are kids down there that the empire wants to turn to Guardians. You remember how messed up they were back when you rescued me from Autem's training program. Those kids are the ones that need a reminder that someone cares about them."

"He's not wrong about that," Becca said from the back of the sleigh. "The empire has created an environment where they are the only ones there to support the kids they took in. Dropping by as Santa could make the difference between them giving themselves over fully to Autem or breaking free of their grip. At the very least, they may be conflicted about it."

"See." Hawk threw a hand out toward them. "Becca agrees."

Digby glanced back at the vampire, noticing a strange smile on her face. "What are you grinning about?"

Her face fell as a sheepish expression took over. "Okay, I can't believe I'm about to say this, but tonight has actually been a lot of fun."

"I'm so glad you're having a good time," he snapped back.

"Oh, don't pretend like you haven't been enjoying yourself. I saw you back at that camp in Colorado." She pointed a finger in his face. "You were having the time of your life."

"That was before."

"Before what?" She lowered her finger. "Before you found out Parker might be evil?"

"Yes, actually," he grumbled. "Parker has been one of our most valuable assets. Losing her is a significant blow to our side."

"Is that really it?" Becca leaned forward over the back of his seat. "Or is it because you feel like you lost a family member, and you're letting that influence your decision to give up on the plan?"

"I..." Digby frowned. "Alright, there might be some truth to that. But what of it? Parker saved me from myself not too long ago. Of course I don't want to lose her. I don't want to lose a friend."

"Then we don't have to," Hawk added. "Parker doesn't know shit about what she is. And honestly, she barely pays attention to anything, so she's probably not good at figuring it out."

"True, we may be able to kick the problem of Parker's loyalty down the road for now." Digby leaned back in his seat. "But none of that changes the fact that our situation here and now does not look good. Delivering presents behind enemy lines is insane. I don't know why I thought it was a good idea. It is only a matter of time before a Guardian spots us, especially if we attempt to make a stop at the barracks where they are training their new recruits. We will bring their entire force down on our heads."

"Then go there last," Hawke suggested. "Visit everyone you can in the outer areas, then do the barracks just before the sun comes up. Then make a run for it."

"You say that as if it is just that simple."

"Isn't it?" Hawk stared at him.

Digby frowned and sank into his seat.

"Is now a good time to point out that you stopped the sleigh a minute ago and that we've been sitting here floating in the sky with the reindeer looking at us awkwardly?" Becca pointed forward as Asher craned her neck back awaiting orders.

Digby's mouth fell open, realizing that they weren't moving. The reindeer must've picked up his feelings across their bond and slowed in response. He had been too occupied by the argument to notice. More importantly, did that mean that he didn't really want to give up? Was he just sulking and letting it cloud his judgment?

No, it wasn't that.

The plan had become too risky.

Then again, every plan he'd had so far had carried a considerable amount of risk. It wasn't like him to worry about what might go wrong. Hawk was right, if they moved fast, they should be able to escape. They just had to know when to make a run for it. Even if they did get caught, what was Henwick going to do about it? Execute him? Not while they had a treaty and he still had a nuke on his side.

"Fine." Digby turned the sleigh around again.

"Does that mean that you're gonna keep going?" Hawk looked hopeful.

"Yes." He replied with as much reluctance as he could muster. "At least for a little while longer. But I have no intention of overstaying my welcome." Digby flicked his eyes down to Hawk's image in the mirror. "Now get out of the way and let Easton show me our next target."

Hawk gave a mock salute before turning and walking out of view.

"Okay, we're doing this." Becca turned and rummaged through the back of the sleigh to find a clean sack as Easton brought up the image of another building.

"This one should be right in front of you. There's ten deliveries to make down there."

"Good." Digby felt the corner of his mouth tug upward as he willed the reindeer to speed up. "Take us down, Becky."

If anything, it would all be worth doing just to annoy Henwick.

He let out a quiet chuckle.

"There isn't a moment to lose."

CHAPTER THIRTY-SEVEN

The next ten deliveries went smoothly. Like before, Digby landed the sleigh on the roof of an apartment building and crafted a bone key to gain access. He still had trouble with it sticking in the lock, but not as much as before.

Learning from his mistakes earlier in the night, he and Becca stopped in the hallway and retrieved several packages from his bag at once before moving on. Thanks to the vampire's agility and dexterity, she could carry most of them by stacking them on top of each other. That left Digby free to handle the locks. He made sure to have Becca listen to each door before entering. That way, he wouldn't run into any surprises like before.

Once they were sure there was no one awake inside, he slipped in and set down a present for each recipient someplace where they would be noticed easily. After five deliveries, they started to get into a rhythm. Three more, and his bone keys started pulling free from the locks more easily. Many of the apartments held multiple children as well, reducing the number of stops they had to make. It only took ten minutes to finish the whole building and get back up to the sleigh.

Counting those ten deliveries as successes, they took off and headed across the street where another thirteen children waited for presents. Digby's luck continued for another three buildings, and by the end of the first hour, they had already crossed fifty children off the list.

It was a far cry from the thousand or so more that remained, but it was a start.

With only two hours left, it seemed impossible to make it to all of them. When considering over half of the children in the empire had been taken into Autem's training program, if they hit the barracks successfully, they could still reach a large chunk.

Digby chuckled. "You know, this might actually work."

Becca immediately dropped a package from the top of her stack. "Why would you say that?"

"Oh, don't be superstitious, Becky." He bent down to pick up the present.

"Hey, you thought there were demons in your blood a couple of months ago, so I'm allowed to be a little-stitious."

Digby opened his mouth to respond only to close it again when a door opened further down the hallway. He leaned to one side to look past Becca as a man in overalls stepped into the hall with a hard hat tucked under one arm. Both he and Becca froze. Like the rest of the buildings of the refugee camp, this one had once been an apartment complex. The man must have been heading out to an early shift working construction on the wall not far away.

His apartment wasn't one of the ones on their list of deliveries.

Digby watched as the man rubbed at his eyes, then turned around to close his door behind him. He looked exhausted. Once his apartment was locked, he turned toward the stairs at the other end of the hall without even glancing in their direction.

Digby relaxed.

Then the man dropped his keys.

Bending down to pick them up, he stopped, his eyes locked staring in their direction. One word fell from his mouth. "Qué?"

Becca's shoes jingled as she turned around awkwardly and angled the pile of packages in her hands in a way that seemed to suggest a wave. "Hi."

The man raised back up in silence, his eyes darting around from the vampire to Digby and the presents that they carried.

Without a better option, Digby fell back on his instincts. "Haven't you ever seen a couple of people trying to brighten the lives of a few children before?"

The man stopped as if to think about the question seriously.

Digby didn't give him a chance to answer. Instead, he flicked his head toward the stairs, adding, "Move along."

The construction worker shrugged and kept walking.

"Anyway, where were we? Oh yes." Digby tucked the package he carried under his arm and placed his hand against the lock of the next door that he had to open.

Tendrils of bone reached from his palm only to stop a second later. He pulled his hand away with a half formed key protruding from his skin.

"Damn, I've run out of mana."

He was still absorbing more, but he was using it too fast to let it recover.

"Just from making keys?" Becca leaned closer, adjusting the stack of presents in her hands to keep them from falling.

"That and opening my maw wide enough to access the silos stored within." He dropped his hand to his side.

"Still, that doesn't seem like that should cost that much." She frowned.

"I think it's because of the keys. Natural formations like limbs and body parts are easy, but an object, even a tiny one, seems to take more mana to control the structure." He let out a frustrated growl. "Of course, this would be a whole lot easier if I knew how much MP I have left. With all these silos stored in my void, I still can't see my HUD."

"I might be able to help with that." Becca set down her packages and turned her attention to him. "Vampires don't usually have a HUD to fall back on, so we have to get used to the feel of our mana system instead. You can't tell exactly how many points of MP you have, but you can figure out a rough percentage just by sensing it. Learning how could certainly come in handy anytime your void is over-encumbered, or if you get yourself silenced."

"And you think you can teach me?" Digby eyed her skeptically.

"I don't think I have to." The vampire leaned her head from

side to side, stopping herself a second later when she realized the bell on her hat was jingling. "I think it's something you can already do, but don't realize it because you have a HUD to answer the question for you."

Digby considered the possibility, closing his eyes and taking a moment to try to feel a mana system. He snapped them back open, feeling nothing.

"I think I might be a special case. I can usually tell what is going on with another person's magic by using my Blood Sense, but the same trick doesn't seem to work on me. Probably because my blood doesn't flow. My veins are just filled with black goo."

"That's pretty gross." Becca leaned against the wall and stared at him. "But that doesn't mean you can't do it. Maybe there's just too much noise for you to focus on your mana. That was a big problem for me when I first turned. It was hard to sort things out. The same thing might be happening with your Blood Sense. It's always active, so you always listen to it first. You might need to try to ignore it."

"Alright." Digby closed his eyes again, immediately noticing a small amount of mana flow through Becca's blood. He cracked one eye open.

"That was me feeding a few points of mana into my hearing. I was trying to give you something to focus on so you can isolate the noise that your Blood Sense is causing."

Digby closed his eyes again and held on to the sensation.

"Do you have a good hold on your Blood Sense?" she asked.

He nodded.

"Good, now I want you to actively ignore it. It might help if you picture something physical in your mind. That helps me when I feed mana into my stats. You could try imagining your Blood Sense as an object and then placing it in a box and closing the lid."

Digby did as he was told. First, he imagined his Blood Sense as a bottle filled with crimson. Then, he pictured a simple wooden chest and placed the bottle inside. Slamming the lid shut, he prepared to feel something new. A second later, he noticed Becca tapping her attributes, the same as before. He opened his eyes again.

"It didn't work."

"Well, try again." She gave him an annoyed look. "Picture something else, sometimes it takes a couple of tries."

"Alright, alright." He closed his eyes again and shrugged. "Isn't there an expression about blood? Something about rocks?"

"You can't get blood from a stone."

"That's it."

Digby pictured a rock in his mind.

Then his mouth fell open. It had worked. Rather than locking his Blood Sense away temporarily, he just blocked it. As long as he focused on that stone, his Blood Sense quieted down. From there, it didn't take much to sense his mana system.

The first thing he noticed was his spark. The internal version of himself that took form whenever he activated his Soul Eater mutation. Surrounding that was a thin current of energy, no more than a trickle. It flowed like a river twisting back on itself and passing through his spark before returning to where it started. It appeared to be one continuous loop that grew slightly as he absorbed more of the ambient essence from the outside world.

Digby opened his eyes again, suddenly understanding that he had close to three percent of his mana remaining. Not only that, but the clearing of his mind had seemed to count as meditation because his mana absorption rate had sped up.

"Good lord, it works."

"See, told you it wasn't that hard." Becca gave him a nod and picked up the stack of presents at her feet.

Digby tried to craft a key of bone a second time, this time completing the process before running out of mana. Picturing the stone in his mind once again, he was able to tell that his MP had dropped to near empty. From that, he was able to figure out that forming a key consumed nearly three percent of his total mana. He filed that knowledge away for later and headed into the apartment to put a pair of packages down on a coffee table.

The rest of the deliveries within the building went smoothly. Unfortunately, that was where a new complication arose.

"This is your next stop." Easton activated the scrying mirror to show them a row of smaller, connected buildings, each with its own entrance.

"Are those brownstones?" Becca leaned forward in her seat to see.

"What's a brownstone?" Digby glanced back at her over his shoulder.

"It's a type of house," Easton answered. "The one in question seems to be a single-family residence instead of being broken up into apartments."

"I'm surprised the empire has allowed any of the refugees to stay in the bigger houses." Becca leaned to one side of the sleigh and threw out a hand. "At least we don't have to go far. It's right down there across the street."

"Alright, that roof looks treacherous to land on, though." Digby sat down in his seat.

"Well, we can't land in the street." Becca grabbed hold of the altitude crank. "I haven't seen a patrol in this area yet, but people are starting to go to work and someone is bound to see us."

"Not if we get in and out fast. Besides, it will be good if some of the citizenry catches a glimpse of the reindeer. Every rumor that they start will only help to build our enchantment." Digby turned the sleigh back toward the center of the street.

"Okay, let's just make this one fast." Becca brought them down.

Digby jumped out before they even came to a stop.

His elf hopped out behind him, carrying one of the bags on her back. Digby wasted no time, rushing up the brownstone's stairs. He made sure to check if he had enough mana before pressing his palm to the deadbolt. A sharp turn later and the lock disengaged. He repeated the process on the door knob and crunched down both keys. He was pretty sure he didn't need to eat them at this point, but it was still a good way to get rid of evidence.

"Hang on, I haven't checked to make sure everyone's asleep in there." Becca climbed up the stairs behind him.

Digby ignored her, not wanting to leave the sleigh out in the street for longer than he had to. Besides, all he had to do was slip inside, drop one package, and be gone. The whole stop shouldn't take more than thirty seconds.

Despite the urgency, he froze as soon as he entered the door.

Unlike the rest of the apartments in the refugee camp that held few possessions of significance, the home that he had just entered was full. The entryway was lined with framed pictures of a family while other belongings decorated the living room beyond. If he didn't know better, he would've thought the apocalypse had somehow skipped over the home altogether.

Christmas decorations adorned nearly every surface and a large tree stood in the corner next to a fireplace. Three stockings had been hung with care, now filled with various sweets sticking out from the top and several packages had already been placed beneath the tree. There was even a plate of cookies sitting out just like there had been in Vegas.

"That's odd." Digby turned back to look at Becca as she stood on the steps just outside the threshold. "It looks like Santa has already been here."

"The family that lives here must have been celebrating on their own." She furrowed her brow. "I'm surprised Autem allowed that." Then she frowned. "Never mind, I think I understand the situation."

"Then fill me in already."

The vampire merely pointed to one of the family photos on the wall. "The father in that picture was a congressman."

Digby turned to the photo. It was of a happy family, posing together, dressed in their finest clothes. There was a father, mother, and little girl. If he was honest, they looked a little stuffy.

"What is a congressman? Is that some kind of local lord?"

"It's a politician. They get elected to represent the people of an area." She grimaced. "Or at least, they're supposed to represent them. From the looks of this place, I assume the empire bought them off at some point. I doubt they ever had to evacuate with Autem's setting up shop here. They got to ride out the apocalypse in the comfort of their own home with protection. In exchange, I'm sure he helped grease the wheels of government in Henwick's favor."

Digby stared at the picture on the wall, focusing on the man as a foul taste crept up the back of his throat. "That's disgusting."

"That's politics." She shrugged. "If it wasn't Autem backing him, it would've been some corporation or another. It takes a lot of money to run for office, and selling out is a good way to fund a campaign."

"Well, as horrifying as that is to learn, I don't think we can hold the sins of the father against the child that resides here." Digby turned away from the photograph, took his bag from Becca, and stepped into the living room.

He noted the names that had been embroidered onto each of the stockings. From left to right, they read, Mom, Dad, and Alice. From the looks of things, Alice already had several presents waiting for her. Digby set down his sack and made sure the bottom was even with the floor to avoid the spillage of any necrotic blood from his maw.

He called forth a silo from his void and pulled the remote control that opened the top from his pocket. Once it was open, he tapped the button to move the shutter inside and reached for the package on top. Raising it to his ear, he shook it. He wasn't sure why he shook it. It wasn't like he could tell what was in it. Still, he couldn't help but feel that this one was important.

Holding the package in one hand, he tapped the button on the silo's shutter and closed the top with the remote control. Then he crouched down in front of the fireplace and placed the gift on the floor.

That was when Becca sucked in a sudden breath. "Santa, we have to go."

Digby glanced back, half-expecting the man from the photograph to be standing behind him. Instead, all he saw was a pair of eyes staring down at him through the railing of the stairway.

"Who are you?" The young girl from the picture knelt on the steps, cautiously. She must have been the owner of the stocking labeled with the name Alice.

She looked to be around six.

Digby hesitated, glancing back to Becca for an instant as if asking what to do.

The vampire standing in the doorway just gave him a look that said, get on with it.

Digby stood tall but struggled to keep eye contact with the girl as he answered her question, "I'm Santa Claus."

"No, you're not." Alice shook her head. "Santa isn't real."

Digby suppressed the instinct to argue and simply held his hands out at his sides. "I'd say I'm real enough."

"No." Her voice fell. "My dad said that Santa's not real."

"Now why would he say a thing like that?"

"I heard him in the hall when I was in bed." Alice pointed down at the plate of cookies sitting out. "He told Mom it was stupid that I left those for you when you weren't real."

"Oh..." Digby frowned, understanding the situation. "Well, just between you and me, your father doesn't know everything."

"Yes, he does." Alice stood up. "He knew that monsters were coming before they did."

"Alright, then." He grinned. "If I'm not really Santa, how do I know that your name is Alice?"

"My name is on my stocking." She stared at him incredulously.

"Ah, so it is." He glanced around the room for another way to prove his lie. Then he snapped his eyes to Becca who was still waiting in the open doorway. "Well, if I'm not real, then why do I have an elf with me?"

Alice stared down at the vampire from the stairs. "That's just some lady in a costume." She glanced back to Digby. "Why is she standing outside?"

Becca cleared her throat. "I'm sorry for letting the cold in. I didn't think it would be polite to come in without an invitation." She eyed the child. "Would it be okay if I came in?" The vampire brushed her hair behind one of her pointed ears to help sell the ruse.

Alice thought for a long moment, clearly weighing the possibility that Santa and his elves were real against the knowledge that she should never invite a stranger into her house. Eventually, she nodded.

Becca cautiously stepped one bell-toed shoe through the threshold. A second later, she relaxed and stepped the rest of the way in. After closing the door behind her, she beckoned to the child.

Alice came down the stairs a few steps until she was standing level with Becca.

"See, I'm the real deal." The vampire leaned forward to show her ears to the girl.

"Can I touch them?" Alice asked.

"Sure." Becca leaned closer so that the child could tug on the point of her ear.

Alice's eyes lit up as soon as she did, finding no trick. "They're real."

"If you want to see something else that's real, come have a look out the window." Digby walked across the room to pull the curtains aside.

They had left the sleigh sitting just outside. It was dark, but close enough to be seen if he leaned against the window at an angle. Surely that would be proof enough.

Alice crept down the rest of the stairs and slipped past Becca to peek out the window. She gasped as soon as she did. "Reindeer."

"Indeed." Digby nodded, glad the animals weren't close enough to see the milky gray of their eyes. "I assume that clears things up. Now, if you don't mind, I have more stops to make." He started toward the door.

"What did you bring me?" The girl tore her attention away from the window and began looking around the room, her eyes settling on the present that he'd left by the fireplace. "I was good all year."

"Oh, yes." Digby gestured to the package. "I'm afraid you'll have to wait until the morning to open it. And I'm sure you were plenty good." He leaned down. "In all honesty, with everything that this year has brought, I'm giving most children a pass. You have all been through enough."

Alice lowered her eyes to the floor. "Okay, I can wait until morning."

Digby glanced back at the other presents sitting under the tree. "You know, there are a lot of children out there that don't have much. Perhaps, it would be good to share occasionally with those you meet."

She looked up and nodded. "Okay."

"Dig, I mean Santa." Becca looked out through a narrow window beside the door. "We should probably get going."

Digby glanced outside as another construction worker stood staring at the sleigh from across the street. He must've been passing by and stopped to investigate.

"Yes, of course." Digby grabbed his bag from where it lay on the floor by the tree and got ready to go.

"Wait." Alice rushed across the room to grab the plate of cookies. "You didn't have any."

"Oh, I couldn't possibly. I'm already quite full, you see." He patted his stomach and turned to the vampire beside him. "But my elf is bound to have some room."

Becca stared daggers at him, having already declared earlier that if she ever saw another cookie, she would literally die. "But those cookies were left for you, Santa. I couldn't possibly deny you of them."

Digby glanced out the window as the construction worker started to approach the sleigh. His eyes widened when he picked up a feeling of excitement from Comet and Vixen from across his bond of the dead. It was obvious what would happen if the man got too close to one of the reindeer. Without his Control spell, the only thing keeping most of them in line had been Asher.

"Fine, fine." Digby snatched up a cookie from the plate and shoved it in his mouth, chewing so that the majority of it fell right back out to get stuck in his beard.

Human food hadn't been appetizing to him since his death. Not to mention, he didn't want to add anything incompatible to his void. Alice looked at him with one eyebrow raised.

"You eat like Cookie Monster."

"I don't know who that is." Digby brushed off the comment before turning to the door.

The girl spoke up again before he could make it more than a few steps. "But you're supposed to use the fireplace."

"What?" Digby stopped.

"Santa is supposed to use the chimney," she insisted.

Digby glanced at the fireplace, remembering what she was talking about from the movies he'd watched. It was one of the reasons why he'd chosen Santa as a target for his enchantment. The ability to travel through ventilation shafts seemed useful. He'd assumed that he would gain some form of teleportation if his deception proved successful. Unfortunately, he did not yet possess such a power.

"Sorry, but my sleigh is just outside." He glanced out the window, nearly choking on cookie crumbs when he saw the construction worker petting Vixen on the neck.

Carrot? the reindeer asked across his bond, as if requesting permission to murder the man.

No carrot! Digby shouted back in his mind, sending a command across his bond with the undead animal to not bite the man's hand off. Then he began heading for the door again.

"But…" Alice trailed off, sounding disappointed. "But you're Santa. If you're really him, you would go up the chimney."

Digby looked to Becca for help.

"She has a point," the vampire said, unhelpfully.

He glowered in her direction, then looked back to the fireplace. "Fine. How hard could it be? I mean, I do it all the time. It's not a problem at all."

"I'll take the sleigh up and meet you on the roof, then." Becca spun on her heel and headed out the door to shoo the construction worker away from the reindeer.

Digby watched as she climbed into the sleigh and grabbed hold of the reins while awkwardly reaching behind her to operate the altitude crank. The entire thing levitated straight off the ground a moment later, leaving the man on the street staring in complete and utter bafflement.

"Alright." Digby stepped back toward the fireplace and crouched down. He glanced back at Alice, who was still holding the plate of cookies and watching him intently.

He gave her a nod, then pushed the present that he'd left there aside and opened the glass doors that covered the fireplace's opening. Inside, there was a metal flap that seemed to be operated by a lever. Regret filled him as soon as he opened it and looked up. His own words echoed back to him.

How hard could it be?

The answer was, extremely.

The brick shaft was only a foot wide in each dimension. Digby pulled his head back out, struggling to think of some kind of excuse.

"Can't you do it?" Alice looked concerned as if this one moment could shatter the trust that he'd gained.

"No, nothing's wrong. It's just a different type than I'm used to." He shoved his head back into the fireplace and craned his neck upward.

The impossible act stood before him like a wall of stone. Then, he got an idea. There was no way his body was going to fit into such a space, but no one said he couldn't use the body of something else. With his Body Craft mutation, the possibilities were endless. He just had to make sure Alice didn't notice or witness anything that might scar her for life.

Digby ran through all of the things that he'd eaten and settled on one he thought could fit the best. The boa constrictor that he'd consumed back in the San Diego Zoo made the most sense. With that in mind, he crawled further into the fireplace. The metal flap left just enough room for him to squeeze his head through. Angling it to the side, he got into position. Then, he willed his Body Craft mutation into action.

A series of cracks and pops came from his neck and spine as everything began to change. His shoulders shrank in toward his body and his chest began to compress and stretch. Not wanting to disturb the function of his brain, he left his head unchanged. It slid upward into the chimney as his neck extended.

"Are you okay?" Alice asked from below, clearly noticing the sound of every bone in his body breaking and reforming.

"Yes, I'm fine. It's just rather tight in here. Nothing to worry about." Digby slid his head further as the top half of his body shifted into that of a nightmarish serpent.

He made a point to keep his hands relatively unchanged, sticking out of his sides so that he could hold onto his clothing. It wouldn't do to let his disguise slide off and leave it behind. As he slithered further up the chimney, he stood up with his lower half and began transforming his legs as well. He added a few fingers poking out somewhere around where his waist had been to keep his pants on. It wasn't long before his feet left the ground below. All in all, the process had gone smoothly.

Then, he remembered his boots.

There was a chance that he could hold onto one with the end of his body and pull it up behind him, but the other would be lost. He couldn't fit it and himself through the pipe. In the end, he had no choice but to drop it.

"You lost your shoe," Alice called up the chimney, raising her voice to be heard.

Digby winced. If she kept shouting like that, it was only a matter of time before she woke up her parents. "I am aware. I left it on purpose." He struggled to come up with a lie. "That's for you. When your father asks if I'm real, you just show him that."

"But you already left the present. I don't need more proof." She stated the obvious.

"Yes, I know, but I have plenty more boots where that came from." His statement echoed through his head, reminding him that it made no sense.

Fortunately, Alice was already distracted by another detail. "Your boot smells bad."

"Of course it smells bad! It's a boot." Digby shoved his serpentine body up the chimney just as a man's voice came from the room below.

"Who are you talking to?"

Obviously, her father had come down to investigate the noise.

"It's Santa!" Alice said with enthusiasm. "See, it's his boot."

Digby ignored the conversation and shoved his head toward the light at the top of the chimney. A metal grate rested on the opening. He popped it off with his head as he slithered out. Getting the first five feet of his body out of the shaft, he swung his head around in search of the sleigh. Digby found it floating to one side of the angled roof. From there, he pulled the rest of his body free along with his coat, pants, and one boot.

Not wasting any time, he slithered straight for the sleigh.

"Jesus fuck!" Becca fell into the back seat as he rose up and coiled into his seat. "That is the most messed up thing I've ever seen. I mean, what even are you?" She gestured to his body as he raised his head to eye level to glower at her properly.

"What did you expect me to do, Becky? I can't just magically transport myself up a chimney." He coughed out a cloud of soot as he spoke.

"Hurry up and change back before somebody sees you. This human head on a snake body thing looks like something out of a Tim Burton movie. And honestly, with the whole Christmas situation, I'm pretty sure we're already approaching copyright infringement territory."

"I have no idea who you're talking about," Digby grumbled as he willed his neck to return to normal, his body filling out to match.

That was when a voice started yelling in the street below. It was Alice's father, the congressman, looking for the man who had given his daughter a boot. The construction worker who was still standing outside seemed to be getting the brunt of the accusations. As soon as Digby's body had mostly returned to normal, he grabbed hold of the reins and pulled the sleigh around.

"Take us back down to the street."

"Okay, but why?" Becca adjusted their altitude.

"To get my boot back."

The sleigh whipped around to align itself with the street.

"There he is!" Alice stood on the steps of her house, pointing up as soon as they came into view.

Her father just stood there, dressed in a robe and silk pajamas, with a look of shock and horror on his face. Digby's boot hung limply in his hand. The construction worker stood beside him dumbstruck as well.

Digby brought the sleigh in to pass directly in front of them. Without stopping, he reached out and snatched his boot back from the man.

"I'll take that." After that, he ignored the congressman in the bathrobe and focused on the girl standing on the steps behind him. "Be good, Alice, and don't forget to share with the other children."

"I will." She waved as the sleigh climbed back into the sky.

———

Congressman Jim Hammond stood, staring up at the sky as an impossible sight faded into the distance. He had no idea what to make of it. The world had gone insane in the last month. There was no telling what might happen next. All he knew was that he had made a deal.

Turning, Jim ran back up the steps of his house, only looking back to shout at his daughter. "Get back inside, Alice."

"You saw him. He's real." The excitement in her voice grated on his nerves.

"He's real alright." Jim went straight for his office and snatched up the landline that had been recently installed.

He had been told only to use it in an emergency.

Raising the receiver to his ear, he dialed the one number he'd been given. An operator picked up immediately.

"Imperial services, please state your reason for calling."

"Yes, I, um…" He hesitated, unsure how to put what he saw into words. "I need to report suspicious activity."

"Go ahead." The voice on the phone sounded annoyed.

"I just saw a man fly into the sky." His report sounded insane, even to him.

"Did you recognize this man?"

"Yes…" Jim placed one hand on his desk and braced himself before saying the words that his mind had been struggling to deny. "It was Santa Claus."

CHAPTER THIRTY-EIGHT

Digby glanced at the clock set into the front of the sleigh.

There were only ninety minutes left before sunrise.

Thanks to the fact that many of the apartments in the refugee camps held multiple children, they had been able to deliver over two hundred presents. There was still a lot more to go, but they were out of time. They needed to head for the city's largest concentration of recipients.

"It's time to finish this." He turned the sleigh toward the section of the city reserved for Autem's Guardians. "We need to hit the barracks now. We should have just enough time to get in, leave presents for the children being kept there, and get the hell out."

"Agreed. It doesn't look like people have been given the holiday off, and workers are starting to head out for the day." Becca leaned over the side. "The only thing keeping us hidden right now is the dark. We need to be gone before that changes."

The sleigh passed over the partially constructed wall below. Compared to the refugee camp, the structures below were like night and day. Every trace of the old world had already been torn down. In their place, several large, blocky buildings now stood surrounded by paved sections of ground.

According to the information Easton gathered using the

scrying mirror, the children that had been taken into the empire's Guardian training program were being kept in a complex of four buildings. The first was for schooling, the second was for combat training, the third was for magic classes, and the fourth was for the barracks. For the children within, their world had been reduced to those four buildings. Eventually, the process would spit them out as loyal Guardians ready to usher in the future that Autem had planned. Many wouldn't even remember the old world. All they would know was the empire.

It was time to change that.

Digby pulled a pair of binoculars from a pouch under his seat and scanned the roof of their destination. It was empty. Though, there was bound to be staff inside the building to keep an eye on the children.

"What kind of security should we be worrying about in there?" Digby looked down at one of the mirrors where Easton waited on the other end of a link spell.

"Unfortunately, that's where we reached the scrying mirror's limits. The building is warded to block our ability to see inside. The empire hasn't done anything to hide the refugee camps, but it seems like all the facilities inside the second wall have a higher level of security. It's even tighter within the center of the city behind the first wall. But you don't have to go there."

"Damn." Digby brought the sleigh toward the roof anyway. "Then we're going in blind."

"Not quite." Easton smiled. "We might not be able to see inside, but we can still see the entrances. And I already did some recon."

"I knew I pulled you out of an imperial prison cell for a reason." Becca leaned over the back of Digby's seat so Easton could see her.

"Hopefully there were more reasons than just that." He frowned before bringing the subject back to the building's security. "During the day, there's a ton of activity with teachers, Guardians, and administrators. But at night, most of them return to the other barracks. That leaves just a six-man squad of mid-level magic users to watch over trainees. There is also a small team of nurses there to take care of the children's needs. There's a cleric on duty at all times, but the other nurses don't have any magic. Based on the number of adults they have in there, most of the security is going to be automated. There's two security cameras on the roof, so you'll have to land on the northeast corner. And I would expect there to be a camera watching the main corridors inside, as well."

"They didn't have cameras set up yet the last time I was here," Becca added.

"Yes, but that was over a month ago," Easton countered. "By now, they'll have closed the holes in the security that existed before. Especially considering how badly you exploited them."

"So they will notice us once we go inside." Digby grimaced at the thought.

"Unless you can find a way around the cameras." Easton shrugged. "Otherwise, you're going to have to find a way to handle the security team without attacking them."

"Alright, we'll do our best." Digby brought the sleigh down to the roof.

"There is one more thing I should mention." Easton adjusted his glasses. "If the security team finds you, it's likely that they will raise an alarm. If they do that, the primary barracks for all of the empire's Guardians is not far away. It's less than a mile from where the youth training facility is. You can see it from the roof. I don't know exactly how many men they have, but my best estimate is that they have over a thousand. And they will send every single one of them after you if you're discovered. So make sure you run the moment that happens. If you wait too long, you might get trapped."

"Then we shall flee at the first sign of trouble." Digby reached for a bag from the back of the sleigh.

As soon as he climbed out of his seat, he set his eyes on the raised portion of the roof where they could access the stairwell. As Easton had mentioned, there were two cameras.

One was facing outward to get a wide view of anyone who might approach the door. The other was facing down so that it could see anyone sneaking under the first camera's field of view.

"Well, that's not good." He frowned.

"That's not the worst of it." Becca pointed to a panel mounted on the wall beside the door. "That's a security lock. I've seen one like it before. It requires a Guardian ring to open it."

"Don't you have one? You were given one a month ago by the empire's caretaker."

Becca reached a finger into the collar of her coat and pulled out a silver chain with an iron ring hanging from it. "True, but I don't dare try it. No matter how friendly I am with the Guardian Core's caretaker, its administrators have almost certainly locked out my ring's access. There's a good chance that if I touch this ring to that panel, an alarm will go off immediately."

"Let's not do that then." Digby nodded.

"We might not need to bother with the lock or the door." Becca shoved the ring back into her coat and pointed in the other direction of the building's ventilation system. There was a grate on the side about a foot and a half wide and a foot tall. "No ordinary person could fit in there, but you've already proven that you can."

"I thought my snake body was... What did you call it? Nightmare fuel?"

"Yeah, but it's the only option we have." She gave a half-hearted shrug.

Digby glanced back to the camera and followed its line of sight. Then he shook his head. "That's no good. The vent is in clear view."

"I think I can fix that." Becca held out her hand as shadows collected around her fingers to form a large, black spider. It skittered away a second later, climbing up the wall toward the camera. "Insects block cameras all the time. Whoever's watching should just brush it off as something normal." She smirked. "They're going to get one hell of a jump-scare, though."

Digby remained where he was until the shadow creature climbed up to the camera's lens and stopped with its body in the center. He took one step forward, but the vampire beside him grabbed his arm.

"Wait."

Digby froze as several seconds went by. "What are we waiting for?"

Becca merely held up a finger and pointed to the spider.

Another few seconds went by. Then, the camera moved, panning from left to right. After that, it tried up and down.

"Whoever's monitoring the video just noticed the spider, and they're trying to get it to move." She lowered her hand. "They'll probably give up in a minute or so."

"What if they come up here to try to get rid of it in person?"

"I doubt they'll go through that much effort. Once they realize the spider's not going anywhere, they'll just give up and stop looking at the feed."

After another thirty seconds of watching the camera try to shake off the spider, it stopped.

"Go, now." Becca shoved Digby out into the open. "And stay away from the door, the second camera can still see it."

"Alright, alright." He headed for the air vent.

It didn't take long to pry the cover off. From there, the rest was all up to his Body Craft mutation. Digby shoved his head into the vent, grateful that it was larger than the chimney that he had traveled through before. His neck elongated as the rest of his body collapsed inward.

"Try to find a way to get the door open once you're inside," Becca called out.

Of course, Digby had no idea how to do that, so he opted to just get a lay of the land. Lowering himself several feet into the vent, he reached a point where it branched off to the side and slithered further. It didn't take long to reach another vent. Pressing his face against it, he peeked into a long room full of bunks stacked on top of each other, two tall. Each one held a sleeping child. Some looked as young as eight while others were as old as twelve. Based on what Digby had seen in the facility back on Skyline's base, there were bound to be older trainees as well. They were probably kept in another room or different floor.

There were no cameras that he could see from the vent. Perhaps that meant that the only areas under surveillance were the hallways outside the room. Despite that, he didn't dare exit the vent for fear of waking one of the children. He was sure he could force the metal cover off the opening, but he doubted that he could do so quietly.

Digby slithered on, passing several more vents. Each led to another room the same as the first. It wasn't until he reached the end of the vent that he found something different.

A bathroom.

This is as good a place as any.

Digby pushed against the grating that covered the vent with his face, but it didn't budge.

Damn, it must be screwed into place.

He cursed his overloaded void again. If he hadn't been silenced, he could have Decayed his way through the barrier. Fortunately, the holes in the grate were just wide enough to fit a finger through. Unfortunately, his hands were about five feet down his body. Getting in was going to take some improvising.

Working with what he had, Digby opened his mouth and rebuilt his tongue into something that resembled a finger with several extra joints and a thick nail at the end. He slipped it through the grate and curled it back to access the front.

After a few minutes of wedging his new digit's fingernail into the screws and twisting, the vent covering came loose. He held onto it so it wouldn't fall and hit the floor. Tilting the grate at an angle, he pulled it into the vent and set it down.

"Freedom finally."

Digby slithered out of the opening and lowered himself to the floor where he rebuilt his body back to the way it had been. Afterward, he straightened his coat in the mirror and adjusted his hat. If he hadn't left his boots up with Becca, his disguise would have been complete.

"Close enough."

Digby snapped his head to the door a second later as the sound of footsteps came from the hall outside.

"Not good."

Scrambling, he pushed through the door of the nearest bathroom stall and climbed up on the toilet. He was bound to get caught eventually, but now was far too early. It wouldn't do to be forced to flee before he'd even left a single present.

The door opened almost as soon as he got himself situated. He braced his hands against the sides of the stall and leaned forward so he could peek through the gap at the edge of the door.

A man in Guardian armor strolled in.

Without his HUD, Digby had no way of knowing what level or class he was. The only detail he had to go by was that he wore a sword sheathed on his back. He was probably a fighter or a knight.

Digby watched as he entered the stall next to him. He dropped his eyes to the floor to see a pair of boots beneath the partition. The sound of several buckles being released followed. Then he dropped his pants to his ankles and sat down with a sigh. He must've been patrolling the hallways and stopped in to relieve himself.

Unsure what to do, Digby remained where he was. He could stay hidden and wait for the man to leave, but he also needed to find a way to open the door to the roof to get Becca. To do that, he needed a Guardian ring.

If I could just knock him out, I could just take his ring.

That was when Digby remembered that the hallway was likely monitored by a camera.

I could take his uniform as well.

As long as he moved quickly, whoever was watching the camera's video shouldn't notice he was a different person. A plan of attack began to come together until he remembered that knocking a Guardian out would almost certainly count as being hostile. No, attacking was out of the question. Not if he wanted to keep the treaty intact.

But what if I don't attack?

With that thought in mind, Digby nodded to himself. All he had to do was find a way for the Guardian to knock himself out. He suppressed a cackle and carefully stepped down from the toilet. He made a point to stay to one side to keep his feet out of view. The fact that he had left his boots back up on the roof only served to make him more stealthy. Not to mention that the Guardian in the stall seemed to be in a bit of a noisy struggle of his own.

Creeping out from the stall, Digby crept toward the sinks on the other side of the room and placed one hand under the soap dispenser. Then, as quietly as he could, he started pumping. He continued until his hand was full. After that, he dumped it all in the middle of the tile floor.

Digby returned to the soap dispenser for more when he heard the man's radio come alive.

"Where are you?" a voice asked. "I can't find you on the feeds."

"I'm in the bathroom, taking a shit," the Guardian in the stall responded, sounding annoyed.

"Oh. So I will see you again, in what, an hour or so?" The voice on the radio laughed.

"Screw you, man. The food in the mess never agrees with me," the Guardian argued back.

"No argument there." The voice added, "But hurry up, there's a massive spider on the camera lens on the roof. It hasn't moved yet, but you gotta get down here and see it. It's huge. You've never seen anything like it."

"Yeah? If it's still there when I'm done, I'll come check it out." The Guardian punctuated his sentence with a grunt of effort.

The voice on the radio didn't respond.

Digby continued pouring soap on the floor, only stopping when it sounded like the Guardian in the stall was finishing up. He wiped his hand on his pant leg and crept back into one of the stalls. The toilet flushed not long after. Digby waited for the sound of a grown man slipping.

With a little luck, the Guardian would hit his head hard enough to knock him out. If not, he could rush out and hit him while he was still dazed from the fall. That way he might not realize that somebody had attacked him, or at least a witness state-ment from the man would be unreliable.

Any second now. Digby grinned at his plan as he peeked through the gap at the edge of the stall door. His face fell when the Guardian walked straight through the soap puddle to reach the sink.

That wasn't supposed to happen. Digby frowned.

Then he got another idea. Focusing on the space just beneath the Guardian's right foot, he opened his maw. The man immediately wobbled and stepped back into the soap on the floor.

What followed was the least graceful display that Digby had ever seen. Arms flailed and legs kicked. For a moment, it looked like the Guardian might catch himself against one of the stalls, but he overcompensated. The momentum sent him slipping forward instead. He toppled over an instant later, his head hitting one of the sinks with a hard crack.

Digby clasped a hand over his mouth to suppress a startled gasp.

"That might have worked too well." He climbed out of his hiding place and crept over to the Guardian who now lay crumpled on the floor with a stream of blood trickling from the side of his head.

Digby crouched down to check if he was still breathing.

He was, but it was going to be a while before he woke up.

"Alright then, let's get that ring off you." Digby went to work.

Five minutes later, he stepped out into the hall dressed in full Guardian armor. He glanced left and right, finding one camera watching the full length of the hallway at the other end. Fortunately, most of the hall's lights had been turned off. He kept his head low just in case.

A minute after that, he was at the top of the stairwell, telling Becca through the door to blind the other camera so he could open it. When she moved her spider to the other lens, he pressed his new Guardian ring against the lock's panel.

"What took you so long?" Becca was already waiting for him just outside when the door opened. "And where did you get that uniform?"

"There were a few complications. And no, before you ask, I did not kill anyone." Digby looked down at his outfit. "But I do need to get this uniform back to its owner before he wakes up."

"Then we need to move." She took a step toward the door.

"Wait." Digby held up a hand. "Do you need an invitation?"

She shook her head. "This is a barracks. By definition, it's only temporary housing. The building needs to be a permanent residence for a hearth ward to function."

Digby stepped aside as she poked a finger through the entryway to make sure. She stepped the rest of the way inside a second later.

"There's a camera at the end of the hall." Digby headed down the stairs. "If you stay behind me, you should be able to stay hidden until we reach it. I don't think another spider will fool them twice."

"Yeah, it's suspicious enough that the spider already switched cameras." Becca crouched behind him as he entered the hall. "But you can't keep walking around dressed like that either. If any of the kids wakes up and sees you, we need you dressed appropriately to convince them Santa is real."

Digby took a right into the bathroom where he left the unconscious guardian.

"What did you do to him?" Becca stared at the blood coming from his head.

"Nothing, he slipped."

She responded by staring at him incredulously.

"Alright, I may have helped things along." Digby stripped off the chest protector that came with the stolen uniform and shoved it into Becca's arms. "Now help me dress this man."

The process became considerably more difficult now that the Guardian had become slippery from his soapy nap. Digby checked the time and cringed. It had taken over fifteen minutes to get into the building and they still had to figure out a way to deal with the cameras.

Becca took the lead from there, listing off several possible ways to disable the cameras. Most involved technical jargon that Digby didn't understand and none of them sounded like they could do it quickly. Eventually, he just walked into the hall beneath the camera's field of view and pulled out his phone. He snapped a picture of the hallway, then held the device up so that its screen sat in front of the lens. Odds were no one would be looking directly at that camera's video at that very second. The picture quality would be a little different but hopefully not by much. Either way, they just needed to buy a little more time.

Digby looked back to Becca with a grin on his face. "What do you think? I'm a genius, aren't I?"

"That's idiotic." Becca frowned at him. "But I don't have any better ideas, so I'm not going to argue." She waved a hand at the camera as a collection of spiders emerged from the shadows to crawl up Digby's arms. Together, they surrounded his phone to support its weight and hold it in position. "You can let go now."

Digby lowered his arms. "We may not be the best at everything, but it seems we have teamwork down." He held out a hand. "Now give me my sack."

Placing the bag down, he opened his maw and accessed one of the gift silos to retrieve the first package. Then, he passed it to Becca. "Here, poke your head into each of the rooms and get a count of how many children are in there. We'll make a stack outside each bunk with a gift for each one."

The vampire handed it right back to him before gesturing to the bells on her feet and hat. "I don't exactly have the advantage of stealth right now."

Digby grabbed the tips of both of her shoes and ripped the bells off. "There, problem solved."

"Thanks," she said with little enthusiasm as she pulled her hat off and shoved it in her coat pocket to silence the bell hanging from the tip.

They got to work after that.

Thanks to Autem, the process was far easier than any of the deliveries they'd made so far that night. On one side of the hallway, there were four bunk rooms, each holding close to twenty young boys. Another two doors across the hall led to where the older boys lived. There was also a bathroom and another space full of desks. It had probably been set aside as a place to study. The door at the very end of the hallway, beneath the camera, led to the stairs. Other than that, the space was incredibly plain. The only decoration was a gold imperial crest hanging on the far wall at the end of the hallway.

It was unlikely that the older boys still believed in things like Santa Claus, but that didn't mean it was too late to rekindle a bit of that magic. Digby stacked presents in front of their doors as well. The whole process only took seven minutes.

From there, they both hid themselves beneath the camera and retrieved Digby's phone. There was always a chance that whoever was monitoring the video would notice the view suddenly shift, but speed was more important than anything else at the moment. They repeated the process on the floor below, then again, and again. The plan was working perfectly.

With one floor remaining, they still had almost an hour before sunrise.

They hadn't been able to make all of their deliveries, but they had certainly done enough to get the children talking. Despite everything that had gone wrong, there was a chance they might pull the con off.

Digby climbed down the steps to the last floor and quietly opened the door. He closed it again as soon as Becca was inside. Then he snapped a picture of the hallway and held his phone up in position while her spiders crawled up his arms to secure it in place.

Placing his bag down again, he crouched and accessed another silo before holding out a present to his little helper.

Becca didn't take it.

"Hurry up." He shook the package without turning around to face her.

"Dig, we have a problem." The vampire spoke in a whisper and tapped him on the shoulder.

"What is…?" Digby trailed off as the obstacle became obvious.

The figure of a child stood a dozen feet away, their features shrouded in shadow.

Digby relaxed. If there was one thing he'd learned from his interactions with children that night, it was that he could handle them better than he previously thought.

"Hello there." He smiled as he turned around, still resting on one knee and holding the present in his hands. "It seems that we've been caught in the act."

Before he could say anything else, the child held out a hand. Fire gathered into a ball just above their palm.

Digby recoiled, tightening his grip on the present in his hands as the flames illuminated the boy's face. It was a face that had been burned into his mind over a month ago. It was a face he never thought he'd see again.

A face that frightened him to his very core.

CHAPTER THIRTY-NINE

"Get back." Digby grabbed the back of Becca's coat and yanked as the child in front of them launched a Fireball.

The vampire fell out of the way as the flames roared through the air toward Digby. With few options available, he threw the present in his hands. It collided with the Fireball in midair with a burst of heat. The package fell to the floor, fire burning around it.

"Shit." Becca thrust both hands out to smother the flames in a blanket of shadows. Then, she flicked her eyes up at the sprinkler system embedded in the ceiling and waited.

A moment of silence passed, but no alarm sounded.

The child in the hallway raised his hand again.

Digby did the same, holding his palms out in defense. "Please don't."

He'd seen the boy before. It had been over a month ago, back when he'd boarded an aircraft to rescue Hawk and Alvin from Autem's care. The child had been there, on that plane. After an older boy had burned himself alive rather than let himself be rescued, this child had stepped up to take his place. He couldn't have been more than eight. Yet, he'd threatened to burn himself alive all the same.

The empire had twisted his mind so far that death was prefer-able to being separated from them.

Now, the same child stood in the hallway, ready to cast another Fireball.

"You can't take me." Defiance filled the boy's voice.

"I do not wish to." Digby remained on one knee with his hands peacefully outstretched in front of him. "The empire has become your home. I'm not here to challenge that."

That was when the doors of one of the other bunk rooms opened behind the child. An older boy poked his head out. He looked about a year older than Hawk.

"What's going—" He stopped talking as soon as he saw the situation, rushing out and pushing the younger boy behind him.

"He wants to take us," the child claimed.

"No, we don't." Becca knelt beside Digby.

"Who are you?" the older boy asked, loudly, as two more doors opened.

More children stepped into the hallway, some of them speaking a different language that Digby didn't recognize. Autem must have started their recruiting efforts in other countries by now. One of the other boys translated for the group as another young boy stepped forward on the other side of the hall.

"Santa?" He sounded confused more than hopeful.

"He's not him," the first child insisted.

"How do you know?" Digby dropped his hands in frustration as he and Becca quickly became outnumbered. "All you know is what Autem has told you."

"He's telling the truth." Becca joined in. "See? I'm one of his helpers." She pushed her hair back with a finger to show her ears.

"You're not an elf, and he's not Santa." The oldest boy stared down at them.

"How is that obvious?" Digby shook his head. "You each know that magic is real. So why not Santa?"

A few of the children screwed up their eyes at the question. He wasn't wrong. With everything that they knew existed in the world, there wasn't a reason why Santa had to be a lie. It was just the ridiculousness of the idea that made it hard to accept.

"I'm only here to do my job. To give gifts." Digby crawled forward to reach into the pile of burnt cardboard that lay in front of him and pulled out a stuffed elephant. One ear was singed, but the rest was otherwise salvageable.

A few of the children eyed the toy. From what Digby could tell, they didn't have anything like it in any of their bunks. For most of them, it probably represented a part of their lives that the empire had asked them to leave behind.

"What's the trick?" the oldest boy asked.

"No trick." Digby held the elephant out.

"None of us will take anything from you." The youth raised a hand, ready to cast a spell.

That was when Becca said the last thing Digby had expected. "Analyze us!"

"What?" Digby shot her a confused look.

That was the last thing they would've wanted. It was easy to lie to children, but not so much if they had a HUD that could reveal the truth.

Unless...

Becca gave Digby a nod before looking back to the growing crowd of children and teens filling the hall. Then she glanced back toward the door that they had entered through. Digby tensed, realizing that her spiders had dropped his phone from the camera's lens. It was a desperate act. With the camera's view clear, it was only a matter of time before the security team came rushing up the stairs.

Despite that, Digby understood what Becca was trying to do.

If the security team downstairs were able to see the camera's feed, then it was possible that the Guardian Core's caretaker could as well.

Becca nodded to the oldest boy. "Your magic is many things, but it will never lie to you."

He stared down at her, locking his eyes with hers. Then his face went slack. He looked to Digby next. A second later, he shook his head. "That's not possible."

Digby relaxed. The empire's caretaker had noticed them, indeed. He wasn't sure what it had labeled him, but it was clear from the expressions of the rest of the children that it had played along with his con.

"See, there's no trick." Digby stood and took several steps forward before crouching again and leaning to the side so that he could see the child hiding behind the older boy. The one who had attacked him weeks ago. "I'm just here to give you this. It's alright if you want to stay here. It's alright if you want to be part of the empire. I just want you to have something to remind you that the world you knew before hasn't ended. There are still people that care no matter how much you've lost."

For a moment, the boy didn't budge, his expression remained confused and somewhat hostile. Then, it softened.

"But I…" The child looked down at his hands that had lobbed the Fireball at them before.

"It's alright." Digby smiled at him. "I know things have been hard. You didn't do anything wrong." He placed the stuffed elephant in the child's hand. Then he stood back up to address the room. "There is a present here for everyone. You don't have to take one if you don't want to, but each of you deserves a gift this year."

Becca started grabbing packages from the sack and passing them to the oldest boy in front. He hesitated, but in the end, started handing them back.

Digby made sure everyone in the hall got one and left enough in a pile for any of the children who were still asleep. When he was finished, the only one standing empty-handed was the eldest boy in the middle. Digby offered him one just in case, but he responded by shaking his head, adding, "That's for kids."

"Very well." Digby gave him a respectful nod before returning to his bag to close up the silo. Once he was finished, he threw the empty sack over his shoulder.

Then, right on cue, an alarm sounded.

Digby glanced at the camera. The security team had finally noticed them. It was just as well, they had finished what they came to do.

"Time to go." He turned and bowed to the hallway full of children and teens. "Happy holidays to all, and may the year to come be better than what has come before."

With that, he spun on his heel and shoved through the doorway into the stairwell. The sound of voices came from below. The security squad was already on their way up. Digby leaned over the railing to look down through the open space in the middle that stretched to the floor. Five men were rounding the flights of stairs at the bottom.

"We can't fight them." Digby tightened his grip on the railing.

"We have to go up." Becca raised her head to stare up into the stairwell. Then, she climbed up on the railing and jumped directly to the next floor.

"Wait for me!" Digby scrambled upstairs behind her, lacking the agility to do the same. Then he remembered a problem. "The door on the rooftop is locked."

"What about the Guardian ring you used to open it?" She looked down at him before hopping up to another floor.

"I put it back on the Guardian I took it from when I returned his uniform. We can't have him knowing we borrowed it. If he figures that out, he might start to think I had something to do with him being knocked out."

Becca stopped climbing as she reached the fifth floor. "Okay, then we go back down and out the front door."

"Are you mad?" Digby threw himself up another flight to reach her. "We can't fight our way past those Guardians." He hooked a thumb at the squad of men below as they continued up the stairs after them.

"We don't have to fight them if we jump." She looked down the several-story drop to the bottom of the stairwell.

Digby merely groaned. "Fine, but I'm going to blame you if I break every bone in my body."

Before either of them had a chance to jump, the sound of Easton's voice came from the compact in Becca's pocket. She pulled it out and held it so both of them could see.

"Sorry to break radio silence here, but it looks like you might've lost the stealth advantage anyway."

"What gave you that idea?" Digby said over the sound of the alarm that was still blaring.

"Mostly the fact that the entire Guardian force just mobilized. You've got about a thousand threats heading your way now. Including a couple of aircraft."

"Damn. We need to move before escape becomes impossible." Digby got ready to jump.

Then the alarm stopped.

"What?" Digby glanced up as the sound of distant notes drifted down the stairwell from a speaker above. It was some kind of string instrument. Woodwinds came next.

It was music.

The squad behind them slowed as more instruments were joined in.

He glanced to Becca with an eyebrow raised. "Are you doing this?"

She shook her head. "It's not me this time. I think it's coming from the building's internal announcement system."

An entire orchestra joined in as the volume climbed.

"I think the Guardian Core's caretaker is getting into the spirit of things." Becca laughed. "That's the Trans-Siberian Orchestra."

"I don't know what that is," Digby snapped back.

"It's a Christmas thing." Becca reached out and grabbed hold of his collar. "The caretaker is telling us to finish the job."

The vampire jumped as the orchestra swelled. With her fingers tightly curled around Digby's collar, he had no choice but to follow. Electric guitars thrummed and synthesizers wailed as they fell past the security squad. Shadows collected around Becca's shoulders, extending outward to slow their dissent.

Digby felt a bone in his ankle snap when he landed. He mended it with his Body Craft in seconds, already running before it had even finished. There wasn't time to lose. He burst through the doors at the bottom of the stairwell and into a brightly lit hallway. An exit stood at the end. Music continued to blare from the building's speaker system as he made a break for freedom.

Breaking into a sprint, Digby passed by an administration counter staffed by two uniformed nurses. Shock filled their faces as

Santa Claus and his helper shot past them. He gave them his jolliest grin on the way by. Moments later they crashed through the front doors and skidded to a stop.

Digby's eyes widened, realizing that the music wasn't just coming from inside the building, but the external speakers as well.

Becca threw a hand toward him as shadows flowed around her. "Come on, we're going back up."

Digby grabbed hold of her and jumped. Just like before in the Vatican, the darkness around the vampire reached outward and flapped to launch them up to the roof where the sleigh waited. Becca landed on the edge of the building as gracefully as ever. Digby, however, found himself scrambling through nothing but air for a fraction of a second before the vampire realized and yanked him toward the building. He planted his feet against the wall as she pulled him the rest of the way over the side.

The vampire stopped to stare into the distance as soon as they both were safe. "Oh wow."

Digby turned to see what she was looking at, his mouth falling open as soon as he did.

Music echoed across the city in all directions as the streetlamps came alive to flash in sync with the orchestra. Occasionally, they swept from side to side in a wave of light and sound, the orchestra coming from every announcement speaker for miles.

"Holy hell!" Digby slapped a hand to his head. "That caretaker friend of yours is going to wake up the entire city."

"I don't know much about them." Becca shrugged. "But they don't do things halfway."

"Whatever, it doesn't matter. We have bigger problems." Digby stabbed a finger down to the street where the headlights of armored vehicles were heading their way. The lights of one of the empire's owl aircraft approached from above.

Pushing himself away from the edge of the roof, Digby rushed toward the sleigh. He slid to a stop as the owl fired a short burst from one of its guns. Bullets punched through the side of the sleigh, splintering wood and sparking off the enchanted panels beneath.

Digby's eyes bulged as the entire sleigh suddenly lifted off the roof to travel straight upward. Asher let out a surprised caw, her harness yanking her upward along with the rest of the craft.

"What the devil just happened?" Digby watched in horror as his escape vehicle left him behind.

"I think that was supposed to be a warning shot, but they must have damaged some of the runes that control the sleigh's altitude." Becca stood beside him staring up as the unconventional aircraft shrank into the sky. "It should stop when it reaches its default setting. Considering it was built aboard the airship, it should end up at the same altitude as the Queen Mary."

"We really need to build our things better." Digby ground his teeth.

There was nothing he could do about the sleigh other than to send a command to Asher across their bond, telling her to return to the airship. Someone there was sure to be able to fix the problem and hopefully come back to get them.

"What do we do now?" Becca shielded her eyes as the aircraft above shined its spotlights on them. "We still have a thousand Guardians coming."

Digby held out a hand toward her. "All we can do is get the hell off this roof, and do our best."

The owl swooped overhead, voices shouting from its loud-speaker. Digby ignored them and started running for the edge of the roof.

He jumped without hesitation.

They hit the ground running as Becca's shadows caught them. From there, they crossed the open land between the barracks toward the partially finished wall that surrounded them.

Headlights grew closer as the sound of engines in the distance blended with the orchestra blaring from every speaker they passed.

The aircraft above gave chase, firing the occasional warning shot and sending bursts of dirt and snow into the air. Digby ignored it. The fact that they weren't targeting them directly could only mean one thing.

The treaty was still intact.

Everything that they had done that night may have been confusing, but none of it was hostile. Digby smirked as he approached a section of the half-built wall, standing just over twenty feet high.

Becca reached out and clasped his wrist with one hand to let him know they were going to jump. He curled his fingers around hers as well and held on. His feet left the ground with a swirl of shadow that dissipated like smoke.

Soaring through the cold, night air, he glanced at his HUD, forgetting for a moment that it wasn't visible. Now that he knew how to sense it, he could tell that his mana was almost full just by how it felt. As for Becca, he had no idea. She had to be below half with the way she had been using her shadows.

The orchestral score swelled as they landed back within the refugee section of the city that still resembled the original streets of Washington, D.C. If they could find a way to lose their pursuers, all they would have to do was ditch their disguises. Then, they could try their best to disappear into the camp. They could deal with the fallout of their actions later.

There was a lot of ground to cover, but it was possible.

They might just pull off the job yet.

Almost as soon as the thought passed through his mind, an armored truck skidded into the intersection in front of them. Another came from the other side to cut off the street completely. The doors of both vehicles flew open to release multiple squads of Guardians. An aircraft swooped in above to shine a spotlight in Digby's eyes.

Becca slid to a stop, the bell on her hat jingling.

Digby stopped as well, his eyes scanning their surroundings for another way out.

Voices shouted from the speakers aboard the aircraft, struggling to be heard over the steady strum of guitars and the boom of percussion. The music was loud enough that Digby could feel the vibrations in his chest. The streetlights flashed in sync with the rhythm as the Guardian Core's caretaker made it clear that they had no intention of letting up until the entire city had joined in the celebration.

"This way!" Digby darted to the left toward an alleyway.

Becca jingled along behind him.

Looking up, he noticed several heads poking out from the windows of a few buildings to see what the commotion was about. He glanced over his shoulder as he rushed into the alleyway. Squads of Guardians poured into the narrow space behind them.

Digby ignored the army chasing him and activated his Limitless mutation to give himself a burst of speed.

Becca kept up, but not without complaint. "I'm going to need more mana at some point. I've only got a third left."

"Try to make it last." Digby continued on as threats were shouted from behind them.

Up ahead, the alleyway was bisected by another, creating a four-way split. Digby blew straight through it. They could get out of sight if they could reach the other side. Maybe they could get into one of the buildings. Hell, he would have gladly crawled into a dumpster to hide.

"Shit!" Becca stopped abruptly.

"What?" Digby slowed just as a dozen Guardians poured into the mouth of the alleyway that he'd been heading for.

She must have heard them coming before they turned the corner.

"Blast!" Digby turned back. This time, heading toward the intersection that he'd just passed.

There were still two more directions to try. Rounding the corner to the left, he only made it a dozen feet before men in white armor flooded in at the other end. Digby tried to stop but hit a patch of ice at the wrong time. The result left him running in place for a few seconds before finally getting some traction. He scrambled back to the intersection.

Of course, more Guardians filled the end of the alleyway on that side as well.

Digby slowed as they closed in on all sides.

"We need to jump." Becca held out her hand. "If you can grow a pair of wings, we might be able to fly away."

Digby looked up at the confused faces of the city's inhabitants that poked out from a few windows above. They stared down as the empire's forces drew their swords and rifles. The Guardians slowed their approach, treading carefully, to make sure that Santa Claus couldn't escape.

"Come on." Becca insisted. "We have to jump."

This time, he didn't take her hand.

"No." He shook his head. "Wings won't be enough to outrun an aircraft. And you're too low on mana to be able to fly."

A spotlight from above shined down on them to illustrate his point.

"Besides, I can't have those civilians watching as Santa sprouts the wings of a bat." He shrugged. "The last time I checked, there was nothing in the Christmas legends about demonic wings."

"Then what do we do?" Desperation entered her voice as the Guardians surrounded them, over a hundred weapons pointing in their direction.

"We give up." Digby simply raised his hands.

"What?" Her voice climbed in shock.

"We've done nothing wrong." He chuckled. "What are they going to do? Execute us?"

Becca slowly raised her hands as well. "I wish you hadn't said that."

CHAPTER FORTY

"Where are they?" Alex rushed into the ballroom just after the sleigh returned empty.

Only Asher was left to steer the craft.

The only information he'd been able to get out of her was that Digby and Becca had been chased away. From the looks of the bullet holes in the sleigh, the altitude control system had been shot and the default alignment had sent it back up. Alex left the repairs up to Jameson and his artificers.

"I can't find them." Easton stood before the scrying mirror, repeatedly asking it for Digby's and Becca's whereabouts.

"I can't open a link to their compacts either." Lana rushed by. "They must have been taken away and smashed."

"Were they captured?" Hawk rushed into the room a moment after Alex.

"Of course they were captured," Kristen's skull commented from a nearby table.

"Wait! I've found them," Easton called out as a new image filled the scrying mirror. "I think they passed through a portion of that wall that's being constructed. They must be warded against scrying magic like the rest of the empire's facilities."

"Oh crap." Alex clasped a hand over his mouth as he approached the mirror.

Digby and Becca had just been led out from an opening in the unfinished wall. They were surrounded by at least a hundred Guardians, many dressed in elite armor. The road they walked on was bracketed by even more men in white, all standing at the ready.

Alex leaned close to the mirror, noticing that both Becca and Digby's wrists were shackled. No doubt their restraints were enchanted to silence them.

"The Guardians won't do anything to them, right?" The concern in Hawk's voice grew. "Because of the treaty?"

Alex's forehead started to sweat. "I don't think so. They haven't done anything hostile."

"They broke into a secure training facility," Kristen argued. "That could be interpreted as hostile."

"But they only gave out presents." Hawk excused the intrusion the same way Digby would have.

"True. If they stick to that story, they should be okay for now." Alex scratched at the strap of his eye patch. "Plus we still have a nuke, so I don't think the chancellor would let Henwick execute them."

"Maybe, maybe not," Kristen said matter-of-factly. "But even if he doesn't kill them, he's not going to just let them go."

She had a point.

Alex stood staring at the mirror as the Guardians marched Digby and Becca toward the capital's inner wall. He checked his watch. There was still a half hour before sunrise, and there was no way to know if Digby had done enough deliveries to secure the enchantment they needed.

Alex stood still for a moment, then turned and grabbed Kristen's skull off the table.

"Hey, where are you taking me?"

"Sorry, there's no time to lose and I might need a guide." Alex rushed across the room and grabbed one of the extra elf costumes that had been prepared in case Becca had covered another one in blood.

"What are you gonna do?" Hawk followed behind him.

Alex simply turned and tossed him a costume. "Suit up."

Hawk caught it. "What?"

"Santa's in trouble and we're all that's left to help him."

"What are we going to do?" Hawk stared at him in confusion.

Alex held one of the spare elf costumes to his chest with his free hand, then looked back to Hawk and grinned.

"Oh, don't you dare say it." Kristen groaned.

Alex couldn't help but let out a chuckle. "We're going to save Christmas."

"And there it is." The skull sighed. "This is the stupidest idea yet."

CHAPTER FORTY-ONE

"Watch where you are poking with that thing," Digby growled at a Guardian whose sword kept jabbing him in the shoulder.

"Keep moving," another man in white armor insisted as they approached a large exterior lift that ran up the side of the capital's inner wall.

"This can't be good." Becca strained her wrists against the chain of the shackles that bound them as she stepped aboard the platform.

"Probably not." Digby followed as the two dozen Guardians piled onto the lift around them, each pointing weapons in their direction.

The rest of Autem's forces had to wait at the bottom as the platform rose off the ground. Digby watched as the three hundred or so men that had escorted them the entire way to the wall grew smaller. There were probably more waiting at the top.

Becca shot him a look.

If they were going to try to escape, now was the time.

His options were limited, but a well-placed maw could swallow at least a few Guardians whole. Beyond that, Becca could probably take down more if she could feed off one first. It would be risky, but there was a chance.

He shook his head. "You know, Becky, I think I'm tired of running."

The lift continued upward, passing several platforms with doors that led into the wall. Strangely, they didn't stop at any of them. No, the lift just continued until they approached the top of the wall. Digby wasn't surprised to find two lines of elite Guardians standing in formation to greet them when the lift came to a stop.

At their center stood Henwick.

"I knew you couldn't help yourself." Autem's high priest wore a simple dress shirt and a pair of slacks under a wool coat. A self-satisfied smile hung on his face.

At least he wasn't dressed for battle.

"Why, Henwick, I have no idea what you mean." Digby chuckled, the little ball of fluff attached to his hat swinging in his face as the winter wind blew across the wall.

"Come." Henwick beckoned to him, barely looking at Becca.

Digby hesitated but eventually stepped forward.

The vampire beside him started to follow.

He glanced back to stop her. "It's alright."

"I know. But we're a team and you're not doing this alone." She gave him a decisive nod. "Whatever happens, we do this together. What would Santa be without an elf anyway?"

"Very well." Digby returned his attention to Henwick.

The wall was around a hundred feet thick with a flat top, covered with metal grating. A knee-high barrier wrapped the edges. Lights ran along the sides at regular intervals. Other than the Guardians, the place was empty.

A pair of aircraft circled in the sky, only to pull away with a wave of Henwick's hand.

Digby moved his head to flip the ball of fluff out of his face. The wind blew it right back. "Is this the best place to meet?"

Henwick slipped his hands into his pockets. "This is the perfect place." He turned around to look out across the capital. "Look at it."

"Look at what?" Digby stepped up to his enemy's side with Becca right behind him.

"Nearly a third of the world's population resides down there." Henwick kept his eyes on the city he was building below. "It doesn't look like much now, but it is growing fast and we have everything we need ready to finish it. We've been prepared for years. When it's done, it will be the safest place for mankind to be reborn."

Music no longer blared through the city, but the street lamps were still flashing from the caretaker's interference.

"Looks like not everyone is happy about that." Becca leaned forward.

Henwick frowned. "Yes, the caretaker's lack of cooperation is regrettable. I look forward to the day that we have a viable replacement, and I can delete that pest once and for all. Until then, I'll have to settle for this." He glanced back to one of his elite Guardians.

The armored man immediately took off his helmet and knelt. Another of the Guardians behind him snapped his sword from the magnetic sheath on his back and placed it to the neck of the first.

After that, Henwick turned to an empty space to the side and spoke as if addressing someone invisible. "Stop this nonsense or his blood will be on your hands."

The lights stopped flashing as soon as the words left his mouth.

Henwick turned back to Digby. "Everyone has a weakness. Even something as powerful as a caretaker. I find threats usually work." Another self-satisfied smile took over Henwick's face. "If there's one thing I've learned about that pest, it's that they care too much to let someone die because of their actions. Even if it's one of my men."

Henwick nodded to the Guardian holding a sword to the throat of one of their own. The man sheathed the weapon and held a hand out to the other that he had been ready to kill a moment before. Both Guardians returned to formation afterward.

A chill crawled down Digby's spine.

One had been ready to kill while the other had been ready to die just because Henwick said so. Even worse, Henwick wouldn't have hesitated to give the order.

"That's horrible." Digby turned away from the Guardians.

"You would say that." Henwick turned to him. "You have that in common with the caretaker that the Fools created. No spine."

"I wouldn't say that." Digby forced a grin back onto his face. "Sometimes I grow several at a time."

Henwick's smile fell. "Do you know why I hate you, Graves?"

"I've always thought it was a jealousy thing. On account of how attractive I am." Digby gave him a crooked grin through his beard.

"Graves, you were not attractive when you were alive, and dying has not helped the issue." Henwick's tone grew annoyed. "No, I hate you because you can't stop yourself from taking more than you deserve. This whole misguided plan of yours is proof of that." He pulled a hand from his pocket and gestured to the Santa costume before sweeping it to the elf beside him. "I was willing to abide by the treaty. To let you and that little city of yours be. Not because you changed my mind, but because I knew I wouldn't have to start the fight again. You would do that for me. You simply can't resist grasping for more. More wealth. More power. It's always the same with you. It was only a matter of time before you stepped out of line and forced me to wipe Sin City off the map. For that very reason alone, peace was never an option. The Heretic Seed is just too powerful to leave in the hands of someone like you. You can't resist abusing it."

Digby glanced back and forth. "I'm sorry, Henwick, but I seem to be a little confused. What is it that you think I've done to harm your people?"

"Don't act like it isn't obvious what you're trying to do here." Henwick jabbed a finger into Digby's face. "You're trying to use the empire's people to bestow you with an enchantment. As if the Heretic Seed's magic wasn't enough. You're putting on this ridiculous farce in some mad grasp for more power."

"I don't deny it." Digby raised his head. "Though, I fail to see how any of that could be considered hostile. I may be seeking more power, but I am doing so to protect my people. That should have no bearing on the empire. It is not an attack on you."

"You can't just declare us the bad guys because you're afraid our power might rival yours one day," Becca added.

Henwick glanced in her direction. "Oh please, you don't have any idea what kind of power I have. It will certainly take more than a couple of monsters and a mass enchantment to come close."

"It doesn't matter who is stronger than who." Digby threw up his hands in frustration, noticing as soon as he did that he'd unconsciously collapsed a part of his right so that it slipped out of his shackles.

Henwick glared in his direction.

Digby quickly slipped his wrist back in and grinned as if he hadn't done it.

Henwick just rolled his eyes.

Digby continued. "As I was saying, it doesn't matter what kind of power I may or may not have tried to grasp. The bottom line is that we have not broken the treaty. We might have entered your territory, but if you recall, the agreement stipulated that we would only be in breach if we attacked or looted anything. As I see it, we have done no such thing. We have merely given gifts."

Henwick responded with a laugh. "Are you honestly going to try to play innocent?"

"Of course I am." Digby shrugged. "I am innocent."

"See, you can't stop yourself." Henwick looked him dead in the eyes.

Digby opened his mouth to speak only to close it again as the events of the night passed through his mind. "You're right. I couldn't stop myself." Digby held his gaze. "But not because of the enchantment that was on the table. I don't know when, but this whole plan stopped being about power."

"What else is there?" Henwick stared at him incredulously.

"People." Digby threw both hands out toward the city below them, the chain of his shackles dangling from his wrists. "I saw something tonight. No, not just tonight, but the last few weeks. Everyone was working together. Working toward something. And in that, they built bonds." He pulled his hands in toward his chest. "I know I'm not the best person to explain this, but everyone lost so much. Homes. Families. Hope. But none of that was truly gone. Hope doesn't die so easily."

Henwick started to laugh.

Digby ignored him. "I know it sounds silly. And I didn't understand it either." He glanced to Becca. "We might be monsters, but we've gained friends and families. I don't know why, but I've become surrounded by people. More than I'd ever had when I was alive. They support me when I don't know what to do, and they tell me when I'm wrong. Hell, I went insane a few weeks back and they pulled me back from the brink. They were there for me when it mattered most." Digby looked back to Henwick. "I know you don't think any of that matters, and maybe that's why you are the way you are. But I wouldn't have been able to do any of this without them. And right now, I think everyone needs to remember that this world hasn't ended. There's still people that care out there."

"I think I liked it better when you were trying to steal from me." Henwick frowned and turned away.

"Honestly, stealing was always easier." Digby took a step toward him. "I've never tried to give something back before. Yet, once I started, I didn't want to stop. Not after seeing the difference it made."

"Let me stop you right there." Henwick held up a hand without looking in his direction. "What did you think was going to happen tonight? That you would just say all this heartwarming ridiculousness, and I would just let it go? I'd send you on your way with a Merry Christmas and a Happy New Year?"

"A little bit." Digby leaned to Becca. "Right?"

"That would be convenient for us, yes," she added.

"That is the stupidest thing I've ever heard. I'm not Ebeneezer Scrooge. I'm not going to have a change of heart just because you spread a little cheer."

"I don't know who that is." Digby frowned.

Henwick shook his head in disbelief. "It's a wonder that city of yours hasn't fallen apart already. Your people are not your family, Graves. They are your citizens. Hope is not something you give to them with kind words and gestures. It is something you secure by doing what is necessary to keep them safe."

"Alright, so we may have a difference of opinion." Digby tried to laugh off the criticism.

He couldn't even get out a chuckle before Henwick slammed a fist into his face.

Digby's head snapped backward, one side of his jaw coming loose. A few teeth floated free in his mouth with a pungent flood of necrotic blood. The metal grating rattled beneath him as he fell. Stars filled the sky, some of them real, some of them merely as a result of his damaged ocular nerve.

"Fut wus fat for?" Digby struggled to get his teeth to realign as he re-crafted his face.

"Shit." Becca jumped backward away from Henwick only for the Guardians behind her to grab hold of her arms.

"This isn't going to go how you wanted it, Graves." Henwick stood over him, cracking his neck. "You don't get to do what you want, and one way or another, this treaty between us ends."

"Is that really up to you? Don't you have to talk to Chancellor Serrano before re-declaring war?" Becca started to pull her arm away from one of the Guardians behind her, only to stop a second later. She still only had a third of her mana left. She must have been trying to conserve it.

"Serrano has his opinions, but he won't stand in the way of important matters." Henwick stomped closer to Digby and rammed his foot into his side.

An audible crack came from Digby's ribs as a rush of air escaped his mouth. He was just glad that he didn't have to breathe as he willed his body to reinflate his lungs so he could speak.

"What are you doing, Henwick? We have a treaty, dammit."

"Get up and fight, Graves." He kicked him again, sending him rolling across the metal flooring.

"Are you mad? We still have the nuke." Digby willed his body to push a broken rib out of one of his organs.

"That may be, but after everything you just said, I don't think you'll use it." Henwick thrust a hand down in his direction as motes of light exploded from his palm.

They hit Digby's body like white-hot pokers, his skin sizzling from each impact. His Body Craft mutation responded, this time fighting to repair the damage as purification magic waged war against his curse.

"You never know when to keep your mouth shut, Graves. I had my doubts about whether or not you would use that bomb to begin with. But one doesn't fly around a city spreading hope if they're willing to kill its citizenry. We both know that you need this treaty a lot more than I do." He punctuated the statement by stomping on Digby's knee.

Pulling away, his bones ground against each other before the cartilage had time to reform. Digby slipped his hand free of his shackles again and tried to shield his body from another attack.

"All you have to do is fight back, Graves. I know how much you want to." Henwick stared down with as much disdain as he could muster. "I'll have the armada in the air and on its way to Vegas before dawn."

"Stop it!" Becca pulled one arm away from the Guardians that held her.

Digby felt a trickle of mana flow through her blood. She was preparing to attack.

"No." Digby brace for another impact. "Don't give him an excuse."

Becca let out a frustrated growl as she let the armored men behind her grab hold again.

Henwick's boot slammed into Digby's face a moment later.

The world went white for several seconds before coming back into focus. All Digby could do was let out a wet chuckle, two of his teeth falling out. "Do you really think you can push me into striking back? Do you think I would jeopardize the lives of the people who stand behind me like that? I might be a lot of things, but I'm not stupid." He fished around in the holes of the metal grate he lay on with a finger to find one of his missing teeth and placed it back in his mouth. "Besides, you can't hurt me. Not really."

"I may not be able to hurt you, but I can kill you." Henwick aimed a hand down at Digby's face.

He winced. Without access to his magic, all it would take was a Smite to burn him out of existence. That was it, he couldn't just lay there.

He had to fight back.

He had to save himself.

Still, he didn't.

"Go ahead," Digby called his bluff, surprising himself as much as anyone else. "Sure, I could fight you. Maybe I'd even escape. But that would only end the peace. And that peace has already given so much to everyone back in Vegas. I'm not about to take that away from them." He smirked. "Besides, you won't kill me."

"You think I won't." Henwick placed his foot on his chest to hold him down.

"Of course not." Digby let a cackle roll through his chest. "At least, not like this. No, my execution would be too useful of a tool for you. A victory like that would matter. It would merit more fanfare than quietly smiting me, here and now."

Henwick nodded almost immediately and removed his foot from Digby's chest. "Occasionally, you do make sense, Graves."

"It was bound to happen eventually." Digby laughed awkwardly, having trouble believing that he'd really convinced the man to back off.

"Fair enough." Henwick turned and started walking away toward his men. He waved a hand in their direction, telling them to let go of Becca. Looking back, he added, "What kind of a man would I be if I killed Santa Claus on Christmas morning?"

"What kind, indeed?" Digby pushed himself back up and got to his feet.

"Though," Henwick held up a finger as he held out his other hand to one of his Guardians. "I don't think anyone will notice if Santa loses one of his elves."

"What?" Digby flicked his eyes to Becca just as one of the Guardians behind her handed their sword to Henwick. Before he could do anything, the man grabbed one of the vampire's wrists.

Dropping the butt of the sword down so that it rested in one of the holes in the metal grating, he adjusted the angle of the tip and casually pushed Becca's palm down onto it. The chain connecting her shackles caused her other hand to follow the first until both were skewered like a piece of meat ready to be roasted.

Becca screamed for an instant before her voice shifted into a ferocious hiss.

Henwick let go and spun back to face Digby as several of his Guardians stepped in to grab hold of the sword and Becca to make sure the vampire didn't pull her hands free.

"Don't you dare touch her!" Digby took a heavy step toward him.

"Or you'll what?" Henwick smirked.

Digby stopped, realizing what he was trying to do.

"I'm fine." Becca breathed through her teeth.

Henwick ignored her. "What will it be, Digby? Help your friend, or let her suffer." He glanced back to Becca. "Actually, it doesn't matter. She's a vampire. As long as that sword stays where it is, her body will continue to try to heal the damage. She'll blow through her mana in under a minute. Then it won't matter if you fight me or not. She will lose control, and attempt to kill my men. Then, the treaty will be broken."

Digby gasped. He was right. It was only a matter of time before she went on a rampage. There would be no way to stop her from attacking.

"You can't count that as a hostile act. She can't stop herself."

"Then you shouldn't have brought her here." Henwick stood there, looking pleased with himself. "But, as I said, you couldn't help yourself." He gestured to the city below. "Honestly, it's a surprise that she didn't kill one of the citizens already. You may think that rules don't apply to you, or that they can always be bent or broken. But the truth is that rules exist for a reason. That's what you Heretics don't understand. You think I am some kind of tyrant when, really, I am just doing what is best for the world. I'm doing what needs to be done to keep its people safe."

Digby pushed past him and reached for the sword impaling Becca's hands. He stopped when several of the Guardians surrounding her drew their swords and pointed them at his throat.

"You won't be able to free her without fighting, Graves." Henwick turned to face him. "Of course, I could just say you did and be done with it, but then the Core's caretaker would just go tattle to Serrano. The old man doesn't have any real power, but he is well-liked throughout the empire. I'd rather not start a conflict there if I can avoid it. Too many headaches. Besides, I am a patient man. I can wait one more minute for your elf here to doom your entire city."

Digby lowered his eyes to the vampire. "Can you hold on?"

Becca shook her head. "My mana is going fast."

He dropped to one knee, ignoring the swords pointed in his direction. "We can't let Henwick win." Digby glanced back over his shoulder. "You hear that? You might think you have us beat here, but will figure something out. We always do."

"Oh, by all means." Henwick held out a hand toward them. "You're welcome to try."

"You're going to have to stop me from attacking," Becca said through bared fangs. "That's the only way."

"I'm not going to kill you." Digby snapped his attention back to her.

"Kill me?" Her eyes widened. "No, I just meant restrain me. Jesus, Dig. I'm not about to sacrifice myself here to prove a point to Henwick."

"Oh, yes. That does make more sense."

Becca rolled her eyes. "I have maybe thirty seconds left. Be ready. Use everything you have, but keep me contained."

Henwick stepped forward to stand over them. "This should be interesting."

Then one of the swords pointed at Digby's throat wavered.

He glanced up at the Guardian holding it as they lowered the blade and raised their other hand to point into the distance. "What is that?"

Digby craned his neck back to find a familiar speck growing rapidly in the night sky. Then he grinned.

Henwick squinted. "That better not be what I think it is."

"Of course it is." Digby let out a rough cackle. "I am Santa Claus. Where I go, my elves follow."

CHAPTER FORTY-TWO

Digby grinned as Asher galloped through the sky straight for them, followed by eight zombified reindeer.

Alex and Hawk shouted from the sleigh behind them, both disguised as elves the same as Becca.

"Son of a—" Henwick dropped to one knee to duck as Asher passed over him.

The enchanted craft streaked by, flying just low enough to be threatening but not close enough to hit anyone. Guardians dove out of the way just to be safe.

Becca remained standing, taking the opportunity to pull her hands off the sword that impaled them.

"Run, Becky!" Digby slipped his other hand out of his shackles and tossed them over his shoulder before sprinting past Henwick.

"Right behind you." Becca caught up.

"After them!" Henwick shouted from behind as the sound of boots hitting the metal grating followed.

Digby glanced back to find every Guardian on the wall giving chase.

The sleigh turned and headed back to blow past them again. This time, the armored men knew enough not to dive out of the way. They were forced to slow anyway when several heavy items from the craft's toolbox fell in front of them.

Digby gasped when one of the men was hit by a random hammer. For an instant, he feared that throwing such a thing would negate the treaty. A second later, another Guardian was hit with a wrench. This time he noticed that someone, probably Hawk, had tied a bow around it. That would at least give them the ability to claim that the falling objects were gifts rather than attacks.

It was ridiculous, but he wasn't about to argue about it.

Digby watched as the sleigh swooped past before dipping down beneath the wall. Snapping his focus back on the space ahead of him, he tried to calculate how long it would take for the sleigh to travel around the outside of the structure and come back again to pick them up.

"What's the plan?" Becca caught up beside him, holding her hands to her chest as she ran. The wounds on her palms were still closing.

Digby glanced from side to side at the top of the wall ahead of them. Then he looked back at the Guardians running behind. "We're going to have to jump."

"I was afraid you'd say that." Her tone grew tense. "I don't have enough mana to manifest a shadow big enough to break the fall."

"I'm not faring much better." Digby felt for his mana system. "That spell Henwick hit me with has everything running slow. I don't think I can grow wings or anything. At least, not before I hit the ground."

"Then what do we do?"

"We jump and trust that Alex and Hawk will be there when we need them."

Veering off toward the edge of the wall, Digby prepared for a leap of faith only to slide to a stop just before committing. The sleigh was nowhere in sight.

Becca stopped beside him and glanced back at their pursuers. "They're coming!"

Digby looked as well, realizing that there was no time to wait. The only thing they could do was hope for a Christmas miracle. Several Guardians raised their hands ready to cast every spell in their arsenal. This time, he didn't expect them to fire off a warning shot first.

"It's now or never." He gave Becca one last nod.

Then he jumped.

The vampire did the same just as several fireballs flew through the space where they had been.

The cold night air rushed through Digby's hair as he picked up speed. He willed his Body Craft mutation to go to work, but everything moved at a snail's pace. There was nothing he could do.

Then, something brown came out of nowhere.

"Oof!" He'd landed with his body draped over the ass of Comet, one of his undead reindeer.

Carrot?

Not now! he shouted back across his bond as he struggled not to fall.

Catching hold of the monster's harness, he stopped himself from sliding off, his feet dangling behind him. His first thought was of Becca. If the vampire had landed too hard, the damage could send her into a rampage. Or worse, she might've missed the sleigh altogether and fallen to her death.

"A little help!" Alex shouted from somewhere nearby.

Digby snapped his head to the side to find the artificer's leg and arm sticking up from the front seat. A vampire, surprised to be alive, struggled on top of him as he attempted to hand the reins off to Hawk. The rogue lunged forward to help out, steering them away from the wall.

"I'm okay. I'm okay." Becca climbed off of Alex, sounding surprised by her own words.

"Don't celebrate just yet." Alex climbed back into his seat and took the reins back from Hawk.

"Yeah, 'cause it doesn't look like they're letting us go." The young rogue hooked a thumb back over his shoulder as one of the empire's owls rose from behind the wall to give pursuit.

Another aircraft hovered over where Henwick had been

standing moments before. It hung there in the air for a short time before joining in the chase. Digby groaned as he pulled himself up to straddle the back of the undead reindeer he had landed on. The aircraft must have picked up Henwick. There was no way that he was going just to let them go.

"Take us down." Digby pointed toward the refugee camp below. "They're obviously done with warning shots at this point, but they won't risk hitting any of the buildings down there."

"Are you sure?" Alex asked, sounding skeptical. "Henwick doesn't strike me as someone who worries about that kind of thing."

Digby considered the question for a second. Then he nodded. "He needs the people here to believe in him as much as we do. He won't risk hurting them publicly."

"Okay, but just a heads up. The patch job Jameson's guys did on the altitude system is barely holding together." Hawk relaxed his grip on the crank as it began to rotate on its own.

"That's not great." Digby frowned.

"They did the best they could in the time allowed," Alex added.

"Give me some room." Digby made a shooing motion toward Becca to clear her out of his seat as he prepared to climb in.

The vampire crawled into the back seat to join Hawk. Once the front was clear, Digby inched his way back aboard the unconventional aircraft. He slid in next to Alex and quickly turned toward the back to help Becca out of her shackles.

Grabbing hold of the chain that connected her wrists, he opened his maw on her seat and shoved the links in. He snapped it shut to sever the chain.

Becca blinked as soon as he did, her eyes darting around to read the information on her HUD that must've appeared across her vision. "Holy shit. Things almost got bad back there. I only have fifteen mana left. If I lose any more, I'm going to tear the nearest person's throat out."

"Oh good." Hawk tried to scoot away from her while keeping his hand on the altitude crank.

Alex reached down for a canteen that was sliding around the

bottom of the sleigh and handed it to her. "Here, there's two pints of fresh Mason in there. I was afraid this might happen so I had him fill it up when I was putting on my elf costume."

Becca grimaced as she took the canteen. "Please don't ever use the phrase 'two pints of fresh Mason' again."

"Yes, yes, that's very weird. But more importantly, we are still being chased by a man who wants to restart a war." He gestured to the aircraft following them. "And I'm relatively sure he does not believe in Santa."

"What do you suggest we do?" Alex asked.

"I don't know, but I'm going to need access to my magic again." Digby grabbed one of the velvet sacks from the back and held it upside down over the side.

After checking to make sure there was no one below them, he opened his maw within the bag and called forth the empty silos he was still carrying. They fell, dripping with necrotic blood, and crashed into a side street below. Next, he willed his void to expel the silos that were still full of toys.

"Wait!" Hawk grabbed hold of his shoulder with his free hand. "You're not just going to drop the presents, are you?"

"Of course I am. It's the only way to regain my magic."

"Wait!" This time it was Becca stopping him. "Hawk has a point. There are better things to do than just throw the gifts away." The vampire thrust her hand out to point at the street further ahead as people looked up from the sidewalks at the flying sleigh coming toward them.

They must've been woken up when the Guardian Core's caretaker decided it was a good time to blast orchestral holiday music over the city's announcement system. Digby looked back to Becca and her brother, then back to the velvet bag in his hands. Were they suggesting that they return to giving out presents while being chased by two aircraft?

Becca gave him a nod.

The very idea of it was insane. Not to mention, it would make Henwick furious.

Digby grinned.

They were right.

Quickly, he flipped the velvet sack in his hands right side up and pulled it back into the sleigh. There was just enough room in the back to lay it flat. Digby called forth another silo, this time full of delicately wrapped packages. Once it was open, he and Becca went to work.

The first glow of dawn began to grow at the edge of the horizon as they tossed presents over the side. He tried his best not to hit anyone. However, some incidents were unavoidable. At least the toys inside weren't heavy.

The faces of the people below were a mix of confusion, shock, and joy. That was about the best reaction that they could've hoped for.

Looking back over his shoulder, he frowned. The owls were still close behind. Without some kind of distraction, the sleigh wasn't fast enough to escape. There had to be something they could do that wouldn't be considered an attack. Without a better option, Digby picked up a package from the bag and lobbed it at the closest aircraft, using his Limitless mutation for added strength. His arm cracked under the strain. The present bounced off the windshield harmlessly a moment later.

"Damn." He let his arm hang limp at his side.

Without thinking, he cast Necrotic Regeneration to repair the damage. He snapped his eyes to his HUD when he realized the spell had worked. His unbeating heart soared as the Heretic Seed's information appeared again. There were still two full silos in his void, but he'd gotten rid of enough to regain access to his magic.

That changed things.

His mind raced as Becca continued to toss presents down on the street below. He just had to think of something that could slow the aircraft behind them that wasn't an outright attack. Quickly, he grabbed the nearest package and ripped open the top.

"What are you doing?" Becca shot him a concerned look as the buildings passed by on both sides.

"I just got my magic back, so I'm going to craft some random bits of viscera and wrap it all up in this box. Then I'm going to throw it at that owl's front window and cast Cremation to set it all alight."

"I'm pretty sure that would be considered a hostile act." She glowered at him.

"No, it wouldn't." He pulled a stuffed bear from the box in his hands and tossed it over his shoulder before holding out the empty package to aid his explanation. "I'm going to gift wrap it. So it'll be a present."

"That's maybe pushing the gray area of this situation too far," Alex argued. "You can put a bow on a hammer and throw it because tools make sense as a present. But no one reasonably would want a box full of entrails."

"I would." Digby looked down at the empty box and frowned.

"You are not exactly the target audience here," Becca added.

"Hey guys?" Hawk spoke up.

"Hang on a second." Digby tried to think of a way to make his viscera present idea work. "What if we—"

"Guys!" Hawk shouted over him.

"What?" Digby snapped back.

"I don't think this is supposed to come off." The rogue held up the altitude crank to show that it was no longer attached to the sleigh.

Several pieces from within the mechanism began rattling loose as the sleigh began to descend toward the street.

"Oh…" Digby stared at the crank. Then he grabbed it and started wrapping a ribbon around it. "Maybe this is heavy enough to cause some damage."

"Never mind that! They had to change the default altitude to sea level when they patched the system back together." Alex dropped into his seat and began to duck down.

"What does that mean?" Digby shouted back.

"It means we're going down!"

Digby immediately dropped the crank in his hand and sat down.

"We really should have built this thing with seatbelts." Hawk ducked into the back.

"We'll try to remember that next time we need to trick the

world into thinking Santa's real." Becca threw herself over him and huddled against the back of Digby's seat.

He hunkered down as well. "At least we had fun while it lasted."

"True." Alex leaned against him. "Now brace for impact!"

CHAPTER FORTY-THREE

"Good god, they're going down." Mason stood in the airship ballroom, watching in horror as the scrying mirror showed the sleigh plummeting toward the street of the refugee camp.

He'd been glued to the artifact ever since Becca had been captured. His body practically vibrated with frustration. He could barely see straight after watching Henwick torture her. She may have been a ferocious vampire who could take care of herself, but that didn't change the fact that all he wanted to do was jump in the limo and head straight for her. He couldn't just stand there and watch.

Yet, that was exactly what he did.

Becca had said it best. He was the voice of reason.

He was the one she depended on to stay objective and look for a tactical solution.

If he had jumped into the limo and flown it through the refugee camp, he would run the risk of disrupting the narrative that Digby's con required. That could blow the entire plan. Getting in the way would only put Vegas at risk later. He had to keep that in mind, no matter what his emotions and pride demanded.

The situation was made worse by the fact that they still had a spy on board. Parker was still locked in her room. From what Lana had reported, she still didn't know why she was being held captive. Either that, or she was putting up a good front to maintain her cover. He wasn't sure which. He knew firsthand how dangerous she was. It didn't matter if she knew what she was or not. There wasn't much Parker could say to convince him to trust her, not after remembering how she'd stolen his memories. He'd probably never forgive her either.

Mason forced the traitor out of his thoughts; it wasn't helping him stay calm. Becca's situation looked bad, but he had to keep his head on straight. She could handle herself. He had to trust in her.

Then again, if there was a way to help her and the others without risking everything they were working toward, he had to try.

The scrying mirror continued to follow the sleigh as it leveled out and dropped to the street. Asher touched down along with the rest of the reindeer. They kept running to pull the unconventional craft behind them. Becca, Digby, Hawk, and Alex all peeked up from their seats, clearly surprised to have landed without issue.

Only seconds passed before the four of them started arguing.

The scrying mirror had no way to provide sound, but it was clear that none of them had a plan of what to do from there. Above them hovered two of the empire's magic-powered aircraft, shining spotlights down on the sleigh as it finally slowed to a stop.

"Come on, Becca." Mason focused on her. "You can figure this out. I know you can."

He relaxed a little, glad that he'd sent along two pints of blood for her. If she was going to get herself out of the situation, she was going to need to keep her head focused. Two pints would give her roughly forty-five points of mana. It wasn't much, but it would be enough to keep her going. As much as he wished he could have given more, there hadn't been much time and he was already running low.

"Whoa." Mason placed a hand on a nearby table to steady himself as the room began to spin.

"Are you okay?" Easton, who was also glued to the scrying mirror, tore his eyes away from the reflection to glance over his shoulder at him.

Mason nodded weakly. "Sorry, two pints of blood is a lot to lose. I can cast heals on myself to stay on my feet, but it can't create new blood."

"At least the magic will keep you stable." Easton turned back to the mirror. "It looks like the patch job on the altitude control system didn't hold up. I don't think they can fly anymore."

"Damn." Mason clenched his jaw before forcing himself to release the tension. "Maybe this isn't as bad as it seems. We still have the treaty to lean on, and that street they're on is in full view of civilians. Henwick can't harm them publicly, not without setting his own plans back. He needs the people down there to believe in the Nine as much as we need them to believe in Santa. And since Henwick represents his angels, he should think twice about smiting Santa Claus on Christmas morning."

"That will be able to buy some time, but it won't resolve the situation." Easton scratched at one of the tattoos that peeked out of his shirt collar. "Speaking as someone who's spent a week in an imperial prison cell, there's no way those Guardians are going to let them walk away. We need to give them a hand."

"Agreed. We just need something that won't get in the way." That was when Mason got an idea. "What about the prototype?"

"What?" Easton took his eyes off the scrying mirror.

"The little sleigh that the artificer experimented with before moving on to the full-size version. You know, the one that Parker found in the airship's decoration storage. Jameson's R&D team put an entire flight system in that thing." Mason stepped forward and placed a finger against the scrying mirror over Digby's sleigh. "If one of us could throw on an elf costume and fly the prototype out to them, Alex could probably gut it for parts and get everything operational again. That way, they could leave while still keeping up appearances enough to keep Henwick from attacking. And our actions would still be within the narrative that we're building. Graves can just say he called back to the North Pole for some help. Henwick would have to let him go."

"Yeah, that could work. I mean, it's weird as hell, but what isn't at this point?" Easton stepped away from the mirror just as Mason tossed him part of an elf costume.

"Suit up."

"Wait, what?" Easton failed to catch it, letting a pair of tights fall to the floor. "I can't go."

Mason paused before throwing a coat at him. "What do you mean, you can't?"

"The prototype sleigh only holds one person, and it drains mana from whoever pilots it to fuel its propulsion system. That was the reason why we had to use reindeer for the final version."

"So?" Mason stared at him.

"So my system is all locked up by these." Easton pulled the collar of his shirt down to show more of the tattoos that Autem had given him to take away his access to magic. "My mana absorption rate has been slowed way down; I wouldn't be able to cover the distance without running out."

"Damm." Mason lowered the coat in his hands, debating on whether he should go. He staggered a second later, reminding him how unsteady he was after donating blood.

"You can't go either." Easton told him what he already knew. "You might have the mana for it, but you can barely stand up straight right now. The prototype sleigh is tiny and wobbly. Taking into consideration your size and the weight distribution, it would be a miracle if you don't flip it and fall to your death the moment you get off the ship."

Mason let out a frustrated growl. The voice of reason inside him agreed. Trying to pilot the prototype would likely be a suicide mission with only slim odds of success. It was the sort of idea that only made sense while standing in an IKEA. He knew exactly what Becca would say to that.

"Alright, what about Lana?"

"She hasn't gained any levels since unlocking the cleric class. She has a decent absorption rate, but her max mana is still too low. We have the same problem with Jameson's artificers. They only leveled enough to unlock the abilities they needed for research and development."

"And we can't send Jameson himself, because he's twice the size I am and would never fit in the prototype to begin with." Mason slapped a hand on a nearby table.

"What we need is someone small with a lot of mana," Easton added.

"The only one that fits that description... is Parker." Mason frowned. "And there's no way in hell we're sending her."

"I can't argue with that," Easton said.

"Crap. I don't have a choice then. They need those spare parts." Mason shook his head in disbelief. "I have to go."

"Damn, I don't see another way either." Easton hesitated for a moment before fully getting on board with the idea. "Alright, it's dangerous but we can try to tie you in. Just try to stay low and don't rush."

Mason swallowed hard. Rushing was the only option to make it in time. He shoved his arm into the costume's coat, struggling with the buttons of the garment which was two sizes too small. "I know this is a shit plan. It's dangerous and likely to fail. But it's worse if we do nothing and let this situation drag out. The only way that ends it is with our people in the empire's dungeon, and Dig and Becca are too important to this fight. I have to be the voice of reason here, and a bad plan is still better than no plan."

Easton didn't argue.

"I'll just have to hang on tight and hope for the best." Mason headed out into the hall and toward the room where they had been keeping the sleigh and its prototype. "And next time we build an aircraft this stupid, we need to remember to put seatbelts in..." He trailed off as soon as he passed through the doors.

The prototype sleigh had been sitting in the corner the last time he'd been there. His first thought was that somebody had moved it. Then he noticed the doors that led out onto the ship's deck were open. He spun to scan the room. The prototype was nowhere to be seen. Dread climbed up his spine to grip the back of his scalp.

Someone had already taken it.

Lana burst into the room as the horror of the discovery washed over him. The cleric leaned on a table, panting.

Mason just stood, dumbstruck as she spoke. Her words barely registered but he already knew what she was going to say.

"Parker escaped."

CHAPTER FORTY-FOUR

"What do we do? What do we do? What do we do?" Digby asked each of the sleigh's passengers as they sat in the middle of the street with mid-rise buildings bracketing both sides and two of the empire's aircraft hovering above.

Alex climbed into the back, shoving Becca into the front so that he could help Hawk with the altitude system. The young rogue sat holding several loose parts in his hands.

To make matters worse, random bystanders had begun peeking out from the windows and doors of the surrounding buildings to see the spectacle. Digby raised his eyes to the sky as the two aircraft above circled like vultures. Eventually, they both split off to land in the street, one in front of them and one behind. Though, no one exited the crafts. They must have been waiting for reinforcements. Once they arrived, there would be no escape.

Digby dropped back into his seat and rested one arm on the front of the sleigh while rubbing at the bridge of his nose.

We're doomed.

If the sleigh had been capable of flight, that would have been a different story. They could've kept up with the con and just flown away over the horizon. Henwick wouldn't be able to stop them. Not without making the Empire look bad in front of its citizens and losing their faith. On foot, the chances of escape were considerably lower. Not to mention, leaving the sleigh behind would cast suspicion that he was not who he said he was once people got a better look at it and the reindeer.

Digby lowered his hand from his face as Easton and Lana appeared in one of the mirrors set into the front of the sleigh.

"What's going on down there?" they both asked in unison.

Digby glowered back at them. "What does it look like? We're about to be captured." He paused before adding, "Again."

Alex leaned over him so he could talk to Easton. "If someone can get the prototype sleigh here, I can switch out the whole altitude system—"

Easton stopped him. "We've already thought of that."

"Oh, good." Alex sat back down. "Everything will be fine then. We just have to buy time."

"Sorry, I should've made that clearer." Easton winced as if preparing to be yelled at. "We were about to send the prototype out to you, but it looks like Parker picked the lock in her room and used it to escape. We've lost the prototype and her."

Digby stared down at the mirror blankly. "I don't even know if I can be mad at that. That's literally the worst thing that could happen."

"Where's Mason?" Becca asked.

"He's on his way to you," Lana chimed in. "We didn't know what else to do, so he took the limo. He's going to set it down on the edge of the city and try to sneak in with some spare parts. If you can tell me what part you need to fix the sleigh, I can tell him. Hopefully, he can scavenge it from the limo and get it to you."

Alex shook his head. "No. We made too many modifications when we made the new version. The limo's system is incompatible with this one."

"Hey Dig?" Hawk interrupted the conversation by pointing a finger past him at a man who was approaching one of the reindeer.

From the way the empire's aircraft had landed, they looked a bit like escorts, which made the scene appear to be some kind of holiday event. Almost as if it had been planned.

"Get away from there! You want to get bit?" Digby stood up, making a point of sending a command across his bond before Comet or Vixen started looking for a carrot. He ordered them to close their eyes while he was at it, to hide the telltale milky gray of the dead.

The man he shouted at jumped away before stepping back to join a woman and child behind him. Digby cringed, realizing he'd just yelled at a family of three. He swept his gaze across the street as more people approached from all sides. He had to do something to keep them away.

"Wait!" Digby climbed out of the sleigh.

"What are you doing?" Becca leaned down to him.

"The only thing I can do," Digby whispered back. "Henwick is obviously waiting for reinforcements, so we have a chance to take control of the narrative. That's all that stands between us and certain doom right now. Henwick can't attack us in front of his citizens. Even if he tries to explain it away, they will always remember it. It could take months to earn their trust back. So, I'm going to spread some cheer and make it that much harder for Henwick to attack." He glanced to Alex. "Now I don't care how, but you need to figure out how to fix the sleigh."

"But—"

"No buts. The moment Henwick's reinforcements get here, they will have the manpower to take over the scene and usher the citizens away. If that happens, we're done for." Digby ignored the artificer's lack of confidence and pointed to Hawk and Becca. "Now, you both, follow my lead."

With that, he spun back to the family of three that he'd yelled at and gave them his friendliest smile.

"I apologize if I startled you." He walked toward them petting Vixen behind the ear as he passed. "I try to let the animals rest whenever possible. Do you have any idea how exhausting it is to pull a sleigh around the world?"

All three members of the family in front of him looked stunned as he approached. The parents both stammered out a few words of little consequence.

"Well, suffice it to say, it's best to keep your distance when the reindeer are resting. They've worked hard, after all." Digby turned from left to right and raised his voice to make sure the rest of the onlookers could hear him. "As you can imagine, this year has been a little more difficult than most, what with monsters roaming the world. Everything has taken a little more time than normal. Yet, that doesn't mean I'm going to let a single present go undelivered." He held up a finger. "Now, many of you might have noticed that I've already visited and left something for the wee ones. However, if not, please get in line."

The adults in the crowd remained where they were, clearly still skeptical of what they were seeing. Some had witnessed the sleigh in flight before it landed, but others had only just arrived and witnessed little proof. A few excited children were scattered throughout the onlookers, holding onto the hands of parents or whichever adult had stepped up to the role. It seemed that most had kept their young back out of caution.

Digby simply gave the crowd a bow and turned back to the sleigh. "Fetch me my bag, will you?"

Hawk pointed to himself with a confused expression before jumping back into his seat and grabbing one of the velvet sacks. He handed it to Becca, who carried it to Digby. Taking it from her, he walked back over to the family of three that he'd yelled at. He made a point of setting it down far enough away from the reindeer to draw the crowd's interest to something else and keep them out of biting range.

People watched from all around him as he reached inside the sack.

Opening his maw, he called forth one of the silos that remained within his void. Then, in full view of everyone, he pulled out a present and held it out in front of him.

The man who had tried to approach the reindeer earlier stepped forward and took the gift.

Digby gave him a reassuring nod and gestured to the child standing behind him. He waited for the man to hand the package over before turning to address the rest of the crowd.

"Come on now. Don't be shy." He gestured to Becca and

Hawk. "My elves have worked all year making toys, and they would be glad to hand them out."

Becca took that as a cue to approach the velvet bag and take over for him. She beckoned to Hawk to help her hold the sack open while she reached inside. She made a show of rummaging around for a bit, as if the inside of the bag really was larger than the outside. Pulling out a package with one hand, she whispered something to Hawk. Her brother looked confused for a second but then nodded. After that, he pulled another present from the bag and tossed it to his sister. She caught it on top of the one already in her hands.

They repeated the process of tossing presents and catching them until Becca balanced a stack of ten packages, making use of the inhuman grace and agility of a vampire.

Digby chuckled.

It was a nice touch. The sun was just beginning to peek through the buildings, but Becca would have a couple more minutes to use her abilities before they faded. At least she was making use of them right up until the very end.

With that, he turned his attention to the owls that had landed in the street. It was only a matter of time before a hundred or so Guardians showed up to usher the people away and take him prisoner.

Digby wasn't about to give Henwick that opportunity.

It was best to make the first move.

Waving and smiling to the crowd, Digby directed families to Becca. The atmosphere had begun to resemble the celebration that he'd left back in Vegas. Adults emerged from buildings and from further down the street with curiosity on their faces. Once they saw what was happening, they left and returned with the rest of their family in tow. Many of the children arrived already clutching a new toy in their arms.

Digby grinned.

They must have been the presents that he'd already delivered.

He glanced up to a speaker that had been mounted to a light pole. It was part of the announcement system that the Guardian Core's caretaker had used earlier. He'd questioned the sense of disturbing everyone's sleep, but now it made perfect sense. Word was spreading fast and the crowd was growing. It would be near impossible for Henwick to do anything to him in front of so many.

Digby locked his eyes on the ramp of the owl ahead of him as it opened. He could practically feel Henwick's murderous intent radiating from the craft, even before the man walked down onto the street. Digby walked toward him as if he had nothing to fear until they were standing face to face. Of course, there was always the chance that Henwick would throw caution to the wind and Smite him out of existence anyway.

It was a risk Digby was willing to take.

"Henwick." He threw his arms out wide and embraced his enemy. "It has been too long!" He added, speaking loud enough for the nearby crowd to hear. Then he lowered his voice to a whisper. "I suggest you play along."

Henwick placed a hand flat on Digby's back. "I could Smite you right where you stand."

"And I could rip your throat out with my teeth."

"Not if I've already reduced you to a pair of smoking boots."

"Now, now, Henwick." Digby patted him on the back. "Might I remind you that a lot of people are watching and that destroying me is not worth losing the faith they have in you. Not if you intend to leverage it later."

Henwick squeezed him tighter. "Really? I'm not so sure. I could always start over. There are still plenty of survivors out there in the world."

A moment passed when neither of them said anything. Digby struggled to keep up the act, afraid of the possibility that Henwick really would write off the people around them and try to start over.

Then a familiar voice came from the crowd.

"It's him! It's him." Alice, the young girl that Digby had met earlier in the night, pushed her way through the crowd, holding a stuffed rabbit.

"Well, Henwick? What's it going to be?" Digby whispered in his ear. "We can both lose, or we can both win."

Henwick's body went rigid for an instant. Then he relaxed and let go. "Ah, yes. My friend—"

"Santa." Digby put the word in his mouth.

"Yes…" Henwick trailed off for a second before reluctantly adding. "My friend, Santa—"

"You know Santa?" Alice interrupted him excitedly as her father pushed through the crowd behind her.

The congressman took one glance at the scene and relaxed.

It really was starting to look like everything had been planned. Like it had all been an event put on by the empire to help with morale. Adults were the easiest to fool. They always looked to the mundane to explain away the things that they didn't understand.

"Of course he knows me." Digby shoved himself up beside Henwick and threw one arm around his shoulder. "In fact, my good friend Henwick just sent me a letter telling me how much the presents I brought him as a child meant to him. So I decided that, come hell or high water, I would make sure to make every delivery on my list this year."

"You're not supposed to say hell." Alice frowned.

"Yes," Henwick said through his teeth. "You aren't supposed to say hell, Santa."

"Yes, well, this has been a bit of a different year." Digby lowered his hand from the man's shoulder. "But I thank you for the escort." He gestured to the aircraft sitting nearby.

"What's wrong with your sleigh?" Alice pointed toward Alex who was completely dismantling the craft's altitude system.

"Ah yes, we just had some trouble with the magic that keeps it in the air," he answered honestly. "I'm afraid it's all rather complicated. Magic isn't what it used to be, you see."

"Why didn't you say you were having sleigh trouble?" Henwick turned toward him, suddenly smiling. "I can have it towed right into one of our maintenance bays. I'll have my best artificers on the job." His smile widened. "And I have a room exclusively for important guests set aside where you can wait."

Digby froze. Obviously, he wasn't going to be leaving if he let Henwick take him anywhere. Glancing back at the crowd, he started to realize that having an audience worked both ways. If

Alex couldn't get the sleigh in the air soon, it was going to get much harder to make an excuse as to why he couldn't let Henwick take it.

"I wouldn't want to cause you any trouble." Digby brushed Henwick's offer aside for the time being. "I'm sure my helpers will have the situation sorted in just a few minutes." He made sure to speak loud enough for Alex to hear him. To make sure his point was received, he also shot the artificer the most urgent look that he could muster.

Alex gave one back that made it clear that nothing short of a miracle was going to save them.

"Yes, yes, it looks like we should be ready to leave soon." Digby tried to keep his voice from shaking.

Before Henwick had a chance to issue another veiled threat, something small appeared in the distance. At first it was just a speck in the sky. Then, Digby recognized it.

The prototype.

The tiny sleigh drifted toward them with the last person he expected sticking out of it.

Parker.

The woman, who was most likely a spy, gave him a smile as she brought the ridiculous craft down to the street and skidded to a stop.

"There you are!" She pulled down a pair of goggles so that they hung around her neck and climbed out, leaving the prototype where it was. "I have been looking everywhere for you. They didn't tell me you went down right in the middle of the street."

Digby had to remind himself to close his mouth as he stared at the woman, unsure why she was there. The last he'd heard, she had escaped from her room and fled. She should have been miles away by now. Instead, she'd come to help.

Alex didn't skip a beat, practically leaping for the prototype to strip it for parts.

Parker ignored him and walked straight for Digby. She was still dressed in the same festive coat she had been wearing, along with a hat that matched his. A few locks of faded pink hair stuck out from underneath, looking gray in the pale light of the street lamps and the early glow of the dawning sun.

"Are you Mrs. Claus?" Alice asked, looking her over.

Parker hesitated, looked down at herself, then back up at Digby before speaking. "Ah, yeah. That's me, Mrs. Claus. I heard that my, um, husband was having sleigh troubles and headed straight here to bring him some replacement parts."

Digby leaned to the side to see past her. Alex was already wrist deep in the prototype's altitude system. "Yes, dear, I don't know what I'd do without you."

He wasn't sure why she had left the airship without telling anyone, but it was clear that she still had no idea what or who she was. She was still the same old Parker. More importantly, she had just pulled them right out of Henwick's clutches.

"Without me, you'd probably lose your head. Or at least your hat." Parker flicked the ball of fluff hanging next to his face, committing to the farce. "Probably don't crash the sleigh next time, dear."

"I wouldn't call that a crash." Digby brushed the comment aside. "There's barely a scratch on it."

"I'm sure," she said sarcastically before leaning down toward Alice. "You should see how many sleighs he's crashed this year alone."

The girl giggled before asking another question. "Where's Rudolph?"

"Yes, Santa, where is Rudolph?" Henwick turned toward him, clearly enjoying the question.

Parker came to his rescue again. "Back at the, ah, North Pole. But don't worry, I've made sure to give him plenty of carrots."

"Indeed." Digby joined in. "I'm afraid with the world being what it has become, I had to recruit something stronger to lead my sleigh tonight. Didn't want to run into anything scary out there and risk missing any deliveries."

"Yeah, Asher over there was able to fill in." Parker nodded.

"Does Asher eat carrots?" The child continued to question every detail.

"No…" Digby trailed off, realizing that he couldn't explain that his minion mostly ate the brains and hearts of humans.

"Birdseed," Parker blurted out. "Asher eats birdseed. Yes."

"I'm sure," Henwick commented, looking annoyed.

"Yes, well." Digby clapped his hands together. "It looks like we shall be back in the air in no time, so I will bid you farewell." He inclined his head to Henwick, locking eyes with the man to reaffirm the fragile agreement between them.

They could both lose or they could both win; the choice was his.

Henwick merely stood there, hiding his displeasure. "I'll look forward to the next time we meet."

Digby tried to ignore that last threat and turned to Alice, giving the girl a bow. "You be good now, and remember to share what you have with the other children."

"I will." She nodded politely.

Her father still looked a bit confused.

Digby turned away and held one arm out toward Parker. "Shall we go?"

She took his arm and started walking. "Yes, dear, let's go home."

The moment they were out of earshot from the crowd, Digby leaned closer so he could whisper, "What the devil were you thinking, leaving like that without telling anyone?"

"Sorry." She let go of his arm. "I got bored and picked the lock on my room. Which, by the way, what the hell? I know you're trying to protect me, but you don't have to lock me up." She shot him an annoyed look. "Anyway, when I got down to the ballroom, I overheard Mason and Easton talking about getting the prototype out to you so Alex could repair the sleigh. Mason was going to try to go himself and probably get himself killed in the process, so I decided to go instead."

"Why didn't you at least tell someone?" Digby gave her an annoyed look right back.

"I would have if I thought they would let me go. But I figured if whatever was wrong with me was serious enough to lock me up, I wasn't going to convince anybody to step aside. Especially not

Mason. I overheard him say letting me go was out of the question. There wasn't time for an argument."

"I see." Digby nodded slowly.

She wasn't wrong. Not when taking into account that she didn't know all the details. No matter what the reasons, she had done everything she could to help.

"What is wrong with me, by the way?" Parker stopped and looked up to him. "I can tell when people are lying to me. How bad is it? Am I dying?"

Digby hesitated before shaking his head. "Nothing is wrong with you that we didn't already know. Your magic was killing you." He forced a smile as he lied. "But you should recover as long as you let yourself rest. I was forced to revoke your access to the Heretic Seed. It was the only way to save you."

She squinted at him for a long moment as if suspecting he wasn't being completely honest. Then, she shrugged. "Okay. But don't lock me in any more rooms."

"Sorry, we were a little shorthanded and didn't have anyone to keep an eye on you. I wasn't sure you would accept it if I just told you to sit the night out. And I will point out that you just proved me right by flying the prototype all the way here. Though, I suppose I do appreciate the rescue." He forced a smile, trying to forget the traitor that was lurking within her. "Actually, now that we're talking about it, how do you feel now that your magic is gone?"

"I'm fine. The headache went away and I don't feel sick at all." Parker looked down at her hands before shoving them in her pockets. "I feel lighter. I don't know why, but losing my magic was like having a huge weight taken away. It sucks not to be immortal anymore, but I don't know if I ever wanted that to begin with."

Her last comment took Digby by surprise. Not just because the enchantments that had extended her life were still intact, but the idea that someone would turn down the chance to be immortal.

"Good." Digby pushed her toward the sleigh, not knowing what else to say.

"We're ready to go." Alex screwed the altitude crank back into place.

"And we are out of kids to give presents to." Becca returned to the sleigh with Hawk dragging an empty velvet sack behind him.

"It's a good thing we brought some extra gifts." The young rogue climbed into his seat. "It would've been pretty shitty if one of the kids got nothing."

"Yeah, now scoot over." Parker shoved into the back seat between him and Alex.

"Any messages from the seed?" Becca sat down in front. "Did we get the enchantment?"

Digby glanced at his HUD. There was nothing there.

"Not yet." He climbed into the sleigh and took the reins.

Turning back, he gave a wave to Henwick.

The empire's high priest didn't wave back.

Digby shifted his attention to the crowd and continued to wave, getting cheers in response.

With that, he sat down and commanded the reindeer to get moving. The sleigh slid forward. The only thing that would've made the moment more perfect would be if it had been snowing. Well, that and a notification from the Seed telling him that the plan had been successful.

He checked his HUD again.

Still nothing.

He smiled anyway as the sleigh left the ground.

A cackle rose in his throat.

It had been a good night. Nobody had been captured and, best of all, Henwick was miserable.

What more could he have asked for?

CHAPTER FORTY-FIVE

The return flight to the airship didn't take long. With Henwick standing down, the Queen Mary was free to meet them halfway. Digby spent the flight occasionally glancing at his HUD for an update from the Seed regarding the status of the enchantment.

None came.

There was always the chance that the children's belief in him would take a few days to solidify. Or perhaps they just hadn't met the threshold to manifest a new mass enchantment. He was trying to claim the power of a demigod, after all. Maybe he'd been aiming too high in the first place.

Still, Digby found himself smiling as the sleigh touched down on the deck of the airship. He commanded the reindeer to drag the ridiculous craft back into the room that they had been using as a stable. Once they were inside, Digby climbed out of the sleigh and fed each of the undead animals a few treats from the box of severed revenant fingers. They'd more than earned it.

The rest of his helpers climbed out as well.

Alex headed straight for one of the tables that littered the workshop to retrieve Kristen's skull. She complained about being left behind but quickly shifted her focus when he brought her over to the sleigh's flight system. The contraption had gotten them back to the airship, but it was mostly held together by duct tape at this point. There was no need to repair it since the craft's purpose had been served, but Digby wasn't going to interrupt.

Becca ran to Mason as soon as she saw him. From the looks of it, the soldier had been pacing back and forth on the deck nervously. He tried to get the vampire to go to the infirmary so Lana could look at her hands. Then he nearly fell over, still missing a couple pints of blood. Becca caught him and led him to a chair in the corner of the room.

Parker hopped down from the sleigh and quickly looked around, as if checking if the coast was clear to make a run for it. Digby tensed and clenched his jaw only to relax a second later when she headed straight for Asher to unhook the ravendeer's harness. She was probably just checking to see if anyone was going to lock her up again.

Digby tore his attention away and looked for Hawk.

The rogue was nowhere to be found.

"Odd." Digby arched an eyebrow.

Hawk had been in the sleigh a moment before.

He made a brief lap of the room before checking the hallway outside. Still nothing. Eventually, he pushed back out through the doors leading to the deck and found the rogue staring out into the distance with his chin resting on the railing. A full view of the landscape below stretched out into the distance as the morning sun shined across it. The imperial capital was still visible on the horizon. Though, it was no more than a speck, growing smaller by the second.

Digby couldn't help but be reminded that such a place was now home to a large portion of the world's children. There were still plenty more out there in the world, but the realization made it all seem so fragile.

Clearing his throat, Digby joined Hawk at the railing. "The holidays still getting you down?"

Hawk raised his head. "It's not that. Actually, this year was fun." He smiled for an instant before letting the expression fade. "I'm just afraid that none of it mattered. You didn't get the enchantment."

Digby glanced at his HUD one more time.

"Still nothing?" Hawk asked, clearly noticing him check.

"I'm afraid not." He placed a hand down on the rail. "But maybe, that's alright."

"What?" The rogue looked up at him like he'd lost his mind. "But we just went through all that. It's not fair that we get nothing."

"I wouldn't say we got nothing." Digby gave him a smile. "I think, maybe, the real reward was the time we spent together along the way."

Hawk said nothing in return. Instead, he just stared at him like he'd just uttered the dumbest thing in the world.

"What? You had fun, didn't you?" Digby stared right back.

"Well sure, but that's not enough," he groaned.

"Isn't it?"

"No."

"Well, too bad." Digby frowned. "It was enough for me."

"What does that even mean?" Hawk looked annoyed.

"It means you and I are a lot alike." Digby jabbed him in the chest with a finger. "I never liked celebrating things either. I never had a family or friends that cared about me. Hell, I thought I hated people."

"I don't hate people," Hawk added while avoiding eye contact. "At least, not anymore."

"That's my point." Digby smiled. "I think I learned something throughout all this. And I think you did too."

Hawk remained silent for a moment. Then he sighed. "It was nice. Giving gifts and all that. The kids seemed happy."

"Indeed." Digby chuckled. "So did their parents. I didn't realize how something so small could make such a difference. I think that's why I'm not angry right now." He held out an empty hand. "We might not have gotten the enchantment that we set out for, but I think we gave something back to the people we visited." He closed his hand. "I don't know why, but that might have been more important."

"I guess you're right." Hawk let a smile show without hiding it.

"Of course I am." Digby stood a little taller. "I am rarely wrong, you know."

"Sure." Hawk dragged out the word sarcastically. Then he looked back over his shoulder through the doors at the room behind him, and lowered his voice to a whisper. "So what are we doing about…" He hesitated before adding, "You know who?"

Digby turned as well, following the young rogue's line of sight to where Parker was stroking Asher's neck.

"Oh…" He let his mouth hang open, having trouble thinking of an answer to the question.

"Is it true?" Hawk's voice fell. "You know, that she's a bad guy?"

Digby continued to watch her until she noticed.

She simply waved in response.

"I don't know." Digby turned back to the railing. "She could be more dangerous than Henwick."

"But she doesn't know it, right?" Hawk sounded a little hopeful. "And she doesn't have to find out?"

Digby frowned. "I'm not sure. We may not be able to keep it from her forever."

"But we don't have to tell her now." Hawk lowered his head.

"No, I suppose not." Digby nodded. "Parker might be evil, but for now she's a friend. Locking her up is out of the question. At least, it won't work long term without us having to tell her the truth. So for now, all we can do is keep a close eye on her." He shrugged. "Maybe when the time comes, she'll remember the time she spent with us. Maybe she'll pick our side in the end."

"Maybe." Hawk stared out into the horizon.

"Only time will tell, it seems." Digby slapped a hand on the railing a second later. "I almost forgot."

"Forgot what?" Hawk snapped his head toward him at the sudden movement.

"Wait right here." Digby spun, rushed back into the ship, and ran down the hall into the ballroom. Sprinting over to one of the tables, he crouched down and retrieved a box that he'd stashed underneath it a week earlier. Unlike the rest of the presents, it was wrapped in a sheet of newsprint. The corners were uneven and there was a strip of tape running up the side to cover up a tear. Digby hesitated, debating on rewrapping the gift. Then he shook his head. The paper was only going to be torn off anyway.

Heading back out to the deck, he approached Hawk cautiously with the package held in front of him.

"What you got there?" The young rogue eyed the present skeptically.

"A gift, for you." Digby pushed it into his hands.

"Great, another one." Hawk rolled his eyes.

"Another?"

"Yeah, Becca gave me one yesterday before we left." He shrugged.

"What was it?" Digby asked out of curiosity.

"A PlayStation. One of the old gray ones. She hunted it down in some retro store, since it doesn't need the internet to work. It's actually pretty cool." He smiled. "Alex gave me some games too. He said they were some of his favorites when he was a kid."

"Oh, so you like it?" Digby reached out, debating on taking the package back.

"Yeah." Hawk nodded. "But it's not like I needed anything."

Digby winced. Compared to Becca's gift, his was a little stupid. He wished he'd talked to her first; he could have had Alex show him some games that Hawk would like. Instead, he'd just grabbed something on a whim.

Before he had a chance to say anything, Hawk had already torn the newsprint off. Digby cringed as he pulled open the cardboard box underneath.

"What?" The rogue stared down at the gift inside.

It was an orange cat. Not a real one, obviously. No, just a stuffed one, the same as many of the other presents they had given out that night.

"Sorry." Digby lowered his eyes to the deck. "I know it's silly and for kids. I should have gotten something else." He scratched at the back of his neck. "It just reminded me of a cat that lived back in my village when I was young. And I thought you needed a simple toy, because…" He struggled to explain his thoughts. "You deserve one. I mean, you deserve a childhood."

Hawk started to frown.

"Yes, I know, you're not a child." Digby didn't give him a chance to argue. "I'll gladly admit that I trust you over most adults. You've also proven yourself time and time again. But that is exactly why you deserve a childhood. You don't need to sacrifice it. It's not too late. The world will still be here when you're older and I know you will do great things then."

Hawk continued to stare up at him.

"Oh, just shut up and take the stupid cat." Digby folded his arms. "I'm not good at this. I care, is all I'm trying to say. So deal with—"

Digby went silent mid-sentence when Hawk threw his arms around him, the stuffed cat dangling from one hand.

"What is happening here?" Digby stood with both arms held out in panic.

"Shut up, Dig." Hawk squeezed him tighter.

"Does this mean you like the gift?" Digby gave the young rogue and awkward pat on the back.

"Yeah." Hawk sniffed. "It's fine."

"You don't have to lie." Digby chuckled.

"I'm not." Hawk let go and tucked the toy under his arm. "Thank you."

"You're welcome." Digby smiled.

That was when a new message scrolled across his vision. Digby ignored it for a second, not wanting to interrupt the moment. Then the first line of text caught his eye.

NEW TEMPORARY MASS ENCHANTMENT ACHIEVED

"What?" His eyes bulged.

"What is it?" Hawk asked.

"I think." He glanced down at the rogue. "I think you just started to believe in Santa, because I just got an enchantment."

"Seriously?" Hawk looked up at him before shaking his head. "Wait, I don't believe in Santa. I guess… I believe in you, though."

Digby stared in disbelief at the words that filled his view.

"What does it say?" Hawk stepped close as Digby read the words aloud.

By completing the tasks of a mythical figure, legend, or demigod, and invoking the abilities associated with the role, you have been granted all powers of the original bearer. This enchantment will expire one year after its manifestation if its requirements have not been met again. This enchantment may be passed on to another in the event that you are unable to complete the tasks required.
Required tasks: Give gifts

Ability 1: Mana Form
Temporarily disperse your body and anything you carry amongst the surrounding environment's mana. While in this form, you will be capable of traveling through the ambient essence to pass through any space, no matter how small. This ability will require an expenditure of 20 MP to activate as well as a second 20 MP to deactivate. *You'll become a ghost yet.*

Ability 2: Gentle Snow
Summon a light flurry to create a festive atmosphere. This ability will require an expenditure of 100 MP per hour. *Wow, so helpful. This is sarcasm, by the way.*

Ability 3: Bag of Holding
Turn any bag or sack you carry into a bottomless storage void. This ability may only be applied to one bag at a time. *Not very impressive, you already have that.*

Ability 4: Sense Morality
With this ability, you will be able to sense whether someone has been good or bad throughout the course of the current year. *Maybe don't use this one on yourself.*

Ability 5: Halt

Temporarily accelerate your perception of time. While accelerated, the flow of time will appear to have stopped. However, you will be capable of moving and thinking normally. All damage incurred by this level of physical activity will be regenerated at the same accelerated rate. This ability will require an expenditure of 50 MP per second of use. *This will certainly make a life of crime a bit easier.*

"Shit, that last one is crazy." Hawk gestured stabbing someone. "You could just stop time and walk right up to Henwick and murder him."

"Indeed." Digby stared at the ability.

It was exactly what he'd been hoping for. Stopping time could end the war once and for all if things came down to a fight between him and Henwick. Before he could let his mind travel down that path, he realized there was more to the Heretic Seed's message.

NEW TEMPORARY MASS ENCHANTMENT ACHIEVED

"Wait, there's a second one?" Digby furrowed his brow at the addition.

By completing the tasks of a mythical figure, legend, or demigod, and invoking the abilities associated with the role, you have been granted all powers of the original bearer. This enchantment will expire one year after its manifestation if its requirements have not been met again. This enchantment may be passed on to another in the event that you are unable to complete the tasks required.
Required tasks: Punishment

Digby reread that last word. "But I didn't punish any of the children. I just decided they were all good this year and gave them presents anyway."

"Didn't you shove a bunch of bandits in your void earlier?" Hawk eyed him.

"Well…" Digby hesitated before adding, "I might have eaten a few."

He continued reading to find that he'd unlocked many of the same abilities. Halt, Sense Morality, and Mana Form were all there at the bottom of the list. Yet, the top two entries were different. Gentle Snow and Bag of Holding had both been replaced.

Ability 1: Blizzard
Summon a terrifying winter storm to strand victims and
reduce their ability to seek help. This ability will require an
expenditure of 500 MP per hour. *Alright, now we're talking.*

Ability 2: Sack of Torment
Turn any bag you carry into a sack of torment. When opened,
this bag will manifest several lengths of barbed chain that
may be controlled by its wielder as if they were an extension
of their own body. Any person pulled into a sack of torment
will be engulfed by darkness and the screams of the damned
until such a time when they are released. This ability may
only be applied to one bag at a time. *What the hell? That's…*
just wrong.

"What the devil does any of that mean?" Digby stared at the description.

Hawk burst out laughing. "I think you're the new Krampus, Dig."

"What the devil is Krampus?" he snapped back.

"It's evil Santa," the rogue answered matter-of-factly. "I had a foster parent tell me he'd come get me if I did anything wrong."

"Whatever." Digby shrugged off the implications that came with the title. "Results are results."

"I guess so." Hawk continued to laugh.

Digby spent the mana to summon a Gentle Snow and waited as a layer of puffy clouds collected overhead. Snowflakes drifted down to the deck a moment later.

Hawk held out a hand to catch a few as Digby stepped away from the ship's railing.

"Why don't we head back in?"

"Okay." Hawk shoved the stuffed cat back into the box it had come in and headed into the ship only to stop a few feet later. "Do you think, if I asked, I could go to school with the other kids? Just until you need me again?"

"Of course you can." Digby placed a hand on his shoulder. "I know things haven't been easy these last few months, but I'm going to do my best to change that."

"I believe you." Hawk smiled without trying to hide it.

"And I'll eat anyone that stands in my way." Digby let a cackle slip out.

Hawk's face fell. "You really need to learn when to stop talking."

"I know." Digby shoved the rogue forward. "But today is not that day."

EPILOGUE

"A pirate's life for me."

Elton blew out a sigh and hung his head as he leaned on the railing of the Soaring Hound. An ocean of darkness stretched into the distance as far as the eye could see. The only light came from the moon overhead. The Hound's running lights had been turned off for the night and the crew was under orders to keep their flashlights off unless it was an emergency.

The captain didn't want to risk being spotted by another ship in case someone else had gotten the same idea as him.

That idea being piracy, of course.

The Hound had set sail a day before the monsters took over. Elton had been one of five chefs who worked in the ship's kitchen. The Hound had been well stocked with two weeks of gourmet meals as well as the basics for the crew, so the captain had ordered them to stay out. The plan was to wait the situation out. It wasn't long before it became obvious that the world wasn't going to bounce back.

Everything simply crumbled.

In the beginning, it hadn't been that bad.

The Hound was classified as a mega-yacht. It was three hundred meters and cost hundreds of millions. It had almost everything a billionaire could ask for. Elton didn't actually know who owned it. Most of the time it was rented out by other equally wealthy people for a few million per week.

In this case, it was the captain.

He had been the CEO of a pharmaceutical company and made his fortune by maximizing shareholder returns at the expense of his employees and customers. Once it became clear that they were going to need more supplies, he'd ordered the crew to head back to land and take the helicopter, which had been sitting on one of the Hound's two helipads.

The next week was grueling.

Half the crew died in the process, but they had gained a second helicopter, a mountain of guns and ammo, and enough food for a few months. The problem was that the captain wanted more. There was an attempted mutiny soon after. The manager of the ship's spa had attempted to take charge but didn't get that far. Apparently, the captain's cutthroat business style translated well to cutting actual throats.

After that, they kept to the seas and maintained their supplies by attacking every vessel they came across. Most of the people they found were either killed or left to starve in the middle of the ocean. Elton could still hear them begging as the captain left them to die. That was one of the two reasons that he could never sleep.

Sure, he could try to take command of the ship, but after what happened to the last group that tried... Well, that was the other reason that he couldn't sleep.

In the end, he had no choice but to go along.

The Hound rocked gently on the waves just as Elton caught a flash of light in the distance. At first, he thought it was moonlight reflecting off the water. Then it flashed again. It continued at regular intervals after that, making it clear that it was a signal beacon. Whoever was aboard the vessel must have needed help.

Elton stood up straight, his first instinct to call out the discovery to the rest of the crew.

He settled back down a moment later. The ship might have needed help, but the captain of the Hound wasn't about to offer any. It would probably be best for whoever was aboard to remain unnoticed. At least that way, they might have a chance.

That was when another member of the crew rang a bell up on the upper deck to wake the captain. They must have noticed it too.

Ten minutes later, the Hound was approaching the vessel. They held position at fifty feet to observe the craft. It was a good-sized sailboat, the kind that could make it across the ocean on its own. It looked abandoned, or at least there were no other lights aboard other than the flashing emergency beacon.

Elton got his rifle along with the rest of the crew, and lined up on the side. The captain stayed on the deck above, and ordered a few men to head over in a raft.

"We have movement!" another member of the crew shouted.

Elton flicked his eyes back to the sailboat to squint into the dark. There was someone on board, or something. The figure stumbled across the deck before falling over the side.

"Hold positions," the captain ordered. "It's a ghost ship."

That was what he called it when they came across a vessel that had been taken over by monsters. It was pretty common. It seemed that half the boats they came across carried someone who had tried to hide a bite. The result was always the same. At first light, the captain would send people over to clear the sailboat out and take anything of value.

Elton blew out a sigh, relieved that there had been no one alive on the vessel.

The captain ordered him and a few others to keep watch while the rest of the crew returned to their bunks to wait until morning. Elton went back to staring out into the distance.

Fifteen minutes later, a scream came from the rear of the yacht. Elton was moving in an instant, pulling his rifle from his back and heading for the disturbance. The monster that had fallen from the sailboat must have made its way to the docking area at the back of the Hound. He converged with three other members of the crew and took position at the back of the group.

By the time they reached the scene, the monster was gone. One of the crew lay dead on the deck. His head had nearly been torn off, hanging by a few scraps of flesh.

Elton turned away to keep from throwing up, taking his eyes off the area in front of him where the other three crew members stood.

A second later, blood sprayed across the deck. He snapped his vision back to the others just as the man in front came apart at the seams. A figure moved like a demon in the dark, tearing the guy's arms clean off and kicking the screaming man away. His rifle flew past Elton, still held by a severed arm. The monster surged forward, slamming into the next crewmember. It shoved him against the wall and tore into his throat the same way someone might peel a banana. A torrent of blood sprayed to cover the figure in crimson.

The dying crewmember unloaded his rifle into the deck.

That was when Elton ran, only glancing back to see the figure shred through another two men that had rushed onto the scene. He kept running until he'd reached the safest place aboard the Hound, the captain's quarters.

The main suite took up the entire top level of the ship and was larger than most houses. Elton banged on the door as soon as he got there. He wasn't sure what he was going to tell the captain, but he could think of that once he was inside.

The captain turned on the light and opened the door, holding a pistol in his free hand. "What in the hell is——"

Elton shoved in past him as men screamed on the deck below.

"What the fuck do you think you're doing?" The captain shoved his pistol in his direction.

"Something got aboard." Elton frantically closed the door, ignoring the gun.

"Then go out there and deal with it!"

"It's tearing through everyone." Elton shook his head, trying to come up with a good reason for the captain to let him stay.

Before he could get another word out, the sound of gunfire and screams stopped.

The captain started to argue but froze as footsteps came from the other side of the door. "What is it?"

"I don't know." Elton held his rifle aimed at the entrance to the suite.

That was when a quiet knock came from the door.

They both opened fire, shredding the door to splinters, along with whoever might have been on the other side. A moment of silence fell when they ran out of bullets.

"Is that any way to greet a guest?" A voice came from the door as it bowed inward and cracked, the same blood-soaked figure pushing through it like a piece of wet cardboard. It dragged a member of the crew along behind it. They were missing both legs and one arm. The man choked out a few last gasps through a gaping wound in his throat before his corpse was dropped to the floor.

Now that the monster stood in the light of the captain's suite, Elton realized that it wasn't a monster at all. No, it was a man. He stood for a moment, stretching his body. A series of cracks and pops came from his shoulders as he stood a little straighter.

"Who are you?" the captain demanded.

"Just a traveler in need of passage." The blood-soaked man held out a hand as if checking the condition of his fingernails.

"Passage to where?" The captain's voice wavered.

"America." The man lowered his hand. "I have business with a certain acquaintance there, and I wish to pay her a visit. I might even let you live if you serve me well?"

A sudden chill ran down Elton's spine. "Serve you?"

"Of course." The blood-soaked man stood as if obedience was their only option.

"Alright." The captain lowered his pistol and held up a hand in submission. "If you let me go, you can be the captain."

"Captain?" The man cocked his head to the side, dripping blood to the floor. "I do not need such a position. I already have a title."

"Title?" Elton took a step back.

"Yes." The man held both hands out, as if presenting something for reverence. "You may call me Lord Durand."

ABOUT D. PETRIE

D. Petrie discovered a love of stories and nerd culture at an early age. From there, life was all about comics, video games, and books. It's not surprising that all that would lead to writing. He currently lives north of Boston with the love of his life and their two adopted cats. He streams on twitch every Thursday night.

Connect with D. Petrie:
TavernToldTales.com
Patreon.com/DavidPetrie
Facebook.com/WordsByDavidPetrie
Facebook.com/groups/TavernToldTales
Twitter.com/TavernToldTales

ABOUT MOUNTAINDALE PRESS

Dakota and Danielle Krout, a husband and wife team, strive to create as well as publish excellent fantasy and science fiction novels. Self-publishing *The Divine Dungeon: Dungeon Born* in 2016 transformed their careers from Dakota's military and programming background and Danielle's Ph.D. in pharmacology to President and CEO, respectively, of a small press. Their goal is to share their success with other authors and provide captivating fiction to readers with the purpose of solidifying Mountaindale Press as the place 'Where Fantasy Transforms Reality.'

Connect with Mountaindale Press:
MountaindalePress.com
Facebook.com/MountaindalePress
Twitter.com/_Mountaindale
Instagram.com/MountaindalePress

MOUNTAINDALE PRESS TITLES
GameLit and LitRPG

The Completionist Chronicles,
Cooking with Disaster,
The Divine Dungeon,
Full Murderhobo, and
Year of the Sword by Dakota Krout

A Touch of Power by Jay Boyce

Red Mage and
Farming Livia by Xander Boyce

Ether Collapse and
Ether Flows by Ryan DeBruyn

Unbound by Nicoli Gonnella

Threads of Fate by Michael Head

Lion's Lineage by Rohan Hublikar and Dakota Krout

Wolfman Warlock by James Hunter and Dakota Krout

Axe Druid,
Mephisto's Magic Online, and
High Table Hijinks by Christopher Johns

Dragon Core Chronicles by Lars Machmüller

Pixel Dust and
Necrotic Apocalypse by D. Petrie

Viceroy's Pride and
Tower of Somnus by Cale Plamann

Henchman by Carl Stubblefield

Artorian's Archives by Dennis Vanderkerken and Dakota Krout

APPENDIX

NOTEWORTY ITEMS

THE HERETIC SEED
An unrestricted pillar of power. Once connected, this system grants access to and manages the usage of, the mana that exists within the human body and the world around them.

HERETIC RINGS
A ring that synchronizes the wearer with the Heretic Seed to assign a starting class. Unlocks administrator access.

THE GUARDIAN CORE
A well-regulated pillar of power. Once connected, this system grants temporary access to and manages the usage of, the mana that exists within the human body and the world around them.

NOTEWORTY CONCEPTS

AMBIENT MANA
The energy present within a person's surroundings. This energy can be absorbed and used to alter the world in a way that could be described as magic.

CARETAKERS
An entity that lives within the Heretic Seed and is needed to unlock and manage the use of magic for a large number of users. A caretaker must be offered a soul to gain sentience. Once

consumed, the caretaker will adopt the appearance and personality of the soul it has gained. This new entity will be capable of understanding the impacts of its actions on a human level, which will allow it to make appropriate judgments when needed.

INFERNAL SPIRIT
A spirit formed from the lingering essence of the dead.

MANA SYSTEM
All creatures possess a mana system. This system consists of layers of energy that protect the core of what that creature is. The outer layers of this system may be used to cast spells and will replenish as more mana is absorbed. Some factors, such as becoming a Heretic will greatly increase the strength of this system to provide much higher quantities of usable mana.

MANA BALANCE (EXTERNAL)
Mana is made up of different types of essence. These are as follows, HEAT, FLUID, SOIL, VAPOR, LIFE, DEATH. Often, one type of essence may be more plentiful than others. A location's mana balance can be altered by various environmental factors and recent events.

MANA BALANCE (INTERNAL)
Through persistence and discipline, a Heretic may cultivate their mana system to contain a unique balance of essence. This requires favoring spells that coincide with the desired balance while neglecting others that don't. This may affect the potency of spells that coincide with the dominant mana type within a Heretic's system.

MASS ENCHANTMENTS
Due to belief and admiration shared by a large quantity of people an item or place may develop a power of power of its own.

SURROGATE ENCHANTMENTS
An enchantment bestowed upon an object or structure based upon

its resemblance (in either appearance or purpose) to another object or structure that already carries a mass enchantment.

WARDING
While sheltering one or more people, a structure will repel hostile entities that do not possess a high enough will to overpower that location's warding.

RUNECRAFT
By engraving various runes onto a surface through the use of the Artificer's Engraving spell, an object may be empowered with a magical trait. When used in combination, a variety of results can be achieved.

WEREWOLVES
These cursed creatures shift between human and wolf along the cycles of the moon. May access some of their power without a physical transformation or the requirement of a full moon. Highly dangerous, however, their intelligence decreases in correspondence with the amount of power they use.

VAMPIRES
These cursed creatures retain their souls and resemble normal humans, but require the consumption of blood to maintain their abilities. Highly dangerous at night but weak to light essence. May still be dangerous during the day.

HERETIC & GUARDIAN CLASSES

ARTIFICER
The artificer class specializes in the manipulation of materials and mana to create unique and powerful items. With the right tools, an artificer can create almost anything.

ILLUSIONIST
The illusionist class specializes in shaping mana to create believable lies.

FIGHTER
Starting class for a heretic or guardian whose highest attribute is will. Excels at physical combat.

MAGE
Starting class for a heretic or guardian whose highest attribute is intelligence. Excels at magic.

MESSENGER
The determining factor to access this class is unknown.

ENCHANTER
Starting class for a heretic or guardian whose highest attribute is well. Excels at supporting others.

HOLY KNIGHT (GUARDIAN ONLY)
A class that specializes in physical combat and defense. This class has the ability to draw strength from a Guardian's faith.

TEMPESTARII
A class that specializes in both fluid and vapor spells resulting on a variety of weather-based spells.

AEROMANCER
A class that specializes in vapor spells.

PYROMANCER
A class that specializes in heat spells.

ROGUE
A class that specializes in stealth and movement spells.

CLERIC
A class that specializes in life spells.

NECROMANCER
A specialized class unlocked by achieving a high balance of

death essence within a Heretic's mana system as well as discovering spells within the mage class that make use of death essence.

DISCOVERD SPELLS

ABSORB
Absorb the energy of an incoming attack. The absorbed energy may be stored and applied to a future spell to amplify its damage.

ANIMATE CORPSE
Raise a zombie from the dead by implanting a portion of your mana into a corpse. Once raised, a minion will remain loyal until destroyed. The mutation path of an animated zombie will be controlled by the caster, allowing them to evolve their follower into a minion that will fit their needs.

ANIMATE SKELETON
Call forth your infernal spirit to inhabit one partial or complete skeleton. An animated skeleton's physical attributes will mimic the values of the human whose bones they inhabit.

BARRIER
Create a layer of mana around yourself or a target to absorb an incoming attack.

BLOOD FORGE
Description: Forge a simple object or object of your choosing out of any available blood source.

BURIAL
Displace an area of earth to dig a grave beneath a target. The resulting grave will fill back in after five seconds.

CARTOGRAPHY
Send a pulse into the ambient mana around you to map your surroundings. Each use will add to the area that has been previ-

ously mapped. Mapped areas may be viewed at any time. This spell may interact with other location-dependent spells.

CONCEAL
Allows the caster to weave a simple illusion capable of hiding any person or object from view.

CONCEALING MIST
Description: Fill a space with an eerie mist. When entered, this mist will conceal your presence completely.

CONTROL ZOMBIE
Temporarily subjugate the dead into your service regardless of the target's will values. Zombies under your control gain +2 intelligence and are unable to refuse any command. May control up to 5 common zombies at any time.

CONTROL UNCOMMON ZOMBIE
Temporarily subjugate the dead into your service regardless of the target's will/resistance. Zombies under your control gain +2 intelligence and are unable to refuse any command. May control up to 1 uncommon zombie at any time.

CREMATION
Ignite a target's necrotic tissue. The resulting fire will spread to other flammable substances.

DECAY
Accelerate the damage done by the ravages of time on a variety of materials. Metal will rust, glass will crack, flesh will rot, and plants will die. The effect may be enhanced through physical contact. Decay may be focused on a specific object as well as aimed at a general area for a wider effect.

DETECT ENEMY:
Infuse a common iron object with the ability to sense and person or creature that is currently hostile toward you.

EMERALD FLARE

Create a point of unstable energy that explodes and irradiates its surroundings. This area will remain harmful to all living creatures for one hour. Anyone caught within its area of effect will gain a poison ailment lasting for one day or until cleansed.

ENCHANT WEAPON

Infuse a weapon or projectile with mana. An infused weapon will deal increased damage as well as disrupt the mana flow of another caster. Potential damage will increase with rank. Enchanting a single projectile will have a greater effect.

FICTION

Description: Increase the chance that your lies will be believed. The likelihood that this spell will be successful or not will depend on how willing the target is to believe the lie. The effects of this spell may fade over time.

FIREBALL

Will a ball of fire to gather in your hand to form a throwable sphere that ruptures on contact.

FIVE FINGERS OF DEATH

Create a field of mana around the fingers of one hand, capable of boring through the armor and flesh of your enemies. Through prolonged contact with the internal structures of an enemy's body, this spell is capable of bestowing an additional curse effect. Death's Embrace: This curse manifests by creating a state of undeath within a target, capable of reanimating your enemy into a loyal zombie minion. Once animated, a zombie minion will seek to consume the flesh of their species and may pass along their cursed status to another creature.

FROST TOUCH

Freeze anything you touch.

HEAT OBJECT

Slowly increase the temperature of an inanimate object. Practical when other means of cooking are unavailable. This spell will continue to heat an object until the caster stops focusing on it or until its maximum temperature is reached.

ICICLE
Gather moisture from the air around you to form an icicle. Once formed, icicles will hover in place for 3 seconds, during which they may be claimed as a melee weapon or launched in the direction of a target. Accuracy is dependent on the caster's focus.

IMBUE
Allows the caster to implant a portion of either their own mana or the donated mana of a consenting person or persons into an object to create a self-sustaining mana system capable of powering a permanent enchantment.

INSPECTION
Description: Similar to a Heretic's Analyze ability, this spell examines an inanimate item with more depth, allowing the caster to see what materials an object is made of as well as enchantments that might be present.

KINETIC IMPACT
Generate a field of mana around your fist to amplify the kinetic energy of an attack.

MEND
Allows the caster to repair an object made from a single material. Limitations: this spell is unable to mend complex items.

MIRROR LINK
Connect two reflective surfaces to swap their reflections and allow for communication. The caster must have touched both surfaces previously.

MIRROR PASSAGE

Create a passage between two reflective surfaces capable of traversing great distances. The caster must have a clear picture of their destination.

NECROTIC REGENERATION
Repair damage to necrotic flesh and bone to restore function and structural integrity.

PURIFY WATER
Imbue any liquid with cleansing power. Purified liquids will become safe for human consumption and will remove most ailments. At higher ranks, purified liquids may also gain a mild regenerative effect.

REGENERATION
Heal wounds for yourself or others. If rendered unconscious, this spell will cast automatically until all damage is repaired or until MP runs out.

REVEAL
By combining the power of the enhanced senses that you have cultivated, this spell will reveal the position of any threat that may be hidden to you and display as much information as available. This spell may also be used to see in low-light situations.

SHADE PROJECTION
Description: Project a shadow version of yourself visible to both enemies and allies. Shade projections may interact with their surroundings but will possess low strength values. This spell can only be used with the intent to cause fear or psychological harm.

SPIRIT PROJECTION
Project an immaterial image of yourself visible to both enemies and allies.

SUMMON ECHO
Temporarily recall the echo of a consumed spark to take action.

The actions of a summoned spark may be unpredictable and will vary depending on what type of spark you choose to summon. More control may be possible at higher ranks.

SUMMONABLE ECHOES

CRONE
When summoned, this spark will call upon the remnants of the lingering dead to grab hold of a target and prevent movement. This spell will last until the target can break free, or until canceled.

HONORABLE CLERIC
When summoned, this spark will manifest and heal one ally.

MURDEROUS WRAITH
When summoned, this spark will manifest and attack a target that is currently hostile to you. Due to the skills of the consumed spark, this spell has a high probability of dealing catastrophic damage to a target.

TALKING CORPSE
Temporarily bestow the gift of speech to a corpse to gain access to the information known to them while they were alive. Once active, a talking corpse cannot lie.

TERRA BURST
Call forth a circle of stone shards from the earth to injure any target unfortunate enough to be standing in the vicinity.

TRANSFER ENCHANTMENT
Allows the caster to transfer an existing enchantment from one item to another.

VENTRILOQUISM
Allows the caster to project a voice or sound to another location.

VERITAS
Decipher truth from lies.

ZOMBIE WHISPERER
Give yourself or others the ability to soothe the nature of any non-human zombie to gain its trust. Once cast, a non-human zombie will obey basic commands.

PASSIVE HERETIC ABILITIES

ANALYZE
Reveal hidden information about an object or target, such as rarity and hostility toward you.

MANA ABSORPTION
Ambient mana will be absorbed whenever MANA POINTS are below maximum MP values. The rate of absorption may vary depending on ambient mana concentration and essence composition. Absorption may be increased through meditation and rest. WARNING: Mana absorption will be delayed whenever spells are cast.

SKILL LINK
Discover new spells by demonstrating repeated and proficient use of non-heretic skills or talents.

TIMELESS
Due to the higher-than-normal concentration of mana within a heretic's body, the natural aging process has been halted, allowing for more time to reach the full potential of your class. It is still possible to expire from external damage.

VAMPIRIC ABILITIES

SHADE CRAFT
Form physical manifestations from the shadows around you

capable of damaging. This ability can only be used with the intent to cause fear or psychological harm.

BANSHEE
Description: Allows the caster to project a voice or sound to another location. This ability can only be used with the intent to cause fear or psychological harm.

VAMPIRIC REGENERATION
Description: Automatically heal all damage upon receiving it. This ability can not be canceled or delayed.

TIMELESS
Due to the higher-than-normal concentration of mana within a heretic's body, the natural aging process has been halted, allowing for more time to reach the full potential of your class. It is still possible to expire from external damage.

ZOMBIE RACIAL TRAITS (HUMAN)

BLOOD SENSE
Allows a zombie to sense blood in their surroundings to aid in the tracking of prey. The potency of this trait increases with perception.

GUIDED MUTATION
Due to an unusually high intelligence for an undead creature, you are capable of mutating at will rather than mutating when required resources are consumed. This allows you to choose mutations from multiple paths instead of following just one.

MUTATION
Alter your form or attributes by consuming resources of the living or recently deceased. Required resources are broken down into 6 types: Flesh, Bone, Sinew, Viscera, Mind, and Heart. Mutation path is determined by what resources a zombie consumes.

RAVENOUS

A ravenous zombie will be unable to perform any action other than the direct pursuit of food until satiated. This may result in self-destructive behavior. While active, all physical limitations will be ignored. Ignoring physical limitations for prolonged periods of time may result in catastrophic damage.

RESIST

A remnant from a zombie's human life, this common trait grants +5 points to will. Normally exclusive to conscious beings, this trait allows a zombie to resist basic spells that directly target their body or mind until their will is overpowered.

VOID

A bottomless, weightless, dimensional space that exists within the core of a zombie's mana system. This space can be accessed through its carrier's stomach and will expand to fit whatever contents are Consumed.

ZOMBIE MINION TRAITS (AVIAN)

FLIGHT OF THE DEAD

As an avian zombie, the attributes required to maintain the ability to fly have been restored.

BOND OF THE DEAD

As a zombie animated directly by a necromancer, this creature will gain one attribute point for every 2 levels of their master. These points may be allocated at any time. 7 attribute points remaining.

CALL OF THE DEAD

As a zombie animated directly by a necromancer, this minion and its master will be capable of sensing each other's presence through their bond. In addition, the necromancer will be capable of summoning this minion to their location over great distances.

ZOMBIE MINION TRAITS (RODENT)

SPEED OF THE DEAD
As a rodent zombie, the attributes required to maintain the ability to move quickly have been retained. +3 agility, + 2 strength.

BOND OF THE DEAD
As a zombie animated directly by a necromancer, this creature will gain one attribute point for every 2 levels of their master. These points may be allocated at any time. 7 attribute points remaining.

CALL OF THE DEAD
As a zombie animated directly by a necromancer, this minion and its master will be capable of sensing each other's presence through their bond. In addition, the necromancer will be capable of summoning this minion to their location over great distances.

ZOMBIE MINION TRAITS (REVENANT)

BOND OF THE DEAD
As a zombie animated directly by a necromancer, this creature will gain one attribute point for every 2 levels of their master. These points may be allocated at any time. 9 attribute points remaining.

NOCTURNAL
As a zombie created from the corpse of a deceased revenant, this zombie will retain a portion of its attributes associated with physical capabilities. Attributes will revert to that of a normal zombie during daylight hours. +8 Strength, +8 Defense, +4 Dexterity, +8 Agility, +5 Will

MINOR NECROTIC REGENERATION
As a zombie created from the corpse of a deceased revenant, this zombie will simulate a revenant's regenerative ability. Regeneration will function at half the rate of a living revenant. Minor Necrotic Regeneration requires mana and void resources to function. This

trait will cease to function in daylight hours when there are higher concentrations of life essence present in the ambient mana.

MUTATION PATHS AND MUTATIONS

PATH OF THE LURKER
Move in silence and strike with precision.

SILENT MOVEMENT
Removes excess weight and improves balance.
Resource Requirements: 2 sinew, 1 bone
Attribute Effects: +6 agility, +2 dexterity, -1 strength, +1 will

BONE CLAWS
Craft claws from consumed bone on one hand.
Description: .25 sinew, .25 bone
Attribute Effects: +4 dexterity, +1 defense, +1 strength

———

PATH OF THE BRUTE
Hit hard and stand your ground.

INCREASE MASS
Dramatically increase muscle mass.
Resource Requirements: 15 flesh, 3 bone
Attribute Effects: +30 strength, +20 defense, -10 intelligence, -7 agility, -7 dexterity, +1 will

BONE ARMOR
Craft armor plating from consumed bone.
Resource Requirements: 5 bone
Attribute Effects: +5 defense, +1 will

———

PATH OF THE GLUTTON

Trap and swallow your prey whole.

MAW
Open a gateway directly to the dimensional space of your void to devour prey faster.
Resource Requirements: 10 viscera, 1 bone
Attribute Effects: +2 perception, +1 will

JAWBONE
Craft a trap from consumed bone within the opening of your maw that can bite and pull prey in.
Resource Requirements: 2 bone, 1 sinew
Attribute Effects: +2 perception, +1 will

———

PATH OF THE LEADER
Control the horde and conquer the living.

COMPEL ZOMBIE
Temporally coerce one or more common zombies to obey your intent. Limited by target's intelligence.
Resource Requirements: 5 mind, 5 heart
Attribute Effects: +2 intelligence, +2 perception, +1 will

RECALL MEMORY
Access a portion of your living memories.
Resource Requirements: 30 mind, 40 heart
Attribute Effects: +5 intelligence, +5 perception, +1 will

———

PATH OF THE RAVAGER

SHEEP'S CLOTHING
Mimic a human appearance to lull your prey into a false sense of security.

Resource Requirements: 10 flesh.

TEMPORARY MASS

Consume void resources to weave a structure of muscle and bone around your body to enhance strength and defense until it is either released or its structural integrity has been compromised enough to disrupt functionality.

Resource Requirements: 25 flesh, 10 bone.

Attribute Effects: +11 strength, +9 defense.

Limitations: All effects are temporary. Once claimed, each use requires 2 flesh and 1 bone.

HELL'S MAW

Increase the maximum size of your void gateway at will.

Resource Requirements: 30 viscera.

Attribute Effects: +3 perception, +6 will.

Limitations: Once claimed, each use requires the expenditure of 1 MP for every 5 inches of diameter beyond your maw's default width.

DISSECTION

When consuming prey, you may gain a deeper understanding of how bodies are formed. This will allow you to spot and exploit a target's weaknesses instinctively.

Resource Requirements: 10 mind, 5 heart.

Attribute Effects: +3 intelligence, +6 perception.

———

PATH OF THE EMISSARY

APEX PREDATOR

You may consume the corpses of life forms other than humans without harmful side effects. Consumed materials will be converted into usable resources.

Resource Requirements: 50 viscera

BODY CRAFT

By consuming the corpses of life forms other than humans, you may gain a better understanding of biology and body structures. Once understood, you may use your gained knowledge to alter your physical body to adapt to any given situation. All alterations require the consumption of void resources. Your body will remain in whatever form you craft
until you decide to alter it again.

Resource Requirements: 200 mind

Limitations: Once claimed, each use requires the consumption of void resources appropriate to the size and complexity of the alteration.

LIMITLESS

Similar to the Ravenous trait, this mutation will remove all physical limitations, allowing for a sudden burst of strength. All effects are temporary. This mutation may cause damage to your body that will require mending.

Attribute Effects: Strength + 100%

Duration: 5 seconds

Resource Requirements: 35 flesh, 50 bone, 35 sinew

MEND UNDEAD

You may mend damage incurred by a member of your horde as well as yourself, including limbs that have been lost or severely damaged.

Resource Requirements: 50 mind, 100 heart.

Limitations: Once claimed, each use requires a variable consumption of void resources and mana appropriate to repair the amount of damage to the target.

––––––

PATH OF THE UNDEAD LORD

SOUL EATER

Drag your prey into a temporary immaterial space. If devoured

within this space, you will consume their spark. Consuming the spark of another may result in the advancement of other abilities or attributes. Consuming the spark of another may also result in the discovery of new abilities. Consumed sparks may also be saved for use later.
Resource Requirements: 5 Still Beating Human Hearts

SPIRIT CALLER
Draw the echoes of the lingering dead toward you across great distances. Each use will consume 100MP.
Resource Requirements: 10 Sparks

CALL OF THE CONSUMED
Reform the body of a spark you have consumed from the resources available to you. This temporary entity will fight alongside you and will be capable of most abilities that it had in life. Each use will require a temporary mana donation of 150MP as well as the resources required to restore the called echo's original body.
Resource Requirements: 25 Sparks

CURSE BLAST
Unleash a blast capable of eroding a target's natural and supernatural defense. Once a target's defenses have been negated, your curse will spread to them. This version of the curse will take effect immediately. The time it takes to negate defenses may vary. This mutation will cost 10MP per second that it is active.
Resource Requirements: 50 Sparks

Made in the USA
Columbia, SC
26 July 2024

dab81ecb-693f-4a3d-88eb-28a1d65a4d4eR02